All She Sought

PUBLISHER'S CATALOGING-IN-PUBLICATION DATA
Name: Johnson, Myra, author
Title: All she sought / Myra Johnson
Description: Second trade paperback edition | Fawn Ridge Press, Georgetown, TX
Identifiers: LCCN 2020916177 | ISBN 978-1-7356107-2-6 (pbk.)

Cover Design © Melissa Jagears
Photo by Grégoire Hervé-Bazin on Unsplash
Photo by Allison Lara on Unsplash

All She Sought

MYRA JOHNSON

www.FawnRidgePress.com

June, 24 years ago
Little Rock, Arkansas

Mama was dead.

Thank you, Lord!

Not that Rennie put much stock in prayer or even God anymore. But three days ago she'd found Mama stretched across her bed, one arm flung across the frayed chenille spread, the other draped in graceful repose across her abdomen. Sightless eyes peered from beneath half-closed lids as if watching, waiting, wishing for that sweet chariot Mama used to sing about to swing low and sweep her out of this cruel, cruel world.

The water glass next to the empty prescription bottle bore Burgundy Nights lip prints. Leave it to Mama to put on her makeup before committing suicide. And dress in her prettiest batik caftan, too.

Oh, Mama.

They should have expected this, especially if anyone had bothered to check the calendar. People said anniversaries were always the hardest. Rennie had tried her best to forget this anniversary, the first one since the accident. How stupid could her parents be? Abandoning the resort, leaving Hot Springs, moving into a dank little bungalow up the highway in Little Rock and pretending that day on the lake never happened?

A day that would haunt Rennie for the rest of her life.

At least now Mama wouldn't be around anymore, piling on the blame, shooting hateful glances. It was all Mama's fault, anyway. Rennie hoped she burned in hell.

Daddy touched her arm. "Rennie, it's your turn."

Her head snapped up. A ripple of surprise coursed through her before she remembered where she was. The cemetery, beside Mama's open grave, on a sultry June morning with rainclouds looming. Stately pines stood motionless, not a breath of breeze to stir their branches. A carpet of neon-green fake grass rustled beneath the soles of Rennie's patent-leather pumps. She'd saved up months of baby-sitting money to buy them for her new friend Linda's "sweet sixteen" dance party at the country club.

Which she'd be missing today, no thanks to Mama.

Sometime during Rennie's woolgathering, the coffin had been lowered into the hole. She cast Daddy a blank stare. "My turn for what?"

Aunt Geneva, on her other side, handed her a long-stemmed, pale-pink lily. "Say your good-byes, honey."

Rennie stepped forward, chin raised. She shredded the lily and flung the pieces onto the coffin lid. "Good-bye, Mama. Good riddance."

"Rennie!" Daddy's voice broke on a sob.

Across the chasm, the preacher in the frumpy suit cast her a stunned frown. The other mourners—what few there were, which served Mama right—lowered their eyes and whispered among each other.

"What? You expect me to be sorry she's dead, after how she ruined my life? You weren't there. You don't know—"

Aunt Geneva seized Rennie's wrist. "Please, child, not here."

"Not *here*? Not *ever*, you mean! Nobody knows how awful she treated me. I did *everything* to try to please that evil woman." She clamped her mouth shut and swallowed unshed tears. No longer would she silently take the blame for something that was *not her fault!*

"Your mama wasn't evil." Aunt Geneva edged closer and drew Rennie into her arms. "She was very troubled, very . . . sick."

"She was sick, all right. Sick in the *head*!" Rennie clenched her fists at her sides and stood stiff as a fence post, hoping Aunt Geneva would take the hint and release her.

But she didn't. Aunt Geneva held on tight and planted kiss after kiss on Rennie's throbbing temple, as if atoning for her own guilt in this madness. Because Aunt Geneva should have seen it, too—Mama's neediness, her violent mood swings, her obsession with perfection. She should have done something. They all should have done something.

Now it was too late. Too late for Mama, too late for Rennie.

Saddest of all, it was a year too late for Jenny.

1

——

JULIE PEARL

Present day
Caddo Pines, Arkansas

"You're late, Julie Pearl."

Flinching beneath my grandpa's pointed stare, I settled onto the barstool behind the front counter of our family-owned indoor flea market. "Sorry, I overslept. Had another bad night."

"Thought I heard you tossing and turning again." Grandpa replaced the waste bin he'd just emptied. "Ain't been sleeping so well, myself."

I shot him a worried glance. "Everything okay?"

He just grunted and headed toward the back of the shop. Didn't even ask what had kept me awake half the night.

Not like it was anything I could share with the sweet old man who raised me. Just my ever-growing sense of restlessness. I wouldn't call it dissatisfaction, exactly. I loved my grandpa and I loved the flea market. Nope, this was all about filling in the holes in my life, finding the missing puzzle pieces that would make my story complete.

5

The problem was I didn't even know where to begin, and at age twenty-seven maybe I'd waited too long to try.

Truth be told, some days I felt like a naïve schoolgirl. Other days, so much older. Folks have often told me I should have been born half a century ago. I've been called an ancient in a young woman's body, a flower child amongst Generation Nexters. Guess that's what comes of being raised around old things. Vintage clothing and costume jewelry. Dented avocado-green refrigerators and antique furniture. Depression glass, a 1956 set of Encyclopedia Britannicas, and don't forget those eight-tracks and cassettes of Carly Simon and the Beatles. You could find all that and more at our drafty, gymnasium-sized warehouse where thirty-seven vendors displayed their wares. Otto Stiles' Swap & Shop (no "s" after the apostrophe, thank you; it'd spoil the sibilance). Otto Stiles. Out of style. Get it? And yes, that's his real name.

Maybe some of the stuff we offered should have been thrown in the dumpster years ago, but most of it could still be useful, or carried sentimental value anyway. Grandpa had been reusing and recycling since the days when "green" meant either a bad case of envy or serious tummy trouble. Yes, indeed, he had a real gift for discerning the hidden worth of a thing.

Not the least of which was me.

I'd lived with my grandpa in a four-room apartment above the Swap & Shop for as long as I could remember. As a school kid, I spent my weekends and summers tagging merchandise, sweeping aisles, greeting customers, and manning the checkout counter. After I earned my community college degree, Grandpa promoted me to manager—which turned out to be a smart move on both our parts, since not three months later, Grandpa landed in the hospital for a quadruple bypass. The thought of losing him scared me spitless, but thank the Lord he came through just fine. Certainly there was no shortage of prayers, including my own and the promise that if only God would let me keep my grandpa around a few more years, I'd devote my life to taking care of him and the Swap & Shop.

No regrets about that promise, I guarantee! Although I will admit managing a flea market is not the most exciting job in the world, even on the busiest days. And we sure didn't get much excitement in Caddo Pines, Arkansas, barely a bulge on the winding back roads between Hot Springs and Little Rock. Nope, Caddo Pines was not exactly what you'd consider a "happening" kind of town. But all in all, it was a good life, a life I cherished, a life I wouldn't trade for anything.

So why couldn't I shake this confounded restlessness? I'd spent most of my life shoving aside unanswered questions about where I came from—the mother I barely remembered, the father who remained nothing more than a scribbled name in Grandpa's family Bible. Why should today be any different?

Except, to be completely honest, a heavy disquietude came upon me about this time every year. Along about Memorial Day, I'd start feeling an edgy kind of dread, like a bunch of nervous frogs jumping around in my belly. I used to blame the onset of summer and the fear that Grandpa would put me in swimming lessons again—which I hated!

But swimming lessons ended the year I turned fourteen, hallelujah, so what was my excuse for the past dozen or so years? By hook or by crook, I made up my mind this would be the summer I put an end to it.

Grandpa appeared beside me and slapped his car keys onto the counter. "I'm fixin' to run some errands, Julie Pearl. You got the bank deposit ready?"

"Just finished." I shoved the cash drawer shut and zipped up the bank bag. "Pretty good weekend, all things considered."

Grandpa tucked the bank bag under his arm. "After I drop this off, I'm gonna check out an estate sale over in Benton. You be okay till I get back?"

"Are you kidding? It's Monday, remember?" The slowest day of the week in the flea market business. And I expected *this* Monday would be even slower than normal—partly the heat, partly the fact that most people already shopped till they dropped the previous weekend over Memorial Day.

"Just the same, buzz if you need me." Grandpa patted the pants pocket where he kept his cell phone—his one concession to the twenty-first century.

"You bet." I flicked him a two-finger salute. "Drive safe."

He tossed a wave over his shoulder and shuffled out through the back, where he usually parked our white 1984 Econoline delivery van. Ancient as the Ozarks, but it still hummed along like a Swiss watch.

Okay, an old, beat-up Swiss watch with rusted gears and a couple of parts missing.

I pursed my lips as I watched Grandpa leave. No doubt about it, part of my unease had to do with him. Normally chatty and cheery, he'd been unusually quiet all weekend. I hoped his heart wasn't worrying him again.

My breath hitched. *Please, dear Lord, don't let anything happen to my grandpa!*

Just then, the miniature brass bells on the front door clanged against the glass, and my heart spasmed like a decapitated chicken. I tried to get a grip and forced a smile as one of our repeat customers breezed in. Charming and pleasant though she was, this woman's arrival never failed to churn up an unsettling sense of déjà vu.

Not exactly what I needed today.

I gave myself a mental shake and straightened the skirt of my orange psychedelic-print mini-dress (circa 1971). "Hi, Mrs. Nelson. You're out bright and early on a Monday."

"You know me—can't abide the weekend crowds." The elderly woman's golden-brown curls, although obviously from a bottle these days, were just a shade lighter than mine, and she still carried herself with posture to rival a runway model. Being tall, myself, she was one of the few women I could look at eye-to-eye. She strode up to the counter and blessed me with a warm smile. "How are you, Julie?"

I swallowed my edginess and tried for a friendly tone. "Fair to middlin'. How about you?"

"Never better." She leaned closer and patted my hand as if I were family. "Mr. Tuttle phoned over the weekend saying he'd found that piece of carnival glass I've been looking for."

I snapped my fingers, remembering. "Got it right here under the counter." Setting the bubble-wrapped candy dish between us, I started to peel back the tape. "I'm sure you'll want to inspect it."

"Oh, leave it wrapped. Mr. Tuttle has never done me wrong."

I winked. "And you *know* you're one of LeRoy's favorite customers. Do you want me to ring this up now, or did you want to look around?"

"Actually, I was expecting someone to meet me here." Mrs. Nelson scanned the shop, then checked her watch. "Looks like she hasn't shown up yet."

"Nope, you're the first customer of the day. Need to call someone?" I pushed the counter phone toward her. Mrs. Nelson was *not* among the elderly who'd embraced the cell phone generation.

"Maybe I should." She dialed a number and tapped her short, shiny nails on the counter. "Hello, dear, I'm at the shop I told you about. Are you on your way?" Her smile drooped. "One o'clock? Oh, my, I wrote down ten. I'm so sorry . . . Well, certainly, you must get that taken care of . . . Yes, dear, I understand. I'll talk to you later."

I propped one elbow on the counter and cupped my chin in my palm. "Your friend stand you up?"

"My niece. Apparently we got our times mixed up. She'd planned to stop here after lunch on her way to an appointment in Hot Springs. And I was so anxious for her to meet you." Mrs.

Nelson heaved a sigh and tugged her wallet from her purse. "What do I owe you, dear?"

I tapped some keys on the register to ring up the sale, then read her the total. "Your niece, huh? Now, if you'd said your handsome young, single *nephew* . . ."

"Why, Julie Stiles, surely you have potential beaux lined up from here to Little Rock." She handed me her charge card.

"I'm sure I'd have better luck in Little Rock. Most of Caddo Pines's eligible bachelors took off for the big city straight out of high school." Not that I'd have been interested. Guys you've grown up with your entire life seem more like pesky brothers than boyfriend material.

We shared a chuckle as I double-bagged the carnival glass, tucked her receipt inside, and wished her a pleasant day. When she left the shop, a twinge of something like homesickness hollowed out my stomach, and the agitation I'd shoved aside for a while came back full force. Before I could stop them, all my age-old questions slithered back into my brain. Mama might be dead, but did I still have a father out there somewhere? And if I did, why hadn't he ever come for me? Did I mean so little to him? Didn't he care? A deep, deep part of me ached to track down my father and force him to acknowledge me, but how could I go looking for him without upsetting Grandpa?

With a tiny shudder, I pressed a fist to my lips. I needed to quit dwelling on such things and get busy doing something productive. As usual, weekend browsers had left displays in disarray, so I spent an hour or so reshelving paperbacks, straightening clothing racks, and generally reorganizing.

Along about eleven, our mailman, Lester Carlson, popped in. "Hey there, Julie Pearl." A bulky cardboard shipping crate stretched Lester's skinny arms to nearly twice their length. He dropped the box inside Katy Harcourt's booth and dabbed the sweat off his forehead with the hem of his pale-blue shirtsleeve.

I moseyed over to peer at the shipping label. "Looks like Katy's purse order. She'll be glad to know it finally came in." Where the woman found a reputable supplier for her knockoff designer handbags, I'd just as soon not ask.

Lester collected a stack of mail from his pouch and thrust it into my hands. "Looks like slim pickin's. The job ain't what it used to be since folks started emailin' and even payin' their bills online." internet"Shame, isn't it? Nothing's quite the same as getting a handwritten letter from a friend—although the bills I could do without!" Anyway, considering Caddo Pines's hit-or-miss internet service, email wasn't much use to me.

Returning to the front counter, I flipped through the assortment of advertising flyers, ads for stuff like gutter cleaning and air-conditioner repair, catalogs from companies I'd never heard of. A fishing lure catalog caught my eye, and I flipped it open. Oh, yeah, just what I needed. A neon-yellow spinnerbait with a tandem blade configuration—whatever that was. Like you'd ever find me on a rocking boat in the middle of the lake. No way, no how. "You fish, don't you, Lester? You're welcome to this catalog."

"Don't mind if I do." He'd ambled over to another vendor's consignment booth and bent to paw through a box of greasy, grimy tools. His knobby spine poked through his shirt like a row of nickel-plated pinballs. "Say, this looks handy."

"Whatcha got there, Lester?"

He pulled out a big orange C-clamp. Or at least it used to be orange. Now it was mostly an icky shade of rust. "Side mirror on my truck's loose. This'd just about do the trick, I'm thinkin'." He turned it every which way and twisted the screw thingy a few times. "How much, Julie?"

"Make me an offer."

"A buck-fifty?"

"Sold." I keyed in the consignment code for Tom's Tools & More and rang up the sale. I wrapped the clamp in a plastic bag and slid the fishing lure catalog in beside it, then handed Lester our outgoing mail.

He tucked the envelopes into one of his mailbag pockets. "Oops, almost forgot your newspaper."

"Thanks, Lester. The whole world would go to pot if I missed the latest edition of the *Caddo Pines Recorder*." Usually four thin pages—eight at the most—the weekly publication promised everything you ever wanted to know, plus a lot you probably wished you didn't, about the goings-on around our homey little town.

Lester headed on his way, and a few minutes later the rear door banged shut, followed by rustling sounds in the storeroom. Grandpa appeared with a broom and dustpan and joined me behind the counter. "Estate sale was a bust—already picked over. Anything important in the mail?"

"Nothing worth keeping. Mostly ads and catalogs." I opened the *Recorder* and smoothed out the creases. "And the paper."

"What's newsworthy in Caddo Pines this week?" Grandpa's voice had a funny edge to it, like his mind was a million miles away.

"Let's see, Lacy Jones won the Memorial Day chili cook-off, a deer wandered into the feed store and polished off half a bag of corn . . ." A headline at the lower right snagged my attention:

25th anniversary: Lake Hamilton regulars recall tragic drowning

Gut clenching, I pushed the paper away. "How awful. Why would they rerun a story about a little girl who died?"

"Sells papers, I guess." Grandpa snatched up the *Recorder* and tossed it into the recycling bin beneath the counter, then swung his broom like he was beating out fires. "Time's a-wastin', Julie Pearl. Hadn't you oughta get some work done around here?"

Now I knew for certain something was up with Grandpa. He never got this riled up without good reason. I snagged his arm and made him look at me. "You haven't been yourself all weekend. Want to tell me what's going on?"

"Must be the heat. Don't bother your head about it." Heaving a shrug, he shuffled back to the workroom to do who-knew-what.

My gaze darted toward the recycle bin, and I shuddered. Just as well Grandpa had tossed the *Recorder*, because the way I felt about water, I sure didn't care to read an article about a drowning victim. Instead, I got busy with the bookkeeping, then polished real and imaginary fingerprints off the display cases, inventoried cups and napkins in the snack bar, and refilled the Coke machine.

By mid-afternoon I'd grown so antsy and out of sorts that I took to rearranging coins in the cash register by the year of their mint. As I paused to admire my neat little stacks, the brass bells on the front door announced another visitor. I jumped about three feet off my barstool and sent a pile of pennies clattering across the counter. While my heartbeat backed off from hyper-drive, I swept up the pennies with my forearm and beamed a nervous smile toward a woman I'd never seen before. "Come on in, ma'am. Welcome to the Swap & Shop."

The chic Jackie Onassis look-alike cast a bland smile my way and stepped inside. Maybe I was the only under-50 person on the planet who'd notice the resemblance, but just yesterday I'd sold a shrink-wrapped 1968 *Time Magazine* with Jackie and Ari on the cover. Slender, thirty-something, and wearing a pale-yellow sundress, our new customer looked as rich as the late Jackie-O and just as mysterious behind wide tortoise-shell sunglasses.

I scooped up the pennies I'd been counting and dropped them into the cash drawer. "Looking for anything in particular, ma'am?" A breathy weariness stole the sincerity from my tone. Hopefully the woman wouldn't notice.

"Just browsing." She folded her sunglasses and dropped them into a butterfly-appliquéd tote draped across a bronzed forearm. Hmmm, tennis player? Or just hours beside her backyard pool paging through the latest issue of *Vogue*? Although, considering all the hype about skin cancer these days, a tan like that probably came straight from a spray-on tanning salon. With a hefty price tag to boot.

Considering how my day had gone so far, I didn't mind at all the distraction our new customer provided. I set my mind to pondering what exactly would prompt a snooty rich lady to bother stopping at our humble establishment. Probably just an interesting off-road diversion, which was how most of our non-local customers found us. It didn't take much imagination to picture the lady arriving at her Little Rock mansion later and telling her husband, "Oh, *dahling*, I came upon the *quaintest* resale shop on my way home from high tea with the racing commissioners at Oaklawn."

Sneezy, our shop cat, wandered over from wherever he'd been snoozing all day and wound himself around the legs of my barstool. With a plaintive meow, he hopped on the counter and snuggled up to the cash register. I scratched him behind one notched ear. "Oh, well, she isn't the first rich lady to cross our threshold *just browsing*, and she won't be the last."

I decided to let her wander on her own—that's often the best approach for those aloof types. She certainly was attractive, trendy, obviously loaded. And tall. Which made me wonder if she might be the niece Mrs. Nelson told me about. Not much resemblance otherwise, but just like sweet Mrs. Nelson, this lady carried herself with the kind of poise and confidence I only dreamed about. I imagined men tripping over themselves to get a nod or smile from beneath her magnificent mane of thick, mahogany-colored hair. She didn't look the type to be very free with her smiles, though.

And she definitely didn't look like she belonged in a flea market.

Giving Sneezy a tickle behind his ears, I glanced down the aisle to see what Ms. Moneybags was up to. She looked away almost too quickly—had she been sizing me up, too?

More likely just making sure the mop-haired, hick-town flea market clerk wasn't stalking her, ready to lay on a cheesy sales pitch if she so much as looked sideways at an item.

Grandpa came up beside me, broom and dustpan in hand. The worry lines around his eyes had eased some. I hoped it was a good sign. "New customer, eh? You keeping an eye on her?"

Kind of a mutual admiration society, I didn't say. "Said she's just browsing."

"Why don't you show her the silver coffee service LeRoy just got in? First customer I've seen in a while who looks like she could afford it." He nudged me off my barstool and moved it so he could sweep around me.

"You just swept here before lunch, Grandpa. I'm not that messy," I said, then cringed when he swept up a couple of stray Lincolns having a tête-à-tête under the counter.

He slapped the pennies into my palm. "What else is an old man supposed to do when business is slow?"

In other words, Julie Pearl, quit ruminating and get to work.

"So you think Ms. Moneybags is the silver tea service type? Shoot, I'd be happy to sell her an heirloom china teacup to match her set of genuine Haviland from France."

"Now, Julie—"

"Although she'd do a far sight better down the road at Maudine's Antiques. Or the Park Plaza Mall in Little Rock." I was on a roll and couldn't stop myself. "Actually, she just oughta hop on her Lear jet and zip across the state line to Dallas. I hear they've got some fancy-schmancy stores at the Galleria."

"That's quite enough, young lady." Grandpa leveled his index finger at my nose. "Remember what James has to say about the tongue. It's 'a restless evil, full of deadly poison.' If you can't say anything nice—"

"Don't say anything at all. Sorry. Guess you and I are both a bit touchy today."

"Then best we both work on our attitudes and go about our

business." Grandpa gave me a five-second massage between my shoulder blades before continuing his sweeping, and I loved him even more.

With a rasping sigh, I tracked down our customer as she exited LeRoy Tuttle's booth carrying a pink "Cabbage Rose" Depression glass plate. "Need any help, ma'am?"

"No, thank you." She gave me the once-over before swiveling in the opposite direction.

"Fine," I mumbled, and strode to the front counter. So Grandpa wouldn't pester me anymore, I got out the calculator and tried to look busy double-checking the weekend sales entries.

I caught another glimpse of yellow, this time at the far end of the building. Now the lady carried one of Hazel Diffenbacher's hand-crocheted tablecloths, but apparently she'd decided against the plate. Oh well, if she bought one of Hazel's creations, at least we could almost declare it a profitable day.

By now she'd worked her way down to Katy Harcourt's Classic Shoes and Bags, where Grandpa plied his broom around a pile of dusty old cowboy boots. Grandpa gave me a pointed glare before smiling at the lady. "Anything we can help you with, you just holler, okay?"

She lifted her nose in the air. "Really, I'm just browsing." She'd probably take one look at Katy's knockoff Louis Vuitton handbags, snort in disgust, and hightail it out of here. *No sale.*

Sneezy sauntered over and draped himself across my ledger page as if to say, *Get over it, Julie Pearl Stiles.*

"You're right, Sneezy. I'm being ridiculous." I stroked his broad head and gazed into eyes the same shade of lima-bean green as my own. "I've got a wonderful grandpa, good friends, a job I love, and a roof over my head." Sneezy mewed and raised a whiskered brow. "And you, of course. What more could a girl want?"

With a pleading glance heavenward, I tried once again to shake off my restlessness and stop stewing over things I couldn't do anything about anyway.

While Sneezy camped out across the ledger, I reached for the dog-eared 1982 copy of *Good Housekeeping* I'd been paging through yesterday between customers. And just when I'd come across a great "new" way to fix ground beef and macaroni, Ms. Moneybags laid the crocheted tablecloth on the counter.

"Exquisite work," she remarked. "Do you prefer check or credit card?"

"Check, if you don't mind. Saves us the card fee." I pushed Sneezy, the ledger, and *Good Housekeeping* to the far end of the counter—didn't think she'd appreciate complimentary yellow cat fur with her purchase. I copied the inventory number off Hazel's tag into the register and totaled the sale.

"Eighty-seven fourteen, including tax," I quoted, and attempted a mental tally of our commission. Move the decimal over one, add half of that . . . Community college degree notwithstanding, math was not one of my better subjects. I came up with a ballpark figure of fourteen dollars. "Just curious, ma'am, what brought you to the Swap & Shop today?"

Well, I had to ask, didn't I?

"I was supposed to meet my aunt here, but she got confused about the time." The lady pulled a turquoise leather wallet from the depths of her tote and wrote out a check.

"I wondered if you might be Mrs. Nelson's niece." Although she sure didn't inherit her aunt's pleasant nature.

"Aunt Geneva was simply adamant that I drop in, and since I had business in Hot Springs this afternoon anyway . . ." She handed me her check along with her driver's license for an ID.

Dutifully I compared the name, address, and signature. "Renata Pearl Channing," I read aloud. "We have the same middle name."

"Pearl is actually my maiden name." She lifted her gaze to meet mine and spoke slowly, as if it were a test or something. "What is your name, dear?"

"Julie Pearl Stiles." A tingle crept up the back of my neck. I felt proud and perplexed and under a microscope all at the same time.

"Julie Pearl Stiles," she repeated, her voice barely a whisper. I could have sworn she stifled a gasp.

I cocked my head. "Do . . . do I know you?"

"No," she murmured, scrunching her eyebrows together. "No, I —it's just too—" She dropped her wallet into her tote, scooped up the tablecloth in the white plastic bag I'd wrapped it in, and pivoted toward the exit.

"Your receipt, ma'am."

Ignoring me, she marched out the door while thumbing in a number on her cell phone. Her silver Mercedes kicked up gravel as she sped out of the parking lot.

"Left in a hurry, huh?" Grandpa joined me behind the counter.

"Weird." I showed him the check. "Any idea who she is?"

He adjusted his bifocals and squinted at the tiny print on the upper left corner. His lips mashed together. "Channing? Never heard of her."

"Wait, aren't the Channings the folks behind GigantaMart?" The name had been bantered about on the evening news often enough the past several years.

"Oh. Right. I'm sure that's it." He reached around me and snatched the feather duster from under the counter. "Just look at all this dust. Cleanliness is next to godliness, you know."

That clinched it. Something was definitely up with Grandpa. I suddenly didn't believe him about not recognizing Mrs. Channing's name.

And now I wasn't so sure the lady had been completely honest about not knowing me.

2

JULIE PEARL

What should have been another uneventful Monday had turned into one crazy day. I knew exactly what had birthed my own lousy mood, but pile on a grouchy grandpa and a mysterious rich lady with an attitude? Please! Perched on my barstool behind the counter, I drummed my stubby nails on the laminate surface. *Busy. Keep busy, girl.*

Across the way, my gaze alighted on that mishmash of cowboy boots Grandpa had been sweeping around earlier. Poor Katy's sciatica was acting up, so helping her tidy up the mess seemed the least I could do. Besides, that pile of ugly old boots had been bugging me for a couple of weeks already. With a groan, I knelt on the cool concrete floor and set to work.

"Boo!"

At the sharp jab to my ribs, my head snapped up so fast I cracked it on the metal edge of Katy's display table. I stood with a huff and tugged at the hem of my dress. "Clifton Carter Doakes! How many times have I told you not to sneak up on me?"

"Yikes. Sorry, Julie, that looked like it hurt."

"Where'd you come from, anyway? I never heard the bells."

"Came in the back. Wanted to surprise you."

"Well, you succeeded." I rubbed my throbbing head and gave perverse note to the fact that Clifton could always finagle a way to catch me unawares in the most embarrassing positions. Like just now, with my backside pointed toward the ceiling. Even worse, he seemed to enjoy it way too much.

Clifton stifled his chortling laughter and thumbed tears off his sunburned cheeks. "So whatcha doin' down there anyway?"

"Doing a favor for Katy. What's it look like?"

He brushed a cobweb off my shoulder—another occupational hazard of working in a flea market. "Julie Pearl, you are so cute when you're mad."

"It's been one of those days." I hid the remnants of my irritation behind a cockeyed grin. "And you'd better watch it, buster, or I'll tell Sandy you were flirting with me."

Something between worry and embarrassment flickered in Clifton's eyes. He and Sandy Monroe and I had been best friends since kindergarten, but along about tenth grade I realized Sandy and Clifton had become slightly *more* than friends. I also knew their relationship had experienced a few ups and downs lately.

I nudged one of the cowboy boots with the toe of my genuine Mexican huarache. "You two need to talk out whatever's going on between you."

"We will. Eventually." Clifton checked his reflection in the polished glass of one of LeRoy Tuttle's breakfront curio cabinets. He ran an admiring hand across bleached-blond hair all spiky and shiny like he'd just worked a quart of styling gel into it. "Doing anything after work today? When Sandy gets back from her job interview, I was thinkin' we could all meet at the trailer park for a swim."

The Caddo Pines RV & Mobile Home Park had the only decent-sized pool in town, and for a dollar fifty a day they let anybody swim there. Only Clifton knew better than anyone that I didn't swim. "Not today, Clifton. My hair will just frizz even worse." It was a lame excuse, one I'd used way too often, and I knew he wouldn't buy it.

"Aw, come on, Julie. I've been practicing my high dive. You gotta see it." He dropped to one knee like he was going to propose. "Pleeeeeeze."

"Oh, okay. I'll come by for a bit. Just to watch." I waved him to his feet. "Now get on out of here so I can finish up."

By ten of five I was more than ready to call it a day. When a local cabinet builder shuffled out with a new pair of vise grips from Tom's Tools & More, I followed close on his sawdust-covered heels with the keys to lock up. The commotion woke Sneezy. He leapt off the counter with a yowl, nearly tripping me on my way back to the register.

"Poor kitty, did I disturb your beauty sleep? Hey, come back and I'll get you one of your fishy treats."

Honestly, that cat had the vocabulary of a precocious three-year-old. Soon as he heard the word *treats*, Sneezy did a quick U-turn and pranced to the counter. I reached for the foil pouch of cat treats on a lower shelf and shook out four of the tuna-smelling morsels. While he munched to the accompaniment of his own deep-throated purring, I tallied the day's receipts and wrote out a deposit slip. Grandpa wouldn't mind my closing up a little early. He'd already gone upstairs for his afternoon nap.

Since Grandpa's bypass surgery, it didn't take much to wear him out. Somehow you take it for granted that the people who matter most in your life are always going to be around, always be there when you need them. Grandpa had sure been there for me, and even though I knew someday I'd have to say my final good-byes, the thought of it collided against my insides like an iceberg hitting the *Titanic*.

Shaking off the nagging fears, I zipped up the bank bag, stuffed it into my "Hazel Diffenbacher original" crocheted shoulder purse, and trudged up the inner stairs.

The apartment lay in shadows. Grandpa snoozed in his easy

chair, legs sprawled across the frayed brown ottoman. His chest rose and fell with soft, snuffling snores. A tender flame kindled under my heart. I tiptoed closer, wishing I could snuggle up to his whiskery chin and kiss him without waking him. I settled for brushing my fingers across the fringe of gray hair over his ears before bending to pick up the book that lay open in his lap. It was an old photo album, and I found myself staring into my own toothless grin.

My first-grade school photo, missing front teeth and all. Same mop of messy, brownish-blond curls poking out all over my head and making me look like a wild child raised by wolves. With a self-conscious groan, I reached up with one hand to twist my long, unruly mane into a thick rope across my shoulder.

Moving to the kitchen, I pulled a chair from the scarred gray Formica table and sat next to the front window. A late-afternoon sunbeam set dust motes aglow and highlighted a streak I'd missed last time I cleaned the windows. I resisted the urge to grab the Windex and turned my attention to the album. Paging backwards from that atrocious first-grade picture, I lingered over photos of myself at younger and younger ages. No baby pictures, though. My official photographic history began somewhere around age three and a half, the year I came to live with Grandpa.

I hadn't looked at these pictures in forever. It always made me a little sad to have no idea what I looked like as a baby, no photos of a first smile, first tooth, first steps. Even sadder, there were so few pictures of me with my mother, and not one single picture of my father—a bitter reminder that I was once unwanted, deserted, discarded.

When I was little, I used to pester Grandpa all the time to tell me more about my parents, but he never seemed willing to talk about them. It looked like it pained him, and I hated seeing Grandpa upset. So after a while I quit asking.

In his own sweet way, Grandpa mostly filled up the empty space my daddy left behind. But growing up without a mother . . . I'd come to think it was why I'd reached my mid-twenties no closer to love and marriage than averting my eyes when Clifton and Sandy stole kisses in the choir loft. A girl needs a mother to teach her things, to guide her gently through puberty and hormones and all the confusing boy-girl stuff. Shopping for a prom dress. Getting her first kiss. Planning a wedding, choosing a gown, addressing invitations. And someday being a doting grandmother to a bunch of little Julies and—

Enough!

Before the longings ate me alive, I slammed the album shut, forgetting my dozing Grandpa. He sat up with a snort. "Oh, Julie Pearl. You about scared the dickens out of me! Is it closing time already?"

"I've got today's bank deposit ready, and then I'm meeting Clifton and Sandy at the pool." I tried for a lighthearted smile as I slid my sagging shoulder bag up my arm and fished out my car keys. "I'll pick up something for supper on my way home. Don't you bother about it, okay?"

I gave him a quick kiss before skipping down the outside stairs. Even beneath the shade of the immense oak tree that sheltered this side of the building, the late-afternoon heat slapped me in the face. It had to be 150 degrees inside my rattletrap '74 Volkswagen Beetle. The vinyl seat sucked against my thighs like hot tar paper. The engine grumbled and bucked a few times, and five minutes later, long before the car's wimpy little rebuilt air conditioner could kick in, I pulled up to the drive-in window at Caddo Pines Bank and Trust, a squat brown building next to the Dairy Queen.

"Hey, Marge." I waved to the wiry, salt-and-pepper-haired teller.

Marge Monroe, my friend Sandy's mother, grinned at me over the rims of rhinestone-studded reading glasses with a wingspan that could rival a 747's. "How's it going, Julie?" Her words sounded scratchy and metallic over the intercom.

"Fair to middlin'." I dropped the deposit bag into the drawer, and she slid it inside. "Is Sandy back from Hot Springs? I'm dying to know about her job interview."

"I expect her back pretty quick. Her shift at the DQ starts at six thirty." She paused to count the cash and total the deposit. "A specially slow Monday, I see. Alrighty-dighty, hang on one sec and I'll have your receipt."

"Most of that is one of Hazel's tablecloths. Wish we could sell one or two of those every day." The drawer slid out and I claimed the bank bag and receipt. "If you hear from Sandy, tell her Clifton and I will be at the pool."

"You bet. And keep your fingers crossed for my girl. She *needs* this job." Marge made no secret of the fact that she and Fred were getting tired of having their daughter living under their roof again, not to mention coming home every night smelling like burgers and fries.

Out of college, Sandy had landed a great job with a telecommunications company in Oklahoma City, but when they started laying people off, her job was among the first to go. The manager position at the DQ was supposed to be temporary, until Sandy found something better.

Of course, Sandy's career moves had a whole lot to do with the problems between her and Clifton. Not being college material himself, it about broke his heart when Sandy went away to school and then took the job in Oklahoma. I'd sidestepped a few too many of their quarrels lately as Clifton nagged her to look for work closer to Caddo Pines.

I waved good-bye to Marge and headed toward the trailer park. Tall Arkansas pines framed the entrance. A narrow blacktop road led between Winnebagos and travel trailers down a hill to the grassy commons surrounding the pool. As I nosed the Beetle up to the chain-link fence, I glimpsed Clifton preening on the high dive while several tanned high-school girls in bikinis cheered and applauded. Even soaking wet, his gelled hair stood in proud, chlorine-green spikes.

I stopped at the whitewashed check-in counter, and the bored-looking attendant waved me on without a second glance. She'd been around long enough to know I never got wet past my shinbones, so no point charging me the dollar fifty. With a nod of thanks, I picked my way along the deck between water puddles and lounge chairs.

"Yo, Julie! Watch this!" Clifton loped to the end of the diving board and cannonballed into the blue-green water. The well-aimed splash drenched Heather Juergen, the bossy lifeguard watching the deep end. Clifton's bevy of bikinied admirers erupted in hoots and catcalls.

Heather let out a shriek I bet they could hear clear to Memphis. "Clifton Carter Doakes, you are *so* out of here!" Pointing toward the exit, she jammed her whistle between her lips and blew three sharp blasts.

"Aw, come on." Clifton rested his forearms on the edge of the pool and grinned at her. "You looked awful hot up there. I was trying to cool you off."

"Yeah, right." Heather's freckled face beamed the same shade of crimson as her Red Cross swimsuit, whether from sunburn or rage it was hard to tell. Her bosom rose and fell with all the drama of Scarlett O'Hara. "I ought to have you permanently kicked out. You're a creep, Clifton Doakes. A conceited, immature *creep!*"

I cast a groan skyward and ambled over to the base of the lifeguard stand. "Now take it easy, Heather. You know Clifton was just playing around." I turned to glare at Clifton and lowered my voice. "Apologize, you dope. And try to act your age for a change."

A flicker of remorse clouded his expression. He mumbled a halfhearted "Sorry."

"Humph." Heather crossed her arms and slumped into her seat. One more Clifton fiasco averted. His insecurities in the romance department had him acting out even worse than normal these days.

I kicked off my huaraches and grabbed Clifton's Scooby-Doo beach towel from his usual deck chair. Making myself a poolside seat with the folded towel, I chose a semi-dry spot at the shallow end of the adult lap-swimming lane, where I hoped to avoid the worst of the splashing.

By the time I'd hiked up my skirt and lowered my feet into the water, I was already having stomach-knotting flashbacks to those humiliating days of childhood swimming lessons. There's not much worse than having six other kids laughing at you because you're scared of water. Not to mention the swim instructor, a middle-aged lady with saddlebag thighs reminding me that if I didn't dive in and paddle across the pool with the other kids, I'd have to watch while they slurped up the grape Popsicles she always brought for after class.

To this day I hate grape Popsicles.

Clifton swam over and hoisted himself out of the pool, after which he proceeded to drip all over the corner of the towel. His mouth twisted into a sheepish grin. "You're not mad at me, are you?"

"For Pete's sake, Clifton, sometimes you act like a dorky teenager." I couldn't restrain my spiteful tone. "If you really want things to work out with Sandy, you're going to have to get your act together."

He winced, and I felt bad for him, sorry I'd used my simmering stewpot of worries as a reason to lash out. Clifton was a decent guy and a loyal friend. Not to mention he knew the inside of old car engines better than I know my own name. He found my Beetle in a salvage yard ten or twelve years ago, cobbled it together with parts from other junkers, and somehow kept the persnickety thing running.

He'd learned the trade from his dad, the owner of Doakes Automotive and Body Shop, but leave the two of them together for long and it was World War III. Clifton could have easily found automotive work elsewhere, but with his mom slowly going blind from macular degeneration, Clifton chose to stay close to home. Instead, he'd cycled through one minimum-wage job after another—his latest sacking groceries at Friendly's Neighborhood Supermarket. Between the lack of local job opportunities and Clifton's underachiever tendencies, seemed he couldn't settle on what to do with his life.

"Hey, you two!" Sandy's perky voice startled me. She looked sharp in her interview attire—slim white skirt, pink knit top with lace edging, white patent-leather sandals. Shoving her sunglasses up through thick brown bangs, she shimmied from head to toe. "I got the job!"

"Wow, that's super!" I pushed up from the pool deck to give her a hug. "So? Details, girl!"

Sandy tugged me over to an umbrella-shaded table. She motioned for Clifton to hurry as he scooped up Scooby-Doo and wrapped the towel around his hips.

"I start one week from today," Sandy said as we pulled out chairs. "My new boss is a real-estate developer. He's planning a resort, but it won't open for several months yet, so he set up a temporary office in a suite at the La Quinta." She exploded in a burst of giddy laughter. "I'll be Mr. Micah Hobart's administrative assistant—can you believe it? Good-bye, Dairy Queen!"

"It's about time! I'm so proud of you, Sandy."

The brief downturn of her lips told me she'd picked up on Clifton's down-in-the-dumps vibes. She squeezed his hand. "The best part is it's just over in Hot Springs. Close enough that I don't even have to think about leaving Caddo Pines."

A relieved grin crept across Clifton's face. "So what kind of *developments* is this dude going to have you working on? Nothin' after hours, I hope."

"Now, Clifton, don't get all jealous on me." Sandy released a girly giggle, and I couldn't help rolling my eyes in embarrassment. If that's what romance did to a person . . .

I shook off a twinge of envy. "Go on, tell us about it."

"It's exactly the kind of career opportunity I was hoping for. Mr. Hobart is building brand new super-modern luxury vacation condos. And I'm getting in on the ground floor—literally!"

"A tourist resort, huh?" Clifton rested his ankle on the opposite knee. "Then he'll be hiring more people down the road?"

"Probably. The place will be called Hamilton Haven. It's on the site of some old lakefront cottages Mr. Hobart bought cheap. He took me to see it. The location's great, but what a candidate for *Extreme Makeover: Resort Edition*—broken-down buildings, weeds and brush overgrowing everything. I'm glad my boss can see the potential, because I sure can't."

Clifton hiked an eyebrow. "Where is it exactly?"

"A few miles off Highway 270 on the way into Hot Springs." Sandy described the turn-off, waving her hand in the general direction. "The setting is gorgeous—hidden away at the end of a private road, with a wide stretch of Lake Hamilton shoreline. Driving by on the highway, you'd never know it was there."

She lifted her sunglasses off her head and cast Clifton a pleading look. "Promise me you won't go poking around, honey. Mr. Hobart just closed the deal today, and the construction fencing isn't even up yet. I mean it, it's a disaster area."

I tried to picture a place that dumpy. "Gross."

"You aren't just kidding. Supposedly it was a popular vacation spot in its heyday, but the owners abandoned it. The place has been sitting untouched for nearly twenty-five years. It used to be called Pearls on the Shore, or maybe Pearls Along the Lake." Sandy waved her sunglasses. "Something 'Pearl,' anyway. I think it was the family's name."

My mind flashed back to the headline in the *Caddo Pines Recorder*—the article I was about to read before Grandpa yanked the paper out of my hand. Pearls Along the Lake—I was pretty sure I'd seen that name in the first line or two of the story. And could there be a connection with our snooty rich visitor at the Swap & Shop? She'd told me Pearl was her maiden name. Remembering the way she'd looked at me, I stifled a shudder.

Sandy checked her watch. "Yikes, I gotta get to the DQ. Can't wait to give ol' George Bradley my one-week notice. I am so ready to *not* go home every night smelling of burger grease."

Rising, Sandy tousled Clifton's spikes, beamed us both a megawatt grin, then raced through the gate in a blur of pink and white. Watching her Honda Civic roar away, Clifton settled back and rubbed his jaw. "Maybe I should apply for Sandy's old job. The pay's gotta be better than schlepping groceries for little old ladies."

I was still stewing over the day's events and wondering how they all fit together—and somehow, I just knew they did, even right down to Grandpa's edginess. What *was* it he so badly didn't want to talk about?

Smiling wanly, I pushed my chair back. "I should be going, too. Gotta stop at Friendly's to pick up a few things for supper."

"I'm off again tomorrow." Clifton stood and tossed his towel across the chair. "Want to check out the old resort?"

"Oh, I don't think so—"

Suddenly I did. An urgency had crept over me, like the buzzing of a bumblebee I couldn't shoo away. It was more than curiosity about Sandy's new job, more than idle interest in a tumbledown old resort.

No, it was the honest-to-goodness, deep-in-my-gut certainty that nothing about today was coincidence. It all meant something, and I needed to find out what. "Sure," I said, keeping my voice even. "The flea market's closed until Thursday, so I've got all day. What if I pick you up around ten?"

RENATA

June, 27 years earlier
Hot Springs, Arkansas

"Rennie, leave that baby alone!"

The girl backed away from the crib, a sharp stream of air escaping between tight lips. "I'm not doing anything, Mama. Just looking at her." She flicked a clump of shaggy, red-brown hair out of her eyes.

Rennie's mother flounced into the nursery, the sleeves of her purple-and-fuchsia paisley caftan flapping like a bat's wings. "Oh, my sweet baby Jenny-girl, what's your big ol' mean sister doing to you?" She swept the nine-month-old into her arms. "Won't she let you take your nappy-pie in peace?"

Rennie lowered her gaze. She spied the mustard stain on her T-shirt, and her face warmed. Turning sideways, she crossed her arms over the spot. "I swear, Mama, I didn't wake her up. I heard her crying and came to see if she lost her pacifier."

"Nice girls do not *swear*." Mama tapped the toe of her slipper on the hardwood floor. "And what are you *supposed* to be doing?"

"Sweeping the cabins."

"Sweeping the cabins, *ma'am*." Mama settled herself in the spindle-backed rocking chair and nuzzled the baby's cheek, then lifted glaring eyes to Rennie. "You're a young lady now, practically a teenager, and it's high time you started acting like it."

"But I was just—"

"You *know* how much I rely on you these days. It's the busy season, and your daddy can't manage the place all on his own." Mama's voice turned all whiny and saccharine-sweet. "Specially now we've got little Jenny, and me still feeling so frail and all. If you don't do your part, why, things will absolutely go to pot around here."

Rennie ran one finger along her baby sister's soft cheek. Jenny giggled and squirmed, sending a delighted shiver through Rennie. "I know, Mama, but—"

"No buts about it. Now you do an extra good job in cabin three. The MacDonohoes are due to arrive this evening, and they always leave a nice tip if things are done up the way they like." The rocking chair creaked rhythmically. "And then you get yourself cleaned up before suppertime. And comb that mop of hair. For goodness' sake, child, you do look a fright."

Rennie's lips flattened. "Yes, ma'am."

"Now be a good girl and fetch me one of my little pink pills. My nerves are botherin' me something fierce today."

So what else was new? "Yes, ma'am," Rennie said again, and dodged around the corner to the bathroom. She returned with the pill and a plastic cup of water, then stood with her chin lowered in case Mama had further orders. Which she generally did.

With a gulp, Mama downed the pill and flicked her hand in dismissal. "What are you standing there gaping for? Get those chores done lickety-split."

"Yes, *ma'am!*" Rennie's yellow flip-flops slapped the polished floor as she marched down the back hall to the maid's closet. The only good thing about cleaning cabins was getting far enough away that Mama couldn't pick on her for a while.

But why did it have to be the MacDonohoes' cabin? They came for two weeks every summer, and Rennie *hated* them. Hated how they acted all sweet and lovey-dovey, hated the way they hung on each other like honeymooners. Their poor little boy was as grossed out by all the mushy stuff as Rennie, so she'd taken pity on him that first year and invited him to tag along with her. And if their smooching all the time wasn't bad enough, Mrs. MacDonohoe was fussy as an old granny. One tiny hair in the bathtub, or a chipped coffee mug in the kitchenette, and she'd be pounding on the front desk five minutes after they unpacked.

Rennie generally hated the resort, period. She was sick to death of cleaning up other people's messes, fed up with cleaning slime out of the ice dispenser, bone tired from hauling cases of soft drinks and snacks to fill the vending machines.

And lately she had to work harder than ever, thanks to her mother's getting pregnant so late in life and then having to stay in bed nearly the whole nine months. Good grief, did people as old as her parents really *do it* anymore? And Mama was crazy as an upside-down cuckoo clock anyway. How Daddy put up with her mood swings was anybody's guess. Not to mention if Mama ever forgot to take her little pink pills. When that happened, things could get twenty times worse.

But then Jenny came along, and oh, how Rennie loved that little baby, thought she was the cutest, most precious creature ever born. Jenny's sweet smile could charm Rennie out of her darkest moods. And that was saying a lot.

But everything else . . . sometimes it got to be just too much.

"Hey, sweetkins." Her daddy, toting a toolbox and some torn shingles, met her on the way down the path to cabin three. "What's that ugly ol' frown about?"

She tapped the wheel of the housekeeping cart with the toe of her flip-flop. "Mama's mad at me again."

"Aw, it can't be that bad." He chucked her under the chin. "She's had a hard time this year. Things'll get better soon."

"I know, Daddy. I just . . ." But Daddy couldn't understand, never would. Rennie sighed and sniffed back a tear. Stiffening her back, she gave the cart a shove and continued on her way.

In cabin three, she made quick work of dusting and mopping, then stripped and remade the beds and hung fresh white towels in the bathroom. She replaced the used dishes and utensils with clean ones, then refilled the oblong wicker basket next to the percolator with complimentary packets of ground coffee, sugar, and powdered creamer.

Halfway out the door, she stopped. An idea slithered into her brain. The very thought made her insides all tingly, and it wouldn't let her go until she acted on it. She reached up and pulled a single brown hair from her bangs, now damp with sweat and smelling like the dust she'd been stirring up all morning cleaning cabins. With demented *Mommie Dearest* laughter, she carried the strand to the larger of the two bedrooms, lifted a pillow, and tucked the hair between the blanket and the top sheet.

"A special gift, just for you, Mrs. MacDonohoe." She pursed her lips in a satisfied sneer. "Enjoy your stay at Pearls Along the Lake."

4

JULIE PEARL

Present Day

"Yes, ma'am, the story on page one yesterday, about the drowning." Back at the Swap & Shop last evening, I'd slipped downstairs and dug out the copy of the *Recorder* Grandpa seemed determined not to let me read. The article was little more than a two-paragraph blurb recapping only the sketchiest details, so this morning I'd parked my VW under an elm tree at the end of Clifton's street to call the newspaper office and see what more I could learn about Pearls Along the Lake.

"Yes, yes, here we go, sugar." The receptionist hemmed and hawed a few times until I thought she was having an asthma attack. "Yes indeed. That's Abe Friedman's story."

Honest Abe Friedman. Guaranteed to print what he knew and make up the rest. I pushed my hair up so the breeze could cool my neck. "I'm curious about that family, the Pearls. Do you know their story?"

"Sorry, honey, I didn't live around these parts back then. See, I moved over this way from Turrell . . . oh, long about 1998, I think

35

it was. My Bennie, he got a job over at the Weyerhaeuser plant and—"

"Then maybe I could talk to Abe?"

"You could, exceptin' he don't usually show his face around here till noonish. I could have him give you a buzz."

"No, that's okay. Thanks for your help." Knowing how well Abe researched his stories, I doubted he could tell me much more than what he'd written in the article. Maybe later I could swing by the Garland County Library and pop on their internet to do some research on my own. With the A/C vent aimed right at my face, I chugged up the street to pick up Clifton.

After over an hour of searching the winding back roads along Lake Hamilton, we finally deciphered Sandy's directions and found our way to the abandoned resort. I found a bit of shade for the car beneath a straggly oak along the roadside. If we ventured up the circle drive, I was afraid I'd blow a tire. All kinds of junk cluttered the way—broken tree limbs, rotting boards, crushed aluminum cans, shattered beer bottles, debris from just about every fast-food joint in a five-mile radius.

My stomach did a swirly thing, like brackish water circling the drain. I gnawed on my lower lip. "Wow, it looks even worse than Sandy described it."

Clifton stared through the open passenger window. "Sure don't look like it'll be open for business anytime this century."

We got out and picked our way up the cracked driveway toward the gabled two-story frame house at the top of the circle. Peeling white paint exposed bare wood weathered to a soft gray. Prickly weeds poked through the splintered boards of the broad porch steps. The smells of age and decay blended with a fishy odor carried on the morning breeze.

Clifton kicked at a broken limb. "Must have been quite a showplace in its time. Ideal location—off the beaten path, great view of the lake." He pointed beyond the big white house toward the chain of lakefront cabins laid out under sprawling pines and oaks.

"Makes you wonder how anyone in their right mind could have let it go like this." An eerie sensation raised goose bumps on my arms. I couldn't seem to stop dwelling on that child who drowned. If there was a connection between the child and the family who'd owned this resort, maybe it was why they up and walked away.

Clifton braved the porch steps, each one creaking under his weight. I held my breath, expecting him to crash through at any second. "Clifton, be careful."

He bounced up and down on the warped boards in front of the door. "See? Solid as a—*yikes!*"

One of the boards gave way with a *crack*. Clifton's left leg sank up to his knee, and if he hadn't lunged sideways and grabbed the door handle, the rest of him would have followed.

"Clifton, hold on!" Hugging the railing, I dashed up the steps as lightly as I could—no easy task in my clunky Dr. Scholl's wooden sandals from Katy Harcourt's booth. I still hadn't gotten used to the weird toe grips and unforgiving soles. I grabbed Clifton's arm and draped it around my shoulder, supporting him until he could free his leg from the jagged jaws of the termite-ridden plank. Easing down beside him on the top step, I surveyed the damage to his leg. "How's it feel?"

He rubbed his shin and kneecap. "Nothing's broken. Prob'ly be black and blue for a few days is all." If he hadn't been wearing his usual cowboy boots and Levis, it could have been a lot worse.

I stood carefully. "We should get out of here. This place is just begging for an accident." I grimaced and glanced down at Clifton. "I mean, an even worse accident."

"No way, man. I ain't done exploring yet." Before I could catch up, he bounded around the side of the big house along a path of broken stepping stones.

"Slow down, Clifton!" As I chased after him, the toe of my

wooden sandal caught on an exposed tree root that had cracked one of the stepping stones. I nearly did the splits trying to keep from crashing face first. If I didn't watch my step, it would be me with the broken neck.

"Hey, most of these cabins are standing wide open," Clifton yelled. I turned the corner in time to see the grime-covered backside of his jeans disappear through a cabin door.

"Clifton, will you be careful, please?" Catching up, I leaned on the doorframe and gasped for breath.

And got a stinging noseful of something best described as rotting compost mixed with a heaping dose of wet dog. The sill felt spongy beneath my feet. A huge hole gaped where the bathroom wall should have been, and the cracked commode lay on its side. Clifton stood dead still in middle of the kitchenette, his boots planted in a sticky yellow ooze.

The snarl from the bedroom beyond revealed the source of the wet dog smells. The poor thing lay curled up in the center of what used to be a mattress.

"Don't move," Clifton whispered. "Just back out slowly."

Most dogs and I get along great, but this bundle of matted black fur didn't look any too happy to be disturbed. Then I heard soft whimpers—puppies! Craning my neck, I counted three fuzzy, dark heads pressed against their mama's tummy in search of breakfast. Mama looked too thin to be making much milk, though. No wonder she was cross—a batch of hungry little ones and no way to satisfy them, much less her own empty belly. "Aw, poor thing."

"Yeah, this 'poor thing' has teeth like a gator. Now move so I can get outta here."

I eased out the door, and Clifton scooted backward to follow me. As soon as he cleared the doorframe, he sprinted several yards away.

"We've got to get her some food." I peered inside. A menacing growl, louder this time, warned me to keep my distance.

"Uh, Julie?" Clifton's voice cracked like he'd hit puberty again. "We've got company."

I pivoted on the rickety landing. Clifton faced me with a nervous grin, while behind him loomed a tall, lanky man wearing a scowl beneath a neatly trimmed black beard. One tanned hand clutched Clifton's shoulder. With the other he pointed an accusing finger directly at me.

"This is private property," the man snarled, doing a good imitation of that angry mama dog. "What do you think you're doing here?"

"Sir, we didn't mean any harm." I edged forward. "We were just—"

"Looking around. Yeah, I guessed that." Glancing down, he tugged a fancy cell phone from the holster clipped to his belt. "This is about to be a busy construction site, and I don't need a couple of kids playing Lewis and Clark on my property. Now get on out of here before somebody gets hurt."

"Yes, sir, we hear you." Clifton ducked from under the man's grip and did a mock salute. "No problemo. We are history, sir. Come on, Julie, let's go."

So much for Clifton's bravado. I wasn't feeling too brave myself, staring into those piercing gray eyes—eyes a good six inches higher than my own. Last time I felt caught in the act like this was after my high-school prom, when Grandpa caught me kissing Everett Buckles good night (more like good morning since it was nearly 4:00 a.m.) beneath our apartment stairs.

More whimpering from inside the cottage and I grabbed what little nerve I had left. The man said he owned the place, right? Then he must be Sandy's new employer. I scanned my brain for a name. "Mr. Hobart, right? Hi, I'm Julie Stiles, a friend of Sandy Monroe's."

"My new assistant." His glare softened somewhere just short of apologetic. "But that doesn't give you and your punk-haired boyfriend an open invitation to go poking around."

Somebody must have gotten up on the wrong side of his bed of nails. "Clifton is not *my* boyfriend, he's—" Best I let Sandy explain that one. I set my hands on my hips. "Excuse me, sir, but did you know there's a dog with puppies in there?"

"Aw, man, I was afraid of that." Hobart brushed past me and peeked into the cottage.

I waited for Mama Dog's growl and Hobart's quick retreat, but instead I heard a soft, anxious whining, as if the dog recognized him. He dropped to one knee just inside the door. "It's all right, girl. Sorry if these nosy kids scared you." He clicked his tongue. "Wow, you've got quite a brood there. You should have come home with me when you had the chance. A pile of blankets on my kitchen floor would be a lot nicer than a dirty old mattress."

I came closer. "Poor thing looks like she's starving. Has she been hanging around here long?"

Hobart eased out of the cabin and stood on the top step. "First noticed her a few days ago. I've been tempting her with dog chow, but she's never let me get too close." He shook his head. "I thought she looked pregnant. Now she needs to eat more than ever."

I couldn't stay riled at the guy for long when he showed such concern for animals. "What are you going to do with her?"

"She won't let anyone near, and I can't just watch her starve to death. Even if I caught her, I couldn't keep her long—there's a 'no pets' clause in my apartment lease." He shrugged and glanced sideways, his jaw clenched. "I should call the humane society, but in the shape she's in, and with the puppies and all, I'm afraid they'd just . . ."

He didn't have to finish his sentence. I reached out, my fingers tightening around his forearm. "Please, you can't!"

His arm muscles tensed. He stared at my hand like it was a giant cockroach, and a second later Dr. Jekyll reverted to Mr. Hyde again. He lifted his steely gaze to meet mine. "Like I said before, you need to get off my property. I'll handle this."

I took a step back, stumbling against Clifton. When I

accidentally hit his bruised shin with the heel of my Dr. Scholl's, he let out a groan. "Come on, Jules, let's get on outta here."

"Your boyfriend's right," Hobart said. "Go home before somebody gets hurt, or before I change my mind and call the cops."

That nailed it. I marched up to Mr. Hobart and aimed my finger at his bearded chin. "You have got to be the rudest man I have ever met in my entire life. Why, if I weren't an upstanding, church-going, decent-as-the-day-is-long Christian, I—I'd tell you right where to get off!"

He gave me an odd look, like I'd hit a nerve. Lifting his chin, which I could have sworn trembled just the tiniest bit beneath his beard, he said, "Don't let that stop you. It wouldn't be the first time a hysterical female gave me a piece of her mind."

"Julie." Clifton's tone became insistent. "I really, really think we should leave."

I wanted to, I really, really did. But this Hobart character was doing weird things to my insides, and common sense seemed to have deserted me. Not to mention the image of that hungry mama dog and her three precious pups kept me planted firmly—or pretty shakily, actually—on the broken stepping stone beneath my Dr. Scholl's.

A plan. I needed a plan. It didn't sound like Hobart would be calling the humane society quite yet. Clifton and I could leave peacefully now, and then tonight I could sneak back here and find a way to get Mama Dog and those pups into my Beetle and take them home with me.

Hobart took a step towards us. "Listen, I'm—"

I raised my hands, palms outward. "Okay, we get the message. We're leaving."

Half a minute later, Clifton and I were in the car. I revved the engine a few times before screeching through a U-turn and zooming down the winding road.

Clifton braced himself against the dashboard. "Easy there,

'Mario,' this ain't a NASCAR race."

By the time we reached the highway, I'd managed to calm down. A little. But it bugged me something fierce when people purposely chose rudeness over good manners. What was the deal with Hobart anyway? He must have the biggest chip on his shoulder ever.

I dropped Clifton at his house, deciding not to let him in on my plan to return for the dog and her pups. Clifton was not a dog person. He would not understand the horrible ache I felt under my ribcage just thinking of that poor hungry dog, lost and alone and living among the ruins.

At Friendly's Neighborhood Supermarket, I splurged on several cans of premium dog food and a box of bacon-flavored dog treats. While I was at it, I remembered to browse the aisles for something for supper. I settled on tuna, cream of mushroom soup, a package of egg noodles, and a wedge of Wisconsin cheddar. Tuna casserole—always quick and easy.

"Hey, Grandpa, I'm home." I kicked the kitchen door closed with one foot and plopped my grocery sacks on the counter.

Grandpa shuffled to the table and pulled out a chair. It happened to be the one Sneezy was sleeping on. Yawning, Sneezy slunk to the floor with an insulted green-eyed glare. Grandpa brushed cat fur off the chair and sat down with a tired sigh. I hoped he hadn't been working too hard cleaning up the shop. I should have been here helping him instead of gallivanting around Lake Hamilton with Clifton and getting yelled at by grumpy Mr. Hobart.

"What did y'all do in Hot Springs?" Grandpa bent to scratch Sneezy's hindquarters.

"Nothing much." Grandpa would only worry if I told him Clifton and I had been poking around in abandoned buildings. I reached into a grocery bag and pulled out the dog food.

Grandpa let loose with a loud cough. "Something you forgot to tell me? Last time I checked, Sneezy preferred cat food."

Cradling the box of dog biscuits as if it were one of those precious little puppies, I sat down next to Grandpa. Might as well be honest. Grandpa would have to know sooner or later, especially when I came home with four new additions to our family. "She's a stray, with three pups. They're at the resort where Sandy just got hired, and I'm worried the owner will call the pound if I don't rescue them."

"Aw, Julie Pearl." Grandpa gave a moan and pressed a palm against his forehead. "You know I could never turn away a stray."

I hugged his neck. "Thanks, Grandpa, I knew I could count on you!"

"Let's go look around, then. Seem to recall some pet supplies in Maddie Barton's booth." Rising stiffly, he gave me one of those understanding smiles that always tugged at my heartstrings. It was a relief to see he didn't seem quite as moody and preoccupied as he'd been yesterday. "You say you found the dogs at a resort?"

"Well, it's going to be a resort. It's . . . under construction." Sort of. Dare I mention it was the same location as the place mentioned in the *Recorder* article? Not if I didn't want Grandpa clamming up on me again—or worse, outright forbidding me to return for the dogs.

"Not sure I like the idea of you fooling around a construction site," Grandpa said as I followed him down the inner stairs to the main floor. He stopped at Maddie Barton's booth and unearthed a leash and a couple of dog dishes from her hodgepodge of garage-sale-quality merchandise.

"It's fine, I promise. I've just got to get the dog and her pups out of there before the demolition crew starts tearing stuff down."

Grandpa shot me a curious look over his shoulder. "Tearing stuff down? I thought you said it was a construction site."

I should have known better than to try to keep anything from Grandpa. I chose my words carefully. "It's a rundown resort on Lake Hamilton, a big house and some cottages that have to be cleared out before they start building."

"I see." Grandpa's voice sounded like his vocal chords had stuck together. His gaze darted sideways with that nervous look he'd had lately. "This place got a name?"

My throat felt like I'd swallowed a bottle of Elmer's, myself. "I think Sandy said Hamilton Haven."

He shut his eyes, then took a deep breath and let it out in one long sigh. When he opened his eyes again, they seemed brighter somehow, less anxious. "Well, then, best get a move on. We'll need some lunch before you head over. The round trip alone will take you nearly an hour, and you want to be home in time for supper and your Bible study tonight."

"But, Grandpa, I—" How was I supposed to tell him I'd intended to wait until the end of the day, when Hobart wasn't likely to be loitering about?

Grandpa stopped halfway up the stairs and looked me in the eye. "All right now, Julie Pearl Stiles, first it was a resort, then a construction site, then a bunch of deserted cabins. What else aren't you telling me?"

I twisted the hem of my tie-dyed T-shirt. "The owner ran us off earlier. If he catches me out there again, he'll have me arrested for trespassing."

"Well, now, I sure don't want that to happen." Grandpa reached the landing and stepped through the door. "Maybe I better go along in case some feathers need unruffling."

Much as I dreaded letting Grandpa see the wreckage Clifton and I had been snooping through all morning, his suggestion made sense. And truth be told, I was not looking forward to stumbling around a trashed out old resort in the dark. No telling what kind of varmints—four-legged, six-legged, eight-legged, or no-legged—I might run into.

"Oh, Grandpa, thank you!" I threw my arms around his warm, wrinkled neck. With Grandpa and me working together, Mama Dog and her pups would be safe, warm, and well-fed by suppertime.

5

Driving Grandpa's delivery van was always an adventure. If you didn't foot the clutch just right, the gears tended to grab and make a horrific grinding noise. Plus, I wasn't exactly thrilled about an afternoon jaunt in mid-June with a broken A/C. We cranked down the windows and let the warm, pine-scented air flow over us. The wetness trickling down my backbone reminded me I'd need another shower before tonight.

I parked the van near the end of the driveway, where a brand new pile of chain-link construction fencing had been dropped off. No telling when they'd be back to install it. At least I didn't see any sign of the shiny maroon Dodge pickup that had been parked out front when Clifton and I took off earlier. I scrambled out the driver's-side door. "Come on, Grandpa. We'd better hurry."

Grandpa slid open the side door and grabbed the dog food. I went around back to retrieve the cardboard box for the puppies, made all comfy-cozy with a soft, worn bath towel. We'd even had the foresight to fill an empty milk jug with fresh water, as I doubted we'd find any working taps on the property. The dog had probably been finding stagnant puddles somewhere or else hanging off the dock to drink from the lake.

As we started up the driveway, Grandpa paused and set one thumb alongside his jaw, rubbing thoughtfully. "Something's awful familiar about this place." He stared a moment longer. "You said it's called Hamilton Haven?"

A warning twinge speared my gut. "That'll be the name for the new place Sandy's boss is building. It used to be something else," I said quickly, then started on around back. Glancing over my shoulder, I realized Grandpa wasn't following me. I turned to see him grimace and haul in a shaky breath, and my own heart threw in an extra beat. "Grandpa? You okay?"

"Fine, fine. Let's just get those dogs."

A low stone retaining wall bordered a weed-infested garden and brick patio behind the house. We stopped there to open a can of dog food and fill the water bowl. I told Grandpa to wait on the patio until I made sure I could coax the little black dog to come with us. Carrying a bowl in each hand, my pockets stuffed with dog treats, I made my way across the cracked stepping stones.

"Hey, Mama Dog. You must be so hungry. Look what I've brought you." From the cabin doorway I could hear the soft, snuffling sounds of the nursing puppies.

As soon as I peeked inside, Mama Dog let loose with a growl. I lowered my gaze and eased down to kneel on the grimy linoleum. "It's all right, it's just me." I set down the bowls and pushed them toward the open bedroom door. "Come on, Mama Dog, this is real good stuff."

Now it was a matter of waiting—waiting for her hunger to overcome the fear, waiting for her to trust me enough to come closer. I made myself as comfortable as I could leaning against the rotting door frame and prepared for a long afternoon.

From where I rested, I could see Grandpa meandering around the rear of the big house, peering in windows, trying doorknobs. I only thought Clifton was dangerously curious. I forgot what Grandpa turned into anytime there was even the slightest chance of discovering some unique flea market find.

I watched the minutes tick by on my vintage Snow White watch, a favorite because of how Snow White charmed first the forest animals and then the dwarves, transforming their dusty, males-only cottage into a real home. Now, if I could sing as sweetly as the fair Snow White, maybe Mama Dog would already be licking out of my hand.

The snarling finally eased off, but those beady eyes held me locked in their gaze. A trickle of drool slipped down Mama Dog's shaggy black muzzle. She licked her lips. The meaty aroma of fresh, moist dog food was working its charm in a way Hobart's dry old dog chow never could.

Maybe if I gave her a little space. Moving as slowly as my stiffening muscles could manage, I stood and stepped outside. I brushed off the seat of my bellbottoms and crossed the yard to join Grandpa on the back porch. "Find anything interesting?"

"Looks like it's pretty well cleaned out." He backed away from a dirt-streaked window.

I licked my thumb and rubbed a smudge off the tip of his nose. "Anything of value the owners left behind, looters probably ripped off."

Grandpa moseyed to the far end of the porch, where a torn screen door hung from one hinge. He propped it open and jiggled the knob on the inner door. We both gasped in surprise when the knob fell off in his hand and the door creaked open. Grandpa dropped the knob into his pocket and gave a nervous chuckle. "Looks like we're invited in."

I tugged at his elbow. "Wait, Grandpa. This whole place looks like it's ready to cave in on itself."

Grandpa ignored me and started down the hallway, sliding one hand along the wall and hunched forward like it helped him to see better. I followed, and as my eyes adjusted to the dim light, I made out vague floral patterns in the faded wallpaper. We passed several doors opening onto rooms of various sizes, mostly empty except for the telltale clutter left by vagrants—musty blankets, empty bean cans, a broken thermos, a shredded feather pillow.

Turning a corner, we came upon a room overlooking the back patio. It must have been a child's room once, judging from the cartoonish ducks and rabbits scampering across the peeling wallpaper. Gauze curtains—I guessed they used to be pale green or yellow—hung in tatters from the window frame. In one corner sat a wooden toy chest. Once upon a time, someone had lovingly clipped duck and rabbit shapes from the same paper that covered the walls and used them to decorate the sides and top of the chest. Now the lid lay ripped from its hinges, as if some scavenger, finding nothing of value inside, had torn it off and cast it to the floor in a fit of rage.

My eyes misted. To think some little boy or girl—maybe even the child who'd drowned—had once resided here, maybe snuggled under fuzzy yellow blankets with a huge stuffed bunny. I imagined a bespectacled daddy reading *The Velveteen Rabbit* while a smiling mother looked on. A happy family, now lost to time, gone forever, leaving only these empty, echoing rooms.

I sighed, a hurricane in the sweltering silence. "This place is so sad, a whole family simply packing up and walking away."

Grandpa shoved past me, as if he couldn't escape the room soon enough. Had he felt it, too—the sadness, the sense of loss? *What was he not telling me?*

I caught up with him in the lobby, where the remains of a reception desk fronted a wall of small, numbered cubbyholes. A few tarnished keys still hung from their hooks. I edged behind the counter, careful not to scrape my arm on the bent and broken nails poking out. "Looks like somebody came in here and tore the top right off."

"A shame, yes indeed." The walls seemed to soak the sound right out of Grandpa's voice. He stood there staring, as if he couldn't quite take it all in.

"I told you we wouldn't find anything worthwhile. Too many people—with a lot fewer scruples—got here before we did."

Something on the floor caught my eye. It looked like a large book, but when I reached for it, I found only the front cover and a few water-damaged pages clinging to what was left of the spine. "I think I found part of the old guest register."

Grandpa shuffled closer. "Julie Pearl, don't—"

I brushed debris off a flat space under the cubbyholes and laid the book open to the first brittle page. In heavy black ink it read:

WELCOME TO PEARLS ALONG THE LAKE

Please sign in with your name and auto license.

The following pages contained fading ballpoint entries in myriad handwriting styles, some faintly readable, others blurred beyond deciphering.

Grandpa edged up beside me and peered around my shoulder. "Pearls Along the Lake." His breath rasped against the side of my neck, and his next words were so faint, I almost didn't catch them. "I should have known."

"Then you *have* heard of it." I squinted to make out some of the guest entries. The ten or twelve surviving pages spanned close to three years. Summers appeared to be the busiest times, with long gaps between dates the rest of the year. A few names appeared regularly. It looked like someone named MacDonohoe spent the same two weeks of June here every year. "Grandpa, why didn't you want me to read that story in the *Recorder* yesterday?"

Grandpa's labored breathing resonated in the stifling silence. I shifted to face him, only to see a strained look deepening the lines around his eyes and mouth. "Grandpa?"

"Oh dear me." He turned away, rubbing his forehead.

"Grandpa, you're scaring me." I stepped in front of him, and even in the weak light filtering through cracks in the boarded-up windows, I could see how pasty his complexion had become.

His expression cleared. "Oh, Julie Pearl, pay me no mind." Fanning himself, he started back the way we'd come. "Whew! It's stuffy in here. And hadn't you better check on your dog and her pups?"

Cocking my head, I gave Grandpa a thorough once-over. Yep, he was keeping something from me—maybe not intentionally, but it couldn't be plainer that whatever had happened at Pearls Along the Lake twenty-five years ago, he didn't like thinking about it. About a dozen possible reasons filed through my brain. Did he know the Pearl family somehow? Did he and Grandma have a child besides my mama that maybe drowned or died some other way, and every reminder of a child's death brought him fresh grief? Maybe if I was patient, he'd finally tell me someday.

With a resigned sigh, I glanced at my Snow White watch and saw it was nearly three o'clock. Where had the afternoon gone? In my hurry to catch up with Grandpa, I brushed against the shelf where I'd laid the guest register and knocked the book to the floor. When I bent to pick it up, a faded snapshot fluttered out from between the pages. The photo showed a dark-haired girl with a pixie haircut standing on what looked to be the front porch of this very house. She balanced a baby on her hip, a tiny thing in a jaunty sailor cap perched atop pale, wispy strands.

Something about the picture made my stomach twist in on itself. Maybe it was because one of these children would never grow up.

Or maybe it was the way those two girls seemed to be smiling into each other's eyes, a sisterly love I would never know.

"Julie Pearl, you coming? Best see to the dog."

Grandpa's call startled me into action, reminding me why we were here in the first place. This was no time to be puzzling over old snapshots. I stuffed it into my back pocket and started down the hall, unable to resist a second glance into the child's bedroom as I passed the doorway. From some unknown source, a breath of air stirred the wispy curtains, and despite the stifling heat, I shivered.

Returning to the cottage, I found the food bowl licked clean. Mama Dog had finished off most of the water too. She lay quietly now on the stained mattress, never taking her eyes off me as her pups squirmed and attempted to nurse. "Good girl," I said. "Want some more?"

With slow, deliberate motions I emptied the can of food into the bowl, then pushed it toward her, closer this time. Her only reaction was lifting her chin and pricking her feathery black ears toward me. Speaking soft encouragement, I inched nearer, all the while gauging her response. I reached the bedroom door before she let out another warning growl.

"Okay, okay, I hear you." But this time, instead of backing away, I sat right where I was, an arm's length from the food dish.

It seemed like an eternity before she finally crept off the mattress in search of the food. The pups hung on tenaciously, dropping off one by one as she raised to all fours and started toward me, one cautious step at a time. Her nose twitched. Saliva dripped from her tongue. Finally she dipped her head and gobbled up the food. She took a couple of backward steps and licked her chops, her gaze slipping from my face to the water bowl, still sitting in the middle of the kitchenette. I could see her weighing her thirst against having to walk past me. Which would also put me between her and the pups—not a risk she'd easily take.

I decided to stay put. Sooner or later she'd have to choose, and I really needed it to be sooner. Hobart or his crew could show up any minute.

At long last, with a fretful glance toward the writhing mass of fuzzy pups, Mama Dog inched past me, so close that her matted belly fur tickled my ankles. I made out the bulges of fat ticks behind her ears and between her toes and hoped I'd soon have the chance to give this poor dog a warm, sudsy bath in the most powerful flea-and-tick soap I could get my hands on. And then a trip to the vet for vaccinations and a complete checkup.

After lapping up some water, Mama Dog stood in the kitchenette gazing at me with sad, hopeful eyes. She whimpered and ran her tongue across her muzzle, her gaze dropping to my pants pocket.

"Ah, you smell those doggy treats." I tugged a biscuit from my pocket and offered it to her. "Poor, hungry thing. Sure wish I knew where you came from, girl."

With each bite she grew more trusting. I inched farther into the bedroom until I knelt at the side of the mattress where the puppies lay squirming, their eyelids and ear flaps still sealed shut. Without so much as a growl or a snarl, Mama Dog ambled past me and curled up around her babies, resting her chin on one tiny rump. Her gentle eyes spoke gratitude.

The time had come. I made my way outside and called to Grandpa, where he rested on the stone retaining wall. "Get the puppy box. We're ready to roll."

We'd just arranged the dog and her puppies in the back of the van when I heard the low rumble of an approaching vehicle. My heart did the cha-cha-cha on its way up my throat. I climbed in the rear door next to Mama Dog. "Get in and drive, Grandpa."

But before he could get his rusty joints moving or I could slam the door, a car pulled up behind us. Not Hobart's maroon pickup. A silver Mercedes.

The driver's door swung open and a long, bronze leg stretched toward the pavement. A thick, mahogany-colored mass of hair appeared above the door, and I found myself staring into the smoky depths of wide tortoise-shell sunglasses.

The air whooshed out of my lungs. "It's *you!*"

6

RENATA

August, 25 years earlier
Hot Springs, Arkansas

Rennie sat on the top step of the front porch, chin resting on her bare knees. Above her head, metal creaked against metal as the "Welcome to Pearls Along the Lake" sign swung from its short chains in the steady breeze. The house behind her stood empty now. The brawny men in their olive-green jumpsuits had carried out the last of the packing crates and furniture—everything except Jenny's toddler bed, matching dresser, and the decorated pine toy box Daddy had built.

Rennie thought back to the day she'd helped Mama cut out six yellow-beaked ducks and eight pink-nosed rabbits from the leftover roll of Jenny's wallpaper. After trying several different arrangements, Mama had Rennie spread craft glue on the back of each figure before she positioned them just so on the sides and lid of the toy box. Then they carried it outside to the patio and coated it with several layers of clear shellac, until it glistened in the afternoon sunshine.

That had been one of Mama's good days—too few and far between.

Now, Mama said she couldn't bear to see those things from Jenny's room again. Aunt Geneva had already packed up all Jenny's clothes and toys and donated them to the Salvation Army. With nothing left of her little sister but a few sticks of furniture and the starched yellow Priscillas adorning the windows, Rennie could almost imagine tears to match her own in the wide, staring eyes of the ducks and rabbits staring down from the walls.

Her father's footsteps echoed behind her. He rested his large, warm hand on the crown of her head. With his callused thumb he smoothed back her sweaty fringe of bangs. "Time to go, Rennie."

Without looking up, she answered, "I don't want to."

Daddy lowered himself to the step next to her. "I know, my girl, I know. But you've seen how hard"—he cleared his throat and blinked several times—"how hard what happened this summer has been on your mother. We need to leave here, for her sake." He sniffed. "For all our sakes."

She'd heard the speech a million times—from Aunt Geneva, Daddy, even their pastor. They'd each explained in patient detail how none of them could be expected to heal from the tragedy if they stayed on where the memories were so vivid.

Rennie swung around to face her father, octopus tentacles constricting her throat. "Please, Daddy, please don't make me come with you and Mama. Let me stay here and live with Aunt Geneva. Send me away to boarding school—anything!"

"Rennie Pearl, you gotta stop such talk. Of course you're coming with us." Daddy drew her close against his chest, and she could hear his thumping heart. His moist, sighing breath whispered across her cheek. "It'll be all right, honey-girl. You'll start at your new high school next week, make new friends. We'll all begin a new life. We'll get through this together, I promise."

"But she hates me, you know she does."

She waited for him to deny it, but he didn't. He couldn't, after all. Mama had spoken it outright the day of the memorial service, said it plainly for all the world to hear:

"I left you in charge, Renata Louise Pearl. And you *killed* your baby sister. I will never, ever forgive you, not even if I live to be a hundred. I will hate and despise you until the day I die!"

7

JULIE PEARL

Present Day

From behind me came the sounds of Mama Dog's soft whimpers as her puppies rustled around in the box. I edged out of the van and closed the door before the lady got close enough to see inside.

"You—you're the girl from the flea market." Ms. Moneybags cocked her head and slammed the door of her Mercedes. She took mincing steps toward me. "What in heaven's name are you doing *here?*"

"Howdy-do, ma'am." Grandpa joined me at the rear of the van and extended a gentlemanly hand, but his voice was tight. "Otto Stiles."

She took Grandpa's hand with limp fingers. "Renata Channing. I was in your shop yesterday."

"Picked out one of Hazel's lace tablecloths." He nodded. His Adam's apple bobbed. "Hope it suits you."

"Yes, it's lovely." She glanced toward the house, and I thought I detected a shiver. "Really, why are you here? This encounter seems . . . entirely too coincidental."

Indeed it did, and I was beginning to wonder what fate had in mind, placing this snooty rich lady in my path two days in a row. Not to mention I had a few questions of my own—like was she connected with the Pearl family who used to own this resort, and why had she left the Swap & Shop yesterday in such an all-fired hurry?

I rubbed my arms, feeling as if I'd caught a chill. She glared at me like she was waiting for an answer, so I thought I'd best give her one. "My best friend just got hired by the new owner. We thought we'd see if there was anything worth salvaging before they start demolition."

The lady bristled. "Ah, yes, the new owner. Micah Hobart."

"So you know him?"

"I'm the one who sold him this worthless pile of trash. We signed the papers yesterday."

"Then you *are* one of the Pearls." She must be one of the children in the snapshot that was now burning a hole in my back pocket. I ached to ask her about the child who'd drowned, why her family abandoned the place, why she'd held onto the old resort for so long while letting things fall into such disrepair.

"It was a long time ago." The woman's eyes took on a distant look. "A very, very long time ago."

"Then why . . . ?" I lifted one hand in a vague motion toward the house.

"I felt the need to see the place one more time before—" She blinked several times and crossed her arms. "Honestly, why is this any of *your* business?"

"Sorry, it's just—"

Grandpa cut me off, his grip biting into my wrist like an ice-cold vise grip. "We best be on our way, Julie."

I couldn't leave, not yet. Not when the woman who might hold the answers I sought stood right in front of me. But I didn't get the chance to say so, because Mama Dog chose that moment to let loose a pitiful whine.

"Is that a child in there—and in this heat?" Mrs. Channing barged past me, her face a mask of righteous anger. She peered through the cloudy rear window, then instantly shrank back. "Oh —a dog! It can't get out, can it?"

I rolled my eyes. I could never understand some people's irrational fear of animals. If a dog is vicious or dangerous, there's usually a logical reason. Like abuse. Starvation. Illness. Abandonment. Conditions likely traceable to a cruel or irresponsible human being. "No, she can't get out," I snapped. "I agree, though—she's probably getting overheated by now. You're right, Grandpa. Let's go."

I could probe Grandpa with questions after we got Mama Dog and her pups safely settled in. All of a sudden I just wanted to get out of there, away from this woman who made me feel as jumpy inside as a frog in a hot frying pan.

Back at the Swap & Shop, I didn't have time to think much more about the resort or the crazy lady who used to live there or the grumpy old guy she'd sold it to. All my attention went to getting Mama Dog and those pups settled in, and I was amazed at how quickly she made herself at home. It convinced me she must have once lived with decent folks, just got lost somewhere along the way and was forced to fend for herself. She seemed plenty happy to hop in the big galvanized washtub out back, letting me lather her up and pick those nasty ticks off with a pair of old tweezers. When I finally rinsed her off, she hopped out of the tub and yipped with pure glee. After a good shaking, she had me almost as wet as herself.

And by then it had gotten so late that I'd never get myself cleaned up, fix Grandpa some supper, and still make it to Bible study on time. I gave Sandy a quick ring and told her to make an excuse for me. "We found another stray," I told her, not saying where. "I just got through de-ticking her, and I'm a mess."

"Then for heaven's sake, *please* stay home," Sandy said with a gasp. "I'll catch you up on everything tomorrow."

Mama Dog and the pups spent the night on a fresh, clean blanket in a box at the foot of my bed, and the next morning we headed to the vet for a checkup and shots. I cradled one of the tiny black pups in my two hands and lifted it to eye level. "What breed do you think they are?"

Doc Wagner chewed her lip. "The mother could be part shepherd, maybe border collie. Hard to say yet what the pups will look like. Want me to put an ad on the bulletin board? This sweet girl will be easy to find a home for, and the pups, too, when they're old enough."

"Let me think on it," I said slowly. Mama Dog had already wormed her way deep into my heart, and I had a feeling I'd be keeping her around.

On the way home I tried out some names for the old girl. "Stormy? Smoky? Blackie?" I flicked a glance toward the rear of the van. "Nope, too ordinary. How about Sylvia? Gretchen. Ashley. Brynna—"

She yipped. Whether I'd accidentally landed upon her original name or maybe one that sounded similar, it was settled. Mama Dog was officially renamed Brynna.

That afternoon, Grandpa and I brought Brynna and the pups downstairs with us while we swept and dusted and generally got organized to reopen for business on Thursday. Brynna seemed a bit uneasy at first with Sneezy sniffing around the puppies, but they soon forged a cautious friendship.

Grandpa and I had some of our best conversations doing busy work around the shop, so with everything weighing on my mind lately, I decided to take advantage of today's opportunity. I maneuvered my broom and dustpan over to where Grandpa was polishing the glass fronts of LeRoy Tuttle's china display cabinets.

Most of our vendors did a pretty good job keeping their own booths clean and orderly, but for a few we had to put forth a little extra effort. A tenant's streaked display case or dusty merchandise didn't speak well for the Swap & Shop.

"How's it going, Grandpa?" I reached the broom under Maddie Barton's front table and swept out a gum wrapper and a few dust bunnies.

He made a clucking noise with his tongue. "If old LeRoy doesn't get his trifocals adjusted soon, I may have to up our commission on his sales. I swear, the man is as blind as a cave-dwelling salamander."

"Now, Grandpa, why are you picking on LeRoy? That's not like you at all." More proof he was bothered about something he didn't want to talk about.

He finished his attack on a smudge and stood erect with a groan. "Just getting old, I suppose. Old and crotchety." He rubbed his back and stretched.

He wasn't fooling me for an instant with his "old and crotchety" excuse. I made a few more strokes with the broom and pushed a pile of litter into the dustpan. Maybe a slightly more direct approach would get him talking. "That Renata Pearl Channing—she sure is a puzzle."

He moved to the next cabinet and spritzed it with Windex. "You sure we have enough dog food for the week? Might want to run over to Friendly's later."

"We're good for another day or two." If Grandpa thought changing the subject would get me off his case, he had another think coming. "Sure would like to know her story."

"Brynna's? Guess we'll never know." Grandpa tore off a fresh paper towel.

He knew perfectly well I didn't mean Brynna, and his avoidance tactics were starting to rile me. "I'm talking about Mrs. Channing. Do you know what happened at the resort all those years ago? Is that where the little girl dr—"

"Julie Pearl." Grandpa stopped his work and fixed me with a desperate glare. "It's not our business, all right? Leave it be."

Obviously, my tightlipped grandpa had no intention of telling me a thing. But the harder he worked to avoid my questions, the more certain I became that he was hiding something important, something that mattered to him a lot.

And if it mattered so much to Grandpa, it mattered even more to me.

Later that evening, as I dried the last supper dish and set it in the cupboard, the phone rang. Grandpa answered it. "How ya doin', Sandy? Yep, she's right here."

I draped the dishtowel over the oven door handle and reached for the receiver. "What's up, girlfriend?"

"How's your new dog? Get rid of all those revolting ticks?"

Brynna came over and nuzzled my hand as I sat down at the kitchen table. "She's great. Sweetest dog I ever met. A real keeper."

"You missed a great discussion last night. I took lots of notes. Can I bring 'em by?"

"I thought you had to work at the DQ on Wednesday nights."

Sandy let out a jubilant laugh. "Not anymore! There was a message from Mr. Hobart when I got home last night. He decided he needed me to start right away. Today was my first day!"

"Wow, Sandy, that's super." I only wished I sounded happier for her, but her news reminded me of the old resort and all my questions about Renata Pearl Channing. The mounting frustration slammed me in the chest like a bucket of Tom's rusty old tools.

"Jules? Something's wrong. I can hear it in your voice."

I chewed on a hangnail. Maybe by now Sandy would know more about the history of the Pearls' place. "You want to meet me at the DQ for sundaes? My treat."

"Great! I'm ready to celebrate!"

Twenty minutes later, Sandy and I picked up our deluxe brownie-and-hot-fudge sundaes at the DQ counter and settled across from each other in the front corner booth. I couldn't help feeling a little sorry for red-faced George Bradley, scurrying behind the counter trying to cover the management duties Sandy had handled so capably.

I licked a swirl of caramel and hot fudge off my plastic spoon. "Well? Tell me all about it. How was your first day on the new job?"

"Terrific. There's so much to learn, but I can already tell Micah Hobart is going to be a dream to work for."

My hand paused halfway between the bowl and my mouth. "I haven't had the chance to tell you yet, but Clifton and I met your boss yesterday."

She raised an eyebrow. "Oh, yeah? Where?"

"At the resort. Clifton wanted to go look around."

Sandy groaned and lowered her head to the table. "And after I outright *told* him not to go snooping."

"Don't be too mad at him. I was curious about the place, too. Besides, Clifton was hoping Mr. Hobart might have some other jobs available."

"So did you talk to him?"

"Mr. Hobart? Yeah, we had a conversation of sorts." I stirred my melting ice cream and tried to think of something nice I could say about Sandy's new boss before grilling her with questions. "He seems to like animals."

Sandy wrinkled her nose. "That's a non sequitur if I ever heard one."

I bit my lip. "The resort is where I found Brynna."

"Brynna?"

"The mama dog." I told her how Clifton and I found the dog and puppies in one of the cabins.

"That explains it," Sandy said with a nod. "I overheard Mr.

Hobart on the phone this morning with the humane society. Sounded like they'd gone out to the place to look for some animal but it was already gone. I thought it was a raccoon or a rabid possum or something." She licked her spoon. "He'll be so happy tomorrow when I tell him you rescued the dogs."

"I'm not so sure about that." I leaned back and crossed my arms.

Sandy narrowed her gaze. "Julie Pearl Stiles, you better not be keeping anything from me. Especially something that could jeopardize my new job."

Her mouth twisted as I described how Hobart practically threw us off the property. I left out the part about catching a glimmer of remorse in his eyes . . . or was it something else? Easier to keep my own emotions in check if I focused on his rudeness.

She shook her head. "That's just not the man I know."

"Well, you weren't there." I finished the last spoonful of my sundae and pushed the bowl aside.

Frowning, Sandy pulled a paper napkin from the dispenser and reached over to blot a dribble of chocolate syrup I'd accidentally dripped onto the table. "I gather things didn't go real smoothly Monday afternoon when he closed the deal on the property. Maybe he was still upset when he ran into you and Clifton."

My skin prickled—exactly the lead-in I'd been waiting for. "You mean his meeting with Renata Pearl Channing?"

Sandy's eyebrows creased. "How do you know her name?"

"She was in the flea market on Monday. And then she drove up at the resort yesterday right after Grandpa and I got the dogs into the van." I shuddered. "I don't like her, Sandy. Something about her gives me the scroochies."

"No kidding. I hear she's been nothing but trouble for Mr. Hobart. Fussing over every little detail of the sale, demanding things be handled a certain way. Before she'd sign the papers, he practically had to get on his knees and swear to her he wouldn't leave any of the original structures. She doesn't want a trace of the old resort left behind."

An image of the child's room with the cheery ducks and rabbits filled my mind, along with the growing conviction that something horrible happened there. Some connection to the child's drowning twenty-five years ago that Grandpa didn't want to talk about. What possible reason could he have for keeping it bottled up inside when it clearly ate at him like acid on metal?

Unless . . . could it have anything to do with my own past? Maybe even my father and why he disappeared from our lives and never returned?

An image of a tall, green-eyed man wasting away in a prison cell filled my brain. What if my very own father had something to do with the drowning and that was why no one ever spoke of him around me?

"Julie?" Sandy tapped my hand. "You look like you're a million miles away."

Giving myself a mental shake, I stuffed the chocolate-smeared napkin into my empty bowl and scooted out of the booth. "I have to go. I'll call you tomorrow, okay?"

Without looking back, I shoved the trash into the nearest receptacle and charged out into the muggy June evening. A death squad of vicious, half-starved mosquitoes caught up with me before I reached my Beetle. One or two managed to follow me inside, and I smacked them with unnecessary force before starting the engine and peeling out of the parking lot.

Maybe it was crazy to feel so obsessed with an abandoned lake resort, as if Renata Pearl Channing and her mysterious past should mean anything to me at all. But it did. And somehow it all seemed bound up together—my father, the Pearl family, Micah Hobart, even my sweet dog Brynna.

Yes indeed, Grandpa owed me some answers, and I intended to press even harder until I got them.

8

JULIE PEARL

The flea market opened at nine the next morning, so my questions for Grandpa would have to wait. At least I had plenty to distract me through another busy weekend, because with all the craziness in my life lately, my brain was on the verge of spinning itself into a black hole of confusion.

Fortunately, my precious Brynna and her darling pups helped bring a measure of peace to my soul. They kept me grounded in the here-and-now, reminding me all over again that the bond with an animal is about as close to true unconditional love as it gets in this life.

Now that their mama provided their fill of healthy nourishment, those pups were plumping out nicely. And Brynna, though her coat was a bit sparse where I'd had to clip out mats and tangles, looked sleeker and shinier every day. I'd parked Brynna and the puppies in a used playpen behind the checkout counter during business hours that weekend, and even before closing time on Saturday, at least ten customers had expressed interest in adoption. Several would have taken Brynna *and* the pups right on the spot, but I turned them down flat.

"Only the puppies are available," I told them. "The mama's a keeper." I took names and phone numbers and told the interested parties to check back in six weeks, at which time I'd decide who could provide the best homes.

At the end of the day, Grandpa yawned and eased his back. "Whew, I'm tired. Thank goodness tomorrow's Monday. Don't think I'd survive another busy day like we've had this weekend."

"Go on upstairs and put your feet up. I'll be up as soon as I'm done here."

"You gonna do your computer entry stuff before supper?"

"Thought I would." I grinned. "Unless you want me to teach you how."

He chuckled and reached for the broom and dustpan. "This dog's way too old to learn new tricks."

Katy Harcourt, one of the last of our tenants to call it a day, had just closed her booth across the way. Carrying one of her genuine imitation Gucci handbags, she moseyed up to the counter and rested her plump forearms on the edge. "What old dog you talkin' about, Otto? Not this cute little thing y'all took in?" She craned her neck to see over the counter, where Brynna lay in the playpen letting her pups nurse while she licked them clean with her long, pink tongue.

"No, no." Grandpa waggled a finger. "Why, me, of course. Julie Pearl keeps trying to talk me into learning how to use a computer."

Katy pressed a hand to her ample bosom and let loose a chortling laugh. "That'll be the day!" Her mouth curved downward in an accusing frown. "High time you joined the twenty-first century, old man. You can do email, store digital photos, surf the Net, all kinds of stuff. I got me one of them fancy little laptops back there in my booth—keep a game of computer solitaire going on it all the time. Only thing that keeps me from being bored out of my gourd between customers."

Grandpa crossed his arms and harrumphed. "Ain't got no

digital photos, don't know anyone to email, and surfin's for those crazies in Waikiki."

"Still stuck in the Dark Ages, you miserable old coot . . ."

I tuned out and let them go at each other. The subjects varied, but it seemed to be their preferred form of after-hours entertainment most weekends. I finished totaling the receipts, made my entries in the consignment ledger, and tucked the cash, checks, and charge slips in a bank bag to take upstairs to the safe.

In the meantime, my brain had latched onto the part about "surfin' the Net." Seemed everybody nowadays had their own website, plus with all the historical and genealogical sites and online newspaper archives, surely I could find something about Renata Pearl Channing or the old Pearls Along the Lake Resort. Besides, it might be easier to get Grandpa to talk if I already had some pertinent facts at my disposal.

I hefted Brynna out of the playpen and transferred her puppies into a towel-lined wicker laundry basket. We took a detour out back so Brynna could relieve herself, then went upstairs. The moment I set foot inside the kitchen, my mouth started watering. My crock pot chicken Santa Fe recipe simmered away, filling the apartment with the aromas of cilantro, green peppers, and tomatoes. I stirred it once before filling Brynna's food dish and refreshing her water bowl. Then Sneezy pestered me until I served him up a big scoop of Kitty Delight mackerel surprise.

Finally, with the bank bag locked up and a pan of Spanish-style Rice-a-Roni started on the stove, I had a moment to myself. I pulled a chair up to the tiny desk in the back corner of the living room and poked the start button on my relic of a computer. Being in the flea market business, I'd learned plenty about finding new life and value in just about anything old. Computers? Not so much. I'd just about dozed off by the time my accounting software opened. I keyed in the weekend sales data and bank deposit, then calculated our commissions and vendor payments.

That done, I decided it was time for some internet research. I clicked on my browser icon and then sat there tapping my toes while the homepage loaded. Blast our rural telephone company internet provider. If I was going to find out anything before next Christmas, I'd need a fast computer with a decent high-speed connection. Sometimes I went over to Sandy's whenever I wanted to look something up online, but I sure didn't need her peering over my shoulder now that her employer was the new owner of Pearls Along the Lake.

I ransacked my brain for other options. Clifton's dad had a computer at the shop, but Clifton, as technophobic as my grandpa, naturally steered clear of it. The nearest library with computer access was over in Hot Springs, and it was too late to get in there on a Sunday evening.

Rats. I crossed to the window and stared down at the parking lot. Grandpa and Katy Harcourt had carried their banter outside, and the sounds of their laughter rose on the summer breeze.

The solution hit me so hard, I couldn't move fast enough. I wrestled the kitchen door open and darted onto the landing. "Katy, wait!" I leapt down the steps two at a time.

She spun around. "Slow up there, girl, before you break your skinny neck."

"What on earth is wrong, Julie Pearl?" Grandpa reached out to steady me as I skidded across the gravel to halt right in front of them.

"Katy—your laptop." I shoved a tangled clump of hair off my face while I caught my breath. "You have one of those mobile broadband thingies, don't you?"

"Only way to get a good internet connection in this backwater town. You need to borrow it, sugar?"

"Would you mind?"

"Not one eensy-weensy bit. I won't be in the shop tomorrow, so you can keep it till Thursday. Click on the little lightning-bolt icon and it'll sign you in to my provider."

I gave her a quick hug. "Katy, you're a lifesaver."

"Oh, pooh." She waved me off and started toward her car. Turning with a wink, she added, "Just don't go lookin' up none of them X-rated websites or computer dating services, you hear?"

I laughed out loud. "Don't worry. Finding the love of my life on the internet is the absolute farthest thing from my mind."

Smells of chicken Santa Fe lingered long after we'd cleaned up the supper dishes and Grandpa had gone to bed. Seven thirty was early even for him, and I had to remind myself he wasn't getting any younger.

The thought sent a shiver up my spine. *Oh, Lordy, don't call my grandpa home to heaven too soon. He's all I have in the whole world.*

Still, with Grandpa in bed and the apartment to myself, I could get started on my internet searches. I moved Katy's laptop to the end of the table and drummed my fingernails while Windows loaded. A tinny chord sounded as the desktop appeared onscreen —a grainy photo of Katy and her grandkids smiling around a candlelit birthday cake. I laughed. The mobile broadband icon had been strategically placed right over Katy's buxom chest.

A couple of mouse clicks later, I found the search engine I wanted and typed in my first request: Renata Pearl Channing.

The top entries had to do with Carol Channing, Pearl Bailey, soprano Renata Scotto, various obituaries for people with similar names, and L.E. Channing, owner and CEO of GigantaMart, Inc. No mention of Renata on the GigantaMart site, which was mainly the store's online portal and location finder. The next dozen or so listings were mainly obituaries and other references to various people named Renata or Pearl or Channing. Halfway down the third page I came across a site for the Channing Children's Foundation, based in Little Rock, Arkansas.

Lo and behold, when I opened the homepage, there before me appeared a photo of Renata Pearl Channing in all her perfectly coiffed glory. Only she was identified under the picture as "Mrs. Lawrence Eugene Channing, Founder and President."

I scanned the introductory paragraph and learned the organization, under Mrs. Channing's "loving direction and personal involvement," provided a variety of services for underprivileged children throughout the greater Little Rock area —school supplies, clothing, daycare, medical assistance, you name it. The foundation also ran a home for unwed mothers and provided adoption services. Links took me to pages with more detail, including photos of Mrs. Channing holding a smiling toddler on her lap, handing out toys next to an enormous Christmas tree, and soothing a crying child who apparently had just been given a vaccination.

And, yes, her husband was the noted L.E. Channing of GigantaMart fame. So she was a philanthropist, dedicating her life (and her husband's bank account) to helping children. I felt hard pressed to reconcile the image with my first impression of the cool, inscrutable woman who'd strolled into the Swap & Shop like she was queen of the world.

On the other hand, it did explain her consternation when she thought we had a child in the back of the hot van. As if Grandpa or I either one could ever do anything so stupid. It was her snootiness more than anything that made me mad, but I guess money can do that to people.

Next search: Pearls Along the Lake.

Some jewelry sites, lake references, but no exact matches. Not even the Hot Springs online newspaper archives turned up anything, and no point hoping an obliging history buff in the area had posted something about it on a personal website. I figured too many years had passed.

I cleared the search box. Okay, why not? *Micah Hobart*, my speedy little fingers typed in. When the results came up—*presto!*—there was my own Mr. Micah Hobart, listed on a "Who's Who in Arkansas" page as a prominent real estate investor/developer. The blurb said he was headquartered in Dallas, with a branch office and several buildings and industrial centers to his credit in Little Rock. Picture of him and everything. His beard showed a little less gray, and he wore a neatly pressed baby-blue shirt and striped tie. When he cleaned up for the camera and actually put on a smile, the guy wasn't half bad-looking. I could almost—*almost,* mind you—understand how Sandy could be so taken with him.

Nothing much in his bio appeared helpful. It mentioned briefly his latest endeavor, the purchase and renovation of some resort property on Lake Hamilton. The final paragraph contained a smattering of information about his background and family. I skimmed it quickly and was about to call it a night and sign off when a line jumped out at me: *Hobart, originally from Fort Worth, Texas, is the son of Mrs. George MacDonohoe and the late Thomas Hobart.*

You don't forget a name like MacDonohoe. I'd seen that name only a few days ago, in the torn, stained register pages Grandpa and I found at Pearls Along the Lake.

"Micah Hobart and Renata Pearl Channing must have known each other even as kids," I muttered as the computer went through its shutdown routine. Brynna came over and nuzzled my hand, and I absently scratched her behind the ear. "Brynna-girl, this just gets curiouser and curiouser."

9

———

MICAH

August, 25 years earlier
Fort Worth, Texas

Micah flipped his sweat-stained red ball cap off his brow and sent it sailing across the kitchen, where it snagged a peg on the hat rack, swung back and forth a couple of times, then settled into place. He made a victory fist. "Yes!"

"That you, Micah?" Edith MacDonohoe emerged from the back bedroom with a brimming plastic laundry basket. "How'd practice go?"

He puffed out his chest. "Guess what, Mom? Coach is starting me in Friday's playoff game."

"Pitching? Oh, son, I'm so proud of you!" She dropped the basket, pulled him into her arms, and planted a wet kiss on his forehead.

"Cut it out, cut it out!" He laughed and squirmed out of reach.

"Wait till I tell George. He'll bust his buttons." Mom wiped her lip prints off his face with the side of her thumb. "Hey, superstar, let's have a snack to celebrate."

Micah pulled out a chair in the breakfast nook and plopped

down at the table while his mother poured him a tall glass of milk. Sipping slowly, he watched Mom arrange apple slices and peanut butter crackers in a neat circle on a flowered paper plate. He bumped his sneakers against the legs of the chair. "Think George can get off work to come to the game?"

"I'm sure he'll try his best—careful, there, don't spill your milk." Micah's mother pulled a napkin from the avocado-green ceramic dispenser and dabbed away his milk moustache. "You know George loves you like his own. Has from the day we got married."

Micah wasn't sure what to make of the funny, tickly feeling in his chest. Yeah, it felt good to know his stepdad loved him, cared about him as a son. George was a good man—patient, understanding. Loved baseball and fishing and telling gross jokes that made Micah's friends double over in loud guffaws (and made Mom cringe).

But Micah would always, always miss his real dad.

If Daddy hadn't died, if they'd never gone to that lake place in Hot Springs, if he'd never met Rennie Pearl ...

Micah twisted apart a cracker and scraped his front teeth over the peanut butter filling. He closed his eyes and made himself think about the feel of sticky peanut butter on the roof of his mouth, the scratch of cracker crumbs as he swallowed.

"Oh, I nearly forgot," Mom said. "You got a letter today."

"Me? It's not even my birthday or anything."

"The postmark is Little Rock, Arkansas." Mom retrieved a plain white envelope off the counter and handed it to him.

The handwriting was girlish—the round, swirling script of a teenager. Little circles dotting the I's, curling tails at the end of each word ...

His stomach did a nosedive. He shoved the envelope across the table as if it were on fire.

"Micah, what's wrong?" His mother planted her hands on her ample hips. "You haven't even opened it yet."

His voice dropped to a tense whisper. "It's from her."

Edith MacDonohoe picked up the envelope and studied it, front and back. "There's not even a return address. How do you know who it's from?"

"I just do," he said. "It's from Rennie Pearl." The name tasted bitter in his mouth, like the memories from last June he tried to forget . . . and knew he never would.

"Oh, my." His mother sank into a chair and pressed a hand to her forehead. "What would possess that girl to write you a letter? Didn't you suffer enough? All because of that little tart and her scheming."

Micah tucked his hands under his armpits. His breath scraped the insides of his lungs. "You open it, Mom. See what it says."

"Humph, as if you should care."

The whole world seemed to tilt sideways, time grinding to a near standstill, while he watched his mother slide a ruby-red fingernail under the seal and gently work open the envelope. The soft ripping sound blended with the ticking of the stove clock, the clothes dryer rumbling, Bob Barker announcing the next prize on "The Price Is Right" on the family room TV.

One thin sheet of lined paper slipped out. His mother unfolded it and read softly:

Dear Micah,

I just wanted to tell you how sorry I am for everything. You were only being my friend, trying to do the right thing for me and my sister. I will always love you for that, so promise me you won't go on blaming yourself. Remember, Jenny's in a better place now.

Love,

Rennie

Micah's mother shook her head. "What's she mean, anyway —'Jenny's in a better place'? The poor child is *dead*, for goodness' sake."

Micah could almost feel the milk curdling in his roiling stomach. "You know how Mrs. Pearl acted so crazy sometimes. Rennie just means she's glad her baby sister didn't have to grow up in that house."

"If you ask me, Rennie's the one who's crazy. Every time we stayed there, I felt like she was always staring at us, giving us the evil eye." Her whole body quivered, and her mouth puckered like she'd bitten into a lemon. "I wish we'd never gone to that place. Thank goodness they've shut it down."

"Rennie was always nice to me." Micah said the words in a secret voice, like he was trying to convince himself they were true. They used to be friends, he and Rennie. Didn't matter that she was a couple years older—Rennie always treated him like he was somebody special. Yeah, she was a little strange, but who wouldn't be in a family like hers? And anyway, who else was he going to hang out with every summer while Mom and George celebrated their second, third, fourth—how many, he'd lost count—honeymoons at Pearls Along the Lake?

The first time they stayed there, Rennie seemed to know how awkward he felt with his parents acting like lovesick teenagers and no other kids his age around. One day she asked him if he wanted to help her clean cabins. It sure beat sitting in the front of George's little motorboat while listening to George and Mom smooching in the back. Completely grossed out, he'd pretend not to notice and instead fix his attention on the tree-covered islands they'd pass. One even had campers on it sometimes—weirdoes in blue-jean cutoffs and shirts with beer logos on the front. The guys had shaggy beards and tangled hair even longer than the girls'. One couple owned a big yellow dog that would dart out to a rock overhang and bark like a maniac at the ski boats zipping by.

The weirdo campers were interesting in their own way, but evidently spent most of their time making out, too, even worse than Mom and George. The sun-browned, half-clothed children running about the island didn't seem to belong to any one set of parents—like kids in a commune.

After three days of those R-rated performances, Micah had decided he'd had enough and gladly took Rennie up on her offer. She'd load his skinny arms with a stack of fluffy white towels, and he'd sniff their crisp, clean aroma as he neatly and proudly hung them on the bathroom rods.

Then one summer Rennie introduced Micah to her baby sister, Jennifer Susan Pearl—an itty-bitty thing, scarcely fifteen pounds at nine months old. Born last September, a month prematurely, Rennie told him, smoothing the silky strands of pale gold hair covering the baby girl's tiny head. Micah saw little of Mrs. Pearl that June—Rennie said the birth had been hard on her —and when she did show her face, it was mainly to yell at Rennie over some forgotten chore or a lodger's complaint, all too often his own mother's.

The next summer, Rennie told him her mother was still ailing and hardly got out at all anymore. Rennie didn't have as much time for Micah, what with so many extra duties around the resort —plus looking after her baby sister, now toddling all over the place. Sometimes Micah volunteered to watch over the spunky, green-eyed little tyke, tossing plush toys to her in the playpen on the back patio while Rennie pushed the rumbling white maid's cart from cabin to cabin. If they got lucky, Rennie's mother would find the energy to play with Jenny for a bit, and Rennie would have an hour or so to swim in the lake with Micah. Towing a small cooler lashed to an inner tube, they'd dog-paddle out to the floating deck and then drink orange sodas and eat Fritos and bean dip while soaking up the sun.

By the time Micah's family visited last June, Jenny had grown even bigger, Rennie's mother was crabbier, and Rennie had become more restless than ever. She stopped being so much fun to hang around with, and Micah found himself left to his own pursuits more and more. Mom and George were over the worst of their honeymoon phase, and now when they went out in the boat, they did more fishing than smooching. The same band of drifters still sat around on the island in front of their little blue tents, smoking who-knows-what and drinking beer while their bikinis and jams dried on a rope strung between two pine trees. Each year George said it wouldn't be long until the lake patrol ran them off permanently, but each year they were back, usually with a new set of wild-haired children toddling about, and the same yellow dog barking as fiercely as ever when boats ventured too close.

That was the summer that changed everything. The summer Rennie pleaded with Micah to help her get Jenny away from their mother's insanity, as far away from Pearls Along the Lake as humanly possible.

The summer Jennifer Susan Pearl sank into the depths of Lake Hamilton and drowned.

JULIE PEARL

Present Day

Early Monday afternoon, while I helped a customer load one of Audrey Guthrie's "antique" made-in-Mexico lamp stands into the back of an SUV, a familiar maroon pickup cruised into the parking lot. The hair rose on the back of my neck.

"There you go, ma'am, fits just fine." I helped her spread an old quilt over the lamp stand before closing the hatchback and tried not to let her see my hands shaking.

"Thanks for your help, miss." She climbed into her vehicle and drove off.

I sauntered over to the pickup as Micah Hobart climbed out. Here on my turf, he looked even taller than I remembered—and at my height it takes a really tall guy to make an impression on me. Just looking up at him made my knees all watery.

"Julie Stiles, isn't it?" He shoved his hands into his jeans pockets. The sun reflecting off his Ray-Bans obscured his eyes.

"That's—" I cleared my throat and lowered my pitch a notch or two. "That's right." I slid my sweaty palms into the pockets of my plaid capris and mimicked his stance.

"Your friend Sandy told me you got the dog."

I figured that's why he was here. Sandy betrayed me. "I couldn't let her and those babies go to the pound."

He looked away. "I didn't want that, either, but I didn't see another choice."

Get me started on neglected animals and nobody intimidates me for long. I marched over, waving my finger under his arrogant nose. "You didn't see another choice because you were too busy to find one. Didn't take me any time at all—just a lot of patience and some TLC—before little Mama Dog was ready to follow me home. She's the sweetest thing ever, and I'm going to keep her."

He shifted his weight. "Are you through?"

I harrumphed. "Yes. I guess I am."

He took off his sunglasses and rubbed his eyes. "You're right, I have had a lot on my mind lately. I was rude to you the other day, and I tried to apologize then, but you left without giving me a chance."

I raised an eyebrow. "So you drove all the way over here just to say you're sorry?"

"Yes—no." He chuckled, a gentle sound like the deep, low rumble of a waterfall, then glanced away muttering, "This is insane."

"You're telling *me*." And yet he looked surprisingly cute standing there all tongue-tied. I crossed my arms and waited.

"Truth is," he went on, "I didn't believe Sandy at first when she told me you'd managed to cozy up to that scared old dog so quickly. You may not believe this, but I really had been trying, every spare minute I had."

Something of the momentary kindness I'd glimpsed during our first encounter showed in the softening of his gray eyes. My heart made a strange flutter, like nothing I'd ever felt before, and for some wild reason I wished I could run upstairs and change out of this dust-smeared white camp shirt. I shifted my arms to cover the worst of the grime. "Like I said, you didn't give her enough of a chance to trust you."

"Believe me, the only reason I called the humane society was to get her out of there before the bulldozers arrive to start demolition. If she'd gone too wild, better an easy death than crushed by falling debris."

"So it's true—you are going to clear the land and start over."

"That's the plan."

"Yeah, I heard Renata Pearl Channing gave you a hard time about that."

He swiveled sideways and snorted a laugh. "I see my new assistant's tongue wags both ways."

My heart hammered. The last thing I wanted was to put Sandy's new job in jeopardy. "You can trust her, I promise. She'd never let anything *really* confidential slip."

"Now that's comforting." He glanced away with a shrug. "Anyway, it's not like my dealings with Renata are any big secret."

I swallowed over a twinge of guilt, thinking about the internet research I'd done on him and Mrs. Channing last night. Yet here was my chance to get the facts straight from the source. I bit the tip of my ragged thumbnail. "I've run into Mrs. Channing a couple of times lately. She's one strange bird."

"To say the least." A dark look clouded his eyes.

"Are you and her—I mean, it's none of my business, but it sounds like you two have a . . . history."

His shadowed gaze turned sad, even pained—not like I imagined a jilted lover would look (okay, so I'd read a few too many paperback romances). No, this was something far more intense. All he said was, "It's complicated."

"So how *do* you know her?"

He seemed to shake off whatever memories held him captive. Again, that rippling, waterfall chuckle. "Julie Stiles, you are way too curious for your own good. I didn't come out here to tell you my life story." He blew out through flattened lips. "Like I said, I came to apologize and to thank you for saving the dog's life after I'd almost given up trying."

His humility temporarily banished all thoughts of Renata Channing and Pearls Along the Lake. Before I realized what I was doing, I grabbed his wrist and tugged him toward the shop entrance. "You should come inside and meet her up close. I bet you won't even recognize her. She's all clean and brushed and de-ticked. And those pups—they're growing like little piglets." I knew I was babbling, but I couldn't stop myself.

The brass bells clanged as we pushed through the door, and Grandpa looked up from behind the checkout counter to see what all the commotion was about. "Goodness' sakes, Julie Pearl, just 'cause Mondays are slow don't give you no cause to go draggin' in customers off the street."

My cheeks flamed. I dropped Micah Hobart's warm, callused hand like it had sprouted cactus thorns.

"You must be Julie's grandfather and partner in crime." Mr. Hobart cast Grandpa a crooked smile. He extended the same hand I'd just released. "Micah Hobart. How do you do?"

Grandpa's eyes narrowed. He reached across the counter to accept the handshake. "Otto Stiles. You got business out this way, Mr. Hobart?"

I'd never seen Grandpa treat a new acquaintance so coolly. Leastwise not since he was officially introduced to Renata Pearl Channing the other day at the resort. The tension between the two men hung thick as the matted fur I'd clipped from behind Brynna's ears.

Mr. Hobart took the tiniest step backwards. "I, uh, thought I'd see how the dog and her pups are doing. I heard from Sandy Monroe that you'd rescued them."

"They're doing just fine." Grandpa scowled and moved aside so Mr. Hobart could see Brynna and the pups in the playpen.

"Hey, girl." Mr. Hobart's mouth widened into a grin. "Glad to see you and those puppies looking so fine and healthy."

Brynna gazed up at him and whimpered. Her tail thudded against the mat.

"She's sorry and forgives you," I translated, not even realizing I'd done it till the words were out of my mouth.

Micah Hobart turned and stared at me, and I glimpsed something otherworldly in his gaze, like I'd touched some deep, hurting place inside him. "That's . . . good to know."

Grandpa bustled around the counter. "All righty, then, if your business is done here, you best be on your way. We're fixin' to close up soon—got lots to do."

My mouth fell open. "It's not even three o'clock yet. We've got two hours till—"

"Now, Julie Pearl, what's the point of staying open when we don't have no customers?" Grandpa shuffled to the front door and held it open. "Like I said, you should be on your way, Mr. Hobart."

Casting Grandpa a stunned frown, I followed Mr. Hobart outside. We stood by his pickup, and I waited with downcast eyes until the brass bells jangled against the closing door. "Sorry, my grandpa's been a little edgy lately. He's usually a lot friendlier."

He scratched under his beard with the stem of his Ray-Bans, then cocked his head and glanced toward the building. "Did I hear your grandpa call you Julie Pearl?"

"Julie Pearl Stiles. That's me. But it's usually just the folks who've known me since I was little who use my middle name. It's a Southern thing, I guess, calling your kid by two names. But just plain Julie is what I usually go by, to other people, anyway, and—"

I could tell by the glazed look in his eyes that I was babbling again.

"So Pearl's your middle name. Not a family name."

"No. Yes." I groaned. Was it Micah Hobart himself, or the possibility his lakefront property might have some connection to my past, that had me so discombobulated? "I mean, it's my middle name. I don't know of anyone else in our family named Pearl. Guess my mother just liked the name."

"I see." He blinked twice and slipped on his sunglasses, hiding those incredible smoky eyes from view.

He was about to get in his pickup when I came to my senses and realized he still hadn't given me the answers I'd been dead set on prying out of him. I laid my hand on his arm. "You know, I—"

"I was just wondering—" he said at the same time.

We both hemmed and hawed for a few seconds. I pulled my hand back and stuffed it into my pocket, but the warmth from his suntanned arm and the feel of those dark, curling hairs tickling my palm lingered on.

"What were you about to say?" he asked.

"No, you first."

"I, uh—" He stared at his boots and gave a nervous laugh. "Wow, this is hard."

There went that twitter in my stomach again. "What? Just say it."

"Okay, here goes." He exhaled a sharp breath. "Julie, would you join me for dinner tonight?"

JULIE PEARL

Somewhere in the Bible it talks about making friends with your adversary on the way to court. Not that I harbored any latent worries about Micah Hobart pressing charges against me for trespassing, but I couldn't quite reconcile the person I'd met today with the bad-tempered man who barely one week ago had practically grabbed Clifton and me by the hair and hauled us off his property.

And anyway, did "making friends" include accepting a dinner date? Lingering over dessert and coffee while the sun sank over the rippling waters of Lake Hamilton? This unexpected conclusion to an otherwise average Monday seemed a lot closer to a scene from one of those cheesy paperback romance novels than I felt comfortable with.

Micah crumpled his napkin beside his plate. "I still can't get over how easily you got that dog—Brynna, you named her?—to make up with you."

I stirred another spoonful of sugar into my decaf. I wasn't much of a coffee drinker, but having something to do with my hands took the edge off my nerves. And besides, nothing else goes quite so well with a slice of key lime pie. "Like I said, all it took was patience. And a couple of cans of gourmet dog food."

He sighed. "Patience, I'm afraid, is not one of my virtues."

"I kind of got that idea."

"Okay, spit it out." He laughed and lifted his hands in mock surrender. "What's it going to take for you to let me off the hook for how I acted last week? I was a jerk and I admit it. I was already having a bad day, and you and your boyfriend caught me by surprise. What more can I say?"

"I told you, Clifton isn't my boyfriend." My lungs deflated along with my ego. Had I completely misread this dinner invitation? Was it only Micah Hobart's extravagant way of apologizing for his rudeness? True, my life in Caddo Pines didn't afford many opportunities for dating, but I normally didn't consider myself *this* naïve.

On the other hand, why had I imagined a rich, attractive real estate mogul could ever be interested in a small-town flea market manager? Besides, he had to be a good ten years older than me— the gray in his beard and sideburns should have been a dead giveaway.

"Dinner was great, but I should be getting home." I slid out of the booth. "And of course I forgive you for last week. Don't give it another thought."

"Wait." He grabbed my hand, leaving me no choice but to sit back down or lose my balance and fall face first into the bread basket.

"What?"

His mesmerizing eyes reflected the gray-green of the lake outside the window. Abruptly he released my hand and broke eye contact. "Sorry, I just . . . didn't want us to leave yet."

"Okay," I said slowly, in direct opposition to the staccato rhythm of my heart. "Um, do you want another decaf refill, or—"

"Sure. I mean, no, that's not—" And I thought *I* had the corner on babbling. He stared out the window, his next words spoken so softly that I had to strain to hear him over the clink of flatware against plates and the chatter of other diners. "It's been a long time for me, Julie. An awfully long time since a woman affected my equilibrium the way you do."

My racing heart stopped stone-cold dead. I couldn't think of a thing to say in reply. Instead, I gaped at him like a dead fish—eyes wide, mouth hanging open. *Good one, Julie Pearl. Real attractive.*

He looked at me again and laughed. "Don't look so shocked. I know I'm out of practice with this dating thing, but give me a break."

So it *was* a date. Okay then. "But you hardly know me."

He took my hand. "Think we could change that?"

Dating my best friend's boss? Would Sandy be okay with the idea? Was *I* okay with the idea? I hardly slept a wink that night, getting up several times to pace and think, think and pace. All the while, Brynna lay in her box with the puppies and cast me a puzzled stare, her onyx eyes shining in the glow of the streetlight outside my bedroom window. Time and again, my thoughts returned to the exhilaration of riding shotgun in that snazzy maroon pickup and smelling the rich leather upholstery, the pungent aroma of day-old coffee left in a Starbucks cup on the console, a whisper of aftershave reminiscent of an ocean breeze . . .

"Cut it out, Julie Pearl. You had it right the first time. You hardly know the guy, and you're not exactly in his league." Besides, had I conveniently forgotten I was on a fact-finding mission, and that Micah Hobart might have some answers for me?

By the time the streetlight flickered out and dawn crept across the horizon, I was a basket case. Thank goodness it was Tuesday and I didn't have to worry about working the front counter and looking perky for customers. Point me toward the janitor's closet, stick a mop in my hand, and maybe I'd manage to get a little work done while I puzzled out this latest twist.

Around mid-morning Grandpa caught me staring into the brown, gritty foam in my mop bucket. "What's gotten into you today, Julie Pearl?"

"Huh? Oh, just tired. Didn't sleep so good." He'd given me the perfect opening to pepper him with my own questions, but I didn't feel clear-headed enough to take advantage of the opportunity. Instead, I gave a halfhearted smile, dunked my mop a few times, then resumed my attack on the stubborn ketchup spill under a table in the snack bar.

Grandpa moved the table to one side so I could get a better angle on the spot. "Nothin' to do with Mr. Micah Hobart, naturally?"

"It was just dinner, that's all. Good grief, what ignorant slob made this mess, anyway?" I knew I sounded like a riled up banty hen, but the events of the past few days had left my nerves feeling like they'd been run through a meat grinder.

"It's quite a mess indeed." Grandpa sank with a groan onto one of the vinyl padded chairs.

"Oh, Grandpa." I plopped the mop in the bucket and bent to kiss the top of his head. "I'm all churned up inside, and I'm taking it out on you."

He took my hand and pressed it to his cool, wrinkled lips. "No cause for you to be so confused, Julie Pearl. It just ain't right."

Was Grandpa finally ready to talk? Instantly alert, I pulled another chair over and sat across from him. "What are you trying to say, Grandpa?"

"I should've spoke up yesterday, when that Hobart character showed up and invited you out." He fixed me with a worried gaze. "Please, darlin', don't get mixed up with that man. Promise me you won't. It can't do nothin' but lead to more trouble."

"*More* trouble?" My stomach flipped around like a washer on spin cycle. I squeezed his hands. "If you know something, then tell me. What is it about Micah Hobart? What is it about Pearls Along the Lake?"

He wagged his head. "It's a long story, Julie Pearl. A long, long story."

There are times when you think you want to know the truth, but deep down you have to ask yourself if you really do. Like two days before Christmas, sneaking under the tree and peeling back the wrapping paper on a package, and either you're so disappointed that on Christmas morning you'd rather not even open the gift, or so thrilled you can't bear to wait.

I had the sick feeling Grandpa's "long story" would be one "gift" I'd be sorry I ever peeked into.

Grandpa looked toward the ceiling. "Oh, Lord, give me the words."

"You're scaring me, Grandpa." I tucked my hands between my knees.

He sighed. "There's much I don't know, can't tell you for certain. But you're a grown-up now, and you should be told . . . before it's too late."

"Too late?"

"Before your old grandpa ain't around to tell you anymore." He seemed to fold in on himself, like a book about to close, a story about to end.

"Oh, Grandpa! Please don't talk like that!" I flung myself into his arms and buried my face in the nubby blue collar of his plaid polo shirt.

He gently pushed me away and dried my spurt of tears with the ball of his thumb. "I'm sure not planning on heading home to heaven anytime soon, but the years have a way of creeping up, and my ol' ticker ain't what it used to be. Honey-pie, you know I can't live forever."

I sniffled and scooted onto my chair. "I know. I—I just don't want to think about it."

"Someday you'll have to—no forty-seven ways to Sunday around it. But for now," he said, thrusting out his jaw, "it's time to tell you what you've been hungering to know."

I didn't dare imagine where this was headed. "Is this about the old resort? Micah Hobart? Renata Channing? *What?*"

He waved a hand to silence me. "Remember when you were in second grade and your teacher asked you to make a family tree?"

"Sure, I remember," I said, his question dragging my thoughts back through time. I remembered how it bugged me so bad that everybody else in my class had whole orchards of ancestors—big, broad branches loaded with brothers and sisters and aunts and uncles and cousins once, twice, and three times removed. All I had was a squatty tree trunk labeled "Grandpa," and a puny little branch sticking out the top marked "Julie Pearl Stiles."

"Now, Julie Pearl," my teacher had said, *"surely you have a few more relations you could add to your tree. You talk to your grandpa about it. Have him help you fill it in."*

Grandpa nudged my toe with his and gave a rumbling chuckle. "I can still see you sitting at our same old kitchen table with that pitiful sketch and your box of broken crayons. I felt so sorry for you."

"It was the first time you ever talked much about our family. You gave me Grandma's name—Julia Caroline Dugan Stiles—and then the names of all my great-grandparents." I remembered how I'd added branches for each of them, feeling more and more like a living, thriving bud on a strong, deep-rooted tree.

"And then you asked about your mama and daddy." Grandpa huffed a shuddering breath and grew silent.

"I remember." I could still see my grandpa's hunched shoulders as he trudged to the polished pine chest under the living room window. Folding back the brightly colored Mexican serape, he'd unlatched the lid and hefted an enormous, well-worn Bible. Once we were snuggled together on the coarse brown sofa cushions, he'd opened the Bible to the gilded flyleaf. An ornate family tree filled the page, each of the spaces filled with the spidery black handwriting I recognized as Grandpa's. There were all the names he'd just given me.

There were the names of my very own parents.

Angela Mae Stiles. John David Jones.

I pinched my eyes shut at the memory. The ache beneath my heart made it hard to breathe. "Angela and John."

"Angie, we called her. She was our little girl, our only child." Grandpa's voice sounded thin and reedy.

"You told me her hair was even curlier than mine." It always comforted me to be reminded of the one trait I shared with the mother I never had a chance to know.

Then the pain of being abandoned pressed in on me again as I recalled the rest of what Grandpa had told me that night. For the first time in my young life, I'd found the courage to push him for answers. And still he'd hemmed and hawed. He said my mother had gotten so sick that she couldn't take care of me anymore, so she brought me to the Swap & Shop and went away. I pictured her fragile and weak, pale against white sheets, my daddy hovering over her, tending her, loving her. Then, once she was all better, surely they'd come back for me.

I looked up to see Grandpa staring off into the rafters. He scraped his palms back and forth on the knees of his khaki pants. "Hardest thing I ever had to tell you was that your mama wasn't coming back, wasn't gonna get well. That your mama had . . ."

"Died." A knot swelled against my larynx. "And then I had to go and ask about my daddy. And you said—"

"I told you he'd gone on with his life somewhere else."

The words knifed through my heart just like they had that night. I hugged myself and shivered. I was a little girl again, with Grandpa taking my skinny face in those great warm hands of his that smelled like Dial soap. And just like that night, he said to me,

"Julie Pearl Stiles, you are loved more than you'll ever know. You're my precious jewel, lost but found, a treasure beyond all earthly riches. You are my 'pearl of great price.'"

Then he sat back and with a sad shake of his head began to paint new pictures for me of the parents I never knew.

1 2

ANGIE

April, 24 years earlier
Texarkana, Texas

Angie's head pounded. She sagged against the bagged-ice freezer outside the 7-Eleven, her vision so blurry, she could hardly see the numbers on the pay phone. Could she even remember the right combination? Lately her mind would go blank sometimes, just empty itself at the most inconvenient moments. Or she'd get confused, start out doing one thing and find herself an hour later in the middle of an entirely different task, her original intentions forgotten.

But this morning she willed her head to stay clear—too much was at stake—and once she started dialing, the numbers she needed came back to her like old friends.

"Otto Stiles' Swap & Shop."

"Daddy?"

Silence, then a tremulous, "Angie, is that you?"

Her reply got tangled in the sobs ripping through her throat. "Daddy, I need to come home."

95

"Oh, darlin', you never had to ask." Now Daddy was crying. "Just come."

She should have known. Just like the father in the story about the Prodigal Son, her father stood ready to welcome her back with open arms, no questions asked.

Except she wasn't coming alone. "Daddy, I have a little girl now."

"You've had a baby?" A quiver of excitement laced his tone. "When? How old is she?"

"She'll be four in September—on Mama's birthday. I named her Julie, after Mama. Julie Pearl Stiles. And Pearl because she's such a treasure to me." She drew the sleeve of her ragged sweatshirt across the wetness of her face.

"Three and a half years old?" His pain and shock echoed across the phone lines. "All this time and you never told me I had a grandchild?"

"I—I didn't think you'd understand." How could she ever explain to him about Ray, about all the promises he'd made, all the wasted years following him all over the country, living like vagabonds? Believing the lie that he loved her, hoping that if only she could get him to love this child, she could tie him to her forever?

Her father gave a harsh, grating sigh. "It don't matter no more. Just come home. Bring the little one. We'll do fine, the three of us together."

Yes, yes. She squeezed her eyes shut and let her knotted mass of curls swing forward, grateful it hid her tear-streaked face from the prying stares of customers traipsing in and out of the convenience store.

"Okay. I'll be home soon, Daddy." *And soon it'll be just the two of you.*

She gazed down at the green-eyed toddler clutching her leg and ran a hand over the soft, springy fuzz of golden curls. *Oh my Julie-love, my precious little turtle dove.*

JULIE PEARL

Present Day

"I'm sorry, Julie Pearl. I don't even know if that was your daddy's real name. Your mama wouldn't tell me about him, said I was better off not knowing, said he never mattered anyways."

All these years of wondering, waiting for the day I could track down this man named John David Jones and make him tell me why he left us! "But I have a birth certificate. It has my parents' names, just like you told me. It says I was born in Big Spring, Texas."

Grandpa's mouth flattened. His glance shifted sideways.

I crumpled against the chair and felt the curlicue design of the metal pressing into my spine. "All those stories you told me when I was little, you made them up."

"I see now the harm it's done, but back then I thought it was for the best." His eyes crinkled downward at the corners. "Couldn't flat out tell you your folks never married, that your daddy up and walked out on your mama, leaving her to suffer alone."

Anger choked me, and now I didn't even have a name at which to direct it. "Is there truth to *anything* you told me about my parents?"

Grandpa sighed. "All I know for certain is how much your mama loved you. She brought you here because she knew she was dyin'. She wanted to be sure you'd be taken care of."

A heaviness settled over me at the thought of what my mother must have suffered. "Dear Lord, a brain tumor. It must have been horrible for her . . . and for you."

"Nothing the doctors could do but ease her pain. I took care of her as long as I was able, but as the end drew near, she needed more tending to than I could give. Without insurance, we finally found a nursing home in Little Rock that would take her in for what I could pay. She passed on there a few months later. You'd just turned four."

Once again the memories came flooding back, real as a 3D movie—my first birthday party! I'd even picked out "Snow White and the Seven Dwarfs" invitations from Wilma Longoria's card and stationery booth at the Swap & Shop. Grandpa said we could have my party right here in the flea market snack bar, with funnel cakes and root beer floats and paper hats.

Then one day I overheard Grandpa on the phone. "I see . . . I see. . . . Thank you, I'll try to get there in time." When he dropped me off at the church preschool later, he said he didn't think the birthday party was such a good idea after all. "Maybe next year, honeybunch. Maybe next year things'll be better."

The next day he left Katy Harcourt in charge of the flea market. Said he had some important business up in Little Rock and I was to go home with Sandy's mom after preschool. He ended up missing my birthday entirely.

I flicked a tear off my cheek. "You hardly spoke three words to me after you came home, just got busy sweeping and dusting and rearranging merchandise till all hours of the night. You couldn't even tell me my own mama had just died."

"You were so little, I—" Grandpa stared at his clasped hands. "Can you ever forgive me, Julie Pearl?"

"What do you want me to say, Grandpa? I just found out I've been clinging to a lie." I stood, gripped the mop handle, pressed it against my sternum and hung on for all I was worth. I guess at some point I figured out my parents weren't married. Why else would my name be Stiles instead of Jones . . . or whatever the creep's name was? Illegitimacy didn't carry the stigma it once did —celebrity couples had kids out of wedlock all the time these days. But the fact that my mother wouldn't even acknowledge the man who'd fathered me? It made me feel dirty, ashamed. More worthless and unwanted than I'd ever felt in my life.

"Don't, Julie Pearl." Grandpa rose and set his hands on my shoulders, his bony fingers biting into my arms. "Don't let this change who you are, the kind and caring person you've always been. You'll always be my 'pearl of great price.'"

"I don't want to hear that right now, Grandpa." I shrugged out of his grip and stormed upstairs to the apartment. *Oh, Julie Pearl, you asked for it, didn't you?*

Then about the time my feet hit the landing, it occurred to me that right before Grandpa told me about my parents, he'd warned me not to get involved with Micah Hobart—because it would lead to nothing but "more trouble."

Micah. Pearls Along the Lake. Renata Pearl Channing.

I was missing something. Something important.

An invisible fist slammed me in the chest. Did any of this have to do with the *real* reason Mama had chosen Pearl as my middle name? I mean, what were the odds she'd give me that name if she *didn't* have some ties to the Pearl family or the resort? Maybe she worked there once, fell in love with my father while he was a guest. But he was already married. To Micah's mother, Mrs. MacDonohoe. Yes, it had to be something like that. And when Grandpa saw the article in the paper about the child's drowning twenty-five years ago, it reminded him about the time Mama had spent at the resort and he worried I'd find out and—

My head reeled. Obviously I was as good at making stuff up as Grandpa, and it only served to muddy the waters even more.

I hugged myself and stood before the kitchen window. The paved parking lot below shimmered in the noonday heat, but all I could feel was cold—colder even than the chilled, musty-smelling air flowing from the ancient Frigidaire window unit in the living room.

The phone rang three times before I registered hearing it. Even then, it took Brynna nudging the back of my knee with her warm, wet nose. *Hey, you, wake up,* her big black eyes seemed to say. *Life goes on. Get with the program.*

"Okay, okay." I scratched her behind the ear with one hand while reaching for the phone with the other.

"Julie? It's Micah."

My stomach twisted. Before I even realized I was going to say it, I blurted out, "Micah, I'm going crazy, and we need to talk. Can you meet me somewhere? Now?"

There was a campground and picnic area nestled in the rolling Ouachita Mountains about halfway between Hot Springs and Caddo Pines. A stream ran through the park, burbling and splashing over mossy rocks, with tiny fish slipping through the shallows and fighting to hold their own against the current—kind of like I felt right now. I got there ahead of Micah and arranged myself on a flat rock under a spreading maple tree, where I could safely slip off my sandals and let the cool water rush across my bare toes.

The park didn't have much activity this afternoon. In the distance I could hear the big logging trucks rumbling along the highway. Nearby, squirrels chattered, their toenails *scritch-*

scritching on the rough pine bark as they raced each other up one tree and down another. A soft breeze played cello with the pine boughs.

Finally I heard his pickup. Funny, I'd only seen it twice in my life, but I knew the sound of it without even glancing over my shoulder. Like we were connected somehow. Like Micah Hobart was already a part of me.

"Hey," he said, joining me on my rock. He crouched down in his stiff, new-looking jeans and tried to sit sideways to keep his scuffed black boots out of the water.

I wiggled my left big toe at three silver minnows who'd swum over to check it out. "Thanks for coming."

"You sounded upset. How can I help?"

I nailed him with a pointed stare. "For starters, you can tell me why my grandpa warned me to stay away from you."

The bewildered look on his face looked real enough. He gave a half-laugh. "I only just met your grandpa. I have no idea what he'd have against me."

"I'm pretty sure it has something to do with Pearls Along the Lake."

He cut his eyes at me. "You mean the old resort? Why would your grandfather think that?"

"I wish I knew!" I stood abruptly, my wet feet almost skating out from under me on the slippery rock. Micah reached out a hand to steady me while I slid into my sandals.

I stalked toward my Beetle. Stupid to think a perfect stranger could tell me anything about my past. Insanity to think a series of coincidences surrounding a termite-ridden, falling-down lake resort could have some connection to my parents.

"Hang on, Julie." Micah caught up with me and seized my elbow. "Now I'm as confused as you are. Tell me what's going on here."

I let him steer me toward the nearest picnic table, and we sat across from each other on the stained concrete benches. Avoiding blobs of bird poop, I rested my elbows on the table and lowered my head into my hands. For several long moments I sat there, unsure where to begin—unsure if I should be telling him at all.

But I did. I poured it all out. All those years of wondering about my parents, feeling abandoned, suppressing the urgency to search for my father and make him explain why he left us. I even confessed the secret story I used to tell myself to ease the pain—that Mama's death had left my father so brokenhearted that he'd gone off on a private quest to find solace for his grief, and someday he'd come back for me.

"Julie, Julie, I'm sorry." Micah pushed aside the mass of kinky hair falling around my face.

I sniffled and tried to pull myself together. "No, I'm the one who's sorry. Here you are being so nice, after I went totally ballistic on you the other day at the resort."

He gave an embarrassed chuckle. "Not that I didn't deserve it."

"Blame it on my concern for Brynna and the puppies, I suppose. I should know better, though. My grandpa's always taught me to look for the good in people."

"Yeah, I almost forgot. You're such a—let me make sure to quote you correctly—an 'upstanding, church-going, decent-as-the-day-is-long Christian.'"

Now it was my turn to cringe in embarrassment. "A 'hysterical female,' I think you called me. Guess I really was over the top that day. You just . . . made me so mad."

"I think we've established that." He folded his arms on the table. "I'm still trying to figure out what your grandfather could have against me. Unless . . ." His gaze clouded. "You suspect it has something to do with the resort?"

"I'm ninety-nine percent certain it does. Please, Micah, tell me what you know."

"Wow." He breathed out slowly. "That's a long, complicated story."

"I'm listening."

MICAH

June, 25 years earlier
Hot Springs, Arkansas

"Come on, Micah, no one will find out you helped me." Rennie Pearl tugged at his arm, her huge brown eyes shining in the beguiling way that never failed to twist him to her schemes.

Micah dangled his long, sun-browned feet off the edge of the boat dock. A leafy cottonwood shaded the upper half of his body, while the hot midday sun baked his bare legs beneath the hem of his swim trunks. "But where will you go?" he asked. "Somebody's gonna find out and come after you. You know they will."

"Once I get into town, I'll call my aunt to come get us. She knows how crazy my mom's gotten. She'll understand."

"Then why hasn't she already done something?"

"Because." Rennie sputtered and stared as if the question were completely ludicrous. "Because she knows my daddy wouldn't ever let her take me and Jenny away. He can't see what's happening." Desperation filled her eyes. "He won't face the truth about Mama, how sick she is, what she's doing to this family."

Micah's insides quivered. Since Jenny was born, he'd watched Rennie grow more and more desperate, and this summer it had peaked. All Rennie could talk about was getting away—getting Jenny away. She wanted Micah to take her and Jenny out on his parents' boat, motor them to the other side of the lake, drop them at one of the busy public marinas, and then pretend to the world he knew nothing of their whereabouts.

Rennie's plan sounded easy enough. Micah's parents had left him at the resort for the day while they celebrated their anniversary at a fancy restaurant over in Little Rock. Two summers ago, George had taught Micah to drive the sleek white fishing boat. The keys were on the dresser in the cottage. The fact that he was only twelve and not of legal age to take the boat out alone didn't seem to faze Rennie.

"Who's gonna know? Besides," she added with an a flirty giggle, "you're so tall, dark, and handsome, you don't look a day under fifteen."

That clinched it. He'd given his heart to Rennie the day she befriended him six years ago. If it would make her smile, he'd risk anything. He shot nervous glances up and down the dock. "Okay. But we have to go soon, so I can put the boat up before my parents get back."

Within twenty minutes Rennie met him under the green awning of the small private marina at the north end of the resort property. Struggling under the weight of an overstuffed backpack and balancing Jenny on one hip, she took Micah's hand for support as she eased into the rocking boat. He handed her the smallest life jacket on board, but it still swallowed the toddler. He frowned his concern.

"Don't worry." Rennie shrugged off the backpack and stowed it under a seat. She slipped her arms into the jacket Micah's mother usually wore. "You drive slow, and I'll keep hold of her. We'll be perfectly safe."

"Go boat!" Jenny clapped her dimpled hands. The lake breeze

lifted the golden wisps off her forehead beneath the gingham sailor cap she wore.

Micah's shoulders drooped. He'd made a promise and now he had to keep it. He started the engine and headed the small craft toward open water. Traffic was thick and noisy on the lake that afternoon. Jet skis, ski boats, flat-bottomed party boats, fishing boats—watercraft of every description skimmed the surface, the wakes crisscrossing and stirring up whitecaps. Steering clear of the busiest areas, Micah kept a nervous hand on the wheel and a sharp eye out for the lake patrol.

A pair of jet skis roared past, too close for Micah's comfort, and the boat pitched like a tidal wave had hit them. He sucked in his breath and waited for the rocking to subside before glancing back to make sure Rennie and Jenny were secure. Rennie's face had paled. She sat with one hand gripping the side of the boat and the other arm locked firmly around Jenny's waist. The laughing toddler bounced on Rennie's lap, unmindful of any danger.

Off to the right, Micah recognized the island where the weirdoes camped. Near the tree-shaded shore, he noticed a break in the traffic. "I'll head over that way," he called over the rumbling motor. "It looks quieter."

Rennie nodded mutely.

Micah aimed the prow toward a spit of land at the near end of the island. As he drew closer, he made out the scantily clothed forms of a man and woman sunbathing on the narrow strip of shoreline. Their dog—the same hairy yellow mutt he'd seen in years past—trotted out to chest depth and barked at the boat until the man sat up and yelled at him to stop.

Jenny laughed with delight. "Goggy! Go see big goggy!"

"No, sweet-pie, no doggy," Rennie told her. "We'll see Aunt Geneva's parakeet soon, how about that? You like Buster. He talks to you."

Rennie's anxiety echoed in her high-pitched tone. Micah's own worries poured out through sweaty palms gripping the slick chrome steering wheel. How much trouble would he find himself in if anyone discovered he'd helped with Rennie's escape plan? Could they send a twelve-year-old to prison for kidnapping?

He slowed the boat and swiveled to face her. "Rennie, I—"

From out of nowhere a flash of metallic green roared past them. Startled, Micah leaned too hard on the throttle. The fishing boat scooted forward, pitching him off the seat. Still gripping the wheel, he yanked it to the left, and the boat flipped up and over. For endless, terrifying moments Micah's stomach seemed higher than his head. Then something slammed against his temple and he sank underwater, struggling against the urge to inhale. Seconds later, his life vest carried him upward. When his face cleared the murky green surface, he sucked in several noisy breaths, then coughed violently, spitting out mossy-tasting lake water.

"Rennie! Rennie!" He paddled in circles, his vision clouded by a red haze. Finally he caught sight of the overturned boat, rough waves lapping at its sides. He tried to swim toward it, but the current thwarted him. His limbs felt limp and useless, his brain as mushy as cold oatmeal.

Fighting through his mental fog, he became aware of yelling, splashing, that noisy dog barking in the distance. Two boats arrived, their occupants shouting to him. "You all right, son? Anybody else with you?"

"My friend"—he coughed again and wiped blood and water out of his eyes—"and a little girl—can you see them?"

"Over here," came a shout. "I found someone."

"Rennie?" Micah kicked his rubbery legs and strained to see.

"Here, son, let me help you." A pair of brawny arms reached over the side of a ski boat and hauled him in. He collapsed in a dripping heap. His face collided with yellow vinyl seat cushion before everything went black.

JULIE PEARL

Present Day

My breath quickened as Micah described the boat accident and how he'd nearly drowned. All I could do was suck in quick, panicked gasps—like the water was closing over my own face and I was sinking down and down and down, into the suffocating green depths.

Micah abruptly broke off his story. "Julie? Are you okay?"

I pressed a hand to my chest and deliberately slowed my breathing. "It's just—I'm terrified of drowning."

He came around to my side of the table and straddled the bench. Absently he rubbed my back, as though his thoughts were still in the past.

"The baby. Jenny. She drowned, didn't she?" I pictured once more the sad, lonely bedroom at the resort, those faded ducks and rabbits gazing on the emptiness.

He sighed, long and painfully. "I'll never get over the guilt."

He went on to describe the aftermath of the accident— shivering with Rennie under scratchy lake patrol blankets, watching as divers searched the depths for any signs of the toddler. They found her empty life jacket floating a couple hundred yards away and figured she'd slipped right out of it, her slight form sinking like a stone in water close to forty feet deep.

Then the endless interrogations, the terrible moment Micah had to face his parents . . . and then Rennie's. The MacDonohoes had packed up and left for home in Fort Worth as soon as the authorities gave them permission. At his mother's insistence Micah went straight into counseling with a child psychologist, but even years later the nightmares persisted.

"Mom and George did their best to help me get over it." Micah's shoulders heaved. "But knowing you're responsible for the death of a child is something you never forget. In one way or another, it's affected every aspect of my life."

I brushed away a tear. "Is that why you bought Pearls Along the Lake?"

He looked at me squarely, his jaw muscles bunching. "When I learned the place was up for sale a few years ago, all I could think about at first was buying the property and setting the whole thing on fire so I could watch it burn to the ground. I wanted to wipe out every last reminder of what happened there."

I swung my legs around so that my back leaned against the hard edge of the table. "But you changed your mind?"

"I realized nothing I do can ever erase the past. The most I could hope for would be to redeem the place. Level it. Rebuild. Change the name. Make it possible for happier memories to be created there."

I laid my hand on his solid forearm and wished I wasn't such a babbler, that I could ease Micah's pain and convince him to forgive himself, convince him that, in God's view, no situation, no matter how tragic, was irredeemable.

Do you believe this for yourself, Julie Pearl Stiles?

My thoughts got all tangled up then—my grandpa's deception, my nameless father. What could possibly be the link between a desperate teenage girl, an innocent child drowning, and the man next to me floundering in a lake of guilt? My head throbbed with the effort to figure it all out. I bent forward and pressed my hands to my temples.

"I'm sorry, Julie." Micah rested a palm on the small of my back. "I don't suppose I've helped much with your problems, just burdened you with my own."

The next few days passed in an oppressive blur. The weather turned cloudy and humid, with thunderstorms rolling in each afternoon as the day heated up. The gloomy skies suited my mood. I kept to myself mostly, conducting my flea market duties with a pasted-on smile for the customers and reassuring Grandpa (without much conviction, I'm afraid) that I forgave him and would eventually get over my shock and disillusionment.

But I began to have nightmares of my own. I dreamed about drowning and woke up drenched in sweat, a silent scream in my throat. More than once, Brynna jumped up from her box, leaving the puppies whimpering and surprised, and planted her paws on the side of the mattress while she licked my face and gazed at me with worry in her sweet, soft eyes.

Her presence was such a comfort. I'd entwine my fingers in her curly black fur, press my nose into the warm spot behind her ear, and inhale the musky-orangey smells of dog fur and flea shampoo.

I didn't hear from Micah again until Saturday afternoon. I was concentrating extra-hard on ringing up a customer's sizable purchase and making sure to correctly record items from several different vendors, so it was Grandpa who answered the phone.

"Swap & Shop. . . . Yes, she's here, Mr. Hobart, but . . ."

My fingers got all knotted, and I managed to ring up a $3.95 volume of Reader's Digest Condensed Books at $395.95. "I'm so sorry," I muttered to the frowning school teacher–type standing across the counter from me. It took three tries to void the entry while I strained to catch Grandpa's side of the conversation.

"No, I won't," Grandpa barked into the phone. "I don't think—" He glanced over his shoulder at me and lowered his voice. "I don't think it's a good idea at all. Leave Julie Pearl alone. *Please.*" He slammed down the receiver and swung his broom with vicious strokes in the area behind the counter.

I couldn't finish with my customer soon enough. "Thank you, come again," I muttered as I shoved the cash drawer shut and dropped the receipt into one of her bags. The gray-haired lady glared from beneath raised brows and marched out, setting the brass bells clanging.

"What was that all about?" I stepped in front of Grandpa. "Aren't I an adult? Can't I decide for myself who I talk to?"

He froze and looked up at me with sad, rheumy eyes. "Of course you can, Julie Pearl. I'm sorry. Sorry for you, sorry for poor Angie, sorry for . . ." His whole frame drooped. "Shoulda known I couldn't hide the truth from you forever. Shoulda never let her convince me to try."

Steeped in such emotional chaos all week, I'd been avoiding the one question Grandpa still hadn't given me a satisfactory answer to—why he so vehemently opposed my spending time with Micah. And I was more convinced than ever that it had something to do with that little girl's drowning.

Across the way, I spotted Katy Harcourt running a feather duster across a rack of her slower-moving merchandise. "Katy, can you watch the front for a bit?"

"Sure thing, sugar-pie."

While she moseyed up to the counter, I took Grandpa by the hand and tugged him toward the workroom at the back of the shop. Amidst racks of cleaning supplies, soft drink cases, and giant cans of nacho cheese, I pried open a folding chair and sat Grandpa down in it.

"Okay, then." I planted myself in front of him. "Tell me

everything. Tell me exactly what you have against Micah, and what all this has to do with the Pearl family and the old resort and the drowning twenty-five years ago."

He rubbed one hand across his dry lips. "Ain't nothing I know for certain, Julie Pearl. Just . . . suspicions. Suspicions I never, ever want to confirm, because . . . because I might lose you forever." He stood and started for the door, then turned. His eyes sought mine, and they were filled with the worst kind of desperation. "So please, honey-girl, if you love me at all, stay away from that ol' resort. Stay away from Renata Pearl Channing. And for the love of God Almighty, *stay away from Micah Hobart.*"

He marched out of the workroom, his words still ringing in my ears.

What was it he didn't want me to know? Didn't he realize the *not knowing* was sending my imagination down pathways I wished I'd never set foot on?

On the other hand, if knowing meant losing my grandpa and everything I held dear . . .

All the rest of the afternoon, on through an even busier Sunday and a halfway decent Monday, it felt like something big and powerful had me by the scruff of the neck, the way Brynna grabbed hold of her pups to line them up in a neat little row for nursing or cleaning. And I needed a good cleaning, because the thoughts I'd been having had been anything but virtuous.

Like wishing Renata Pearl Channing had never set her designer-sandaled foot inside the Swap & Shop. Contriving ways I might persuade Sandy to quit her cushy new job as the dubious Micah Hobart's administrative assistant. I'd even thought about packing all my worldly goods into the back seat of my Beetle and heading off for parts unknown in search of the useless, no-good father who'd abandoned my mother and me—a man who I prayed with all my heart was *not* Micah Hobart's stepfather.

Long about Tuesday morning, while I restocked the napkin dispensers on the snack bar tables, Grandpa came over and pulled out one of the filigreed chairs. He sat backwards on it and rested his wrinkly, spotted arms across the curved metal back. "Don't you think you've moped around here long enough, Julie Pearl?"

"Long enough for what?" The words flew from my mouth with the force of a bazooka. I pressed my lips together in a hopeless attempt to stifle a sob. I'd been doing way too much crying lately, and that just wasn't like me.

"Ain't there no way I can have my own sweet Julie Pearl back?" Grandpa made a funny choking sound. "Oh, Lordy, what I wouldn't give to turn back the hands of time and make you smile again."

I sank into the chair opposite him and stared at the faded knees of my vintage Guess overalls. "I don't even know who I am anymore, Grandpa. Ever since *she* showed up two weeks ago, nothing's been the same. It's like Renata Pearl Channing laid a curse on my soul, and now—"

Grandpa shuddered. "Don't say such things, Julie Pearl."

"But it's true, isn't it? Admit it. The day she walked into the shop is the day my life started falling apart."

Grandpa removed his bifocals and pinched the bridge of his nose. "I been thinking, Julie Pearl. You need to get away, go find whatever it'll take to bring you peace."

I sat back, surprised to hear him suggest the very thing I'd been contemplating. The very thing I simply could not do. "Leave you by yourself? But you need me here, Grandpa. Who'll man the cash register? What about the bookkeeping? Who'll fix your supper and do the laundry and—"

"I'll be fine." He tipped his head toward Katy Harcourt's Classic Shoes and Bags. "Katy will look after me. She knows all that fancy computer stuff too. She won't mind at all helping me take care of things for a while."

Though I resisted, the idea of getting away rolled around in my mind and slowly gathered steam. It'd been years since Grandpa and I had taken a real vacation. Other than the occasional jaunt with Sandy to Eureka Springs or Memphis or Tulsa, I'd never traveled by myself. A road trip to think and ponder and seek out whatever answers might be waiting for me? Could I do this? *Should I?*

I began a mental list of the preparations I'd have to make, starting with giving Katy the password to my accounting software and explaining my bookkeeping system. I could stretch my cash by packing several days' worth of food in a cooler and camping out at state parks. Maybe I could even phone a couple of old friends who actually made it out of Caddo Pines.

Rising, I paced the small area between our chairs. "But if I did take off for a while, I don't even know what I'd expect to find. Maybe nothing at all." I didn't have to say aloud what we both knew, that unless he could give me my father's real name, that search would be futile.

"You're a smart girl. You'll figure it out." He slid off the chair and wrapped me in his arms. "Go, Julie Pearl. Find your truth. For both of us."

Truth. The word struck a crazy kind of terror in my heart. I sat in my Beetle, parked next to the gas pump outside Doakes Automotive, while Jimmy Weber, possibly the last of the true-blue full-service station attendants, filled my tank with regular. He shuffled behind the car to check under the hood, then hunched next to each tire to check the air pressure.

"Lookin' fine," he drawled. "Clifton's done you good with this ol' thing."

"Thanks, Jimmy." I leaned my elbow on the hot metal lip of the door and handed him two tens and a five. "Keep the change."

He gave me a two-finger salute and a toothless grin. "Where you headed, Miss Julie? Long trip? This buggy's in good shape, but it sure ain't up to no cross-country drivin'."

"Don't know for sure." I gazed through the windshield. From here I could see Caddo Pines's central intersection and the mileage signs pointing one way to Little Rock, the other to Hot Springs. Would I find my truth in either of those places? Were there even answers to be found?

"Well, you be careful, you hear? And don't stay away too long, or we'll get to missin' your pretty smile around here."

I waved good-bye and rolled up my window against the steamy noonday heat. So much for getting an early start. It had taken me all of yesterday evening and this morning to decide what to pack—no easy task having no idea how long I'd be gone or where I'd end up, and not at all sure I wanted to leave in the first place.

Earlier, as I'd stuffed the last suitcase into the back seat, Grandpa pressed a wad of cash into my hand. Then he slid a lumpy, stained manila envelope between the piles of luggage.

"What's that, Grandpa?"

"Something for you to look over once you're a little farther down the road. If you get stuck and don't know where else to turn, maybe it'll help."

Knowing Grandpa, I figured it was a collection of scriptures, or maybe inspiration-filled clippings from his favorite magazines, something to lift my sagging spirits along the way.

What I needed just now, however, was clear direction. I pulled up to the stoplight at Main and First Street, glad the signal had chosen that moment to turn red and give me a few more seconds to decide.

Right, to Little Rock? I could look up Renata Channing there, find out what more she could tell me about Pearls Along the Lake or Micah or any other possible connection between us.

Or I could turn left, toward Hot Springs, and drive straight into the arms of the man I couldn't seem to get off my mind or out of my heart.

JULIE PEARL

"Hi, Micah."

"Julie." He stood in the doorway of his Hot Springs La Quinta suite, a lopsided grin crinkling the edges of his beard. "You're the last person I expected to see this afternoon. Actually, I wasn't sure I'd ever hear from you again."

"Well . . . here I am." I'd rehearsed a million things I wanted to tell him when I saw him face to face. Now I couldn't remember a single one.

"Come in." He motioned me through the door, and we sidestepped stacks of files and boxes. "Excuse the mess. Can I get you a soda?"

I followed him into a small sitting area flanked by two massive conference tables layered with papers, blueprints, and more files.

"Julie?" At the sound of Sandy's surprised voice, I whirled around. "What in the world are you doing here?"

Why hadn't it occurred to me she'd be here too? "Hi, Sandy."

She darted around the table. "I've been trying to get hold of you for days. You never returned my calls."

"I've had a lot on my mind." She was my best friend. I should have told her everything. "I'm sorry."

My knees wobbled. My mouth tasted dry and cottony. I realized I hadn't eaten since breakfast—half a piece of toast that I could barely choke down. "Do you have any Diet Coke? No, make that regular. I need the sugar." I fixed my sights on a barrel-shaped armchair and staggered toward it.

"Be right back." Micah disappeared into an adjoining room.

Taking the chair across from me, Sandy planted her palms on the creased legs of her navy slacks. "You don't look so good, Jules. Did something happen? Is it your grandpa?"

"No, he's fine." I closed my eyes and slumped lower in the chair, resting my head on the back.

"Then what's wrong? I've never seen you looking so—so—"

Lost? Scared? I sat up and tried to pull myself together. Micah stood near me with a frosty can of Coke in his hand. I reached for it with a nod of thanks. The sweet, fizzy liquid tingled all the way down, and the coolness revived me.

Micah wiped the dampness from the soda can onto his jeans and propped a hip against one of the conference tables. "Julie, does this have anything to do with . . . with what you told me last week at the park?"

I took another sip of cola. "Actually, it has everything to do with it."

"What are you two talking about?" Sandy looked back and forth between us.

"I didn't know how to tell you before, Sandy. It's about my—" I broke off and shook my head, afraid the next words out of my mouth would bring with them another torrent of unwelcome tears.

Micah looked at me with understanding. "Want me to give it a try?"

At my silent nod, he moved closer and laid a hand on my shoulder. "Julie found out last week that her mother died without ever identifying Julie's real father."

"But you told me his name once." Sandy's brows drew

together. She gave her head a quick shake. "You always said you'd go looking for him someday, after . . . you know."

"That was the plan." I combed shaky fingers through my mass of tangled curls. "But apparently the name on my birth certificate, the same one Grandpa wrote in his big Bible, is a phony. There is no John David Jones. My mother probably pulled the name out of thin air."

Sandy's face twisted into a mixture of shock and sympathy. "Oh, Jules, how awful."

I finished the last of my Coke and stood, strength returning to my voice. "So now I'm on a quest to find out who I really am."

"But if you don't even know your father's name . . ."

"Actually, there may be another avenue I can try." I nailed Micah with a pointed stare.

He spread his hands. "Oh, no, you're not back to that again?"

Sandy cocked an eyebrow. "Julie, what's he talking about?"

"There's a connection somehow, a connection with Micah and Renata Channing and Pearls Along the Lake. I don't know yet how this puzzle all fits together, but I intend to find out."

Before the afternoon ended, I'd persuaded Micah to tell Sandy the full truth about his history with Renata Pearl Channing, including the boating accident and the child who drowned. We sat around the round coffee table, now littered with empty Chinese takeout containers, and sipped from Styrofoam cups of iced tea.

Sandy finger-combed her heavy bangs off her forehead. "Oh, Micah, what a horrible burden to carry all these years."

"There has to be more to it. Something my grandpa is afraid for me to find out." I poked the straw into my cup to break up the ice chunks. I wasn't sure I was ready to share my theory about my mother knowing Micah's stepfather.

Micah reached for a fortune cookie and ripped off the

wrapper. "Maybe your grandfather remembers reading about the accident in the papers and thinks I'm bad news—dangerous, irresponsible. What else could it be?"

"My grandpa's always given people the benefit of the doubt. He'd realize you were just a kid then. He wouldn't hold it against you."

"Julie's right," Sandy said. "Her grandpa is the kindest, most understanding man I know."

Micah gave his head a doubtful shake. He methodically broke open his fortune cookie and flattened the small slip of paper, studying it as if it might hold the answers we sought. He gave a harsh laugh and crushed the paper in his fist.

Sandy and I exchanged glances. "What's it say?" I asked.

"'The past holds the key to a brighter future.'" He tossed the wad into the empty mu shu pork container and stalked to the window. The western sun knifed through the slit in the sheer white curtains, striping Micah's face with harsh light. "Because of me, an innocent baby went to her death at the bottom of a lake. Where's the 'brighter future' in that?"

"It was an accident," I said tiredly. I felt a headache coming on. "You can't keep blaming yourself."

"Julie's right, Micah. And who knows?" Sandy cast me a desperate frown. "Maybe all this is coming out now for a reason. Maybe it's God's way of saying you and Mrs. Channing both need to finally let go of the past and move on."

Micah swung around. "Sorry, ladies, but your platitudes aren't making me feel any better."

I rose with a groan and gathered up empty containers and plastic utensils, then deposited them in a nearby trashcan. "I'm exhausted. Maybe I'll see if I can get a room here for the night."

"You're serious, then." Sandy gripped the arms of her chair. "You really did leave home."

"I'm dead serious. My luggage is in the car." I found my

shoulder bag where I'd dropped it next to the door and fished out my keys.

Micah held out his hand. "Give me your keys. I'll get your bags while you check in."

La Quintas are not exactly budget motels. Even with the discount Micah finagled for me, my room cost a big chunk of the cash Grandpa had given me. Still, it was a luxurious treat to settle into a clean, comfortable room decorated in soothing, natural shades of beige and brown. I filled the pristine white tub and soaked for nearly an hour, replenishing the hot water as the temperature cooled.

And I tried not to think.

Dressed for bed in a cotton sleep shirt, my damp hair plaited in a loose braid, I stacked pillows against the headboard and flipped through the TV channels with the remote—another luxury. At home, we used one of those digital converters for our ancient RCA, and then we had to tweak the rabbit ears just right to tune in. Finding nothing of interest, I pressed the off button and rested in the silence of the darkening room.

My glance fell upon the luggage Micah had carried in for me. The larger suitcase sat unopened next to the dresser. Poking out of the front pocket was the envelope Grandpa had stuck in the car before I drove away this morning. I didn't know if I could stomach whatever bromides Grandpa thought might help.

I rolled over and snuggled under the covers. I squeezed my eyes shut and prayed for sleep to come quickly.

"Julie, Julie, my little love. My sweet little turtle dove."

My pillow grew damp with tears. "Oh, Mama, Mama . . ." Her face floated across the blackness behind my eyelids, the image of the pale, thin woman in Grandpa's old family photo album.

Tired as I was, sleep had deserted me. I tossed back the covers and swung my feet off the side of the bed. I felt my way to the bathroom and pawed through my toiletries by the glow of a tiny orange nightlight. I felt sure I'd packed some Tylenol in there somewhere. After scattering hand lotion, makeup, shampoo, and a handful of hairpins across the counter, I remembered I'd thrown the Tylenol into the big suitcase as an afterthought just before I zipped it shut. Leaving the mess, I found the switch on the dresser lamp. The glaring bulb momentarily blinded me.

When I could see again, I muscled the heavy suitcase onto its side, but as I felt for the zipper pull, my arm caught the edge of the manila envelope. I sank to the floor and stared at it for a long moment. Bleary-eyed, I slid it from the pocket and shook the contents into my lap—two smaller envelopes, one a bulky brown business packet, the other a plain number-10 thick with folded papers. I held them both to the light. On the front of the white envelope I recognized Grandpa's broad, flowing scrawl.

Save for Julie, he had written. Nothing more. I laid it aside.

The lumpy packet bore no markings. The contents gave beneath the pressure of my probing fingers. I unwound the string securing the flap.

Why is it, when you've wanted something so badly for so long and it's finally staring you in the face, all at once you're paralyzed? Maybe it's realizing that actually having the object of your desire could be even more painful than merely wanting it. Like craving a frosty milkshake and then slurping it down so quickly that you get brain-freeze and it feels like it'll never end and all you can do is press your tongue to the roof of your mouth in agony until it passes.

No amount of tongue-pressing would make the contents of this envelope go away. I knew then, knew in my deepest core, that the secrets it held would hurt, maybe even more than I could bear. But I had no choice. I had to know, once and for all.

I tipped the envelope sideways, and a small, blue-gingham sailor cap slipped out. It must have been mine long ago. Why else would Grandpa have saved it? The cap even bore my own faded initials—JPS—in heavy blue embroidery across the brim.

But something wasn't right. The P was much larger than the letters on either side, the way you usually see items monogrammed, with the initial for the person's last name larger and centered. Meaning the owner of this cap rightly should have had the initials JSP, not JPS, unless the person doing the monogramming made a pretty stupid mistake.

I laid the sailor cap on the carpet and pried open the seal of the other envelope. Inside, brittle onionskin paper surrounded a collection of creased, yellowed newspaper clippings. My pulse throbbed beneath my jaw as I separated the fragile pages.

Again, Grandpa's spidery script on the onionskin. I reminded myself to breathe.

My precious Julie Pearl,

If you are reading this, it means you're all grown up now, and something you've learned, or remembered, or maybe needed to know for health reasons—who knows?—has got you asking questions again about your parents. I prayed this day would never come—and maybe I'm worried for nothing, because even though you're just a little thing as I write this, I can see you're a strong girl. And I know the Lord will help you through whatever comes of this.

Your mama died without telling me the whole story, so I can only guess at what really happened—but I've a pretty good idea. I saved all these clippings so maybe someday you can ferret out what's true and what isn't. One thing is true, though—your mama loved you with all her heart, loved you till the day she breathed her last. Everything she ever did was out of love for you.

I hope you can forgive us both for keeping this from you all these years. Right or wrong, I love you like my own, my treasure, my "pearl of great price."

Love always,

Your Grandpa

Forgive them? *For what, Grandpa? What did you know all these years that you never told me?*

A chill shook me. I shifted to kneel at the foot of the bed and spread the newspaper clippings across the floor. The headlines screamed at me:

Popular lake resort is site of tragic drowning: twelve-year-old driver of boat being questioned, search for child's body continues

No charges filed in toddler's death; drowning officially ruled accident

Pearls Along the Lake closes, family grieving loss of daughter

The drowning wasn't news to me, but why had my grandfather saved all these clippings? And why had he given them to me now? "What are you trying to tell me, Grandpa?"

The last clipping was a death notice for Jennifer Susan Pearl, dated twenty-five years ago, almost to the day:

. . . The child's tragic drowning occurred June 21 near the family-owned resort, Pearls Along the Lake. Jennifer Susan is survived by her parents, Everett Roy and Lucille Marie (McLain) Pearl, and sister, Renata Louise Pearl, of Hot Springs; and one aunt, Geneva Pearl Nelson . . .

A memorial service is scheduled for June 27 at 2 p.m. at Mountain Valley Christian Fellowship Church. In lieu of flowers, the family asks that memorial gifts be made to the church's building fund for the new Sunday school wing. . . .

My gaze drifted from the page as images zigzagged through my brain. Images of a little girl who drowned twenty-five years ago. Images of a golden-haired toddler whose body was never found.

JSP—Jennifer Susan Pearl.

JPS—Julie Pearl Stiles.

Goose bumps rose on my arms, and it felt like every breath of air had been sucked from the room. Grandpa *knew*. Deep in his heart, he had to have known. But he let a family keep on grieving, mourning the death of their precious little girl. He let them blame a desperate and confused teenager, whose only real crime was desiring a safer, saner life for herself and her baby sister. He let a young boy grow up believing he was responsible for a little girl's death.

A little girl who wasn't dead at all, who'd grown up believing her name was Julie Pearl Stiles.

JULIE PEARL

Along about 3:00 a.m., tears all used up and the initial shock finally easing off, I trudged downstairs to wait for Micah outside the door to his office suite. I wouldn't call him at home to say what I had to tell him. No sense both of us losing a good night's rest. But I wanted to be the first person he saw when he arrived.

A subtle vibration stirred me awake. Not that I'd done more than lightly doze, my arms wrapped around one of the thick foam pillows from my hotel room. My spine was in knots and my seat bones felt numb from sitting on the floor half the night.

"Julie, what on earth—" Micah dropped his briefcase and knelt beside me. "How long have you been waiting here?"

I forced a laugh. "Don't ask. Would you help me up? I don't think I can move."

He got to his feet, then lifted me. I groaned as my back unkinked. Natural as breathing, I wrapped my arms around his waist and pressed my cheek deep into the cleft of his shoulder. It felt good to lean on someone warm and solid, someone tall enough to look down on me, someone who could make me feel safe and protected.

"Julie, you're shaking. What's wrong?" He stroked my hair, and his fingers got all tangled up in my mess of a braid.

I didn't want to let go of him, not ever.

But we had some talking to do. Taking a half-step backward, I pulled my hair over my shoulder and tugged off the loose rubber band. I wrapped the band around two fingers and popped it over and over, as if the activity would drain some of my agitation. "Can we go inside? I need to tell you something. Something important."

Eyebrows drawn together, Micah pulled a card key from the pocket of his oxford button-down and slid it into the reader. When the green light blinked, he shoved open the heavy door. The suite lay in semi-darkness, the drapes billowing over the humming air conditioner. Micah flipped a light switch, and two wall lamps flickered on.

I went to the window and pushed back the drapes. Beyond the parking lot, cars wrangled for lane space on Highway 7 in Hot Springs' version of morning rush hour—not a safe place to be this time of day.

Was anywhere safe anymore?

I heard water running at the wet bar, then a burbling sound as Micah filled the reservoir of the coffeemaker. "Need some breakfast?" he asked. "I can have room service send something over."

"She didn't die, Micah." I spoke the words without looking at him.

"What?"

"The little girl. Jenny Pearl. She didn't drown."

A drawer slammed shut. "Are you trying to convince me there's a God? That Jenny's happily playing in heaven now?"

"No, that isn't what this is about." I went to him, took the unopened foil coffee packet out of his hand, and pulled him over to the window, where the morning light could shine bright and full upon my face. "Look at me, Micah. Take a good, long look."

His face contorted in confusion and anger. "Whatever this is about, just stop it. I've told you what I went through back then."

"Please, Micah, *look at me*." I grabbed tufts of his beard and forced him to make eye contact. "Isn't there something about me you recognize?"

He stumbled backward, catching his thigh on the corner of the conference table. Wincing, he rubbed a hand along the seam of his blue jeans. "You're talking crazy. I mean it. Stop."

"No, listen. It's true. I was so sure we were connected somehow, but I couldn't have been more wrong about how and why." In a rush of words I told him about Grandpa's letter and the newspaper clippings. An image grabbed me. "It was the dog, I bet, the one you told me about. He must have swum out and dragged me to shore. Everybody else was so busy rescuing you and Renata, they probably didn't see—"

"Now you're *really* imagining things." Micah slumped into one of the barrel-shaped chairs and pressed his palms into his eye sockets. "I don't want to hear any more of this."

"You have to, Micah, because it all makes perfect sense." I sat across from him, hands clasped. "It explains so much—Grandpa's reservations about me getting to know you, my terrible fear of drowning. It explains why Mama lied about my father on my birth certif—"

I grabbed my head to keep it from spinning right off my neck. Of course. I was the proud owner of a forged birth certificate. Could you get arrested for that?

Micah leaned back and stared at me. "But there were boats all over the lake that day. How could nobody notice?"

"I don't know." I lowered my hands and forced a breath. "Maybe the current carried us out of everyone's sight by the time the dog got me to shore. My mother—I mean the woman I've always believed was my mother—must have found me."

He crossed his arms. "This woman witnesses a boating

accident, then finds a half-drowned baby, but she doesn't report it to the cops?"

When he said it like that, I realized how foolish it all sounded. No one in their right mind would even think about running off with someone else's child, unless . . .

Staring into space, I pictured the woman in the few photographs I'd seen of my—of Angie Stiles. I imagined a restless, rootless young woman camping on an island with a bunch of freewheeling ne'er-do-wells. I imagined her desperation and loneliness, wishing she'd never turned her back on her own family. I imagined her finding a lost baby girl and seeing me as a gift meant just for her, the answer to years of yearning for something that would give her life meaning.

I tried to voice these thoughts to Micah. "Maybe she thought if she had a child, she could turn her life around. Everybody thought Jenny was dead, so if my mother kept her—me—then left Hot Springs, changed my name, and somehow faked a birth certificate to prove I was hers, who would know?"

"Good story, Julie, but what proof do you have? A bunch of newspaper clippings and an ambiguous letter from your grandfather."

My voice thickened. "I have this." I pulled the blue gingham sailor cap from my back pocket. In the brighter light of morning, I could make out the mud and water stains, still faintly visible even after repeated washings.

For long minutes the only sounds were the whirring air conditioner and Micah's slow, labored breathing. He gazed at the cap, his eyes crinkling at the corners and wetness pooling along the bridge of his nose. "Jenny?" The name came out like sandpaper on rough wood. He crushed the sailor cap to his chest as he took the Lord's name in vain and repeated, *"Jenny."*

Micah's murmured words didn't begin to convey the whirlwind of emotions I read in his eyes. Hope that the little girl he never meant to harm hadn't drowned after all. Gratitude for a second chance at making things right. Utter amazement that Jennifer Susan Pearl might be sitting across from him right this minute, all grown up and alive as she could be.

My own eyes filled with tears—from sadness, relief, or joy, I couldn't say. Probably all those reasons and then some.

But one question kept running through my head, begging for an answer:

Now that I know, what happens next?

Micah rose like an old man and rubbed the back of his neck. "This is a lot to take in so early in the morning. I need some coffee. How about you?"

Snow White was back in my hotel room, so I reached for his wrist to read the time on his watch—8:25. My stomach growled. "I think I'm ready for breakfast."

He stared at me, shaking his head, laughing softly. "You just hit me with the most incredible possibility I could ever hope for, and you're thinking about food? Honestly, Julie—Jenny— Good grief, if this really is true, what do I call you?"

"Let's stick with Julie." I paced to the wood-framed mirror over a credenza. "I don't have a clue what Jennifer Susan Pearl is all about."

Micah stood behind me, his hands on my shoulders. "Are you planning to find out?"

"I think I have to." Our gazes met in the mirror—his forehead creased with a million questions, my eyes wide and jumpy with questions of my own. I swung around to face him. "I need to go—right now. I'll get breakfast later."

"Wait. We need to talk more about this."

"Oh, Micah, I can't." I hugged him again, briefly, then hurried to the door. "You're not the only one who needs to know the truth."

"You're going to see *her*?" His voice had a strange catch in it.

Pulling open the door, I glanced back at him with a smile that was half exultant, half terrified. "She is my sister, after all." After years of believing I was an only child, it felt strange to say it, to realize I had a living, breathing sibling.

Micah strode toward me and shoved the door, ripping the knob out of my hand. "Julie, don't. You have no idea what you're getting yourself into."

I rubbed my palm. "What I'm getting myself into is reconnecting with the family I never had a chance to know. What's wrong with that?"

"You don't know Renata. You don't know what she's capable of. If you really are Jenny, she'll—"

"You keep saying *if*. Micah, don't you *want* it to be true?"

"I told you, nothing would make me happier, but—"

Voices echoed in the corridor, Sandy calling a greeting to one of the housekeeping staff. I glanced toward the door to the adjoining room. "Can I get out through there? I don't have the strength to repeat all this to Sandy just now."

Micah looked sideways at me. "Yeah, sure. Just don't leave the hotel without telling me. Promise me that much."

I didn't answer. I couldn't promise. Not if he intended to talk me out of seeing Renata. I slipped into the next room and out the other door.

Renata Pearl Channing. Mrs. Lawrence Eugene Channing. Neither listing appeared in the tattered Little Rock phone directory I'd borrowed at the McDonald's where I'd stopped for a late breakfast. I shouldn't be surprised a family as rich as the Channings had an unlisted number. I did find a listing, however, for the Channing Children's Foundation. Parked in the sweltering sun outside the McDonald's, I used my cell phone to call the number.

A cheery receptionist answered. "Hi," I said. "I'm trying to reach Mrs. Channing."

"She . . . isn't available at this time."

"Okay, when should I call back?" Leaving a message didn't sound like the best option, under the circumstances. I fanned myself with the folded daily newspaper housekeeping had poked under my hotel room door this morning.

Throat clearing, papers rustling. "Excuse me, ma'am, I'll have to transfer you to our manager."

Elevator music, just what I needed. I hummed along with repeated golden oldies by Barry Manilow, John Tesh, Neil Diamond . . . I swore if "You Don't Bring Me Flowers" played one more time, I'd hang up and head back to Caddo Pines.

"Good morning, this is Dana Ellis. May I be of assistance?"

As patiently as I could manage, I expressed my urgent need to contact Renata Channing.

I didn't care for the condescending tone of Ms. Ellis's response. "I'm sorry, ma'am, but Mrs. Channing does not maintain an office here."

"But she's your founder and president. Your website says so."

"I realize that. But Mrs. Channing's . . . involvement . . . takes place outside the scope of these offices."

In other words, she just showed up for the picture. I drummed my fingers on the steering wheel. This was getting me nowhere fast. And I'd already lost twenty-five years.

"Okay," I said, "can I leave my number with you? Can you have her return my call?"

"I suppose so . . . if she checks in, that is."

Ms. Ellis's tone suggested it wasn't very likely she would.

"Can you call her? Text her? Send her an email?"

"Mrs. Channing prefers not to be disturbed unless it's absolutely necess—"

"It *is* absolutely necessary." Annoyance and fatigue threatened to strangle me. The adrenaline high that had kept me going since last night was quickly winding down.

I inhaled a calming breath. "Please, I *need* to talk to her." I reeled off my cell phone number. "Tell her it's about Pearls Along the Lake. She'll know what you mean."

RENATA

October, 10 years earlier
Arkansas Philanthropic Association Annual Gala

Renata's heart stammered. She willed her voice to hold steady. "Micah Hobart, is it really you?" She swept aside the shimmering train of her beaded mauve satin gown and stepped toward the tall, handsome man in the tuxedo.

He turned. The smile he'd just flashed his over-processed blond companion slowly faded. His brows locked together in astonishment before his expression softened into unconcealed approval. "Renata?"

Exactly the effect she'd hoped for. She knew she looked drop-dead gorgeous tonight. Her stomach had been in knots all evening as she scanned the crowd and waited for Micah's arrival. "I saw your name on the invitation list. Micah, darling, it's wonderful to see you again. And congratulations on your new business venture. Barely out of grad school and already the entrepreneur." She linked her arm through his, discreetly guiding him a few steps away. Let the drab wannabe in the Von Furstenberg knockoff cool her cheap rhinestone-studded heels for a bit.

Micah angled a nervous glance toward the woman staring dumbly after them. "It's good to see you, too, Renata, but I—"

"The beard makes you look distinguished. I like it." She tweaked the corner of his moustache. "But then you always did look roguishly mature for your age."

Shrugging off her arm, he gave an uneasy laugh and stuffed his hands into his pockets. "I shouldn't leave my fiancée . . ."

Renata lifted a hand to her mouth. "Forgive me, I had no idea." She forced a tittering chuckle, hoping it masked her disappointment—her sudden, seething jealousy. "Well. Congratulations again."

A long, slow breath eased the tense set of his shoulders. "It's good to see you, Rennie. It's just . . . you're the last person I expected to run into tonight."

Her heart clenched. "Rennie—no one except family has called me that in years." She could barely speak over the tightness in her throat. "I've missed you, Micah. There's so much I've always wanted to say . . . and never had the chance."

His Adam's apple worked. "Give me a minute, okay? I'll explain to Tori—tell her I've run into an old friend. Then we can go somewhere and catch up. But just for a while."

She nodded and watched while Micah kissed away the puzzled look on his fiancée's face and whispered something in her ear. The blonde smiled up at him and minced over to a nearby table, where she joined a gossiping brood of women about as tackily dressed as herself.

Honestly, the nouveau riche—or those who wished they were. No class at all.

Unlike you, of course.

With an angry shake of her head, she silenced the annoying voice that took such pleasure in pointing out her flaws. *Shut up, Mama.*

At least Rennie had married well, attached herself to someone who could lift her out of her miserable past and give her the life she deserved, the life she'd fantasized about since her days of pushing that creaking old maid's cart from one dusty cabin to another. And Lawrence Channing was old money, the eldest son of one of the richest families in Arkansas and CEO of the thriving GigantaMart corporation.

But Micah . . . oh, Micah, what a charmer. I always knew you had it in you to succeed.

She hadn't been able to get him off her mind since the day she came across his name listed among the Arkansas Philanthropic Association's top fifty contributors. As president of the Channing Children's Foundation, she served on the APA board and helped coordinate the $350-a-plate invitation list for this year's gala.

If things had been different—but it didn't bear thinking about.

"There's a bar on the first floor," Micah said, returning. "It shouldn't be too crowded right now."

"Your fiancée—Tawny, you said? She can't possibly begrudge two old friends catching up?"

"Tori. She'll be fine." Taking Renata's elbow, he escorted her to the glass-and-chrome elevator, brushing past a border of potted sago palms and pink hibiscus heavy with forced blooms.

She plucked a blossom as they waited for the elevator car. "Brings back memories," she murmured, holding the soft, tropical-scented petals against her cheek. Behind her closed lids she pictured the brick patio at Pearls Along the Lake, her mother's geraniums, impatiens, and hibiscus parading in clay pots along the retaining wall. She remembered the day nine-year-old Micah had stood before her on the stone path, grinning shyly as he brought a fistful of sweetly pungent hibiscus blooms from behind his back and presented them to her.

You once thought I hung the moon, Micah Hobart. Can I still make you believe it?

Three vodka cocktails later for her, one snifter of brandy that Micah never quite managed to finish, and Renata couldn't hold her emotions in check any longer. She reached across the table to lay a hand on Micah's ink-black coat sleeve and ran a finger along the narrow satin stripe. "My life has never been right, Micah. Never. Not since that day—"

"Don't, Rennie." His voice was gentle, tender. He pushed the brandy snifter aside and clasped her hand. "Nothing will change what we did, but it's in the past and we have to leave it there."

"I've tried, believe me, and for years I pretended I had. But long ago I had to admit that I'll never be able to let it go. My baby sister"—she stifled a sob—"we killed my baby sister."

"You can't think of it that way." He slid his chair closer, close enough to encircle her in his arms, just like she'd planned. "It was a mistake, a horrible, tragic accident. Every day of my life I have to remind myself we were just kids."

"Two incredibly stupid, naïve kids." She buried her face against his neck, weeping softly, knowing she'd leave behind a smear of beige powder, a streak of Keepsake Rose lipstick. She tilted her head to look up at him, her eyes brimming. "No one understands me the way you do. No one else knows the pain I live with."

"Rennie, Rennie." The sound of her name on his lips made her tremble. He brushed a strand of hair away from her damp cheek.

She snuggled deeper into his embrace. "I don't want to go home alone tonight. Larry's away on business, and that huge house will seem so cold and empty. Micah, seeing you has . . . it's brought back so many memories, so many emotions I thought I'd long since put behind me."

"Rennie, no . . . I can't." And yet she heard the hesitation in his voice.

"Please."

He sighed, swallowed, ran nervous fingers up and down her spine. "Let me make some excuse to Tori, and then I'll see you home. But I won't stay. Do you understand?"

19

———

JULIE PEARL

Present Day

Just like I thought, I didn't have to wait long for Renata Channing to return my call. I'd parked the VW in the shade of a sprawling oak in War Memorial Park, off I-630 near the Little Rock Zoo. Seemed like a calming place to hang out while I figured out my next move.

"Exactly who is this?" came her crisp greeting.

I sucked in a loud, shaky breath. I couldn't exactly pop right out with, *"This is your long-lost sister, Jennifer Susan Pearl,"* now, could I? "Mrs. Channing, this is Julie Pearl Stiles. From the flea market in Caddo Pines."

"You." An exasperated groan slammed against my eardrum. "Why on earth would you be calling me? Even more appalling, why did you find it necessary to bother the employees at my foundation? Certainly my check didn't bounce?" Her voice dripped Southern sophistication at its arrogant best.

No way would she make this easy. I got out of the car and leaned against the fender, welcoming the light breeze that lifted

137

damp ringlets off my forehead. "Is there any chance we could meet somewhere? I have something important I need to tell you."

A snort. "Did you forget to give me the laundering instructions for that relic of a tablecloth you sold me?"

I pushed away from the car and paced across the grass. "Hazel's tablecloths are fine, handmade works of art."

"Perhaps so, but when I unfolded it yesterday—in preparation for a hugely important dinner party, by the way—I must have sneezed at least fifty times from all the dust that flew."

Okay, so Hazel's expensive creations didn't sell very fast, which meant a lot of shelf time. But I couldn't let Ms. Moneybags get in the last word here. "Yeah, right. With all the servants you surely have at your beck and call, I just bet you were working your delicate little French-manicured fingers to the bone."

Oh, great, if my grandpa heard me talking like this, he'd be all over my case.

My grandpa—right. Was I making a huge mistake? I mean, I had a really good life in Caddo Pines. Maybe it had all been a sham, but it was the only life I knew, and I loved it. Loved my grandpa with all my heart. Could I ever be happy as Jennifer Susan Pearl, especially having a sister as stuck up and ill-tempered as Renata Channing?

"I—I'm sorry. I had no right being so rude." I hoped the stone-cold silence on the other end didn't mean she'd hung up on me. "Mrs. Channing, are you there?"

Her breath caught. "I apologize as well. I'm not myself lately—so much on my mind. Now, if you'll please tell me what you called about?"

On the way back to my car, I dodged a jogger and inhaled a nauseating odor of sweat. "Like I said, I'd prefer to talk to you in person. What I have to say is—well, it's major."

She gave a sardonic laugh. "All right, if you think it's *majorly* important. But I'll have to ask you to come to my home. My seamstress is here, and we're in the middle of a dress fitting."

Twenty minutes later I stood shifting my feet in the dressing area adjoining Renata's elegant bedroom. A servant (housekeeper, lady's maid, chief cook and bottle washer—whatever her actual title might be was out of my range of experience) had escorted me along about a half-dozen hallways, up winding staircases, through paneled doorways. I hoped she'd be available when it came time for me to leave. Otherwise I might be wandering the maze of rooms and corridors of this castle fortress till the day I died.

And that's what it seemed like—a fortress. A high brick wall surrounded the estate, with ten-foot wrought-iron gates and a guardhouse barring the driveway. I wondered what the poor man checking IDs did between visitors. Play computer solitaire like Katy Harcourt?

"Well, don't just stand there." Renata motioned me into the room. She stood on a low platform, arms extended at an awkward angle. "The chair in the corner—pull it closer and tell me what you came to say."

"Stand still, *por favor*, Mrs. C. You don't want trousers with uneven hems." Even with a mouthful of straight pins, the kneeling seamstress spoke with a polite Hispanic lilt.

I didn't feel right planting the seat of my faded jeans onto the fancy gold brocade chair Mrs. Channing had indicated. "That's okay, ma'am. And anyway, I'd rather we spoke in private."

"We are in my private suite—ouch! Isabel, be careful with those pins!"

"Sorry, Mrs. C."

"How much more privacy do you need?"

The fine hairs on the back of my neck rose. She'd shown her seamstress about as much respect as she probably gave the family dog.

Oh, yeah. Renata Channing was deathly afraid of dogs. Maybe she kept people as pets instead.

Micah's warning rang in my ears. This lady was definitely someone to be wary of.

Even so, she was my sister, and she believed I'd died. Look what the accident had done to Micah—turned him bitter and cynical, made him want nothing more than to wipe out every reminder of that horrible day. Maybe living (and acting) like queen of the world was how Renata dealt with her grief.

I felt a sudden compulsion to bring the seamstress into the conversation, to let her know she wasn't invisible. "Hi—Isabel, is it?" I plopped down on the floor beside her. "I'm Julie Stiles, from Caddo Pines. Wow, did you make this outfit? It's gorgeous!"

The thin, brown-haired woman looked at me in surprise. "*Sí, muchas gracias*—thank you."

"Have you been working for Mrs. Channing very long?"

"Yes, many years." She flicked a glance my way as she resumed her measurements and pinning.

I fingered the flowing black fabric of the wide-legged slacks. "Must be for a really special occasion."

Above my head I heard an impatient sigh. "A vastly important dinner party, as I mentioned on the phone. Now, will you please let Isabel get on with her work? I have other things I need to attend to before this evening."

With a sympathetic smile, I lightly touched Isabel's arm. Her eyes spoke gratitude.

I pushed up from the floor. "Mrs. Channing, when I tell you the reason I came, it's going to make your *vastly important* dinner plans seem like the most trivial event of your life."

With Isabel excused to finish hemming the trousers, Renata finally granted me the private audience I'd requested. I chose my words with care, leading her as gently as I could to the news I was about to spring on her. I sketched the background—the newspaper clippings my grandfather had given me, the things I'd learned from Micah Hobart about Pearls Along the Lake and the boating accident.

But all the while I talked, she continually glanced at her watch, the polished toe of one beige pump tapping nonstop on the plush ivory carpeting. I could tell she wasn't going to sit still for much longer. She pressed her eyes shut for a moment and then interrupted me with an upraised hand. "I can't begin to fathom why you've taken such interest in my personal tragedy. I must say I am highly offended."

"Okay, I'll come to the point. But don't say I didn't warn you." I sucked in a rattling breath before reaching into my crocheted shoulder bag and tugging out the monogrammed sailor cap. "Recognize this?"

Her face paled. She flinched as if I held a loaded pistol. "Where did you get that?"

"It was something my mother kept." My voice softened. "I . . . I think it's mine. I think I'm your sister. I think I'm Jenny."

I watched a wild parade of emotions skitter across her face, just like I'd seen with Micah. Then, finally, rage won out.

"What is this, some sort of extortion attempt? The poor, downtrodden flea market clerk thinking she can worm her way into my generous heart and stake a claim on my bank account?" She rose, paced to the window, fingered the filmy curtains. "A few ancient newspaper clippings and a dirty old cap, and you think you can march in here and convince me my baby sister didn't drown after all?"

My turn to rise in indignation. "The last thing I'd ever want is your money. And the *very* last thing I'd ever want is to be related to you. You're the most obnoxious, conceited, self-centered person I've ever met."

She let the curtains fall into place and turned to glare at me. "And you are the most outspoken person *I've* ever encountered." Then she seemed to rein in her thoughts before adding in a choked voice, "Except that you look—*sound*—so much like her, it's uncanny."

She couldn't be talking about Jenny. She'd—*I'd*—been not quite three years old when the accident happened. Maybe our mother? Then it hit me—the woman who sparked that eerie sense of familiarity every time she visited the flea market. "You must mean Geneva Nelson."

Her mouth puckered. She reached for a framed photograph on a side table and stared at it with a sad smile. "Everyone always said Jenny would undoubtedly grow up to look like my father's sister, Aunt Geneva."

I rose to peer over her shoulder at the five-by-seven color photo of a smiling couple, a ship railing behind them and the shimmering blue of a glacier wall in the background. The woman's cheeks were ruddy from the cold. She had sparkling green eyes and a light brown cap of short, curly hair.

And she stood a good three inches taller than the man next to her.

I bent closer, that same sense of déjà vu stealing the air from my lungs.

"Aunt Geneva said so often how much you remind her of herself at a younger age, until I finally had to see for myself the day I stopped in at your flea market." She shuddered, nearly dropping the photograph as she set it back on the table. "But I never thought, never dreamed in my wildest imagination . . ."

"It can't all be coincidence. And please believe me when I say I don't want anything from you." I reached for her hand and pressed the little sailor cap into it. "I . . . I only hoped to bring you some peace."

She clutched the cap with both hands and looked deeply into my eyes, her mouth working. "But how? How can this be?"

I explained my theory about the big yellow dog.

"Oh, the dog, that horrible dog!" She backed away, her face twisted. "He came at me in the water, barking, splashing, snapping his big teeth. He grabbed my shirt and pulled me under. If I hadn't fought him off, he'd have drowned me."

A tremor of conviction rushed through me. "Renata, he wasn't trying to drown you. He was trying to *save* you—just like he saved me."

A cloud of lavender-scented steam enveloped me as I settled into the huge marble tub in Renata's guest suite. Pulsating jets swirled around me and massaged away the tension of the last life-changing twenty-four hours.

And I thought the La Quinta was luxurious!

Over the rumble of the Jacuzzi I heard someone tapping on the door. I reached for the shutoff. "Renata?"

"Sorry to disturb you." I recognized the voice of the woman who'd announced my arrival earlier. The door opened a crack. "Mrs. C thought you might care for some refreshment while you bathe. May I come in?"

I sat up nervously. "Um, I'm not exactly decent." This had to be a first—someone I hardly knew invading my bathroom privacy. Was this common practice for the rich?

I looked around for something to cover myself with. All I found within reach was an oversized teal-blue washcloth. The door inched open. The washcloth would have to do. I sank lower in the tub and spread the cloth over as much of me as I could cover, hiding the rest with my arms and thankful for the layer of sudsy white froth the Jacuzzi had whipped up.

The small, stiff-backed woman minced across the tile floor, an oblong silver tray balanced between her steady hands. "Mrs. C thought perhaps a soft drink would be to your liking. Would you prefer Coca-Cola or Dr Pepper, diet or regular, with or without caffeine?"

I noticed she carried every possible combination of the above on her tray. Plus a tall, clear tumbler filled with ice. She set the tray on an antique mahogany dresser with a marble top—a lot like one I'd seen pass through the Swap & Shop awhile back, one that sold for the hefty sum of $1,375. You don't forget a figure like that when you're calculating the commission. Somehow the dresser didn't look right under a tray—even a silver one—of dollar-a-can soft drinks.

"Miss?" The woman cast me an expectant look. She seemed a bit younger than Renata, equally sophisticated but in a more businesslike way. She looked stunning with her pale blond hair smoothed back in a French braid, the end tucked under at the nape.

"Um, Coke, please. Diet. No caffeine." I didn't need anything else boosting my adrenaline.

She turned her back, and I listened to the snap of a pop top and the fizz of liquid hitting ice. "That's real nice of you, ma'am," I said, "but I'm sure not used to this kind of service. And I don't even know your name."

"Felicia Beaufort. I'm Mrs. C's personal assistant." She handed me the glass but kept her gaze averted. "I'll leave you to your bath now." She hefted the tray and nudged the door open with the toe of her shoe.

The ice-cold glass was already turning frosty in my hand as I held it over the steaming tub. "Um, thank you, Felicia." I hoped it was okay to use her first name. What *was* the protocol for situations like this?

She stopped in the doorway and gave me her profile, the tray balanced against her waist. "Miss . . . Stiles, I believe you said . . . I hope you're as sincere as you make yourself out to be. Because if you're here to swindle the Channings, I'll make sure you live to regret it."

She reached for the doorknob. "Oh, and Mrs. C asked me to tell you that dinner will be served at seven. Please dress appropriately."

JULIE PEARL

Dress appropriately? I was still reeling from her previous warning. Talk about employee loyalty. I hoped she wasn't packing anything more lethal than those high-gloss acrylic nails.

Across the room I glimpsed my reflection in a wall of mirrored tiles. The patterns in the gold-leaf swirls made my nose look like it was coming out of my left cheek—fitting for as mixed up as I felt.

"Okay, Julie Pearl, what are you *really* doing here?" Besides the obvious, of course. Soaking (literally) in the lap of luxury, preparing to hobnob with Little Rock elite at an elegant dinner party? What did I honestly hope to gain by proving myself to be the sister of rich and fashionable Renata Channing? Certainly not money. I wouldn't take one red cent off that snobby woman if my life depended upon it.

I opened the drain, and my heart swirled round and round with the water whooshing out of the tub. I missed my grandpa so bad, it made my chest hurt. What had I done, leaving behind everything and everyone I held most dear? And for what—a soak in a Jacuzzi and an endless supply of the beverage of my choice served on a silver tray?

Once more, Micah's warning ricocheted through my thoughts. What if by pushing for the truth I managed to ruin not only my own life but that of everyone I cared most about?

A plush white velour robe draped from a hook behind the bathroom door. Hoping it was there for guests, I wrapped myself in its softness and wandered into the bedroom. I plopped onto the yellow tropical-print comforter atop the four-poster bed. On the nightstand a bonnet-top Seth Thomas chimed five o'clock.

Two hours until my dinner party debut. I wondered how Renata intended to introduce me.

Dress appropriately.

I doubted jeans fit the bill.

I should let Renata know I hadn't exactly packed for such an occasion, but I was too afraid of getting lost if I went exploring the nether regions of this castle in search of another living, breathing human.

Where was Clifton the brave explorer when I needed him? Back in Caddo Pines—where else?

My glance fell on my shoulder bag, where I'd tossed it earlier at the foot of the bed. I dug through it for my cell phone, brought up the last call received, then hit redial.

"Yes?"

"Hi, Renata, it's me."

"Jul—Jen—?" She made a squeaking sound in her throat.

I studied the ceiling. "It might be easier if we stick with Julie."

"Yes, I suppose. But why are you phoning me? I'm downstairs."

"Wasn't sure I could find my way. And anyway, I didn't want to go traipsing through the house in a bathrobe." I ran my fingers down the velvety-soft lapel and felt like Cinderella.

"Did Felicia talk to you about dinner?" She sounded almost childlike. "It would mean so much to me if you'd join us."

"That's why I'm calling. I'm, uh, a little unprepared for dressing up."

She laughed knowingly, and I didn't know whether I should

feel insulted or grateful. "Isabel will be there shortly with a selection of clothing for you to try on. If anything needs altering, she'll take care of it."

I stared at myself in the full-length mirror on the closet door—a walk-in closet as spacious as my entire bedroom over the flea market. Isabel had outdone herself. In barely over an hour, she'd managed to tailor-fit me into a slinky red Vera Wang tank top over shimmering white capris. She tied a multi-colored geometric-print scarf around my hips and topped it with a gold chain belt. Shoes proved more challenging, as neither my sloppy brown huaraches nor my graying Keds with the frayed toes quite complemented the look we were going for.

Which was . . . what, exactly? I'd been expecting Isabel to show up with something along the lines of a sequined evening gown or a chic little black cocktail dress. Instead, I looked like I was headed out for a night of disco dancing.

We finally pried my 9Bs into a pair of Renata's 8½AA white leather sandals. Then another lady showed up—Yvette was the only name she gave me, a gorgeous Black woman with perfect skin and reddish-brown hair tied back in a fat ponytail of beaded dreadlocks. She did my hair and makeup, and by the time she finished taming my spirals into some semblance of style, I didn't recognize myself.

The prim Felicia Beaufort, now clad in a gray pantsuit, returned for me promptly at 6:50. "My goodness," she murmured with a raised brow. "You do clean up nicely."

Index finger on my chin, I grinned and faked a curtsy. "Why, thankee, ma'am. And yer lookin' as purty as a speckled pup in a red wagon, yerself."

If looks could kill, I'd have been six feet under in less time than it took Sneezy to polish off a bowl of tuna-mackerel surprise.

Felicia's appraising glance found its way to my left wrist. She gave a scornful sniff. "I suggest you remove your cute little toy. It doesn't quite complement Vera Wang."

I slapped my hand over my Snow White watch and glared at Ms. Felicia Beaufort. "Well, excuse me. Let's not offend Vera."

Laying Snow White in a shell-shaped porcelain dish on the dresser felt like leaving the last vestiges of *me* behind. Lifting my chin, I followed Felicia downstairs to the candlelit dining room.

"Here she is, Mrs. C." Felicia guided me by one elbow into the room and sent Renata a meaningful look.

Renata looked cool and elegant in the silky black trousers from this afternoon and a violet mesh poncho over a black shell. As she turned from adjusting a place setting, her mouth fell open, then spread into a wide smile. "Julie, you look fantastic. That outfit looks a thousand times better on you than it ever did on me. You could be a model."

"Really? Thanks." Happy little butterflies danced behind my belly button. I used to play make-believe and prance around the Swap & Shop in vintage outfits borrowed from the Glad Rags booth. By the time I was fifteen, I knew I had the height to be a model, and people told me I was pretty enough. But pursuing such a dream would have meant trading the flea market for big-city life and leaving Grandpa behind, and I just couldn't do it.

I gave myself a mental slap. *Wake up, Julie, and look at where you're standing now.*

I rubbed my arms and glanced around the dining room. The first thing to catch my eye was the centerpiece, a teddy bear–shaped crystal vase containing a "bouquet" of giant decorated cookies. Then I noticed the miniature fuzzy white bears next to each plate. The bears sat with outstretched paws holding embossed place cards. Colorful satin bows with curling streamers adorned each chair.

I mashed my lips together. "Dinner party? It looks like you're expecting a bunch of kids for high tea."

She gave me a dubious smile. "Since you tracked me down through the Channing Children's Foundation, I assumed you'd realize how deeply I care for young people."

Somewhere in the house a doorbell chimed, and moments later Felicia ushered in the first arrivals. I stood to one side, watching in awe as Renata greeted a laughing young couple and their two children, all decked out in their Sunday best. Before they'd even said their hellos, three more families arrived. Soon the dining room sounded like a big, happy family reunion.

I edged over to where Felicia stood in the arched doorway. "Who are all these people?"

She cut her eyes at me. "Families Mrs. C has brought together through the foundation's adoption program."

I recalled the doubts that had run through my mind while trying to contact Renata at the foundation offices. *Wrong again, Julie Pearl.*

"Each of these children had been originally considered unadoptable," Felicia continued. "Health, age, siblings who needed to stay together—a variety of reasons. But through Mrs. C's efforts, deserving and qualified parents were found for them. And once a quarter, Mrs. C hosts a dinner for several families to honor the one-year anniversary of their adoptions."

"That's wonderful." And she looked so . . . blissful. So perfectly at ease as she flitted from one laughing child to the next.

Renata had a heart for needy children. I couldn't turn my back on a stray dog or cat. Were we more alike than I'd imagined?

For introductions that evening, I remained Julie Pearl Stiles, Renata's "new and already very dear friend." Which was fine with me. I had my hands full trying to guess which of several forks, knives, and spoons were appropriate for each course the white-smocked caterers set before me. Thank goodness the two little girls I was seated between had no more clue than I did, so we shared a few giggles behind our napkins and relied on their parents to set us straight.

By the time I fell across my pillow-top mattress that night, every muscle and brain cell in my body felt like I'd been squeezed like a wrung-out mop. I pushed my toes deep beneath the buttery-soft Egyptian-cotton sheets and snuggled into a lavender-scented down pillow that bore not even the faintest hint of mustiness. I felt like I could sleep for days.

It was utterly peaceful. And so . . . *quiet.*

No traffic noises from the highway.

No snuffling snores coming from the next room.

No jerk and grumble as the refrigerator cycled on and off through the night.

No cat's purr or puppies' whimpering or dog's warm, wet nose nuzzling my arm in the dark.

I sat up slowly and hugged my knees to my chest. Silent tears flowed down my face.

Oh, Lordy, how I miss the Swap & Shop!

Over the next couple of days, I felt more and more like I'd stepped from real life into the pages of some bizarre fairytale. I kept thinking I ought to say my good-byes and head on back to Grandpa—except it looked like he wasn't really my grandpa after all. But did that stop me from loving him and missing him? I thought about calling, but what would I say? "Having a ball. Wish you were here," like some cheesy postcard from Pismo Beach?

No, before I phoned home—if indeed the Swap & Shop could still be called my home—I needed a little more time to adjust to my new identity, a little more time to get to know my sister. Except I didn't see much of Renata, and when she did make an appearance, it always came with an apology. "Julie, sweetheart, just give me a few days to clear my calendar, and I promise, we'll have plenty of time to spend together."

In the meantime, Isabel spent hours altering selected items from Renata's closet to enhance my wardrobe, while Yvette coached me on hair, skin, and makeup routines. After watching me mince around at the dinner party in those too-tight sandals, Renata must have sent Felicia shoe shopping. Miss Tight-lips herself appeared in my room Friday afternoon with stacks of shoeboxes, making me try on style after style and returning the ones that didn't fit.

It slowly dawned on me that Renata wouldn't be ready to claim me as her sister until I looked the part, until I looked as polished and perfect as her credit cards and personal shoppers could make me. My homesickness swelled into a festering loneliness, the kind I imagined rich people might feel—at least the ones who based their entire existence on wealth and prestige. I wondered if I'd ever measure up to Renata's ideal.

And did I even want to try? Sure, I wanted my sister to like me —to *love* me—but how much was I willing to change to make that happen?

Early one morning, dressed in a blue-flowered sundress that skimmed my ankles (I learned quickly that my jeans and vintage flea-market finds were not appropriate attire in the Channing household), I found my way downstairs to the breakfast room, a sunny alcove overlooking a brick terrace and sloping gardens. The table was set as usual—pristine white cloth, pastel-print placemats and matching runner, a bowl of fresh-cut flowers in the center. A coffee urn and a selection of cute, sugary foreign pastries waited on a buffet, along with a chafing dish of buttery scrambled eggs.

With a sigh, I poured a glass of orange juice from a frosty cut-glass pitcher and dreamed of raisin bran and whole-wheat toast spread with Katy Harcourt's homemade mayhaw jelly.

"Finding everything to your liking, Miss?"

"Oh, hi." I smiled at the tall Black gentleman who'd just entered from the kitchen. He was new to me. Until now a middle-aged woman and a plump, acne-scarred teen had served the meals. I cast the man a pleading gaze. "You wouldn't happen to have something *plain* back there? Something that comes in a box or cellophane wrapper?"

His brows lifted, and he gave me a knowing smile. "Why certainly, Miss. Let me see what I can find for you."

As he turned to go, I touched the sleeve of his white jacket. "And would it be okay if—I mean, this is so—" I flicked my fingers in a helpless gesture. My shoulders drooped. "I seem to be dining alone this morning, so could I have breakfast in the kitchen with you?"

His hearty guffaw took me by surprise. "I won't tell if you won't." With a furtive glance toward the hallway, he extended one arm and directed me through the swinging door.

We entered an enormous kitchen furnished with an eight-burner gas range and a stainless-steel refrigerator big enough to store food for everyone on the *Queen Mary*. The granite countertops were lined with every modern appliance imaginable. Glass-front cupboards held an array of dishes and serving pieces that LeRoy Tuttle would have paid top dollar for to resell in his Swap & Shop booth. I could only guess at the contents of the massive pantry.

"Why don't you have a seat over here, Miss?" The white-coated man guided me around a vast center work island toward an oak pedestal table near the far windows. He pulled out a chair for me at one end. "What can I interest you in? We stock a fairly broad selection of packaged breakfast cereals, mainly for the staff, of course, but you're welcome to any of it."

I shook my head and remained standing. "Thanks, but you really don't have to wait on me. Just point me to the right cupboard and I can help myself." I offered my hand. "By the way, I'm Julie Stiles."

A flicker of uncertainty darkened his gaze before he smiled and accepted my hand. "I'm Walter. So glad to make your acquaintance, Miss Stiles."

"Hey, Julie is just fine, Walter, and it's nice to meet you, too." Good grief, the man was old enough to be my father. I couldn't use his first name and have him calling me Miss Stiles. Just didn't seem polite.

But then I reminded myself this was a whole new world. It would be a long time yet before I learned all the rules.

Walter showed me to the pantry shelf where the boxed cereals were kept. I filled a bowl with Wheat Chex and insisted Walter pour milk over it right from the jug—wouldn't let him fetch one of those dainty little pitchers like he started to. We had a pleasant conversation while I ate and Walter puttered around the kitchen, though I couldn't for the life of me convince him to use my first name. I finally gave up and settled for Miss Julie.

Walter told me he worked at the mansion Sunday through Thursday, and Mrs. Klein and her daughter Lindy covered Fridays and Saturdays. "I'm assistant pastor at my church," he said. "I preach at Saturday evening worship. Mrs. C gives me Friday and Saturday off so I can prepare."

"Oh my goodness. Today's Sunday, isn't it?" I shoved my chair back and tossed my napkin onto the table. All I could think about was Grandpa and Sandy and Clifton all heading off to church in Caddo Pines . . . *without me.*

Walter folded his polishing cloth and laid it on the counter. His eyes softened. "You're a church-going woman, Miss Julie?"

"All my life." At least as long as I could remember.

Then the words from Jenny's—*my*—obituary came back to me, the part about memorial gifts for the church's Sunday-school wing. So church must have been important to the Pearl family at one time, too—another piece of my history to be filed away.

I rinsed my empty bowl in the sink, then stared out the window toward the garage. My VW bug wasn't anywhere to be seen. Shortly after my conversation with Renata my first day here, she'd requested my keys so her chauffeur could "park the car in a safe place." No doubt she'd wanted that rattletrap moved off her front drive and out of sight ASAP.

Without turning from the window, I said quietly, "How much do you know about me, Walter? Has anyone told you who I am, why I'm here?"

A long, tense silence met my ears before he finally spoke. "There are rumors floating around—can't avoid it in a big ol' house like this. But it's none of my business, Miss Julie, and I don't stick my nose in where it isn't supposed to be."

The horrible, overwhelming sense of loneliness swept through me again. Why had I come here, when *nothing* was turning out the way I'd hoped? Renata and I hadn't even taken a meal together since her dinner party for the adoptees—she always had some function or business to attend to. How was I supposed to get to know my sister if she was always too busy for me?

Walter came up beside me and gently took the bowl from my hands. "Let me, Miss Julie. It's my job, not yours. You should go now. Mrs. C will not be happy to know I fed you cold cereal in the kitchen." He gave a low chuckle, but there was no humor in it.

Truth be told, it sounded more like pity.

The house echoed with silence this lonely Sunday morning. My car keys hadn't been returned yet, and I hadn't a clue how to track down the chauffeur to ask for them. I should have asked Walter while I had the chance. Now I felt trapped and isolated.

"There you are." Appearing out of nowhere, Felicia Beaufort snagged my arm as I went in search of the library and something to read to help pass the time.

At least with Renata's petite watchdog I had the advantage of height. I stared down my nose at her. "Sorry, didn't know anyone was looking for me."

"I searched the entire house. Where have you been?"

"Having breakfast." Obviously the *entire house* didn't include the servants' areas. I held my arms out from my sides and turned slowly. "Want to search me? I promise I haven't swiped the heirloom silver. Walter can vouch for me."

Felicia made a rumbling sound in her throat. "Mrs. C will see you in her private suite. She doesn't like to be kept waiting."

"And *I* don't like being ignored. I don't see her for days, and now *she* doesn't want to wait? Well, she can—" I bit off my retort and took several deep breaths while Felicia gave me the evil eye.

Once I'd calmed down a mite, I folded my arms across my ribcage and spoke slowly. "Ms. Beaufort, I honestly don't care what you think of me, whether you believe I'm Jennifer Pearl or not. But you'd *better* believe that I have no deceitful intentions whatsoever. I came here for one purpose only—to show Renata she's not responsible for her baby sister's death. And maybe, somehow, help her forgive herself and let go of the past."

"That is, *if* you really are her sister. The family attorney will be here first thing tomorrow to arrange for a DNA test." She nodded toward the main staircase. "Now please, don't keep Mrs. C waiting any longer."

Trudging up the curving stairway, I couldn't help wondering why Renata hadn't insisted on a DNA test from the get-go. I'd caught almost every episode of *CSI* and all its spin-offs. What better way to prove or disprove my claim? And once my identity was confirmed, maybe Felicia would get off my case and Renata and I could concentrate on getting to know each other and make up for lost time. DNA test? Bring it on!

I was practically skipping by the time I knocked on the partly open door to Renata's sitting room. I peeked inside. "Hey, it's me."

"Come in, Julie, dear." She beckoned from the satin-striped chaise, a polished wooden lap desk propped on her thighs. "That dress looks charming on you—suits you perfectly. I promise we'll go shopping together soon. I would have had Felicia bring you some outfits to try, but her tastes run a bit too conservative for me. I trust the shoes she selected were suitable, though?"

"Oh, yes, fine." I lifted my skirt to display the silver Cole Haan ballet flats I'd slipped into this morning. I didn't mention I'd be afraid to wear them beyond the front door for fear of sullying their pristine soles.

Renata capped an expensive-looking fountain pen and set the lap desk on the Oriental carpet. "Do sit down, darling. I apologize again for leaving you on your own so much."

"I understand. I've tried to keep myself occupied." More like *preoccupied*. I pulled over an ottoman upholstered in cherry velveteen and sat across from her. "Do you think we could spend some time together today? There's so much we—I—"

A tidal wave of emotions washed over me. I leaned forward and hugged my knees, afraid I'd be sick to my stomach all over Renata's expensive rug.

She swung her legs off the side of the chaise and knelt beside me, taking me in her arms. "Oh, my Jenny, my precious, precious Jenny-love."

"My sweet little turtle dove." The distant echo from my childhood sang through my thoughts, a little rhyme my mother—Angie, that is—used to croon to me. Or had my memory deceived me? Did the words belong to my real mother, or maybe even Renata, instead?

My cheek pressed against the lapel of her pale green satin robe, and I inhaled the crisp, floral scent of Amarige. When Sandy and I were teens, we used to sample all the expensive fragrances at the Dillard's cosmetics counter in Hot Springs Mall—until some grumpy sales clerk banished us.

I wondered what Sandy would think if she could see me now.

I wondered what Grandpa would think.

And I felt like a traitor.

JULIE PEARL

Turned out Renata did have plans to spend some quality time with me that day. While I pulled myself together, she padded into her dressing room and spoke to me over the sounds of hangers sliding across closet rods and drawers opening and closing.

"I thought we'd drive over to Hot Springs this afternoon," she said. Laughter bubbled from inside the cavernous closet. "I can't *wait* to see Aunt Geneva's expression when I tell her our news!"

I smoothed the rippling folds of my skirt. "Maybe you should give her a little warning. She might need to adjust to the idea." I didn't want sweet Mrs. Nelson collapsing of a heart attack.

Renata's smiling face popped around the door frame. "I've already told her we're coming."

I sauntered over and leaned against the wall outside the door. "And who exactly did you say *we* were?"

"Just said she's going to be very, very surprised." She tweaked my chin before giving me her back so I could zip up the same perky yellow sundress she'd been wearing the first time I saw her.

A knock sounded on the outer door and Yvette swept into the

room. "'Mornin', Mrs. C, you ready for me? How are you, Julie, honey?"

"Fine, thanks. You?" In the presence of such glamour I could only hug myself and avoid my plain-Jane reflection in Renata's closet-door mirror. Did Yvette ever have a bad-hair day—a bad *anything* day?

"Start with Julie, why don't you?" Renata plucked at my mass of curls. "Oh, honey, we've just got to tame that hair."

"Believe me, I've tried." I ogled Renata's chestnut waves, flowing across her shoulders like a satin cloak. "I'd give anything to have gorgeous hair like yours."

Hard knots formed on either side of her jaw. "I've had my share of bad perms, too. Yvette, see what you can do for this poor girl. Don't take too long, though. I want to leave within the hour."

Yvette winked. "My clients don't call me a miracle worker for nothing." She ushered me into Renata's bathroom and seated me in front of a lighted mirror. A wide array of gels, mousses, sprays, and electric styling devices cluttered the marble countertop.

Renata finished dressing and excused herself, leaving Yvette to experiment with my hair. She pushed it this way and that, brushing, dampening, blow-drying, and finally attacking it with a wide ceramic flat iron. But five minutes after she unclamped the device, my curls sprang back faster than a Slinky toy.

"Oooh, girl, I'm beginning to believe you." Yvette tut-tutted and shook her head. Lifting a strand of hair, she twisted it around her finger. "Baby, what you need is dreadlocks. You would look *très chic*, I'm telling you."

"Oh, no, no way!" I cringed. "I mean, they look great on *you*, but I couldn't—"

"Hey, you think white girls can't carry off the look? Who's that famous lady writer—Anne Lamott? She finally quit fighting her kinky hair and went with dreads. It'd be so easy for you to take care of. When you get back later, give me a call and we can get started, what do you say?"

I had to admit, the idea sorely tempted me.

But there'd been a few too many changes in my life already. I didn't need one more.

The chauffeur met us out front in Renata's silver Mercedes. She explained she usually preferred to drive herself, unless she had calls to make or paperwork to handle while en route. Today she slid into the backseat with me so we could chat on the way to Hot Springs.

And *chat* about summed it up. Definitely nothing deep or insightful—and Renata did most of the talking. She told me all about the Channing Children's Foundation, the various charitable boards she served on, where she liked to shop, the latest theater event she'd attended—

"What about your husband, Renata?" Interrupting her was about the only way I could get a word in edgewise. "Am I going to meet him anytime soon?"

"Oh, I doubt it. Larry's always off on some GigantaMart business of one kind or another."

I ran a fingernail along a seam in the upholstery. "Sounds like Larry's business keeps him on the road a lot."

She gazed out the window at the pine forests and craggy hillsides. Her rigid posture spoke louder than her words. "We don't see much of each other at all, in fact."

"If I was married to somebody who traveled all over the country, I think I'd find any excuse to tag along."

"I used to." She crossed one bronzed leg over the other, dangling her strappy yellow fake-crocodile slide.

She left it at that, and so did I.

Besides, we'd turned onto the back highway and were nearing the Caddo Pines turnoff. When I saw the billboard with the big blue arrow pointing south to Otto Stiles' Swap & Shop, my heart swelled to three times its normal size. It was all I could do to keep from yelling at the driver to pull over and let me out. I started to check the time on my Snow White watch before remembering I'd left it on the dresser back at Channing Castle. The dashboard clock read 11:24. Grandpa would be home from church by now, changing out of his Sunday clothes and grabbing a sandwich or bowl of soup before opening the Swap & Shop at noon.

At least I hoped he was getting himself something decent to eat. He usually left me in charge of groceries and cooking, and I had this nagging fear that without me around, he wouldn't take proper care of himself.

Why hadn't I at least called to check on him? It had been four whole days now, and I hadn't even had my cell phone on since my first day at Renata's. Maybe it was because I knew I couldn't have it both ways—remain Julie Pearl Stiles, small-town flea market manager, while finding my way as Jennifer Susan Pearl, sister of Little Rock society queen Renata Pearl Channing.

So when I glimpsed the Caddo Pines water tower in the distance, I hunkered down and squeezed my eyes shut. Tears puddled in the creases alongside my nose, but I brushed them away before Renata could notice.

"Aunt Geneva, honey, how have you been?" Renata stepped into the foyer and wrapped her arms around the slender woman, while I held back just out of sight, peering through the red-tinged leaves of a photinia bush.

"My goodness, Rennie-girl, ease up on these old bones." Mrs. Nelson—could I ever get used to calling her Aunt Geneva?—gave Renata a pat on the back and squirmed out of the tight embrace. She laughed heartily. "You were just here for lunch a couple weeks ago. You're acting like you haven't seen me in a month of Sundays."

"I know, but I'm so excited, I could burst."

"I can see that!" Mrs. Nelson set gnarled hands on her hips. "All right, then, who is this surprise guest you brought?" She peered around Renata and cast me a curious grin. "Hello, there—oh, it's you!"

Mrs. Nelson beckoned me inside as she reached for the wall switch and flicked on the ceiling light. The small foyer glowed yellow. "What a surprise, Julie! Renata, why didn't you tell me you finally met the young lady from the flea market?"

On the hall table I noticed the candy dish I'd rung up for her a couple of weeks ago. It saddened me to realize my very own aunt had visited the Swap & Shop so many times and I hadn't even known we were related. When I glimpsed our side-by-side reflections in a gilt-framed mirror, the resemblance was even more obvious. I could see the amazement in her face too. She clicked her tongue. "Didn't I tell you, Renata? Is Julie the spittin' image of me in my younger days, or what?"

Renata's eyes brimmed. Her voice sank to a whisper. "That's because she's Jenny, Aunt Geneva. *She's Jenny.*"

Geneva Nelson's take on the announcement was somewhere between Renata's fervor and Felicia Beaufort's icy distrust. And honestly, that made me a whole lot more comfortable than either extreme.

Geneva smiled at me across the glass-topped wicker table on her screened back porch. Her eyes held kindness and compassion . . . and the memory of great sadness. A light breeze lifted the curls from her temples, revealing salt-and-pepper roots. We'd been talking for over an hour now, the salad lunch she'd served almost untouched. She'd listened quietly as I explained how I'd pieced everything together.

Renata kept nodding in silent agreement and wiping away an

occasional tear. "Isn't it a miracle, Aunt Geneva? If you hadn't kept pestering me to stop in at the flea market, we might never have discovered Jenny's alive."

I took a deep breath and glanced at Renata. "I know it's a shock, and there'll be a DNA test, of course—"

"Which is completely unnecessary." Renata reached over to pat my arm. "No one has to prove what I already know in my heart."

Geneva swirled the melting crescent-shaped cubes in her glass of iced tea. "Renata, would you mind fetching the tea pitcher from the refrigerator? And bring a bowl of ice, too."

"Sure, honey." Renata planted a kiss on the crown of her aunt's head as she rose.

When we were alone, Geneva turned to me. "It truly would be a miracle if you *are* our Jenny. You have no idea what the loss of that little girl did to Rennie—to the whole family."

I pushed a spiral of spinach pasta around my plate. "I know what it did to Micah Hobart."

"You have feelings for him, don't you?"

My voice became gravelly. "Yes. I think I do."

She touched my arm. "He's a good man. I always felt so bad for him, for how he got caught up in Renata's misguided escape plan."

"You knew she was running to you?"

"Oh, yes. It was such a difficult time. Lucille—Renata's mother —could be quite emotional. Controlling. Critical. Some days she'd be just fine, and others—" She broke off, her lips pressed together in a frown.

My skin tingled. "What exactly was wrong with her?"

"We didn't talk much about such things, but I think nowadays they call it bipolar disorder. I know she took pills for years." Geneva's eyes took on a faraway look. "She got worse after Jenny was born, and fools that we all were, we wanted to believe it would pass." She gave her head a small shake. "Forgive me, I don't mean to talk about Jenny as if I don't believe you're she."

"It's okay, I understand. Please go on."

"Well, it was extremely hard on Rennie, barely a teenager and so confused about everything. So many of the day-to-day responsibilities of the resort—things Lucille usually handled—fell to Rennie. Not to mention taking care of little Jenny when Lucille was having a particularly bad day. And it got to be too much."

I paused at the clatter of ice cubes spilling into a glass bowl. My next question came out with difficulty. "If you knew how bad it was, why didn't you do something?"

"I've asked myself the same question more times than I can count." Geneva plucked at the fringed border of her placemat. "I was young, too, recently married and wrapped up in my own concerns. And I was reluctant to meddle in my brother's affairs."

Renata's shoes clicked on the hardwood porch floor. "Here we are. Let me top off your glass, Julie. More ice, Aunt Geneva?"

The DNA test was a simple thing. Just like on TV, the lab tech the Channings' attorney brought had Renata open her mouth and scraped the inside of her cheek with a cotton swab, then did the same with me.

Felicia's polished acrylics did a tap dance on her crossed arms. "How long will the results take?"

The tech capped the vial containing Renata's swab and wrote something on the narrow label. "Since both parents are deceased and we don't have their DNA for comparison, this test won't be conclusive. However, I should be able to determine a probability index for siblingship within forty-eight hours."

Renata, seated on a brocade armchair across the living room, heaved a noisy breath. "Honestly, Howard," she said to the attorney, "this whole DNA rigmarole is overkill."

"Can't be too careful in these situations, Renata." Howard Kirby, Attorney-at-Law, hefted his bulk off the white sofa and snapped his briefcase shut. Casting me a dismissive glance, he ushered the lab tech out of the room. "I'll be in touch as soon as I hear anything. In the meantime . . ." He paused in the tiled foyer next to an urn of white daylilies. He lowered his voice as Renata joined him, and I couldn't hear what he said next.

As if I couldn't guess. *"Don't be so quick to trust this perky young gold digger. She's probably nothing more than a money-grubbing pretender."*

My spine prickled, and I turned to see Felicia staring me down —sort of, since I was the one looking down on her.

She sneered like a snippy little rat terrier. "I suggest you leave now before the test comes back and proves you're a fake. It'll save you and Mrs. C both a lot of embarrassment."

The rat terrier ought to know better than to tangle with a Great Dane. "Maybe you ought to polish up your résumé, Ms. Beaufort, because when those results come back, *you're* likely to be the one who's embarrassed."

RENATA

June, 25 years earlier
Hot Springs, Arkansas

The baby's screams sliced the morning stillness, and over them an angry shout: "Sit still, Jenny. For heaven's sake, *sit still!*"

Feet dangling off the floating platform twenty feet from shore, Rennie pressed her hands to her ears and shuddered.

Micah shot a glance toward the main house. "What's your mama doing to her?"

"Giving her a permanent." Rennie lowered her hands with a groan.

"Sounds like Jenny's getting her hair torn out by the roots."

"The poor thing's not even three years old. She doesn't understand."

The screaming only got worse, along with Mama's hysterical shouting that anyone within a mile of the resort must have heard. "I mean it, Jennifer Susan Pearl! I will tie your hands and feet to this chair if you do not hold still!"

Rennie had all she could stomach. In one motion she pulled

her feet out of the water, curled her toes around the edge of the rocking deck, and launched herself headfirst into the lake. With angry strokes she beat her way to shore.

Her hair and swimsuit dripping, Rennie careened across the brick patio and lurched into the kitchen. "Mama, stop it! Leave her alone!"

Mama grasped Jenny by the shoulders as the frightened child squirmed on the red vinyl stepstool. A Tupperware container of skinny permanent rods sat on the table. The floor was strewn with small white tissue squares of end papers. The house reeked of ammonia.

"Jenny-baby, it's okay, Rennie's here now." She shoved her mother out of the way and swept her sobbing sister into her arms. The poor thing's face was beet red—whether from crying or the stinky permanent solution, Rennie couldn't tell. She wet a dishcloth with cool water from the sink and dabbed Jenny's forehead and temples. "She's too little for this, Mama. Why couldn't you wait till she's older?"

"What do *you* know?" Mama sounded crazed, hoarse. Her eyes held a wild look. "You run around here all day looking like a ragamuffin, not caring a whit about how you look, how it reflects on me and your daddy. I'm so *ashamed* of you, Renata Louise. You're an *embarrassment* to me. You're a pariah, an ugly, worthless, lazy *wretch*."

Rennie's skin crawled. She felt like she could throw up. "Mama, did you take your pills—"

"And heaven only knows what goes on between you and that MacDonohoe boy. I've seen you out there on the lake, your heads together like you're plotting something. Against me, no doubt."

Tears threatened. Rennie's voice climbed an octave. "Mama, *please*! People can hear you clear across the lake." She found the box of grahams in the pantry and broke one in half for Jenny. The treat temporarily quieted the little girl. "And there is nothing going on between me and Micah. How can you say such a thing? He's only a kid, Mama!"

Except right now he was her only connection with sanity.

Oh, God, why can't I get someone to see what's happening here!

But God didn't answer, and Daddy acted oblivious. Either he wouldn't allow himself to see how much worse Mama had gotten since Jenny was born, or the resort kept him too busy to notice. He spent all his time keeping the books or staying on top of the never-ending cottage repairs.

If only Aunt Geneva would step in and do something—but she'd just started a new job as a nursing home dietician, and she and Uncle Burt were trying to have a baby of their own. They sure didn't have time for Rennie's problems. And the grandparents were no help, Mama's parents a thousand miles away in Boise, Daddy's folks retired to a beach condo in Florida.

Rennie had never felt so alone and helpless. She had to think of something, and soon.

JULIE PEARL

Present Day

"The DNA results are back."

At the sound of Felicia's clipped words, I jerked my head sideways and almost slipped off the top step of Renata's huge, kidney-shaped pool. I grabbed for the edge and hoped Felicia hadn't noticed my momentary panic. "That was fast."

She shot me a squint-eyed smirk. "Thought you should know in case you'd like to start packing. Howard Kirby will be here at two thirty." Turning brusquely on her sensible size-4 gray pumps, she marched back inside.

I shaded my eyes to peer at the ceramic clock on the cabana. Already almost two. Glued to the top step, I'd kept my lower half cool in the naturally purified, chlorine-free water, but the rest of me had grown hot and clammy despite frequent splashing. A shower was definitely in order.

And I wanted to look my absolute best when I watched Ms. Felicia Beaufort get her comeuppance. People like her, acting so smug and superior, they flat made me crazy. Grandpa would have a word or two to say about my attitude, I'm sure, but—

Are you Julie Pearl Stiles or Jennifer Susan Pearl? You cannot *have it both ways.*

I felt a little rip in my heart, a physical pain. I could only pray that once those results were announced, my way would finally be made clear.

Shades of Monday, minus the lab tech. Renata sat in the same fancy armchair, looking serene and elegant in iridescent-green silk slacks and matching sleeveless sweater. Felicia was her usual businesslike self in a tailored ice-blue pantsuit. For once I was grateful for clothing options other than my vintage flea market apparel. I thought I looked the picture of style in the navy slacks Isabel had hemmed to capri length and a bold, patriotic-print tunic top. I struck a confident pose against the antique limestone mantel.

Apparently the effect was lost on Felicia. "Aren't we a bit early for the Fourth of July?"

I ignored her as Howard Kirby, seated on the sofa, cleared his throat, reached into the inside pocket of his suit coat, and removed a sealed envelope. "Renata, are you ready?"

She stalled for about three centuries while examining an enameled fingernail. In the meantime, nervous sweat trickled down my spine. "Howard," she said softly, "I trust you have abided by my wishes?"

"Of course." The stout attorney pressed his lips together. "As you instructed, no one other than the lab technician, including myself, has seen the contents of this envelope."

"Good." Catlike, Renata rose and stood before Kirby, hand extended. He laid the crisp white envelope in her palm. "That's all we need from you today, Howard. Thank you so much for your assistance." Pinching the envelope between her thumb and index finger, she gave a dismissive nod.

As Kirby rose with a confused frown, Renata turned to Felicia. "Please have Martin bring the car around. And fetch my purse and cell phone, will you, dear?"

"But, Mrs. C—" Renata's personal assistant looked even more flustered than the attorney, and despite my own confusion, I couldn't help relishing that fact. Felicia's leather soles scuffed across the Oriental carpet as she rushed toward the foyer to catch up with Renata and the attorney. "Wait, what about the test results?"

Renata paused and gave Felicia a look that I can only describe as utter serenity. I edged closer, and Renata's placid gaze drifted to me. I shivered under its coolness. "I have no intention of looking inside this envelope," she said. "I am going right now to lock it away in my safe-deposit box, and there it will stay."

Kirby and Felicia both stared at Renata, their jaws practically dragging the floor.

"Renata, this is stupidity!"

"No, Mrs. C, you can't be serious—"

"I am *deadly* serious." She looked from one to the other as if daring them to argue. Then her eyes locked with mine once more, and she smiled. "I have no need for a piece of paper to tell me what I already know is true."

Five seconds after Renata left, Felicia stormed through the house slamming doors, drawers, and phone receivers. I had no idea who all she called, or what all that banging around was intended to accomplish, but I had to admit, her loyalty to Renata was impressive.

And I had to wonder about it.

I mean, why should my true identity be such a big deal with Felicia, a mere employee . . . unless for some reason (maybe her faithful service and devotion?) she expected a sizeable bequest from the childless Renata Pearl Channing?

Talk about gold diggers!

I followed the din to a third-floor office suite. Felicia stood with her back to me between a burnished bamboo desk and tall windows framed by built-in bookcases. She yammered away on a cordless phone. "Larry, I mean it, you *have* to do something. You can't let her get away with this. It's absolutely outrageous!"

Larry? As in, Lawrence Eugene Channing?

I sauntered into the paneled room and plopped my rear into a thickly padded armchair. The slick, bronze leather felt cool against my back—probably just what I needed to lower my temperature a few degrees before I laid some heated words on Ms. Beaufort.

"No, next week is *not* soon enough." Her tone became wheedling. "I *need* you, Larry. Please, you've got to put a stop to this nonsense before—"

My loud "*Ahem*" got her attention in a hurry. Spinning around, she pressed the phone against her abdomen. "How long have you been sitting there?"

I lifted an accusing eyebrow. "Long enough to hear you whispering sweet nothings to *Larry*."

If I'd thought she looked flustered earlier, now I read sheer panic in her darting glance. She recovered quickly with another of those haughty looks she was so good at. "I don't know what exactly you *think* you heard, but you'd do well to keep your meddling nose out of it."

"That sounds mighty like a threat." I did my best imitation of Renata calmly inspecting her manicure. "Seems to me, someone with nothing to hide wouldn't be so nervous about what she's *not* hiding."

She lifted the phone to her ear and muttered, "I'll call you back," before pressing the disconnect button and laying down the phone.

I stood and rested my fingertips on the polished expanse between us. "So tell me, Felicia, what exactly *is* going on between you and Renata's husband? Are you the reason their marriage is on the rocks?"

She stiffened. "What gave you the idea the Channings' marriage is in trouble?"

"Larry's never around, Renata hardly mentions him, and when she does, the look in her eyes . . . well, let's just say it doesn't take Dr. Phil to interpret the signs."

I could hardly bear to look at the scheming hussy. A Blue Delft vase of fading yellow roses adorned the corner of the desk. I plucked a wilted petal and crushed it between my fingers. "Hmmm, seems I'm not the one Renata needs to be worried about."

With the musky scent of decaying roses filling my nostrils, I turned to leave.

Before I'd taken three steps across the carpet, Felicia grabbed my arm. The panicked look had returned full force. "Where are you going? What are you planning to do?"

I jerked my arm free. "Don't worry, I'm not running to Renata to expose your little secret. She's smart enough to figure it out on her own, if she hasn't already." With a shudder, I made another move toward the door. "And you had the nerve to accuse *me* of deception."

"Mrs. Channing may be convinced you're her dear departed sister returned from the dead." Venom crept back into Felicia's voice. "But I know your type—poor white trash looking for an easy way out of the gutter."

I mimicked her stance of crossed arms and nose in the air, mine hovering a good eight inches above hers. "Tell me, Ms. Beaufort, what gutter did *you* crawl out of before you latched onto the Channings?"

She opened her mouth to respond and then froze, her staring eyes fixed on something beyond my shoulder. She sucked in a tiny, sharp breath. "Mrs. C."

I spun around to see Renata standing in the doorway. She set her hands on her hips. "What on *earth* is going on here? I could hear the two of you shouting all the way downstairs."

"Mrs. C, I—it's just that the DNA results—" Felicia's arms jerked like the forelegs of a nervous spider.

Renata released an exasperated huff as she stepped forward and lightly touched Felicia's cheek. "I appreciate your concern, darling. But my decision in this matter is final."

She turned to me. "And you, Julie dear, try to get along with Felicia. She's been my assistant for almost nine years now, and I don't know what I'd do without her. There are . . . things you don't know, things you don't need to bother yourself with." She cast Felicia a strangely sympathetic look.

As if I weren't confused enough already. Larry? Renata? Felicia? I had to wonder what more there was to know.

Over the next couple of days, Felicia and I kept our distance. I decided neither her doubts about my identity nor her sordid personal secrets were worth getting myself in a snit about. And anyway, Renata wasn't leaving me much time to think about such things. She kept me pretty well occupied helping her finalize arrangements for the big Fourth-of-July bash she'd been planning for this weekend.

"It'll be your coming-out party, in a way," she said on Friday morning as we lingered at the breakfast table poring over lists and schedules.

I laughed nervously. "Coming out of *what?*"

"It's just an expression, sweetie." She signaled Lindy over to refill her coffee cup, and when she didn't offer the timid girl even a nod of thanks, it felt like a tiny death inside me.

"A coming-out party," Renata continued, as if explaining complicated social graces to an illiterate hillbilly, "is a traditional rite of passage for a debutante, an occasion to introduce her to society as an eligible young woman. Usually it's a formal dinner and dance—ball gowns, tuxes, string quartet. And of course every handsome unattached young man in town is on the guest list, but—"

I shoved my chair back. "If I'd known *that's* what you had in mind—"

Her laughter echoed off the high ceiling. "I promise it'll be nothing nearly so formal. But I do want everyone to meet you. My gracious, I want the *whole world* to know my sister is alive!"

An image of that sealed white envelope flashed through my mind. I fingered the hem of a mauve linen napkin. "Are you sure it's a good idea? I mean, do you really want to make an announcement like that without knowing for certain, without . . . seeing those DNA results?"

She sniffed. "I've already told you, I don't need test results to convince me. You're here, and that's all that matters."

"But people are bound to ask questions—how you found out about me, what proof you have. The last thing I want is all your friends thinking this is some prank, that all I want is your money."

"I am beyond caring what other people think," she said, and her tone gave me chills.

The thing is, I cared a lot—more than I wanted to admit. It was why I came here in the first place—the need for authenticity, the need to understand where I fit into this crazy, mixed-up world. It wasn't enough that Renata accepted me. Felicia didn't believe I was Jenny. Howard Kirby clearly had his reservations. And unless Renata could show positive proof that I was her sister, doubts would linger in the minds of everyone she introduced me to.

Then I remembered my one possible ally, the only person who, so far, had maintained any semblance of perspective. Just as Grandpa could always soothe away my anxieties, I'd sensed the same calming spirit in Aunt Geneva.

And since I'd declared Grandpa and everyone else from my old life off limits until I got my head wrapped around all this, I felt an overwhelming need to talk to Geneva—alone, away from Renata's manipulations and blind belief.

I'd seen the file containing the party guest list among the folders and paperwork scattered across the breakfast table. Certainly Geneva's name would be among the invitees. I could get her number and then later call her on my cell phone.

As soon as Renata returned to perusing the caterer's menu, I casually thumbed through the stacks until I found the file. Sliding it into my lap along with one of Renata's favorite decorating magazines, I rose and stepped toward the French doors leading to the terrace. "I'm going to sit outside and read for a bit before it gets too hot."

"Good idea, honey. Here, take this." She handed me a pad of sticky notes. "Our next project will be to redecorate your suite. If you come across any ideas you like, mark the pages so you can show me later."

"Um, okay." *Redecorate my suite?* I hadn't even decided how long I'd be sticking around.

I let the door swing closed behind me and sauntered over to a patio chair just beyond her range of vision. The July morning had already grown warm and humid. My skin felt tingly, as if the heat were penetrating every air-conditioned nerve fiber and telling it to relax, let go. I breathed deeply and closed my eyes.

Micah's warning, never far from conscious thought since the morning I steered my VW out of the La Quinta parking lot—was it only last week?—weighed heavily on me this morning. Already I felt myself being sucked into Renata's world, Renata's lifestyle . . . Renata's control.

But she was my *sister.* How could I learn to love her unless I understood her? Unless I gave myself a chance to experience her world, walk in her shoes? Although, remembering my sore feet after the dinner party my first night here, I realized I'd never intended that part literally.

Yes, I definitely needed to talk to Geneva. Of all people, she seemed to know Renata best—or at least had the clearest perspective. Which was what I needed, and badly.

Making sure I was alone on the terrace, I laid the magazine aside and pulled the guest list from the file folder. There had to be twenty or more pages here, a two-column computer printout in alphabetical order by last name, including mailing address and phone number. I began a brisk page-by-page scan looking for *Geneva Nelson*.

What I *hadn't* expected was the name that did catch my eye.

Micah Hobart.

Renata had invited *Micah*? Last I heard, they weren't exactly on speaking terms.

I cut my eyes toward the French doors to the breakfast room. I couldn't see Renata directly, just the shimmery pink toenails of one arched foot casually swinging under the corner of the tablecloth. "Renata Pearl Channing, what exactly are you up to?"

JULIE PEARL

With the guest list tucked between the magazine pages, I marched inside through the side door to the kitchen. I made myself slow down long enough to offer the weekend cook a smile. "Good morning, Mrs. Klein."

The plump woman looked up in surprise as she set a jam-smeared plate in the dishwasher rack. "Miss Julie! Did you need something?" A horrified look on her face, she started toward the breakfast room. "That Lindy—what did she forget this time?"

"Oh, no, Lindy's doing a great job." I kept forgetting my place, apparently. Which was *not* the servants' areas. "I just wanted to tell you in person how much I enjoyed the . . . the scrambled eggs. You must have a special secret for making them so tasty and moist."

"Goodness me! Why, thank you, Miss Julie!" She pressed a hand to her bosom, and her florid complexion turned even redder. "Must be the extra pat of butter in the skillet, and of course not overcooking them."

"I've got to remember that next time I—" I started to say, *scramble eggs for Grandpa.* I covered the heart-stopping surge of homesickness with a cough. "Anyway, thanks again for the delicious breakfast, and tell Lindy, too."

With a cheery wave, I hurried through the back hallway and found my way upstairs. In my bedroom, I flung the magazine onto the bed and flopped down beside it, head in my hands. With every day that passed, I grew more and more certain I'd never fit into Renata's world.

And now, for reasons I couldn't fathom, she'd invited Micah to her barbecue. What if he came? What would I say to him?

One step at a time, Julie. I would not turn tail and run from this situation. I was made of sterner stuff.

Step one: Consider the possibility that Renata wanted to make peace with Micah. That would be a good thing.

But terribly awkward for me. How would he see me now? As the woman Julie Stiles who was just beginning to open her heart to him? Or the grown-up version of Jennifer Susan Pearl, the baby sister of Rennie Pearl, the teenager who'd all but ruined his life?

Deep breath, and on to step two: Find out whether Micah had accepted the invitation. Then, at least, I could begin to prepare myself.

I figured Sandy would know. She spent more time with him than anyone else these days. I pulled open the bottom drawer of the mahogany nightstand where I'd stashed my crocheted shoulder bag and fished out my cell phone. When I powered it on, it immediately flashed the messages waiting icon.

And *guilt, guilt, guilt* flashed across the backs of my eyeballs. What if something had happened to Grandpa? Steeling myself, I thumbed the voicemail button.

"Hey, Jules, it's me." Sandy. I gave a small sigh of relief. *"Just checking up on you, girlfriend. I miss you. And I'm worried about you. And I'm not the only one, if you get my drift. Call. Soon. Okay?"* The time stamp indicated she'd left the message one week ago today.

"Me again. Why haven't you called? I know you're probably living it up with the rich and famous in Little Rock, but don't forget about us

back in Caddo Pines. We miss you, Jules. And we love you." Monday, 4:57 p.m.

"Don't you ever check your voicemail?" The cajoling tone in Sandy's earlier messages had given way to urgency. *"Or are you ignoring us on purpose? Julie, I mean it, please call."* Yesterday morning.

Finding no messages from Grandpa and nothing from Micah, I felt strangely let down. Not even so much as a "Hey, how U doin'?" text from my old buddy Clifton.

I couldn't blame them. I was the one who'd cut ties with my former life, and they were obviously leaving it up to me to decide when and if I wanted to reestablish the connection.

And I did. Oh, how I wanted to, with every fiber of my being.

I punched the call icon next to Sandy's name in my contacts list. She answered on the second ring.

I spoke timidly. "Hi. It's me."

Static on the line, then a raspy, "Jules—thank God!" More static while she asked me to hold on a minute, then her muffled words, "I'm taking my break now, Micah. Back in fifteen."

A door creaked. When Sandy spoke again, she had that breathy sound of someone talking and walking at the same time. "Okay, I can talk now. Julie, how are you? Is everything okay?"

"Things are . . . weird. Sorry I didn't call you sooner. I haven't had my cell phone on since I got here."

"I assume you mean Renata Channing's place? Micah told me you went to find her. So is it true? Is she really your sister?"

I kicked off my amazingly comfy Cole Haan flats and melted into the pile of down bed pillows. "Renata believes it. Except her attorney set up a DNA test, and when the results came back, she didn't even look at them—wouldn't let anyone else, either. She locked them in her safe-deposit box."

"Seriously?" Another whoosh of a door opening and closing. Then children's laughter, water splashing. Sandy must be outside by the hotel pool.

"Sandy, I was going to call you this morning anyway. I was wondering about Micah. Did he by chance—"

"Get an invitation to a certain society lady's Fourth-of-July barbecue? It arrived by special courier three days ago. And if he wasn't already a basket case, he sure is now."

Mrs. Klein's scrambled eggs started clucking beneath my sternum. "What did he say? Is he coming?"

"I doubt if *he* even knows yet. Julie, Micah's a mess. Since you left, work on the resort has virtually stopped. I've spent the last several days stalling contractors demanding to know when they can put their crews to work and expecting to get paid while waiting for Micah's go-ahead."

"I don't understand. What's the holdup?"

Sandy remained silent for several long seconds. "I think he's having second thoughts about the whole thing."

"The whole—you mean the new resort?"

"Tearing down the old one, building the new one. It's like he's completely lost interest."

My fingers caught in the tangle of curls at my temple. "What exactly *has* he been doing for the past week?"

"Mostly just moping around, mumbling, shuffling papers. And cursing. A lot. I need a fire extinguisher for my poor blistered ears! If it gets any worse, I may have to quit . . . if he doesn't fire me first."

"Fire you? Why?"

"Well, if he's not planning on going ahead with the resort, he doesn't need an administrative assistant for the project."

I hiked up my straight gabardine skirt—propriety be hanged—and sat cross-legged on the comforter. "If you lose your job because of me—"

"Hey, you have no control over what's happening. It's just something that has to play itself out." Another pause. "So how is it there? Really?"

Inhaling a shaky breath, I described life at Channing Castle—

everything from the nightly four-course dinners to all the servants and staff crawling out of the woodwork every time I so much as blinked. Even told Sandy about my run-ins with Felicia Beaufort, including those nagging suspicions about her and Lawrence Channing.

"Hmmm, maybe the Lord meant you to find Renata for purposes you haven't even suspected yet. Julie, as much as we all want you home with us, I think—"

I switched the phone to my other ear. "Oh, Sandy, tell me everything that's happening back home."

I listened hungrily as she filled me in on the doings in Caddo Pines—seeing Grandpa in church last Sunday, stopping by the Swap & Shop to say hello. "Oh, and your grandpa hired Clifton part-time to help out around the shop. You wouldn't believe what it's done for Clifton's work ethic. Having somebody believe in him like that, he's like a completely different guy."

"Good ol' Grandpa. Clifton's working there can only be good for both of them. And did you see Brynna and the pups? And Sneezy—is he doing okay?"

"They're fine, all just fine." She gave a sympathetic laugh. "I've been wondering how you stand it being separated from your pets. I heard Renata hates dogs."

Sandy's statement reminded me how I'd ended up here in the first place. "Renata's afraid of dogs, I'm afraid of water. Even without the DNA results, there's plenty right there to make me believe I'm Jenny Pearl."

"Maybe so, but you're still Julie Stiles to me. You always will be. Don't forget it."

I choked up again. "You can take the hick-town girl out of the flea market, but you can't take the flea market out of the girl. Is that what you're trying to say?"

She didn't laugh. "Even Cinderella had to come home from the ball eventually."

"Until the glass slipper confirmed her identity." I wasn't real sure where we were going with this analogy, but I desperately hoped Renata would turn out to be more like my fairy godmother than an ugly stepsister.

As for Prince Charming . . . ?

I closed my eyes and let my thoughts carry me back to that last morning in Micah's arms. His bristly-soft beard grazing my forehead, the spicy scent of his aftershave, the cottony texture of his shirt against my cheek.

Sandy exhaled sharply. "Jules, I hate to cut this short, but I need to get back to work, or Micah really will fire me."

I swung my legs off the side of the bed. "Are you going to tell him you talked to me?"

"Do you want me to?"

I pondered the idea. "Yes. Tell him I'm doing okay. Tell him I haven't forgotten what he told me. Tell him I . . . miss him."

By the time I made it down to breakfast Saturday morning, the house was buzzing with activity. I watched a crew battle a stiff breeze as they attempted to erect a gigantic canopy at the far end of the pool on the only flat stretch of the Channings' rolling lawn. An extended-cab pickup had towed a massive barbecue trailer onto the property, parking it next to the canopy. Billowing white smoke carried the savory aromas of beef, chicken, and pork slow-cooking over mesquite coals. My taste buds, trying to wrap themselves around a toasted bagel, were thoroughly confused.

As I sipped a latte Lindy Klein had whipped up from the hissing cappuccino maker, her mother handed me a note from Renata stating that both Isabel and Yvette would be waiting for me in my room.

Naturally, Renata wanted me primed, painted, and polished for command performance number . . . ? By now I'd lost count.

And I still had no idea whether I'd be seeing Micah this afternoon, or what I'd say to him if I did.

As I pushed open the door to my room, Isabel looked up from the ivory settee at the end of the bed. "Good morning, Miss Julie. Are you ready for your fitting?"

Something white and feminine lay across her lap. Her sewing basket rested on the coffee table atop one of those massive photography books that normal people can barely afford, let alone take time to look through. This one contained photos of actual coffee tables. I never knew there were so many different ways to photograph them.

I sprawled in an armchair across from Isabel. "Actually, I really liked that red, white, and blue outfit I had on the other day—or is it a huge faux pas to be seen wearing the same thing twice in the same decade?"

Isabel cast me a sympathetic frown. "You are not so happy here, Miss Julie?"

I gave a harsh laugh. "What's not to like? Anything I want or need, all I have to do is ask. I'm living like a princess—and dressing like one, thanks to you." I beamed her an appreciative smile. "Too bad Yvette hasn't been able to tame my mane. I'm sure this mop is a colossal source of embarrassment for Renata."

"No, Miss Julie, that is not true. I have never seen Mrs. C happier than since you arrived."

"Do you mean it?" I clasped my hands between my knees. "About Renata being happier?"

"I have never seen her smile so much in all the years I have been working for her." Isabel stood, shaking out the white dress. "Please try this on. Mrs. C ordered it especially for you to wear today."

Maybe my being here was making a difference after all. If Renata could finally be at peace with the past, if she was ready to reconcile with Micah so that both of them could be free of their ghosts, then I could certainly deal with whatever high-society awkwardness it caused me.

I carried the dress into the giant closet-slash-dressing room and slipped out of my jumper. And I admit, wearing the slim-fitting white embroidered Oscar de la Renta, the ruffled hem skimming my knees, I did feel like a princess.

When I modeled the dress for Isabel, she gave a satisfied nod. "I do not believe anything needs to be altered, Miss Julie. The fit is perfect." She went to the closet and retrieved a pair of stiletto-heeled sandals with ankle straps. "Here, you should wear these."

I didn't remember the shoes among the ones Felicia had picked out for me, but apparently Renata had special-ordered them to go with the dress. I grimaced. "I normally don't wear heels. I'm tall enough as it is."

But Isabel insisted, so I reluctantly slid my feet into the shoes, and she knelt to fasten the ankle straps. Again, a perfect fit.

Wobbling on the spiky heels, I turned to view my reflection in the full-length mirror on the closet door.

And I gasped.

Even before Yvette plied her talents with makeup and hairstyling, I couldn't believe how amazing I looked—how amazing I *felt*. It was more than the way the winter-white dress complemented my skin, more than the lacy trim accenting the narrow waist and kicky hem.

Nope, it wasn't the dress at all. I couldn't take my eyes off the lean, toned look of those mile-long legs. If I'd known heels could have that effect on my bearing, I'd have been wearing them all along. And to think, I used to make fun of the Miss America contestants mincing across the stage in swimsuits and stilettos—like anyone would ever wear heels to the pool.

Wow! Now I understood. *It's all about the legs.*

I swiveled one way and then another, striking various poses before the mirror while Isabel watched with a knowing smirk.

Yvette arrived, and by the time she finished with me an hour later, I really could have passed for a runway model. This time she didn't bother trying to tame my curls, but pinned my hair into an artfully tousled updo, leaving strategically selected ringlets framing my forehead and temples.

Not long after she left, dear ol' strictly-business Felicia rapped on my door. Same nondescript neutral-color pantsuit with sensible shoes, blond hair tucked into a braided chignon. Her only concession to fashion was the lacy camisole peeking out between the lapels of her jacket.

"Mrs. C asks that you to join her downstairs to greet the arriving guests," she stated. Then her stunned gaze traveled up and down all five-foot-eleven-inches of me. More like six-foot-two with the heels.

I asked God to forgive me for taking pleasure in her unabashed envy. Staring down my nose at her, I said with my most charming smile, "Thank you, Felicia. Tell my *sister* I'll be right down."

"As you wish, *Miss Stiles*." Touché. Glaring, she backed out the door and yanked it closed.

I didn't realize how much she'd rattled me until I turned to check the mirror one more time and nearly fell on my keister. As I lunged for a chair, a taunting voice rang in my head: *Julie Pearl Stiles, when are you going to get it? You can play dress-up all you want, but it will never change who you are inside.*

2 5

MICAH

Christmas, 10 years earlier
Fort Worth, Texas

Micah stuffed sweaty hands into his jeans pockets and searched his fiancée's gaze. "You've been quiet all evening, Tori. What's wrong? Did I say something?"

"This—us—it's not working." Tori Varten crossed her arms over the tiny silver bells decorating her navy sweater and turned toward the blazing fireplace. "Think about it, Micah. Things haven't been the same between us since that night."

That night. The night he'd made the biggest mistake—no, make that the *second* biggest mistake of his life. The night he drove Renata home from the Arkansas Philanthropic Association gala and almost allowed his boyhood crush to morph into full-blown lust.

"I never meant to hurt you." He touched Tori's shoulder and felt her muscles tense as she edged away. "It's just that Renata and I have this . . . unfortunate history together. Seeing her again brought it all back, for both of us. We needed to talk."

"Talk?" Tori spat out the word. She whirled around and glared

189

at him. "Yes, I'm sure that's *all* you did. Too bad you don't have the decency to talk to *me*. You don't even love me enough to confide in me what this 'unfortunate history' is all about. Which of course leaves me to torture myself with ugly scenarios from my own imagination."

Micah reached for the fireplace poker and stabbed at a flaming log until it split open and collapsed in a sizzling mass of red coals. Sparks popped and crackled and danced up the chimney. He wished his memories of the past would do the same.

"It's better you don't know," he murmured. "Believe me."

"So you're choosing your private pain over our love, is that it? You're going to let something that happened years ago come between us now?"

"I didn't *choose* this pain," he said, even as it gripped him once again. He clawed the back of his neck and sank onto the sofa. "I did something I'm not proud of. Can't we leave it at that?"

Tori gave a heartless laugh. "Are you talking about what happened in the obscure past, or the night of the gala."

"Tori, I love you. I'm telling you, nothing happened that night—"

"That's *bull!* You're lying to yourself, Micah." Angry tears spilled down Tori's cheeks. "Admit it. You're really in love with *her.*"

"Renata? No! You've got it all wrong—"

"I saw the look in your eyes when you first saw her at the gala." Brushing the wetness from her cheeks, Tori gave a disgusted growl. "You went trailing after her like a lovesick puppy."

He couldn't deny it, not completely. He'd idolized Rennie Pearl from the first day she befriended him that summer at the resort. How else could he explain the fatal lapse in judgment that had changed both their lives forever?

And yes, when she'd called his name at the gala, when he'd turned and looked into those seductive, gold-flecked hazel eyes, for one crazy moment he'd felt eight years old again. Only this wasn't the old Rennie, the skinny teen with tousled hair and sun-reddened cheeks. Renata the woman—elegant, sophisticated, knockout gorgeous—sent his senses reeling.

He pounded a clenched fist against the plaid sofa cushion. She was doing it again, turning his life to shambles. He'd been crazy to believe the past could remain in the past. Crazy to believe something as horrifying and inexcusable as what he and Rennie had done could be permanently locked away in his mental safe-deposit box. Now his connection with Renata was coming between him and Tori, ruining perhaps his one and only chance for lasting happiness.

"Tori, please." He rose, went to her, tried to pull her into his arms. "Don't let the past destroy what we have. I love you."

She pressed her hands hard against his chest. He could feel them trembling. "No, Micah, I can't compete with your ghosts, past or present. It's over between us." Silent tears streaming down her face, she backed away. She slipped off her engagement ring, laid it his hand, and closed his fingers around it. "Good-bye, Micah."

JULIE PEARL

Present Day

Four-inch heels may do wonders for a woman's sex appeal, but they weren't made for traipsing across a spongy lawn. I had to totter around on tiptoe to keep my stilettos from sinking into the ground and sending me sprawling. Once Renata released me from obligatory mingling, I filled my plate with a sampling of appetizers from the buffet table and abandoned the crowded party tent for the more stable surface of the terrace.

Extra tables had been set up under the lattice roof, with most seats already occupied. Avoiding the misting fans, I spied an empty chair and asked if I could join the threesome already seated at the small, square table.

"Please do. Lovely party." The matronly-looking woman at my left lowered her sunglasses and peered at me beneath the brim of a massive straw hat. "Renata does know how to entertain."

I smiled and unfolded my napkin. "Sure looks that way."

"Tell me your name again, dear?"

"Julie Stiles."

"I'm Madeleine Orbach, chairwoman of this year's APA gala. And how are you acquainted with our hostess?"

I had no idea what APA stood for, and decided not to embarrass myself by asking. "I'm . . . a friend from out of town."

"How nice." She nodded to the other two guests, a balding man with glasses and a slender redhead in a tangerine halter dress. "Arthur, Caroline, have you met Miss Stiles?"

"I believe we were introduced when we arrived." Caroline gave me a toothy smile. "Where'd you say you're from, sweetie?"

"It's a very small town. You probably never heard of it." Renata had yet to make any kind of formal introduction of me as her sister, which made these conversations extremely awkward.

Worse, I'd been keeping one anxious eye on the terrace doors in case, by some remote chance, Micah showed up. I honestly didn't expect him to, but a furtive last-minute check of the RSVPs showed nothing beside his name. A hasty call to Sandy's cell phone just before noon got only her voicemail. Maybe now would be a good time to run upstairs and check my phone to see if she'd returned my call. Finishing the last bite of a crabmeat hors d'oeuvre, I washed it down with a swallow of ginger ale.

I scraped my chair backward across the mossy flagstones. "It's been nice chatting with all of you. I should probably go find Renata."

"Oh, but you only just joined us." Mrs. Orbach touched my arm, her jeweled rings glittering. "And look, Renata's over there visiting away with the director of the Little Rock Wind Symphony. I'm sure she wouldn't mind if we kept you awhile longer."

"Well, you know, I—I—" I froze, one hand grasping my glass buffet plate, the other gripping the arm of the chair. My mouth started doing that fish thing it does when I'm halfway between surprise and panic.

Micah.

He ambled through the French doors onto the terrace, slipping on mirrored aviator sunglasses as he got his bearings. He hadn't noticed me yet, half hidden by Mrs. Orbach's wide-brimmed hat and Caroline's over-teased hairdo. And all I could do was drink him in—the seductive tilt of his head, the masculine curve of his bearded jaw, the lean lines of his torso beneath a navy striped shirt.

I felt a hand at my elbow. "Are you feeling all right, Miss Stiles." Arthur, the bald guy. "You can never be too careful about crab, you know. I avoid it myself—seafood allergy. I break out in this horrible—"

"Excuse me, please." I rose and started around the table.

Then my heel caught in a crack between the paving stones and this time I really did go sprawling. If Arthur hadn't jumped to his feet and caught me, I'd have landed in Mrs. Orbach's shrimp cocktail.

"Steady there." Arthur wrapped his arms around my waist—a bit too tightly, as far as I was concerned. A sunbeam reflecting off his bald spot nearly blinded me.

I disentangled myself from his chivalrous grip. "Thanks, I'm fine—*really.*" With a jerk, I freed my heel from the jaws of the shoe-eating pavers, but by the time I recovered enough composure to remember where I'd been headed in the first place, Micah was nowhere to be seen.

Instead, another man stood near the French doors, and he looked even less thrilled about being here than Micah.

"Well, well," Arthur murmured, "looks like Larry's back in town."

"Larry?" My gaze followed the broad-chested man with the shock of silver hair as he strode toward the guests clustering around Renata under the party tent. "Larry, as in Lawrence Channing?"

Mrs. Orbach lifted the brim of her straw hat and gaped at me. "You haven't met Renata's husband?"

"Never had the pleasure." I sank into my chair and tried to figure out what my next move should be.

"It's rare of him to attend one of Renata's functions," Caroline said. "Running GigantaMart keeps him so busy."

"Heard he just opened a new store in Tupelo." Arthur picked up his and Caroline's drink glasses. "Refill, darling? Gin and tonic, wasn't it?"

Caroline's response was drowned out when the string ensemble performing under the tent interrupted their music-to-munch-and-mingle-by with a resounding fanfare.

"My dear guests," came Renata's amplified voice. I glimpsed her through the crowd as she stepped to the front of the small stage and shook back her glorious mane. "Thank you all so much for coming to my little get-together. It's a delight to see so many dear, dear friends again."

She rambled for several minutes thanking the musicians, caterers, and household staff for their contributions to the affair, then began introductions of honored guests. I promptly tuned her out, resuming my visual scan of the area in hopes of finding Micah. How could he simply disappear?

"And now I'd like to officially introduce someone who is very, very important to me," Renata said into the microphone. "Many of you have met her already, but—" Her voice broke. "Julie, where are you, dear?"

"Oh, that's you." Mrs. Orbach patted my arm with one hand and waved frantically with the other. "Here she is, Renata!"

My head jerked around. I gulped.

Renata spotted me. She beamed a smile in my direction and motioned me over, silencing the last remnants of conversation. I rose slowly, the rasp of my chair across the terrace resounding like an explosion in the silence. As I made my way along the pool deck toward the party tent, I could feel everyone's eyes on me. Was this the moment for the big announcement?

Curious murmurs now rose among the guests. Brushing past

them, shutting my mind against their nosy stares, I somehow managed to stay on my toes as I crossed the grass. Renata took my hand and helped me onto the stage. Her eyes shone with moisture. Her lips trembled.

"Everyone, please welcome Jennifer Susan Pearl, my sister."

I felt my face freeze into something between a grimace and a nervous grin. Anyone within two feet of me had to hear my heart thundering like a stampede of startled billy goats.

"I know this is a surprise," Renata said as the crowd grew quiet once more. "It certainly was to me. It's a long and complicated story, and unimportant, really, in the grand scheme of things." She lifted my hand in a manner reminiscent of Arkansas' own Bill-and-Hillary victory salutes. "The only thing that matters is that my sister is alive and well and back with me where she belongs."

A smattering of applause broke out and swelled to a thunderous ovation. Renata signaled the musicians to resume playing and tugged me off the stage into the mass of congratulatory (if confused) party guests. I followed numbly as half-whispered comments rose around me.

"But didn't she say her name was Joanie?"

"No, I'm sure it was Sally."

"Well, what do we call her then?"

"Do you see any resemblance? I'd never have guessed . . ."

"Julie."

My heart stopped dead still, and so did my feet. I looked to my left and there he was.

Micah!

I reached out to him, touched the solid rock of his muscled forearm. His gray eyes, deepened with raw pain, searched mine.

A split second later, a cascading curtain of mahogany hair filled my vision. Flung aside by Renata's sudden motion, I staggered backwards and watched helplessly as she threw her arms around Micah's neck. "Oh, darling, you *did* come!"

Micah clasped her shoulders and eased her off him. "Rennie, stop—"

I'd barely regained my footing when a massive body and a flash of silver hair blocked my view. Larry Channing gripped Renata's arm and spun her around. "What kind of crazy stunt is this, Renata? Are you off your meds again?"

"How dare you!" Renata's shocked whisper hissed between clenched teeth.

"As for you, Hobart, all I can say is you've got some nerve showing up here." Though Larry faced away from me, the quiet force behind his words made my stomach clench.

"I'm surprised *you* showed up at all," Micah shot back.

All around me I sensed Renata's guests edging away, making room, just in case this turned ugly.

Like it hadn't already.

Before my spiked heels sank any deeper into the spongy lawn, I took two giant steps over to the pool deck. "Micah, maybe you should—"

"Stay out of this, young lady"—Larry cut his eyes at me —"whoever you are. Trust me, I'll deal with you later."

Fire blazed in Micah's eyes. "Don't threaten her. None of this is her fault."

"Larry, please!" Renata clutched at her husband's shirtsleeve, a sick, desperate smile contorting her mouth. "Why don't we go inside, darling. This isn't a discussion we should be having in front of our guests."

"It isn't a discussion we should be having under any circumstances." Chest heaving, Larry gave Renata his full attention. "But seeing as how you've been engaged in all kinds of questionable behavior behind my back—" He jerked his head toward Micah.

Micah gave an annoyed huff. "Get a grip, man. How many times do I have to tell you—"

"Don't try to deny it. You've been lusting after my wife since you were a hot-blooded pubescent twerp." Larry thrust his face into Micah's, jabbing a stubby finger at his chest. "Now get off my property before I have you thrown out."

"You conceited creep." Straightening his shirt collar, Micah sidestepped the bully. "If you'd ever stopped chasing skirts long enough to give your wife the attention she craves—"

"Don't you *dare* presume to tell me how to handle my wife!"

"Larry, darling, it's all right." Renata's feeble pleas weren't convincing anybody, but that didn't stop her from trying. She hooked her arm through Larry's and nudged him a few steps away.

While she worked on placating her jealous husband, I shot Micah a desperate plea of my own. "You should go, before things get any worse."

He gripped my hands, and I saw all kinds of turmoil smoldering behind his eyes. "Let's both go, Julie. You don't belong here any more than I do."

I was millimeters away from admitting how right he was. But I had to see this through. I had no choice. My gaze dropped to my French-manicured toenails, and I guess my silence was all the answer Micah needed. I felt his lips brush my forehead before he strode past me toward the house.

In the wake of his leaving I felt the stares of a hundred pairs of eyes. Slowly I lifted my head, catching glimpses of a few of the guests slinking away. A scarce few were brave enough to approach Renata for the requisite "Thank you, good-bye" to the hostess. Not with her and Larry still sniping at each other.

Then with a shudder, Larry narrowed his gaze at me. Jaw clenched, he headed my way.

Yep, if I'd had any sense at all I'd have left with Micah.

"So Renata thinks you're her long-lost sister, does she?" Larry loomed over me. "Well, we'll see about that."

I took a shaky step backward. "I—I had a DNA test. Ask Renata if you want proof." I wished I sounded more confident, but confidence didn't come easy with two hundred fifty pounds of testosterone glaring at me like he wanted to chew me up and spit me out. I backed up another step.

And felt nothing but air beneath my heel. Gasping in panic, I tipped backward into the pool. My head grazed something solid, and I barely heard the splash over the sound of my pulse thundering in my ears. The last thing I remember before the silky coolness enveloped me was seeing Felicia Beaufort standing primly on the far side of the deck, her eyes narrowed in a self-satisfied sneer.

JULIE PEARL

One summer—it was just before I turned eight, and Grandpa had enrolled me for another round of swimming lessons with Madame Thunder Thighs—my short life passed before me in quick review beneath the aquamarine waters of the Caddo Pines RV & Mobile Home Park pool.

That was the day Thunder Thighs (her real name has deserted me) decided to hold a penny-diving contest, and whoever surfaced with the most pennies in one breath would get to sit on the lifeguard stand for the remainder of the hour and bark out drills to the rest of the class.

Naturally I was torn. I could cling to the wall and refuse to participate, thus incurring even more ridicule from my peers. Or I could choke down my fears, pour all my nerve into winning the contest, and enjoy a few glorious minutes of high-and-dry freedom. As the teacher held a plastic cup full of pennies aloft and cocked her arm to fling them into the pool, I gazed up at that lifeguard stand, its green plastic seat shimmering in the morning sun, and my decision was made.

"On your mark, get set, *go!*"

A hundred pennies flew over our heads, and eleven splashing

bodies leapt off the shallow-end step in quick pursuit. I filled my lungs and battled downward, grabbing pennies right and left while dodging feet, knees, elbows, and heads. Clutching two bulging handfuls of pennies, my lungs burning, I reached for one more as the writhing waters lifted it off the bottom and propelled it closer to the deep end.

Then someone's heel caught me square in the breadbasket, and all my remaining air rushed out of me. Unwilling to let go of my cache, I clawed my way toward the surface with clenched fists. I could see the sun up there somewhere, a yellow ripple in a watery mass of blue, but I just couldn't get there. I swam through an ever narrowing black tunnel. I didn't think I'd ever reach the surface, never take another clean, full breath of air. I'd never get my chance to look down from that lifeguard stand in victory.

My short life would come to an end right there in the pool, with nothing more to show for my efforts than a fistful of tarnished pennies.

Which was exactly what I had when I woke up several minutes later, spitting and coughing and wondering why Thunder Thighs had been "kissing" me. My stomach and chest felt bruised, my throat ached, my eyes burned. I made out Sandy's high-pitched wailing, and Clifton's worried query, "Is she dead?"

"For goodness' sake, no, Clifton, she is not *dead*. Children, please, calm down!" Thunder Thighs sat me up and patted my back. "Julie Pearl, are you okay, honey-child? Can you *breathe*?"

I slowly opened my hands, letting the pennies clatter to the concrete deck. A few of them stuck to my wet palms, and I shook them off. "How many?" I rasped. "How many did I get?"

The big, burly woman hugged me to her pillowy chest and laughed. "Oh, honey, you got plenty. Plenty, plenty, plenty!"

And when I stopped coughing and found my land legs again, she personally helped me climb up the chrome ladder to the lifeguard seat, where I presided over the rest of the class in all my glory.

Coughing and sputtering, I struggled to open my eyes against the glare of bright sun. "Did I win?"

A deep laugh, an unfamiliar voice. "Win? I don't know about that, ma'am. And I'm guessin' you won't be qualifying for the Summer Olympics anytime soon."

"Is she going to be all right?" A familiar woman's voice.

"Don't worry, Mrs. Channing. Reflexes are good, she's breathing normally. They'll check her more thoroughly at the hospital, but she should be fine."

I forced my eyes to focus on the face hovering above me. Light brown hair closely cropped, concerned smile. The plastic nametag clipped to the pocket of his pale blue shirt read J. Canby, EMT.

"Let's see what you're holding onto so tightly." He gently pried open my clenched fist, his latex gloves squeaking against my wet skin. "Nothin' here. Whatever you were diving for must still be on the bottom of the pool."

"But my pennies . . ." Then I remembered that was twenty-some-odd years ago. I tried to sit up, only to find myself strapped to a body board, my head immobilized between foam blocks. Another coughing spasm shook me, and I strained against the straps..

"Take it easy, ma'am." J. Canby, EMT, patted my shoulder. "You may have a concussion. We'll be transporting you to the hospital in a few minutes, but I think the police want to talk to you first."

"Police?" My head throbbed. I winced against the bright sun overhead.

"Yeah, apparently someone called nine-one-one to report you'd been accosted by a large, angry man."

Unable to move anything but my eyes, I tried to look around, but a wave of nausea made me gag. If I threw up lying flat on my back, it would *not* be pretty, so I took a deep breath and swallowed. With a cautious sideways glance, I spotted Larry between two cops in uniform. He gestured wildly and kept pointing at me.

And I noticed he was dripping wet.

"He didn't . . . accost me," I muttered through tight lips. Something rancid burned my throat. Had Larry been the one to pull me out of the pool? "Tell them it was an accident."

Another face filled my vision, this one wearing a black cap with gold trim. "That true, miss?" He nodded toward Larry. "The man over there didn't push you into the pool?"

"No." Not on purpose anyway. "I stepped off the edge and fell."

"We need to transport her now, officer." J. Canby and another EMT lifted me onto a gurney and tucked warm blankets around me. I gave in to the compelling urge to sleep and didn't remember another thing until I awoke later in a hospital bed.

The room lay in twilight, a shaft of moonlight silhouetting the head and shoulders of someone dozing in a chair by the window. The soft, snuffling snores seemed out of place yet strangely soothing.

Then on the opposite side of the bed, I felt a hand on my arm. "Finally waking up, sleepyhead?"

I swiveled toward the voice and tried to make out the face in the dim light. "Sandy?"

She chuckled. "I'd have thought you learned your lesson back when we were kids. Katie Ledecky you are not."

The snores coming from the figure by the window turned into snorts. The chair creaked, and then I heard the voice I'd been starving for. "Julie Pearl, oh, my Julie-girl. How are you, darlin'?"

My arms were around Grandpa's neck before he could shuffle across the space between us. I buried my face in the softness of his cotton shirt and inhaled the spicy-musky scent of his aftershave. "Grandpa, Grandpa, I've missed you so much."

"Not half as much as I've missed you." He eased me into bed and sat on the edge beside me. With his warm, work-roughed hands, he brushed away my happy tears.

"But how'd you know? Who told you I was here?"

"Got a call from the hospital." A proud and grateful look warmed Grandpa's eyes. "Seems you gave 'em my name when they asked you for next of kin."

"I did?" Truth be told, I couldn't even remember being asked.

Sandy squeezed in on my other side. "Smart girl. Even half-drowned."

I stared at her, even more confused. "Then how did *you* find out?"

"Your grandpa called me, of course." She gave me a sad smile. "You think wild horses could keep me away when my best friend's in trouble?"

I mentally ran through everything I could remember, which was very little from the moment I toppled into the pool. "Am I okay? How long have I been sleeping?"

Sandy patted my hand. "You're going to be fine. They think you must have grazed your head on the side of the pool when you fell. That's why they wanted to keep you overnight." She glanced at her watch, turning her wrist to catch the pink glow of the nightlight over my bed. "And it hasn't been that long. It's just now a little after ten."

"Still Saturday?"

She nodded. "The doctor said you can go home in the morning if everything checks out."

I didn't allow myself to think about where "home" was at this point. A beige telephone sat on the bedside table, just out of reach. "I need to talk to Micah. Sandy, would you—"

"Best you forget about Micah Hobart, young lady." Jaw firm, Grandpa rose and paced to the window. "Bad enough he nearly drowned you as a baby. His meddlin' about got you killed again."

"It wasn't his fault, Grandpa. Not then, not now." At his indifferent shrug, I turned to Sandy. "Just get him on the phone for me, okay?"

With a sidelong glance at Grandpa, she lowered her voice.

"Maybe you should give Micah some space. He was pretty shaken up after Renata's party."

"You know about his confrontation with Larry?"

Sandy gnawed her lower lip as she plucked at a thread on the blanket. "I was there."

"Then you saw what happened."

"Afraid not. I needed to use the powder room, and there were several ladies in front of me. By the time I started out to the terrace, Micah met me at the door and said we were leaving. It was obvious he was upset, but I had to drag an explanation out of him." She peered at me from beneath lowered lids. "After your grandpa told me what happened to you, I wished we'd stayed."

In slow motion I relived my fall into the pool—the sudden awareness of stepping off into thin air, the clutch of panic in my belly, a sweep of blue sky reeling across my vision just before a dull thud and then the splash.

Then, just like how you remember a dream, my brain started working backward. The ugly scene between Larry and Micah. Renata's attempts to placate her jealous husband.

Her jealous husband. Up to now, my mind had conveniently blocked out the part where Renata had inserted herself between me and Micah. The part where she'd fawned over him like a long-lost lover.

Lover?

My stomach twisted.

"Where is he?" I tossed the covers aside. "I have to see him. I have to see Micah." I swung my legs off Grandpa's side of the bed and tried to stand.

Sandy grabbed my shoulder. "Julie, don't. You need to stay right where you are."

"Don't tell me what I can or can't do. I *need* to talk to Micah." Before I could stagger around the end of the bed, a swirling cloud of dizziness sidelined me. Grandpa caught me moments before I hit the floor. With Sandy's help, he manhandled me back into bed, but not before I put up a good fight.

"That's quite enough, young lady." He shook a gnarly finger under my nose. "I'm still your grandpa till the Good Lord relieves me of the job, and you *will* stay in this hospital until the doc gives you a clean bill of health."

"And I'm his backup," Sandy said with a glare. "Julie Stiles, you are not going anywhere tonight."

Out of breath and only then realizing my entire backside had been exposed to the world thanks to my skimpy hospital gown, I cowered beneath the blankets. I'd have to concede temporary defeat at the hands of my self-appointed jailers, since obviously Marshal Dillon and Miss Kitty were not about to let me out of their sight.

"Good *morning*, sunshine! How are we feeling this bright, sunny day?"

I swam upward through vague but troubling dreams as the cheery alto voice invaded my brain. When I opened my eyes, a buxom nurse in green scrubs stood over me. She balanced a tray with one hand while punching buttons on my bed control with the other. "Let's get you ready for some breakfast, young lady."

I groaned feeble protests as the top half of the bed sat me upright. Grandpa, still camped out in the chair by the window, yawned and stretched. Sandy emerged from the bathroom, hairbrush in hand. Her face looked freshly scrubbed.

"Now you eat up," the woman ordered with a grin. "Get some meat on those skinny ol' bones." She plopped the tray on my bed table, whisked off the plate covers, and sashayed out the door.

The combined smells of coffee, oatmeal, and toast conspired to nauseate me. I pushed the table away and tried to get up.

Once again, my keepers restrained me. "Eat something, Julie,"

Sandy insisted. "You need your strength." She spread strawberry jam across a slice of whole-wheat toast and handed it to me.

Yes, I would definitely need my strength for what lay ahead. Eventually I'd have to face both Renata and Micah, and I had no idea what I'd say to either of them.

Grandpa and Sandy took turns going to the cafeteria for their own breakfast while I nibbled at mine. I tried to convince them they could trust me alone for that long, but neither of them was buying it. Around eight, a nurse came with a wheelchair and said we were going down for "another" MRI. Interesting that I couldn't remember having the first one.

"Soon as your doctor gets the results," she said, "he'll probably let you go home." In the meantime, she gave me permission to shower and dress.

When I saw myself in the bathroom mirror, I nearly gagged. My hair was one giant mass of tangles, and whoever cleaned me up yesterday had left Yvette's model-perfect makeup job in streaks.

Sandy knocked on the bathroom door while I was drying off. "Thought you might want some clean clothes." She passed some things to me in a plastic grocery sack. "I helped your grandpa pick out some stuff for you before we came over yesterday."

I recognized the faded bell-bottom hip-huggers and embroidered dashiki tunic I'd been admiring in Dovie and Royce Buckles' Glad Rags booth. Fresh undies, too. By the time I'd dressed, raked through my snarls, and brushed my teeth, I felt almost human.

And more normal than I had since driving out of the La Quinta parking lot ten days ago.

"Now that's the Julie I know and love," Sandy said when I came out of the bathroom. She wrapped me in a hug.

"Yes indeedy." Grandpa shuffled over. "How's my girl?"

I planted a kiss on his lined cheek. "A little worse for wear, but I'm alive and kicking. Thanks for bringing—"

The door whooshed open, and Renata swept into the room. "Julie, dear, so sorry I didn't come by last night, but I had a million things to attend to. After the party, the caterers left things in an absolute *mess*. And I had so many calls to make—ruffled feathers to smooth, apologies for that unfortunate little interruption—"

"*Interruption?*" My brain was about to strip a gear. "Renata, do you realize I nearly drowned?"

"Now, now, don't exaggerate. Just a little accident, that's all." She eyed me up and down. "Oh, dear, that outfit is absolutely prehistoric! Well, not to worry. I'll wait while you change." Turning toward the bathroom, she deposited a small suitcase on the tile floor and hung a black garment bag on a hook opposite the sink.

Sandy's face reddened. I was afraid she'd say something *I'd* regret, so I beat her to the punch. "It was thoughtful of you to bring me something, Renata, but these are the clothes I'm comfortable in."

She looked hurt, but only for a moment. "Very well, then, as soon as the doctor signs your release papers, I'll take you home."

I wasn't quick enough to stop Grandpa from belting out his retort. He stood toe-to-toe with Renata, chin jutting. "Now see here, Miz Channing, you got no right to be making decisions for my gran—for Julie Pearl. She's a grown woman, and she can make up her own mind."

Renata edged back a step. "Yes, of course, but—"

Grandpa's finger waggled under her nose. "Haven't you caused enough trouble for my Julie Pearl? Whether she's your blood sister or not, it's her choice what she does about it. And I don't take too kindly to you running roughshod over her, taking charge of her life like she's still a toddler who don't know her own mind."

My heart swelled to be defended so gallantly. I hated to interrupt Grandpa, but I had to.

Laying a tender hand on his shoulder, I whispered close to his ear, "It's okay, I can take it from here."

He gulped and ran a hand across his face before stepping aside.

"Renata," I said, leading her by the elbow toward the door, "Grandpa is only trying to look out for my best interests."

"Well, naturally, poor man." She cast him a sympathetic frown. "I understand it's enormously difficult for him to accept you're not his granddaughter and to realize your life is going in a completely new direction."

"No, Renata, that isn't the way it's going to be." We stood in the corridor now, and I pulled the door closed behind us. "I don't care if you showed me a thousand DNA tests confirming I'm Jenny Pearl, that man in there will *always* be my grandpa. He raised me, gave up everything for me. He's the only parent I've ever known, and I love him with all my heart."

In the ensuing silence, I watched a series of confused emotions play across Renata's face, and before my eyes she seemed to shrink by a foot. I knew then that she *didn't* understand— would never understand the bond between me and Grandpa, the unassailable love that's possible only in the purest and best kinds of families.

The kind of love that's thicker than blood.

JULIE PEARL

It was nearly eleven before a baby-faced intern pronounced me fit to be released. Grandpa bustled about, helping Sandy pack up what few things I'd arrived with—my pool-soaked undergarments and the Oscar de la Renta, now stained and torn beyond repair. In the meantime, I fetched the garment bag and tote Renata had brought. Couldn't simply leave those things behind. Peeking into the tote, I was glad to see she'd brought my purse—except I sure was sorry she'd overlooked my Snow White watch.

As I set the suitcase and garment bag on a chair by the door, I turned to see Grandpa slouching in front of the window, hands stuffed into his pockets, staring into space. His forlorn look brought an ache to my chest. Even though I'd sent Renata on her way and told her I'd be in touch later, he must have assumed I'd be returning to the Channing house.

I pulled Sandy aside. "Could you give me a few minutes alone with my grandpa?"

"Sure thing." She tossed me one of those smiles you only get from your very best friend who knows all your secrets. "I drove myself, so I'll head on home, maybe check on Micah. Knowing him, he's probably at the La Quinta working like a madman."

I firmly believed she was right. "Let me know how he's doing?"

"You betcha. In the meantime"—she grabbed me by the nape of the neck and touched her forehead to mine—"don't do anything dumb, okay?"

Rolling my eyes, I gave her my promise.

"Come sit down, Grandpa," I said as the door closed behind Sandy. I led him to the chair by the window and then sat on the bed across from him.

He pulled off his bifocals and rubbed his eyes. "Now don't you be fussin' over me, Julie Pearl. I'll be fine, now that I know you're okay. Soon as you're on your way to the—" He swallowed hard. "Soon as you check out, I'll head on back to Caddo Pines. I can still get there in time to open the Swap & Shop by noon, and—"

"And I'll be there to help you." I reached for his hand. "I'm going home with you, Grandpa."

I'm not sure exactly when I made that decision, but I knew it was the right one. I might be a Pearl by birth, but unlike Renata, I never signed up to be a Channing. Her high-society ways would always be an awkward fit for this small-town girl, and I was one reluctant Cinderella who'd grown tired of tiptoeing around in those woefully uncomfortable glass slippers.

Besides, I'd about given up on things ever working out between me and Prince Charming.

"Now, Julie Pearl," Grandpa said, his brow furrowed, "you still got things to straighten out with . . . with your sister, don't you? I mean, I don't want you troubling over how I'm getting on with you being gone and all."

"You're not listening, Grandpa." I knelt beside his chair. "You and the Swap & Shop—that's where my home is. Where my *heart* is." My arms crept around his warm, wrinkled neck, and I snuggled against his unshaven cheek. "I wish with all my being I'd never heard of Pearls Along the Lake or Renata Channing or—" It hurt someplace deep inside me to say the words. "Or even Micah Hobart."

Grandpa took me by the shoulders and pushed me to arm's length. "Now you listen here, young lady. Much as I've wished the exact same thing, I been praying hard about it, and I got the strongest feeling deep in my soul that the Lord has a higher purpose for what's happened here. It ain't my place, or yours, to go forcing our own wills on the situation."

My jaw muscles clenched. This was *so* not what I wanted to hear just now. Seeing Grandpa when I awoke last night had made me realize how badly I wanted to go home to the flea market. And it wasn't just Grandpa I missed. I missed Katy Harcourt's brazen laughter. Maddie Barton smelling like Coty perfume and garage-sale castoffs. LeRoy Tuttle and his flirtatious wink. Lanky ol' Lester Carlson delivering our mail and the *Caddo Pines Recorder*.

Not to mention how badly I missed the feel of warm fur beneath my fingers, the smell of doggy breath and fish treats, the click of toenails across a hardwood floor.

Yes, that had to be it. Renata's appearance in my life was supposed to be a wakeup call, a reminder that precious things are too easily lost if you don't hang on tight. "I've been praying about it, too, Grandpa, and I think I understand now."

"That's good, Julie Pearl." Grandpa stood and pulled me to my feet. "So now we both got to trust the Lord to work all this out. You get on over to the phone and call Miz Channing. Tell her you're ready for her to pick you up and—"

"I told you, I'm not going back there."

"Don't argue with your grandpa, Julie Pearl." He kept right on nudging me closer to the nightstand where the beige telephone sat, and I kept right on digging in my heels.

Then the confounded thing rang and about planted me on the ceiling. Out of sheer habit, and before I could second-guess who might be calling, I whirled around and grabbed up the receiver. "Hello?"

"Julie? It's Renata." Her singsong tone carried the merest hint of uncertainty. "I'm downstairs in the lobby whenever you're ready."

I stared at my bare toes sticking out at the ends of the Dr. Scholl's sandals Grandpa had brought. He was right about one thing—now that this can of spaghetti had been opened, I needed to ride the horse all the way to the finish line. Or something like that.

Looking slant-eyed at Grandpa, I had a flash of inspiration. "Hey, Renata," I said, hooking a thumb in my jeans pocket and cocking my hip, "I've got a proposition for you."

"Aw, Julie Pearl, what have you gone and done?" Grandpa had to shout over the wind whipping through the open windows of the rattling old Econoline van.

I laughed out loud as we chugged along Interstate 30 toward the cutoff to Caddo Pines. "I think it's a perfect idea, Grandpa. Come on, admit it, you'll enjoy this as much as I will."

"*Enjoy* ain't exactly the word I'd use," he muttered, then shook his fist at an eighteen-wheeler roaring by us in the left lane. I surmised the GigantaMart logo on the side only added fuel to the fire in Grandpa's belly.

I reclined the creaky passenger seat a little farther. "Anyway, I'll believe it when I see it. How much you want to bet she's already chickened out? Two dollars and a bottle of root beer says Renata Channing doesn't have the gumption to spend two hours —let alone two weeks—living and working with us at the Swap & Shop."

Which was exactly what I'd proposed to her. The rationale being, of course, that I'd just spent a week and a half with her in Ritzville, so it was only fair for her, as the devoted sister she claimed to be, to experience life on my terms. She'd hemmed and hawed for a good ten minutes—or at least it seemed that long—while I did some serious arm-twisting. Grandpa, hearing only my side of the conversation, could only stare at me in horror.

When she finally realized I wasn't kidding, Renata gave in. "All right, *all right.* Give me time to take care of a few arrangements and pack a suitcase. I'll be there later this afternoon."

"Oh, and one more thing, Renata. Why don't you drive over in my VW? We don't have covered parking at the Swap & Shop, and I sure would hate for anything to happen to that fancy Mercedes of yours."

Although her Mercedes sure had a lot smoother ride than this old van. Shifting against the sticky vinyl seat, I gathered my windblown hair and tucked it down the back of my shirt to keep it from getting more tangled than it already was.

Grandpa angled me another of his disbelieving stares. "I hope you know what you're getting into, young lady. The woman's liable to be more work than she's worth, you know. Bet she's never lifted a broom and dustpan in her life."

I had to remind him what Micah had told me, that Renata used to sweep, mop, and a whole lot more at Pearls Along the Lake. Had to be like riding a bike . . . didn't it?

Ten miles outside Caddo Pines, Grandpa's cell phone rang. Since he was driving, he passed it to me. It was Sandy. "I was right," she said when I answered. "Micah's slaving away on paperwork. I just left the La Quinta."

Casting Grandpa a sidelong glance, I shifted closer to the passenger door and lowered my voice. "Did you tell him what happened after y'all left the party?"

"Yeah, but I broke it to him real gently. He looked like he hadn't slept all night."

"What did he say?"

She didn't answer right away. Finally she murmured, "Nothing. He just waved me out the door and told me to leave him alone."

My head had started throbbing again. I squeezed my eyes shut, but all I could see was Renata falling into Micah's arms yesterday. Why hadn't I picked up right away on her feelings for him—or his for her, considering their history? Why couldn't I accept that in Micah's mind I'd always and ever be Rennie Pearl's baby sister, the kid they'd nearly drowned?

It was too much for my tired brain to ponder. We were rumbling along the back highway now, winding through small towns and pine forests. In less than fifteen minutes we'd be in Caddo Pines.

I could hardly wait.

"Sneezy! Brynna!" I knelt by the kitchen table as my two favorite animals in the universe about bowled me over with their furry welcome. Purring like a motorboat, Sneezy rubbed against my thighs first one way and then the other, while Brynna lavished wet doggy kisses on my face. I wove my fingers through her soft, curly coat and sniffed back tears.

"Those two are mighty glad you're back," Grandpa said, his voice trembling.

"And I'm mighty glad to be here." Clambering to my feet, I kicked off my Dr. Scholl's and padded barefoot into the living room, where the puppies whimpered in their basket. I picked up each one in turn, snuggling it against my cheek. "Oh, Grandpa, they've grown so much."

A big ol' boa constrictor tightened itself around my heart. It wouldn't be long until the puppies grew big enough to go to new homes. Good thing I came back when I did, because no way these pups were going anywhere without my express approval.

Grandpa shuffled to the kitchen. "Best get some lunch, Julie Pearl. We open in twenty minutes."

By five after twelve, I was counting money into the cash

drawer while Grandpa shook out the welcome mat outside the front door. All my dear friends—Katy Harcourt, Maddie Barton, Hazel Diffenbacher, and so many others—had stopped by to greet me as they arrived to open their booths. I'm sure they'd all heard from Grandpa about why I'd been away, but nobody said a word, just treated me as if I'd been off on vacation or something.

And I was glad. I didn't want to be fussed over, didn't want to be different. I ached to be plain old Julie Pearl Stiles again.

Promptly (for him) at 12:08, Clifton arrived for work. Wearing a black *Lord of the Rings* T-shirt with Gandalf on the front, he didn't notice me at first. He headed straight to the snack bar, where Grandpa was filling the slow cooker with nacho cheese. "Sorry, got caught in the lunch rush at the DQ," Clifton told Grandpa. "I can take over now."

I had to smile. So Clifton had gone from sacking groceries at Friendly's to dishing out nachos at the Swap & Shop.

"I got it covered for now, son," Grandpa told him with a wink. "You might want to say howdy to the cashier we got working today."

Clifton swiveled his head in my direction. I wiggled my fingers in a shy wave.

"Julie Pearl!" He leapt over the two-foot-high wrought-iron railing surrounding the snack bar, skidded around the end of the checkout counter, and collided with me in a monster bear hug.

"Clifton, I—can't—breathe!" Laughing, I squirmed out of his embrace. "I'm happy to see you, too, you dork!" I took his guileless face in my hands and planted a kiss on his forehead.

Turning fourteen shades of scarlet, Clifton jerked away. He glowered and studied me from one end to the other like I was a used car. Any minute he'd be kicking my tires. "Well, at least you didn't come back looking all citified. I hope you didn't let nearly two weeks of living high on the hog go to your head."

Leave it to Clifton to say what I'm sure everyone else had been thinking. "I'm the same person I was before, Clifton. I promise."

Even so, I spent the rest of the afternoon trying to convince myself and everyone else that I really was the same Julie Pearl Stiles they all knew and (mostly) loved. And all the while I kept one eye on the front door and wondered when—or if—Renata Channing would show up and once again turn my peaceful little world upside down.

RENATA

February, 9 years earlier
Little Rock, Arkansas

Perusing the society pages of the morning paper, Renata barely glanced up when her husband entered the breakfast room. "Weren't you supposed to be on your way to the airport by now?"

"O'Hare's iced in. The flight's been delayed until early afternoon." Larry Channing slid into the chair across from Renata and signaled Walter to pour coffee.

Renata pasted on a sugary smile, but her tone was venomous. "I'm sure that pleases Nadine to no end. You two will have the whole morning for extended good-byes." Ignoring Larry's stony glare, she laid the newspaper aside and stirred skim milk into her artificially sweetened coffee. "Oh, and by the way, don't expect Nadine to be here when you get back."

Larry's cup clattered against the saucer, coffee spilling over the rim. "What's that supposed to mean?"

"It means I'm letting her go. I've already begun interviewing replacements."

"You have some nerve." Larry grew silent, his gaze following Walter as the white-coated butler carried a tray of empty dishes to the kitchen. When the door whisked closed, Larry continued with a sneer. "After your rendezvous with your old flame Hobart, you don't have any business meddling in *my* affairs."

At least he had the decency to look chagrined at his own choice of words. Renata pressed both hands on the table. "What will it take to convince you? *Nothing* happened between us." Not that she hadn't tried.

"I'm supposed to believe that? After finding the two of you locked in each other's arms on the living room sofa?"

Renata seethed. Served him right for coming home unexpectedly at four in the morning. Her gaze drilled holes into his back as he strode to the buffet and heaped a plate with sausage links and French toast casserole, to which he added a huge scoop of butter and a generous dousing of maple syrup. "You know your doctor doesn't want you eating like that. If you don't be careful, you're going to have a stroke."

Larry gave a cruel laugh. "I should think you'd be thrilled—but only if I didn't survive, because wouldn't it be too awful if you ended up shackled in marriage to a drooling invalid."

"Not to worry." Renata shifted sideways and hooked her arm over the back of the chair. "Your stock portfolio will buy a lot of years of private nursing."

"Humph. A big, strong, good-looking *male* nurse, if you had your way." Larry took his seat across from her and shoveled in a mouthful of the eggy casserole.

Revulsion filled her as she watched melted butter ooze from the corners of his lips. "It would serve you right, you pompous control freak."

"Sounds like the pot calling the kettle black." He shook his head in disgust as he sawed a juicy sausage link into bite-sized pieces. "Honestly, Renata, I worry about you," he said with a sneer. "Have you taken your pills this morning?"

She skewered him with a glare. "Don't you talk to me about my *pills*. All the pills in the world won't change the fact that I'm married to an egotistical bully."

Larry snorted. "Since you insist on resorting to name calling, here's one for *you* to try on: narcissistic, psychopathic b—"

Renata silenced him with a resounding slap to the table. "Just shut up and eat your breakfast. The sooner you finish, the sooner you'll leave me alone."

"Good idea. That's the first sane remark you've made all morning."

Fuming, Renata shifted and wished she had the fortitude to get up and walk out. But this was her house, too. She'd earned the right to sit at this table, to reign supreme over Channing Manor.

It didn't use to be this way between them. Once upon a time they'd actually loved each other. At least she'd thought it was love. She couldn't forget the night she'd first met the strikingly handsome Lawrence Eugene Channing, newly appointed vice-president of GigantaMart, Inc., and first in line to inherit the Channing fortune. If not for her best friend from college, Janet Slaughter, inviting Renata to share hostess duties at a charity dinner-dance hosted by her parents, Larry would never have given Renata a second look. But of course he had no way of knowing when he asked her to dance that she wore a borrowed dress, borrowed shoes, borrowed jewels—that everything about her was counterfeit. She'd never even allowed him to call for her at her father's house, that dreary little two-bedroom bungalow with the pale green vinyl siding and cracked sidewalk. She always arranged to be in town visiting at Janet's so that he could pick her up there.

Then things started getting serious between them and he'd pressed to meet her family. Ultimately she'd had to confess the truth, even if it meant he'd never want to be seen with her again. "I'm poor, Larry. I'm a nobody," she'd told him with tears in her eyes. "My dad sells insurance, and my mother—she—" Her throat closed, her heart twisted. How would she ever get the words out?

But Larry had been patient and understanding, at least in those days. As they sat shoulder to shoulder in the bucket seats of his tiny German sports car, he'd stroked her hand until she could continue.

"My mother . . ." She swallowed, drew a bolstering breath. "My mother was mentally ill. She committed suicide. Oh, Larry"—sobs wracked her body—"I'm scared, so scared I'm going to go crazy someday too!"

She didn't tell him about the disconcerting symptoms she'd already begun to experience—the jumping thoughts and moments of reckless abandon, the freakish episodes when she could go seventy-two hours or more without sleeping. She didn't mention the crashes that came afterward, when she couldn't drag herself out of bed for days. At least the little yellow pills the doctor gave her helped keep the monsters at bay.

Larry hadn't acted the least bit concerned about her family background, promising he'd make Renata the most admired woman in Little Rock society. They married less than a year later, and Larry's parents immediately began pressing them for a grandchild and heir. Otherwise, the family fortune would go to Larry's ne'er-do-well younger brother, whose embarrassingly fertile wife popped out babies like she was trying to populate her own country.

But after three years of fertility treatments and as many miscarriages, Renata's OB/GYN advised them to stop trying. Heartbroken, she lapsed into a deep depression, worsened by the discovery that Larry had been sleeping with his secretary. He claimed the "clinical sex" he and Renata had been having in an effort to conceive had destroyed whatever love he may have once felt for her.

Desperate to keep her marriage intact, she convinced Larry to consider adoption, but when they began the process, Renata learned they'd both have to undergo a psychological evaluation. During one of her interviews, while the counselor stepped away for more coffee, Renata had stolen a glance at his notes. The words *narcissistic tendencies* and *possible bipolar disorder* jumped out at her. It couldn't be true—she'd inherited her mother's sickness!

Then the final report had come back declaring them unsuitable as adoptive parents and strongly urging Renata to consult a psychiatrist. Neither Larry's money nor a new prescription regimen could repair the damage already done to their marriage, and two weeks later Larry moved out of Renata's bedroom for good. If Renata's mother weren't already dead, Renata would have strangled her on the spot. Leave it to Mama to ruin Renata's life even from the grave!

Well. She'd show Mama *and* Larry. Publicly, she immersed herself in fundraisers for children's advocacy groups, support centers for unwed mothers, various adoption and foster-care agencies, and eventually established the Channing Children's Foundation.

Privately, she vowed Lawrence Eugene Channing would never hurt her again.

Sipping her rapidly cooling café au lait, Renata closed her eyes against the sight of the man she had grown to detest. She could never leave him, of course, nor he her. His wealth made possible everything she did for the less fortunate women and children her foundation assisted—not to mention securing her enviable reputation among Arkansas society. And were he ever to ask for a divorce, she'd only have to remind him of several incriminating photos locked away in her safe-deposit box.

Ah, Nadine, I suppose I should thank you for luring my husband into your bed. You weren't the first, and you certainly won't be the last.

Unfortunately, the gossip had already filtered back to her about his infidelity with her personal assistant, and Renata had her reputation to protect, after all. Time to end Larry's latest flirtation and introduce a new player into the mix.

Larry tossed his napkin onto his syrup-smeared plate. With an icy glower, he rose and strode from the room. A moment later, Renata reached for the manila envelope tucked beneath the corner of her lace-edged placemat. She pulled out the stack of résumés she'd collected and once more perused the one she had found most intriguing.

"Felicia Beaufort." She fingered the attached photo of the attractive blonde, a well-educated woman in her late twenties. "Yes, I think you're the one."

And once again she wished something *had* happened between her and Micah. Why should Larry have all the fun?

JULIE PEARL

Present Day

"Thanks, Miss Hart." I handed my former sixth-grade English teacher a heavy paper bag containing her latest purchase of used books from Herman Trapp's Paperback Place. "I'll remind Herman to give you a call when he locates that Nicholas Sparks novel you're looking for."

"You're such a sweetheart, Julie Pearl." The prim, bespectacled woman reached across the counter to tweak my chin. Continuing in a stage whisper, she said, "But, honey, I thought you'd gone off to the big city to meet a nice young man."

I lifted an eyebrow. "And who told you that, Miss Hart?"

"Well, talk around town and all . . ." She cast a furtive glance in both directions, then leaned closer. "Pickin's are pretty slim in a small town like Caddo Pines. Why else do you think I ended up a crotchety old spinster?"

"What?" I slapped a hand to my chest and barely suppressed a grin. "Correct me if I'm wrong, but rumor has it you and LeRoy Tuttle have been seen—what's the word?—*spooning* on the Hot Springs Promenade."

Reddening, Miss Hart drew herself up to her full five feet. She clutched the bag of paperbacks to her bosom. "Humph, Katy Harcourt's the only one coulda let *that* cat out of the bag. Ooooh, you just let me get a-hold of that gossiping old biddy."

I winked and nodded across the way toward Katy's Vintage Shoes & Bags. "I do believe she's working her booth today. Why don't you mosey on over and say hello?"

As she tromped off to give Katy a piece of her mind, Grandpa joined me behind the counter. "You stirring up trouble already, young lady?"

Hooking my arm through his, I leaned my head on his shoulder. "Gotta do something to keep from wondering when Renata will show up." I glanced at my watch—the plain gold Timex Grandpa had given me for my high-school graduation and another of my favorite treasures. "Or I guess I should say, *if* Renata shows up. It's after four thirty already."

"Still think it was a crazy idea, expecting the woman to give up her high-falutin' ways and come live in a flea market." He popped open the cash drawer and exchanged several one-dollar bills for quarters. "Clifton's about out of change at the snack bar."

I turned to watch Clifton hand a customer a hot dog and a Coke. "He seems to like working here. I'm glad."

"Always was a good kid. Right honorable of him stayin' at home to help his mama." Grandpa planted a kiss on my forehead before returning to the snack bar.

I knew there was no dig intended about my recent departure from Caddo Pines. It just felt so good to be home and to see Grandpa smiling again.

The brass bells clanged as the front door opened. Just like I'd done all afternoon, I jumped, hoping and dreading it might be Renata. Another false alarm. Sandy flounced into the Swap & Shop. Sliding her sunglasses up over her dense brown bangs, she paused to glance around.

Catching my eye, she waved. "Hey, Jules, how's it going?"

I waved back. "Couldn't be better. I was—"

Clifton's baritone rang out. "Hey, beautiful, you're early. I still gotta shut down the snack bar and clean up."

Sandy glanced at me with a sheepish grin. "No hurry. I'll visit with Julie for a few minutes."

I winked at Sandy. "Sounds like you two are back on solid ground."

A steamy blush rose up her neck and into her cheeks. "Clifton's like a new guy since he started working for your grandpa. He's matured, more settled somehow." Her gaze drifted in Clifton's direction. "All he needed was—"

"Someone to believe in him," I finished in a hushed voice.

She looked back at me, her eyebrows twisting into sideways question marks. "It's no secret I've been falling in love with Clifton since we were sophomores at Caddo Mountain Consolidated High, but it's only been in the past couple of weeks that I could actually see myself married to the guy."

My heart did a little flutter dance of happiness for her. Plus a teensy bit of surprise. "Seriously? Has he proposed?"

"Not officially. But I've started dropping hints that I sure might be open to the idea."

Sandy and Clifton. My, oh, my.

And I understood my grandpa a little bit better just then. Otto Stiles, the man who turned trash into treasure, the man who valued the valueless. The man who taught me everything I knew about life and love and hope. Why did I ever think the answers I sought could be found anywhere but right here at the Swap & Shop?

We'd long since closed up shop, and Grandpa and I were watching *Masterpiece Mystery!* on the PBS channel, an "Inspector Lewis" rerun. With Sneezy curled up on my lap and Brynna snoozing with the pups in her box beside the sofa, I tried to follow the plot while quietly wondering what Lewis and Hathaway would make of the mysteries unraveling in my life this summer.

Then the phone rang. I looked at Grandpa and he looked at me, but neither of us made a move to answer it.

"Come on now, Julie Pearl, you know it's prob'ly her."

I crossed my arms. "I'm not in the mood to listen to her excuses. Let the answering machine pick up." Nose in the air, I pretended to be engrossed in the program.

Grandpa watched me for a moment, then sighed and mimicked my posture.

The phone kept ringing until the machine clicked on, and Grandpa's recorded voice announced, *"Howdy, you've reached Otto Stiles' Swap & Shop, open Thursday through Monday. We're closed now, but you can sure leave us a message, and we'll be right happy to return your call."*

After the beep came Renata's voice. "Oh dear, where are you, Julie? I tried your cell phone, but apparently it's turned off."

Oops. It was still in my purse, crammed into the tote I'd brought home from the hospital.

"Anyway, I've had a bit of car trouble. I called Triple-A, but the utter *idiot* I spoke with must have been from Upper Berserkistan and I couldn't understand a word—"

My stomach plummeted. I heaved myself off the sofa and sprinted to the phone. "Renata? I'm here."

"Thank goodness! It's getting dark, and I'm hopelessly lost. I know I took the right exit off the Interstate, and I made it to Caddo Pines but my GPS lost the signal and I must have taken a wrong turn in town—I've only been to your place that one time, you know—and now I'm out in the middle of nowhere, and your little car started making a strange noise, and I managed to get to the side of the road before it died, but now it won't start up again and—for heaven's sake, Julie, why doesn't this thing have OnStar?"

I pinched the bridge of my nose. "It's okay, Renata, don't panic." Turning to Grandpa, I mouthed, *The Beetle died.*

He pushed off the sofa and shuffled to the kitchen. "We need to go get her? I'll get my keys."

"She has no idea where she is." I tilted the receiver so Grandpa could listen in and then spoke into the phone. "Renata, tell me exactly what kind of noise the car was making before it died."

"Well, it was kind of a long, whistling whine, and then a rattle and sputter, and then it just quit."

Good, something simple. Clifton had once shown me an easy fix. "No big deal. Just go around back and pop the hood. You'll find—"

"Wait! You mean, open up the engine? I can't do that!"

"Hmmm. Then maybe you'd better stay in the car and wait for somebody to find you." I winked at Grandpa. "Oh, and keep the windows rolled up. This part of Arkansas is bear country, you know. And I heard talk about a mountain lion stalking the woods around here."

"Bear? *Mountain lion?* Are you *sure?*"

Grandpa had to step away and press both hands to his mouth to keep from laughing out loud. I cleared my throat to mask my own laughter. "I haven't actually *seen* any bears or mountain lions, but I sure wouldn't want to be outside alone in the dark on the back roads."

Short, sharp breaths pulsed in my ear. "Well, it's not *quite* dark yet. If I were to, um, *try* to fix the engine, how long do you suppose it would take?"

"Oh, just a second or two. I can have you back on the road lickety-split."

Dead silence. I wondered if we'd been disconnected. Then she burst out, "All right, talk me through it." The car door slammed.

In my mind's eye, I pictured the Beetle's engine parts and tried to remember the exact steps Clifton had shown me. I didn't know all the technical terms for the car parts, but she wouldn't have recognized them anyway. We got through it with references like "the orange doohickey" and "the black box with the red cap on top," and then I had her get back inside and try the key. I breathed a sigh of relief along with her when the VW started right up.

"Oh, and here's the Triple-A truck. They will *definitely* be hearing from me about their *atrocious* service." Back to her obnoxiously arrogant self. I didn't know whether to be glad or scared.

"Good, then they can point you back to town and get you to the Swap & Shop. We'll have the porch light on at the top of the stairs for you."

I hung up and fell into the nearest chair like a sack of rotten potatoes. "She's coming, Grandpa. She's really, really coming."

JULIE PEARL

It wasn't twenty minutes later when I heard the familiar rumble of my little green car. Knowing how Renata felt about dogs, I didn't see any sense adding to the commotion of her arrival, so I hurried Brynna and the pups into Grandpa's room and closed the door. I caught up with Grandpa on the landing outside the kitchen door, and we watched Renata park under the oak tree and wrestle her suitcase out of the back seat.

Make that two extra-large suitcases and a bulging wheeled tote.

"Best go down and give her a hand." Heaving a sigh, Grandpa trudged downstairs.

I reached the bottom step a couple of paces behind him, about the time Renata dragged the tote bag around the front of the car. The yellow glow of the porch light made her look sallow and gaunt. She stared at me with a dazed expression not unlike the look I'd seen in Brynna's eyes the day I found her half-starved in the rotting old cabin. Noting the black grease marks streaking Renata's face, arms, and hands, I almost felt sorry for her.

Almost.

She released the tote handle, and the whole thing toppled over. "I do hope you have hot and cold running water and a bathtub."

I sent a pleading glance heavenward and shook my head. "This may not be the Ritz-Carlton, but I promise, we won't make you wash up out back in the rain barrel."

It took Grandpa and me straining together to manhandle all her luggage to the top of the stairs. Renata headed straight for the bathroom and started filling the tub. While Grandpa and I arranged her suitcases as best we could in the confined space of my tiny bedroom, several loud sighs and groans emanated from behind the closed bathroom door. Seemed like she intended to stay in there all night, but after nearly an hour the hot water must have finally given out.

The bathroom door cracked open, and a cloud of steam seeped out. "Julie, honey, I need you to bring me a few things from my tote—the blue flowered lingerie bag and a cosmetics kit."

"Coming right up." I gave Grandpa a resigned smirk as I started toward the bedroom.

"Hold on a minute, Julie Pearl." He tugged at the hem of my dashiki. "I thought the whole point of asking her here was so she could see how life looks from your side of the highway. Bad enough you're giving up your bed for her. You go waiting on her hand and foot and you're setting yourself up for trouble."

I gave him a reassuring hug. "Don't worry, Grandpa. After tonight she's on her own."

"Here you go, Sneezy." I set my empty cereal bowl on the floor so the old yellow cat could lap up the last few drops of milk. Brynna plopped her furry bottom down beside him, her tail sweeping the linoleum in broad strokes. She whimpered softly.

"Hang on, girl, almost done." Grandpa scooped up the last spoonful of his raisin bran. As he put his bowl down for Brynna, he glanced toward the clock above the stove. "Shouldn't her ladyship be up by now? We open in half an hour."

About that time, a door creaked. Renata stifled a yawn as she groped her way to the bathroom, her pink satin dressing gown flowing like a royal train behind her.

Grandpa clucked his tongue. "Well, speak of the—"

"Bite your tongue, Grandpa." I carried our now spotlessly clean cereal bowls to the sink and rinsed them. Couldn't help wondering what Renata would have to say about people who let pets eat off their dishes. But hey, a good dousing of hot, sudsy water and any germs to be concerned about get sent right down the drain.

I'd just sat down at the table with a mug of steaming coffee when Renata came padding across the living room carpet. She halted beneath the archway leading to the kitchen and sucked in her breath.

"Oh, no! The *dog!*" Her eyes were two full moons with dark centers. "I—I forgot about your dog."

A throat-tightening quiver shook me, the kind I get around people who don't understand or respect animals. "She won't hurt you, Renata." I knelt beside Brynna, who edged behind me and stared up at Renata. "See, she's as scared of you as you are of her."

"Yes, as well she should be." Renata took a giant sidestep to position herself behind one of the kitchen chairs. "I'm warning you, little doggy," she said with a shaky laugh, "I am not a pleasant person to be around before I've had my morning coffee."

Her feeble attempt at humor eased the tension. I rose and went to the cupboard for another mug. "You like a little skim milk, don't you, Renata?"

Grandpa gave a small cough. "Julie Pearl, we'd best get a move on. Almost time to open."

"Oh, right." I set the mug on the counter and told Renata where to find things in the kitchen. "We take the animals downstairs with us, so they won't bother you. Come on down when you're ready."

Pausing at the door, Grandpa shot her one last warning glare. "Sooner the better, Miz Channing. We got plenty of work ahead of us."

As the day progressed, I could see Grandpa getting hotter and hotter under the collar. He forbade me to interfere, while he assigned Renata one menial chore after another, starting with sweeping the aisles, dusting LeRoy Tuttle's conglomeration of china and knickknacks, and reshelving the misplaced paperbacks in Herman Trapp's booth.

"The woman works slower'n a slug," Grandpa muttered as he helped Clifton carry a tub of ice to refill the snack bar drink machine.

"She is definitely some piece of work." Clifton cast me a toothy grin. "So she's your blood sister, huh, Julie Pearl? I see now where you got your uppity ways."

I resisted the urge to bop one spike-haired, bleach-blond dork over the head with my 1992 *Woman's Day* and slammed it on the counter instead. "I seriously wonder what Sandy sees in you, Clifton Carter Doakes."

His only response was a chortling laugh.

"I'm finished with the books." Renata came up behind Grandpa. "What next, Mr. Stiles?"

Noticing the dust smudge across her nose, I pretended to study the magazine cover to keep from chuckling out loud. This was a side of Renata I'd not seen before—the simple khaki slacks, periwinkle blouse, sensible canvas espadrilles. She'd pinned her gorgeous mass of hair into a neat French twist.

"You go on, Uncle Otto," Clifton said. "I'll finish with the ice."

My head shot up. *Uncle Otto?* When had that started?

Grandpa shrugged, one corner of his mouth lifting in a half-smile. "Kid's spent so much time here over the years, figured it was high time he thought of us as family."

I cringed beneath a sudden spasm of jealousy, like I'd already been replaced. It hadn't taken long to realize Grandpa had pretty much turned the snack bar over to Clifton. What next—the cashier's job? Or was Clifton setting himself up for my position as assistant manager of the Swap & Shop?

What is your problem, Julie Pearl?

It had to be all the stress I'd been under these past few weeks. Either that, or maybe I'd inherited whatever madness infected Lucille Pearl . . . and probably Renata? I shuddered to even imagine such a possibility and prayed with all my might that I'd been spared those genes. Because in the short time I'd known Renata, it was clear *something* wasn't right about this woman who claimed me as her sister.

Besides, if her actions weren't enough to convince me, there was that interesting array of pill bottles I'd glimpsed next to the bathroom sink this morning. But before I could read any labels, Renata had scurried in and swept them all into her Kate Spade designer makeup bag.

My mind flashed back to the day Renata's attorney delivered the DNA results, and my fingers itched with stifled regret that I hadn't yanked the envelope out of Renata's hands to see the results for myself.

Dear God, please don't let me go crazy!

By the end of another typically slow Monday—which was probably a blessing, being Renata's first day and all—Grandpa had clearly changed his opinion of her. At least where her work habits were concerned. She might be slow, but she was thorough. *Obsessed* might be a better word. She'd do just about anything Grandpa asked of her, so long as her chores kept her far away from Brynna and the puppies.

As I tallied the bank deposit, Clifton meandered over, a damp, food-stained cleaning rag slung across his shoulder. "Me and Sandy are meeting at the pool around six. Wanna join us?"

I stifled a tremor. "Thanks, but you know me and swimming pools."

"Oh, yeah. I forgot you nearly drowned again." He tilted his head. "You doin' okay, Julie Pearl? You been awful quiet since you came home. Your grandpa's mighty worried about you."

"He said so?"

"Didn't have to. Seen it in his eyes." Clifton plucked the pen out of my hand and playfully poked at Sneezy, dozing next to the cash register. The old cat raised to his haunches and batted at the pen a few times, then yawned and returned to his nap.

Clifton twirled the pen between his thumb and forefinger. "We're friends, right, Julie Pearl?"

"Of course we are." I straightened a stack of one-dollar bills and started recounting them.

"And friends tell each other the truth. Even if it's hard to hear."

I nodded. "Eighteen, nineteen . . ."

"Truth is, if anyone I know deserves better'n what Caddo Pines has to offer, it's you."

I sucked in a shaky breath. "Twenty-six, twenty-seven . . ."

"You're way smarter'n me, or even Sandy. You're the one shoulda gone off to college and made something of yourself."

"Stop it, Clifton. Thirty-two, thirty-three . . ."

"And you would have, too, if you'd had the life you started out with." Laughing quietly, he gave his head a shake. "I can see you now, prancin' around in high heels and fancy duds, a pair of brainy-lookin' glasses on the end of your nose. A big ol' framed parchment would be hanging over your genu-wine solid oak desk —Julie Pearl Stiles, Attorney-at-Law. Or maybe *Doctor* Stiles, Licensed Veterinarian, since you love animals so much. Why, you'd have a whole string of clinics from here to Atlanta."

With a frustrated groan, I slammed the rest of the bills onto the pile. "You're talking crazy. What exactly are you getting at?"

He took my hands, stroking my palms with the sides of his thumbs. "What I'm trying to say is, maybe you were never meant to have that other life."

I gaped at him. "But you just said—Clifton, you're not making any sense." On the other hand, I realized he made perfect sense, in his own convoluted way. I closed my eyes and let him explain the truth I knew deep in my soul I'd already figured out.

"It's like your grandpa is always saying, there ain't no such thing as a coincidence. If you really are that Jennifer Pearl kid, and if you really did get rescued and raised by Uncle Otto's daughter —even if what she did was wrong—then it's because right here's where God meant you to be." He stabbed the countertop with his index finger. "Right here, in Caddo Pines, Arkansas, doing what makes you happiest. And I know for dang sure you couldn't have been happy keepin' your fingernails clean while you strutted around in designer clothes and dined on caviar and filet mignon."

I stewed for days over Clifton's homegrown wisdom—even though his logic might be a bit flawed. As Jenny Pearl, I might have grown up getting my nails dirty cleaning vacation cottages and learning the resort business right alongside my sister. If I'd never "drowned," if Renata hadn't carried that guilt all her life, who knew where either of us would have ended up as adults?

In the meantime, Grandpa kept right on showing Renata all the tiresome but necessary aspects of the flea market business. And she kept right on surprising me with her fanatical urgency to do whatever Grandpa asked—but not without some complaining over her ruined manicure. It was like she had to prove something, prove she could work as hard and long as the rest of us. I'd never forget the maniacal look that would come over her as she scrubbed a piece of stuck chewing gum off the floor or washed down and squeegeed the front windows inside and out.

When Grandpa wouldn't even let me help with the routine cleaning and reorganizing on the two days we were closed, I decided to back off and let Renata exorcise her demons—if that's what she was doing. In the meantime, I took advantage of the free time to get alone and ponder what all the changes this summer really meant. I didn't feel like I fit in anywhere anymore, like I was caught in some kind of weird limbo between two lives.

One sultry evening, as I sat hugging my knees halfway down the outer stairs to our apartment, the door opened and closed above me, followed by the *tick-tick* of doggy toenails on the landing. A second later, Brynna licked the inside of my ear with her warm, wet tongue. I couldn't suppress a laugh as I flinched and drew my arm around her. Those big, dark eyes looked up at me, and it was almost like she beamed her doggy thoughts straight into my brain: *You're not alone, Julie Pearl. I know what it means to feel lost. Don't let yourself be lost to those who need you most.*

3 2

JULIE PEARL

I was only fooling myself if I thought I could drag Renata to church with us Sunday morning. I looked in on her once as Grandpa and I got ready to go, but she appeared dead to the world, one of those velvety black sleep masks covering her eyes and all my bedroom window shades pulled tight to the sill. I said some extra prayers for her that morning. And quite a few for myself as well.

We came home from church to find a four-course meal laid out on our kitchen table. Roasted chicken, glazed carrots, buttered baby peas, the works.

"You cooked?" I blurted a split-second before noticing the aluminum takeout containers poking out of the trashcan.

"I know a lovely restaurant in Hot Springs that delivers." Renata set an iced-tea pitcher at one end of the table. Her eyes narrowed, and her nose lifted just a tad. "Sunday dinner is the old-fashioned family tradition, isn't it?"

Grandpa huffed and brushed past her. "Julie and I usually just grab a sandwich or somethin' so we can get on down to open the shop."

"Well, this sure beats the canned soup and toasted cheese

239

sandwiches I'd have whipped up." I caught up with Grandpa and chastised him with a meaningful eye roll as I dropped my purse on the serape-covered cedar chest. If an "old-fashioned" Sunday dinner made Renata feel more at home here, we'd eat it and enjoy every bite.

At twelve sharp we opened the shop to admit a bevy of die-hard antique hunters and sunburned vacationers looking for weekend bargains, and the pace kept up most of the afternoon. When we finally hit a lull, Grandpa excused Renata from her temporary duties helping Clifton dish up nachos and told me to teach her how to work the checkout counter.

I'd already walked her through my record-keeping system three times when she tossed her pencil aside and lifted her hands in frustration. "This is utterly pointless. At least I *know* how to mop and dust."

I narrowed one eye and stared at her. "You manage a house bigger than my entire high school. You run a prominent charitable organization. You plan extravagant dinners and huge fundraising events. And you expect me to believe you can't do a little simple bookkeeping?"

Renata picked at a tiny blob of dried nacho cheese stuck to the sleeve of her lace-edged knit top. "Darling, are you so naïve? The secret of success is to surround yourself with highly competent people who know how to make *you* look good."

"Like Felicia Beaufort?" The bitter-sounding words popped out before I could stop myself.

One eyebrow lifted in a catlike sneer. "Like Felicia Beaufort."

I tapped my stubby fingernails on the counter. "I know you know something's going on between her and your husband. How can you keep her on?"

The arrogance faltered for maybe half a second while a sad vulnerability crept into her eyes—a look that reminded me of the young Rennie Pearl holding her baby sister in the snapshot I'd found. Then just as quickly she became stuck-up Renata

Channing again. "Why should I explain myself to you? You couldn't possibly understand."

Resentment and hurt rose in me like bile acids. "A hick-town girl like me? You're probably right. Obviously the rich and famous have a whole different set of principles."

"How dare you pass judgment on my principles! You have no idea what I sacrificed to get where I am today."

"Oh, I have a pretty good idea. You want something, you go after it, the cost be hanged." The image I'd tried so hard to erase from my thoughts came surging back in 3D—Renata draping herself around Micah's neck.

She must have seen it in my face. Something between pity and triumph darkened her gaze. "I certainly never meant to hurt you. If I'd had any idea how you felt about Micah, I'd have explained—"

The clanging brass bells on the front door interrupted her. Both our heads jerked toward the sound, and my heart did a roll and thud as Micah Hobart ambled in. Pausing at the entrance, he slid off his aviator sunglasses. His eyes met mine—briefly—and then he saw Renata. It seemed to my befuddled brain that she melted into a puddle of quivering passion. Nausea rocked me, and I tasted the popcorn and Diet Dr Pepper I'd had for a snack an hour ago. If Micah hadn't already seen me, I'd have slid beneath the counter to hide.

Grandpa cut him off, his greeting anything but cordial. "Something we can help you with, Mr. Hobart?"

Micah spread his hands. "I'm not here to cause trouble, Mr. Stiles. If I could just have a few minutes with Julie . . ." He cast me a desperate, pleading look, and then I was the one melting into a puddle.

Renata took a tiny step backward and crossed her arms. "Go on, Julie," she whispered. "He's here for you, not me."

Despite Grandpa's warning look, I edged around the counter. My legs felt as if I were wading through hardening concrete. Four feet away from Micah, I stopped. "What do you want?"

He hesitated until Grandpa cleared his throat and stalked off to help Clifton with something in the snack bar. "I thought maybe you'd call . . . or something."

The Swap & Shop stood in rapt silence, like a packed auditorium just before the curtain opens for the main attraction. That would be me, obviously. I could tell by the scroochy feeling of several pairs of eyes boring holes through me. I stuffed my hands into the pockets of my plaid capris. "Why? What's there to say?"

Staring at the floor, he shifted his weight and sighed. "I thought we had something between us."

"Oh, excuse me," I said, loud enough for anyone in the farthest corners of the building to hear, "you must have mistaken me for someone else." I turned to signal Renata. "You were wrong, sister-dear. He's here for—"

Micah's hand clamped down on my extended arm. The brass bells jangled, and he jerked me outside into the heat of the July afternoon.

Yanking free of his grip, I stumbled across the gravel parking lot. "You've got some nerve, Micah Hobart. Who do you think you are, anyway?"

He closed the space between us and seized me by the shoulders. "I'm the man who's falling in love with you, that's who."

The next thing I knew, I was drowning. Drowning in a kiss deeper and scarier than the deepest swimming pool. And I never wanted to come up for air.

If, as Shakespeare said, all the world's a stage, then I must be performing for one wildly entertained audience. And right about now, I ached to get my hands on the author of this script and give him what-for.

Micah steered his maroon pickup toward the picnic area

where he'd first told me the story of Jennifer Pearl's supposed drowning. He drove to the far end of the parking area, away from the Sunday-afternoon picnickers with their laughing children, Frisbee-chasing dogs, and greasy-smelling buckets of fried chicken. When he pulled into a parking space, the drooping branch of an oak tree scraped its twiggy fingers along the roof, sending chill bumps up my arms. Micah lowered the windows and shut off the engine.

And sat there in utter silence until I was ready to climb out of my skin. "Okay, just say what you brought me out here to say. The suspense is killing me."

He undid his seatbelt and hooked his forearms over the steering wheel. Something beyond the windshield held his gaze. "I'm no good at this, Julie. I've got a string of failed relationships behind me, and I have no right to expect this to be any different."

My heart felt like a lump of raw meat on a skewer. I couldn't look at him. "Why not?"

"Because of who I am. Because of who you are. Because . . ." He lowered his forehead to his arms.

"Because of Renata." A lava-spewing volcano erupted within me. I jerked open the door and marched across the patchy grass. Then I swung around and marched right back. I slammed the pickup door with a violent heave, then leaned in the window, breathing hard. "What exactly *is* going on between you and Renata? Do you even *know*?"

Micah raised his head and looked at me with the sad eyes of a confused puppy-dog. I bit the inside of my lower lip to keep my heart from cracking in two. No *way* would I ever again allow any man to manipulate my emotions like this!

"All I know is, I don't ever want to lose you, Julie."

Okay, except maybe this once.

I opened the door and climbed into the cab. "Then help me understand."

He told me then about the string of sleepless nights he'd spent trying to figure out exactly what had happened at Renata's that day. Coming to the party mainly to see me, to find out if I had, as he put it, "gone over to the other side." Then Renata in his face, and Larry showing up out of nowhere and lighting into him.

"When Sandy told me the next day that you nearly drowned—again—I wanted to find Larry Channing and throttle him."

I shivered. "He's not worth it."

"But you are, Julie." His smoky-eyed gaze stabbed me where it hurt. "What I feel for you—it's—"

That grinding irritation raked through me again. "Don't even talk to me about feelings, Micah, not until you're ready to be completely honest."

Disbelief flickered across his face. "I thought I did a pretty good job of showing you a little while ago outside the Swap & Shop."

The memory of his lips on mine made me weak. I wanted more than anything to fall into his arms again and lose myself in the taste of his kisses, the scratchy-soft feel of his beard against my cheek. I wanted to forget the past and the future and everything that didn't include Micah Hobart loving me, me loving him.

But I had to be strong now, strong enough to make him face the truth about himself, about me, about Renata. I drew a steadying breath. "You kiss me like there's no tomorrow, and then you turn around and tell me our relationship is doomed. I'm already confused enough about my life, so I don't need another seesaw ride with you. Either you lay it all on the line, or you get this pickup in gear and take me home."

He faced me squarely, and I could see by the way his throat worked how he struggled to find words. "Like I told you before, something about you started worming its way into my heart the day I learned you'd rescued Brynna. But then I found out you could be Jenny, and it changed everything."

I laughed out loud. "If you think it changed things for *you*—"

"I know, I know. I can't even imagine what you've been going through."

We fell silent for a moment, while a hangnail on my left thumb suddenly became of monumental importance. "You want to hear the *really* interesting part? Renata hasn't let anyone see the DNA results. So I still don't know if I'm really Jenny Pearl."

Micah seized my wrist, forcing me to look at him. "You're kidding, right?"

"It's the truth." I swallowed the baseball clogging my throat. "I don't even know if Renata has looked at the results."

"That's crazy. Can't you insist she tell you?"

"Her money paid for the test. She gets to decide what she does with the answers." Once again I itched to get my hands on the report. Renata may not need proof, but now I needed it more than ever.

"It's getting hot. Let's walk." Micah swung open his door and met me on my side of the pickup. Taking my hand, he led me along a well-worn path that wound along the stream under shaggy, shedding pines.

The breeze lifted damp strands from my sweaty forehead. I inhaled the mingled scents of trees, earth, and water. The path followed a steady incline, so neither of us spoke again until we came to a weathered stone bench where the path widened at the top of the hill. Winded from the climb, I brushed aside pine needles and bird droppings before I plopped down.

Micah paced in front of me, sweat sliding into his beard. Half-moons of wetness under each arm darkened his plaid shirt. "My life is turning out like some big cosmic joke. Every time I meet someone I think I could easily spend the rest of my life with, somehow, some *way*, Renata Pearl Channing manages to mess it up."

Spend the rest of his life with? *Don't go there, Julie Pearl, not yet.* I kicked at a rotting pinecone, and it disintegrated in a puff of brown dust. "You can't blame Renata for everything."

"So who should I blame?" He raised his hands skyward and gave an ugly laugh. "God?"

Just hearing him talk like that brought a strange quietness to my spirit and banished the crazies. "Sit down, Micah."

He stared at me.

"Sit down."

He did.

I stood and faced him, finger pointed like an exasperated schoolteacher. "You can't blame God for what goes wrong in your life. But you *can* believe that everything happens for a reason. Like my grandpa always taught me, nothing is hopeless. No matter how bad things look, something good can come out of it."

He slid to the other end of the bench. "You can't convince me anything good has, can, or ever will come out of what happened on the lake that day twenty-five years ago."

I folded my arms. "Then I guess you lied to me."

His head jerked up. "What?"

"You lied. About falling in love with me. Because love is a good thing, isn't it?"

"Yes, but—"

"And if I am Jenny Pearl, then if I'd really drowned, I wouldn't be standing here right now and we wouldn't be having this conversation. And you'd have gone right on hating yourself and Renata for the guilt you carried. So even though the truth has confused things between us, at least now you can close the chapter on the past and start writing a new one. You and Renata can both look at life with fresh eyes."

Micah drew both hands down his face. "And on the off chance you're not Jenny Pearl? What *good* can come out of that tragedy? In that case, I will still have let a little girl go to her death at the bottom of the lake."

ANGIE

October, 25 years earlier
Somewhere in West Texas

"Julie Pearl, don't you wander off now." Angie Stiles tilted a smile toward the elfin, wispy-haired toddler playing beneath the roadside picnic shelter. Her own voice clanged like a gong between her ears.

"Let the poor kid have a little fun." Ray popped the tab on another can of Coors. His Adam's apple bobbed as he guzzled half the can. He belched long and loud, a staccato, machine-gun sound. "You worry too much, Angie. Loosen up. Get a beer outta the cooler."

"I told you, beer only makes my headaches worse." Slowly, carefully, so as not to jostle her exploding brain, Angie stretched out on the concrete bench and rested her head on Ray's blue-jeaned thigh. On the underside of the metal roof above them, an ugly brown spider circled a wasp caught in its web. Angie watched the spider creep closer to its prey, then begin the slow, methodical process of weaving a cocoon around the struggling wasp.

I know just how you feel. Scared. Trapped. Looking into the jagged, venomous jaws of death.

Dying wouldn't be so bad, if she could only be sure Julie Pearl would be okay. But Ray had never wanted the child, not like Angie hoped. She moved her head slightly—paying the price with a stab of pain—and found herself staring through Ray's shaggy yellow moustache into dark, cavernous nostrils. Not a pretty sight.

He wore his tangled mass of sun-bleached hair in a low ponytail that hung halfway down his back. And he had that look in his eye, the one that said he was ready to take off again. Her worsening headaches had put a damper on the fun they used to have, cruising in Ray's rusty yellow Chevy Nova with the windows down and the stereo blasting, jaunting across the U.S. from one trashed-out campground to the next.

Angie's favorite was still the little tree-covered island near Hot Springs. Even more so because that's where her sweet baby Julie Pearl had come into her life. The first time she thought she might be pregnant, Ray had been furious. "No way, Angie! I ain't havin' no kid around. They're dirty and whiny, and they gotta be fed on time. Next you'll be hounding me to get sober and toss out my weed."

"I promise, Ray, I won't let the baby be any trouble. Don't make me get rid of it. Please!"

Her tears had softened him, but not on one issue. "Okay, okay, keep the brat if you want to. But if this is your plan for getting me in front of a justice of the peace, forget it. I told you when we hooked up, I ain't about to get conned into marriage. Not by you, not by any woman."

Then he had left, stranding Angie in Yellowstone Park until she hitched a ride south with a trucker who kept wanting to touch her in places she didn't want to be touched. She'd been wandering the streets of Phoenix, high on marijuana, when she realized something was wrong. Three days later, she woke up in a hospital charity ward, where a beleaguered intern coldly told her she'd miscarried.

Brokenhearted and alone, she'd found work at a local diner. She stayed only long enough to earn the price of a bus ticket to Arkansas, where she headed straight back to the island in hopes of finding Ray there. He showed up three weeks later with a tattooed redhead hanging on his arm.

"Angie, my woman, you're lookin' mighty fine! Hey, you didn't have the kid already?"

She shot the redhead a suspicious glare. "Something went wrong. I lost it a couple months ago."

No sympathy, no comfort, just a guttural laugh. "Well, then, you and me got some catchin' up to do. Angie, meet Donna. Now you two don't fight over me. There's enough man here for both of you."

But Donna wasn't interested in sharing, so she hadn't lasted long. Pretty soon it was just Angie and Ray again, back to their rootless, laid-back lifestyle. She wanted it to be enough, but it never was. And she wondered often, as she lay in the crook of Ray's arm under the starry Arkansas sky, exactly how she'd gotten to this point.

To this aloneness. This estrangement from everything she used to take for granted. Mom. Dad. The daily routine at the Swap & Shop. Her dull, boring, wasted life in Caddo Pines.

Or at least that's how she used to think of it. How could she ever imagine she'd find anything better beyond the Caddo Pines city limits sign? How could she turn her back on the genuine love of family and friends for . . . *this?*

Now, after all she'd done, how could she ever go back?

For two years after the miscarriage, Angie had endured Ray's mercurial moods, his drug- and liquor-induced highs, his frequent absences.

And then Julie Pearl came along and changed everything.

34

JULIE PEARL

Present Day

One week later, at precisely 5:02 p.m., I watched Renata release a heavy sigh as she flipped over the CLOSED sign on the front door of the Swap & Shop. She turned to me, her nose in the air. "That's it, Julie. Two weeks, as promised. I'm going upstairs for a long, hot bath. Then we need to talk."

Not that we hadn't talked over the past two weeks, but as usual, our conversations always had more to do with Renata than me. And—as usual—the glimpses she gave me into herself rarely went beyond the superficial. If not for my own observations, combined with insights gleaned from Micah and Aunt Geneva, my sister would have remained little more than a casual acquaintance.

An acquaintance I'd never in a million years ever keep as a friend.

On the positive side, after learning I'd started seeing Micah again, Renata had relentlessly assured me there'd never been anything more than friendship between them. For the most part I believed her, and I fully believed Micah had done his part to keep

251

everything platonic. But I couldn't shake my convictions that she'd always wanted it to be more, and still would, if only Micah had shown the slightest interest.

Sibling rivalry? The bizarre connection between me and Renata had shifted the concept into a whole new dimension.

After closing out the cash register and tallying a deposit to take to the bank in the morning, I gathered up the puppy basket—getting heavier every day—and trudged upstairs, Brynna and Sneezy at my heels. The squirming pups wrestled and play-growled at each other, making the box even more unwieldy. I couldn't help but laugh at their clumsy antics. "It's almost time to find homes for these guys," I told Brynna over my shoulder.

And then I burst out crying. I sank to the landing outside the apartment door, puppy basket propped on my knees, and sobbed as if I were losing my best friends. One by one, I held each warm, furry body against my tear-streaked cheek, inhaling those sweet, milky puppy smells. Brynna whimpered and stared at me, head tilting one way and then the other. I was glad Clifton and Grandpa had left to deliver an antique table to a customer, so they weren't here to witness my sentimental breakdown.

"Oh, Julie Pearl, you are a case." I wiped the back of my hand across my wet face. This wasn't the first batch of puppies I knew I'd have to say good-bye to, and though I always got a little sad watching littermates move on to their new homes, I'd never reacted quite this irrationally before.

It had to be Micah. We hadn't really settled anything last Sunday, except to agree to continue exploring where a relationship between us might go. But he still kept a part of himself closed off from me, the part that stubbornly refused forgiveness for a childhood mistake.

Snarling his impatience, Sneezy sidled past me and paced on the landing. With a warbling meow, he stretched his forelegs up and batted the doorknob.

"Suppertime, I know." I clambered to my feet and opened the

door, careful to watch my balance as Sneezy and Brynna rushed into the kitchen ahead of me.

A gasp alerted me to Renata, who stood behind a pile of luggage beside the kitchen table. I skimmed past my usual annoyance at her chronic anxiety around the dog and dove straight into my surprise at seeing her packed and ready to leave.

I set the puppy basket down next to the door. "Wow, when you said your two weeks were up, you meant it literally."

"It's been an interesting experience, I'll give you that. But I must attend to pressing matters back in Little Rock, things that require much more attention than I can manage over the phone." She checked her diamond-studded Rolex. "I know it doesn't allow much time for good-byes, but Martin will be here at six with the car."

"So that's it? I thought you wanted to talk."

She cocked her head with a questioning look that reminded me of Brynna. "I meant we could talk on the way to Little Rock."

"On the way—" I staggered like she'd punched me in the gut. Queen Renata had taken it for granted I'd be returning with her to Channing Castle.

"If you want to shower first, you'd better hurry. I laid out one of my sundresses for you. I think it should fit all right." She pulled her cell phone from the front pocket of her handbag. "It was just plain thoughtless of me not to bring along a few of those nice outfits we bought you. I was simply too rattled by your suggestion —or maybe I should call it your *ultimatum*—that I spend two weeks working in a flea market."

Too stunned to speak, I sank into the nearest chair and watched as she thumbed some buttons on her phone, then informed her chauffeur we might need a little more time.

Two weeks. Two wasted weeks of trying to get beneath Renata's high-society façade. Now that her tour of duty was up, seemed she couldn't get out of here fast enough.

She tucked the cell phone into her purse. Noticing I hadn't

budged, she shot me a frown. "What are you waiting for, Julie? Don't you want to freshen up before we leave?"

I leaned back in the chair and stretched out my legs in a wide angle. Toying with the hem of my tie-dyed T-shirt, I glared at her. "How'd you ever get so manipulative, Renata? Does it just come naturally?"

Her eyes widened, and for a split second she appeared genuinely hurt. Then her gaze turned steely. "Control is everything. Someday you'll learn it for yourself."

"I hope you're wrong." My palm smacked the tabletop, the explosive sound sending both Brynna and Sneezy cowering behind the sofa. "Because I'd never want to live in a world where everything I got came at someone else's expense. Where the rule is to do unto others *before* they do it to you. That's the total opposite of what my grandpa raised me to believe, what everything in me tells me is right."

"Jenny, Jenny, how can you be so naïve?" Renata turned away, one hand pressed to her forehead, the other resting on her cocked hip. "You're pretty good at the manipulation game, yourself, in case you hadn't noticed."

I was too incensed by her accusation to take much notice of the fact that she'd called me Jenny. I rose in a huff. "What are you talking about?"

"Oh, please." She angled a contemptuous smile in my direction. "I concede the importance of my seeing firsthand the life you've led up until now, the sacrifices you had to make because of your upbringing. But don't try to convince me you didn't have ulterior motives. Admit it, you enjoyed watching me endure such awful drudgery again."

"*Enjoy?* No!" I stepped toward her, hands extended. "What I hoped more than anything was that you'd rediscover something of who you really are. Rennie Pearl, from Hot Springs. The girl who used to hope and dream and . . . love."

Her jaw trembled. Her mouth twisted into something hideous.

"Rennie Pearl doesn't exist anymore. And whatever hopes and dreams she may have had are at the bottom of Lake Hamilton with—"

The slamming of a car door interrupted her. She hurried to the door and peered out the glass. "Martin is here," she said without looking at me. "I assume I'll be returning alone?"

In two long strides I was at her side. I seized her elbow. "Finish what you were saying. At the bottom of Lake Hamilton with Jenny, is that it? Renata, have you looked at the DNA results?"

"I told you, I don't need to. I meant—" Shaking off my grip, she closed her eyes in silent despair. Martin appeared on the other side of the door and tapped softly. She drew in a rasping breath and reached for the knob. "Come in, Martin. My bags are over there."

I had no choice but to back away and allow the chauffeur inside. Renata held the door as he hefted her luggage and started downstairs. When he was out of earshot, she slid her gaze toward me, and a strange, mad smile curved her lips. "You're my sister, Jenny. Nothing will ever change that. *Nothing.*"

Before I could blink twice, she'd closed the space between us and wrapped her arms around me. I stood stiff as a two-by-four as she planted a kiss on my cheek and whispered sweetly in my ear, "Do come for a visit soon, dear. Your room will always be ready."

A moment later she was gone.

"I think she's crazy. I honestly think she's certifiably insane."

It was Tuesday, and Sandy asked me to meet her for lunch at Applebee's in Hot Springs. She sliced off a bite of her crispy battered fish and swirled it through tartar sauce. "Then you're lucky she's gone. I suspected it from the start, Julie. And Micah warned you too. The woman is nothing but trouble."

"I know, but . . ." I pushed my practically untouched hamburger away and stared through the front window as noontime traffic crept along Central Avenue. "If she really is my sister, I owe it to her to try to help somehow." The memory of all those pills on the bathroom counter brought a twinge to my belly. I still wrestled with unspoken fears that if both Renata and our mother suffered from mental illness, I might someday be in the market for a straightjacket myself.

"Key word—*if* she's your sister. And even if it's true, you can't help someone who doesn't want to be helped. Renata Channing may be too far gone even for someone as persistent as you. Face it, Julie. She isn't another one of your strays that you can win over with patience and affection."

Our waitress came over with a pitcher of iced tea. "Can I get y'all anything else? Dessert? Coffee?"

"I'll have a brownie and ice cream." Sandy took a gulp of iced tea. "And some decaf, please."

"Nothing for me, thanks." As the waitress sauntered away, I grinned at Sandy and shook my head. "Only someone with your metabolism could get away with fried fish and a brownie a là mode in the same meal."

Sandy polished off the last of her fries. "Couldn't keep eating like this if Micah didn't have me hopping around all day like a jackrabbit on steroids."

Even though Micah and I had been spending more time together, we seemed to have reached a tacit agreement not to discuss Renata or anything connected with the past, so I'd avoided asking where things stood with the resort. I twirled the straw in my iced tea glass. "What's he got keeping you so busy?"

"Are you kidding? I've been running redrawn plans and documents back and forth to city hall, contractors, architects, you name it."

"Redrawn—? I don't understand."

She shot me a wide-eyed stare. "You really don't know?"

I crossed my arms, irritation lacing my tone. "If I did, would I be asking?"

"Let's see." Looking toward the ceiling, Sandy tapped her jaw with her index finger. When she met my gaze again, her reply dripped with sarcasm. "Only *completely* revising every plan he'd ever made for the resort."

Something told me I should be worried. *Very* worried. "Revising how, exactly?"

Chewing her lip, Sandy studied me as if she couldn't quite decide how to answer. Finally she said, "If Micah hasn't told you, I'm not sure it's my place to say. You should hear it from him."

"But you're my best friend." I reached across the table and grabbed her wrist. "Sandy, please!"

"I'm sorry, Jules. I love you, but I value my job too much." Her apologetic frown only went so far in soothing my extremely ruffled feathers.

I ground my teeth. "Then at least tell me when this all started."

She dropped her gaze. "Exactly one week ago yesterday."

One week ago yesterday. The day after Micah had admitted his feelings for me.

Micah Hobart, what in heaven's name are you up to?

I snagged my purse and shoved out of the booth. "Are you finished? Let's go."

After dropping Sandy at the La Quinta, I drove straight to the old resort. I'd had enough of Micah's secrets, and if he didn't care to fill me in on his change of plans, I'd have to see it for myself.

Only there wasn't much left to see. Beyond the chain-link construction fence, Micah's crews had leveled the cabins, bulldozed the cracked driveway into a pile of concrete rubble, ripped out tree stumps, and planted surveyor's flags in a hodgepodge pattern only an expert could interpret. The only original building still standing was the main house, but with the rotted porches torn away and the windows boarded up, it gaped like a toothless monster.

A temporary access road had been carved along the south side of the house. Down the hill where the road branched off to the boat dock, I spotted Micah's pickup. He stood on the dock with another man in a yellow construction helmet, both of them poring over a fat wad of curling blueprints. I shuffled down the road, red dirt sifting through the weave of my huaraches. When I called Micah's name, he looked up, his initial surprise morphing into a boyish grin.

"Don't let me interrupt," I said with a wave. It took great effort to keep the irritation out of my voice. "Just thought I'd see what all you've done so far."

With a funny half-smile, Micah returned to his conversation, and I picked my way across the demolition debris until I was standing about where I thought the cabin used to be where we'd found Brynna. A sadness crept into my heart, like I was missing something I'd never really had the chance to know.

I felt Micah's hand on my shoulder. "Looks different, huh?"

"I hardly recognize the place. You've done a lot since the last time I was here." My gaze swept the back of the house, and I noticed the brick patio and retaining wall were gone, leaving a wide swath of bare ground. I released a shaky breath.

Micah drew me to his side. "I know it looks bad right now, but when we finish, it'll be like new." A strange light came into his eyes. "Like nothing ever changed."

"Like new?" I shot him a puzzled frown.

"Come with me, Julie. I've got something to show you." Taking my hand, Micah strode toward his pickup. He reached in the open driver's side window and pulled out a long cardboard tube. Uncapping one end, he withdrew a rolled drawing and spread it open across the hood of the pickup.

Looking past his shoulder, I studied the architect's full-color rendering of the completed resort. It looked nothing like the modern split-level condominium complex I'd seen in the drawings Micah had posted in the La Quinta suite.

It looked everything like how I'd pictured Pearls Along the Lake in its heyday, from the sky-blue gingerbread trim on the main house to the string of pristine white cabins marching along the shore.

And in the legend at the bottom right corner, instead of HAMILTON HAVEN, the artsy block lettering read PEARLS ALONG THE LAKE.

"Micah, it's beautiful." Prickles danced up my spine. I stared at him with puckered brows. "But . . . why?"

He leaned against the front grill of the pickup, tucking me under his arm as he gazed across the lake. "For you, Julie. To give you back what was stolen from you. And for me. Because I realized it's the only way I'll ever put the past to rest."

35

JULIE PEARL

Work continued on the resort through the rest of a long, sultry summer, and I visited often to check the progress. Micah seemed so proud of his work. He smiled more and laughed freely, as if some neglected garden deep inside him were springing to life. In mid-August he canceled the lease on his Hot Springs apartment and rented a small house with a fenced yard, then selected one of Brynna's puppies as his own. The other two also went to loving homes, I'm happy to say, one to my pastor's family and the other to the Swap & Shop's own Maddie Barton. (Maddie's five cats raised a protest, but I was told they adapted quickly.)

I sat next to Micah on his back stoop one evening enjoying the quietness, his company, and a few stolen kisses that made my lips tingle with the hunger for more.

Much more.

We drew apart from one such blissful moment to see Micah's puppy, aptly named Pepper because of the black-and-white flecks on his chin, chasing a grasshopper across the lawn. He tripped over his own big feet, tumbling like a roly-poly bug, and Micah and I both laughed out loud.

Then a shivery sigh shook me, and I reached for Micah's hand.

He squeezed back. "What are you thinking, Julie?"

"Oh, same as always."

"Renata?"

"Who else?" I propped one elbow on my knee and rested my chin in my hand. "I was just thinking it's a shame she'll never know the joy of loving on a puppy." I'd given about five minutes' consideration to driving one of the pups over to Little Rock and offering it to Renata. What better way to show her what a devoted companion a dog could be . . . and maybe breach the stone-cold wall she'd erected between us?

Except I figured the puppy and I both would get the same chilly reception.

Pepper got bored with the grasshopper and presented his belly for Micah to scratch. Micah willingly obliged. "Have you heard from Renata even once since she spent those two weeks at the Swap & Shop?"

"Believe me, I'd have told you if I had." The only word I'd gotten from her after she left was a big brown UPS truck pulling into our parking lot to deliver a large parcel addressed to me. Inside were the clothes I'd arrived with that first day, plus all the shoes and outfits she'd given me. Those items I'd promptly turned over to Dovie and Royce Buckles to be tagged for resale in their Glad Rags booth. I needed no reminders of my bizarre and thankfully short-lived stay in the lap of luxury.

Micah's jaw muscles worked beneath his beard. "It's for the best, her leaving you alone."

"I know, and I'm trying as hard as I can to put it behind me and move on." My shoulders sagged under a weight that only grew heavier, no matter how hard I tried to shrug it off. I leaned my head against Micah's arm. "You—us—it's the one good thing that's come out of this mess."

Pepper yipped and nibbled my bare toe. Laughing, I tickled him behind his ears. "And you and your mama dog, of course."

"Speaking of dogs . . ." Micah shifted so our knees were touching. A shy grin lit his face. "I've been working on a surprise. I hope you won't be mad that I went behind your back, but I didn't want to say anything until . . ."

"Micah?" I tilted my head to stare into the shadowy depths beneath his thick, dark brows.

He lowered his gaze, and his voice softened to barely above a whisper. "In the short time we've known each other, it's become pretty clear what's most important to you. Your grandpa. The Swap & Shop. All your friends in Caddo Pines." He glanced at me out of the corner of his eye and smirked. "And your pets, naturally."

His words made me smile deep down where all my best memories reside. I sat straight as a broomstick and tucked my hands into my lap. "You're leaving out one hugely important thing."

"Oh, yeah? What's that?"

"You."

Grinning, he pulled me into the crook under his arm and released a huff, his breath hot against my cheek. "Are you going to let me tell you my surprise or not?"

"Okay, okay. Tell me your surprise."

"Humph. If *that's* your attitude—"

"Micah!"

His raspy chuckle drained some of my crabbiness. "Okay, here goes. I've asked my architect to draw up some plans to remodel the Swap & Shop."

Not exactly the surprise I was imagining. My eyes got wide, and I pulled in a long breath through my nostrils. "Wow, that's really nice of you, Micah, but we can barely cover our expenses as it is. There's no extra money in the budget for remodeling."

"You don't understand. I want to do this for you."

"But you're already rebuilding the resort for me. I can't let you—"

"Now hear me out, okay? Instead of those flimsy plywood booth partitions, I'm thinking office-grade cubicles with adjustable shelving." He spoke with his hands, his eyes taking on a distant look. "And we can enlarge and modernize the apartment, add some conveniences to make life easier for your grandpa. I've seen how he huffs and puffs going up and down the stairs, so we'll put in an elevator shaft accessible from inside or out. Then maybe a deck and pergola out back, and a fenced yard where the pets can play . . . Julie?"

My mouth must be doing that fish thing again. There were a jillion things I wanted to say, but I couldn't seem to put two sensible words together.

Micah just laughed. "Is my Julie finally speechless?"

"No—yes—but why—?" While I tried to decide whether I should be thrilled or annoyed or downright terrified at having him move into my life in such a huge and tangible way, one teensy part of me got stuck on those two little words—*my Julie.*

"Because I love you, that's why."

"Oh, Micah, I love you, too!" For a while we just sat there, me clinging to his neck and trying to catch a full breath, Micah rubbing his hands up and down my back like he was trying to ward off chilblains. Which maybe he was, because I couldn't stop shaking. My eyes started welling up, so I pulled away before I soaked Micah's plaid button-down.

He lifted my chin with one finger and brushed away my tears. "So you'll let me go ahead with this?"

I shook my head. "I don't know, Micah. This is no small thing. And Grandpa—I can't even imagine his reaction."

"Maybe he'll finally understand how much I care about you, about everything and everyone who's important to you."

The alarm beeped on Micah's phone, signaling it was time to go in and check the frozen lasagna I'd put in the oven. I agreed to think on the idea, and Micah agreed to let me find the best time to spring the offer on Grandpa. The secret smile he gave me as we shared salad-tossing duties made me wonder if the Swap & Shop remodeling project was only one phase of a much larger renovation plan, one that would tie Micah and me together for the rest of our lives.

In the meantime, life at the flea market went on as usual—life so good I could hardly stand it sometimes. For now at least, Grandpa, Sneezy, and Brynna were the only family I needed or wanted. Micah and I, though growing closer day by day, were both still feeling our way through a maze of mixed-up emotions.

I did slowly introduce Grandpa to the idea of making some improvements to the Swap & Shop, mentioning just a change or two at a time so as not to overwhelm him. When I explained the ideas were Micah's and that he wanted to give it to us as a gift, Grandpa balked at first.

"Think of it this way, Grandpa," I suggested over our raisin bran one morning. "Just like the joy you get from finding new homes for castoffs, Micah will take great pleasure in breathing new life into this old building."

"Yes, but I'd feel so beholden to him. Seems an awful big investment of time and money for someone who ain't got no stake in the place."

I pushed a bran flake around the edge of my bowl. "I think maybe he'd like to have a huge stake in this place. If you'd let him, Grandpa."

One corner of his mouth pulled downward. He tugged on his earlobe. "Is that what you want, Julie Pearl?"

"I think it is."

A hurting place in my heart found healing as Grandpa moved nearer to accepting Micah as part of my life, part of *our* lives. And while love bloomed between me and Micah, I also took great joy in watching the deepening romance between Sandy and Clifton.

They did indeed seem like a match made in heaven. What Clifton lacked in polish and education, he more than made up for with his charm and wit, and Sandy had always brought out the best in Clifton in a way no one else ever had.

Sandy and my grandpa both, that is. The more Clifton learned about flea market operations, the more responsibility Grandpa gave him. Clifton's auto mechanic skills easily adapted to small appliance repair, which meant higher profits for the Swap & Shop when we could sell an oldie-but-goodie toaster or record player that actually worked.

Summer eased on into September. My twenty-eighth birthday snuck by with not much more fanfare than a dinner cruise aboard the *Belle of Hot Springs* with Micah. Afterward, we joined Grandpa, Sandy, and Clifton at the apartment, where we gorged ourselves on vanilla ice cream and the lopsided German chocolate cake Sandy baked especially for me.

My gift from Micah was the blueprints for the new and improved Swap & Shop, and when I unrolled the pages across the kitchen table, all I could do was stand and stare in awe. "Look, Grandpa, it's just like I told you. There's the elevator, and a fancy new snack bar, all those nifty cubicles for our vendors, and even a porch out back with a glider where you can watch the sunset."

Grandpa tucked his arm around my waist and squeezed. "It's the way I always pictured it, Julie Pearl. The way I'd've done it up years ago if I'd had the wherewithal." He looked across the table at Micah and gave a solemn nod. "This is a fine thing indeed, and I thank you."

I thumbed away a tear and let the laughter bubble up through my chest. "Yep, now the real fun begins—figuring out how to stay in business while all this work is carried out."

"Not to worry," Micah said. "We'll do it in stages, keep the dust and disruption to a minimum."

So it was that along about mid-September, the Swap & Shop began its transformation. As promised, the crews Micah hired tackled only two or three vendors' areas at a time, and always on a weekday when we were closed or weren't expecting much business. Installing the elevator was the biggest challenge, requiring us to give up a big chunk of storage space behind the front counter. But the tradeoff was well worth my peace of mind in knowing Grandpa could continue living and working here for as long as his dear old heart would allow.

At the end of a long, exhausting Tuesday in early October, when Grandpa, Clifton, and I had finally finished cleaning up and restocking after a horrendously busy weekend, I hauled myself out of the shower, pulled on a clean pair of jeans, and dragged in fifteen minutes late to our weekly young adult church gathering.

Pastor Ed, the only one over thirty-five in our group, looked up from his Bible as I sidled into an empty folding chair. "Glad you could make it, Julie Pearl. We've been talking about what the Bible says about wealth."

How apropos, considering how wealth had played into my confusing summer. I wasn't sure I wanted to go there again, but discussion continued, and I tried to contribute the occasional insightful tidbit. More often than not, though, my thoughts wandered into areas I'd tried too long to avoid. Like the fact that Micah seemed way too wrapped up in fixing my life. Apparently, recreating Pearls Along the Lake just like it used to be hadn't been enough—and whatever Micah did, he did in style. Both at the resort and at the Swap & Shop, he'd ordered top-of-the-line materials so everything would be perfect. He'd even ordered a glittery new Swap & Shop billboard for the highway turnoff and placed glitzy half-page ads in the Hot Springs and Little Rock newspapers announcing the "grand reopening of Hot Springs' most picturesque and enchanting lakeside resort" scheduled for late next spring.

It suddenly hit me. Micah's obsession wasn't about putting the past to rest, or the impossible idea of giving me back my lost childhood. It wasn't even about making life easier for Grandpa or boosting our flea market business. No, Micah's extravagant gifts were really about buying forgiveness, paying for his and Renata's mistake. I had to wonder what the going rate for a clear conscience amounted to these days. Would Micah ever be satisfied he'd spent enough?

I hung out at the close of the evening just long enough to nibble one of the chocolate-chip cookies one of my friends had brought, but my interest in socializing had vanished. Then Pastor Ed caught me on my way out. "Hey, Julie Pearl, when are you going to bring your gentleman friend along? Everyone here's really anxious to meet him."

Trapped. So far I'd sidestepped the issue of Micah's disdain for all things God-related. And though Sandy was all too aware of the fact, at least she'd been tactful enough to keep it to herself.

"Micah's just so busy with all his construction jobs." I tugged the strap of my shoulder bag up my arm and forced a laugh. "I bet he's out at the resort right now, burning the midnight oil."

Freckle-faced Everett Buckles ambled over. "Don't he know all work and no play ain't good for a body? Come on, Julie Pearl, us country bumpkins are just dyin' to rub elbows with your rich, successful beau."

The former class president and Arkansas State University grad wasn't fooling anybody with his fake hick talk. Assistant manager of Caddo Pines Bank & Trust, Everett was about as successful as anybody in our little community could ever hope to be.

"Give Julie a break," Sandy interrupted, stepping in to rescue me. "You think she'd honestly want to subject a nice guy like Micah to your backwoods brand of humor?"

Everett lifted his palms. "Didn't mean anything. Seriously, Julie Pearl, you know we look out for our own around here. I think I speak for all of us when I say we just want to make sure this Micah Hobart character is good enough for you."

"That's nice, Everett. I appreciate your concern."

Pastor Ed rested a hand on my shoulder. "He's right, Julie

Pearl. We're all your friends here. We all want what's best for you, and—" He stopped short of coming right out and saying it, but the look in his eyes told me he wasn't so sure my "best" included Micah.

They all knew by now that I might very well be Jennifer Susan Pearl, the little girl thought to have drowned all those years ago. Poor Grandpa had received a boatload of sympathy over the "loss" of his only granddaughter. He was always quick to explain, however, that he hadn't lost anything, that I'd be his own Julie Pearl for as long as he lived.

And I was just as quick to assure them all that Otto Stiles was dearer to me than any blood-kin grandfather could ever be.

So even though I knew how hard Grandpa worked to accept my growing feelings for Micah, I also knew Grandpa shared the unspoken concerns of my friends. The crux of the matter came down, finally, to just one thing: was Micah's relationship with me one of genuine love, or of guilt?

Sleep came hard that night. I felt like Jacob wrestling with the angel—knowing what was right, what I ought to do, and fighting it all the way.

I woke up the next morning with an achy hip and an answer I didn't want to face.

"Come to the young adult meeting with me tonight, Micah. Please. My friends are all asking to meet you."

We sat on the recently restored front porch at the resort, hip to hip in an oak swing that still smelled like fresh varnish. The chains made a rhythmic creaking sound, a soothing counterpoint to the ringing of hammer against nail as workmen labored to rebuild the cabins behind the house.

"Can't, Julie. I've got crews working overtime to get the cabins roofed before winter. We need to be ready to work on the interiors by the time the weather turns bad."

"But it's not like you have to oversee every detail. What's a couple of hours?"

He pushed out of the swing and stood at the porch railing, staring up through the crisp orange leaves of an ancient oak tree. "They're your friends, not mine. I don't think I'd fit in."

"They could be your friends, too, if you'd give them a chance." I moved to stand beside him, our hands brushing. "Or is it really you're afraid of how they'll see you—a man who can't stop living in the past?"

His cold, gray eyes met mine. "Is that how *you* see me?"

"I love you, Micah. More than I can say. You know I do!" My heart wrapped around itself until I could hardly catch a breath. "But until you can accept forgiveness—until you can forgive yourself—I'll never know for sure whether your feelings for me stem from love or guilt. And I—" Oh, God, this was hard! "I can't go on living like this."

A long, shuddering sigh tore from his throat. His fingers tightened around the porch rail. "So what are you trying to tell me? That it's over between us?"

I gazed at Micah's tanned, work-roughened hands, the hands of an artist and craftsman, a builder. Coarse, dark hairs curled above his callused knuckles. Wood stain outlined the blunt-trimmed nails of his long, strong fingers, the same fingers that so often lately had stroked my cheek, tucked a stray curl behind my ear, caressed the nape of my neck.

I would miss those hands, their tender touch. I would miss the warm, heady feeling of his lips on mine, our kisses hello and our kisses goodnight. I would miss Micah Hobart more than words could say.

"Yes, Micah, it's over." With a last lingering glance at the hands of the man I loved, I turned and walked away.

JULIE PEARL

Tears streaming down my face, I climbed into my VW and started the engine. My grip tightened around the gearshift knob, but I couldn't make myself release the clutch. Maybe I was waiting for Micah to miraculously experience a change of heart and come chasing after me.

But he just stood there staring, his silence a boulder crushing my heart. Finally I drove away, so blinded by tears that I could hardly see the road.

Reaching the highway, I turned toward downtown Hot Springs, just driving, driving, with no other goal than to lose myself in the city. I passed the Oaklawn racetrack, crawled through tourist traffic along Bathhouse Row, then took the turn onto Whittington Avenue just beyond the stately yellow Arlington Hotel and cruised past the Dryden Pottery building with its colorful murals. Spotting the sign for West Mountain, I made a quick left turn and wound my way up to the scenic overlook.

I yanked my keys from the ignition, slammed the door shut behind me, and jogged up the hiking trail, stopping only when the sharp pain of exertion knifed through my side. I sank onto a stone, sweat dripping from my forehead to mingle with the tears.

I stared upward through whispering pines at a crystal blue sky and asked the heavens how I'd ever ended up like this.

I never asked to fall in love with Micah. I never asked to be Jenny Pearl.

No, but you weren't content being Julie Stiles, either. You wanted answers about your past and you found them.

Not the response I wanted, but obviously the only one I could expect. With the October breeze whistling through the pines and chilling me through my fisherman's sweater, I heaved an exhausted sigh and trudged down the trail to the car.

On the way back through town, I felt an overwhelming urge to see Aunt Geneva. Crazy as things had become since last summer, I hadn't had another chance to visit with her since the day Renata took me to "officially" meet her, but I well remembered the calming influence she'd been, an island of objectivity in a churning sea of confusion.

After only a couple of wrong turns, I recognized the neighborhood Renata's chauffeur had driven us through, then the tree-shaded street, then the modest '50s-era white frame cottage. I parked in the slanting driveway, then plodded up the brick porch steps. Standing with both hands stuffed into my jeans pockets, I listened as the doorbell echoed through the house.

The door swung open, and Geneva's look of surprise quickly melted into one of joy and welcome. "Julie. Come in." She reached for my arm. "I've so wanted to talk to you again, but . . . Well, I heard how things ended between you and Renata, and I felt a bit awkward about getting in touch."

"Same here." I followed her down the hall to a small den at the back of the house. Outside the wide picture window, cardinals and blue jays vied for the best morsels at bird feeders hanging from a multilevel verdigris pole.

Geneva offered to make tea, but I shook my head and perched on the edge of a tweed armchair. "Maybe you knew I've been seeing Micah Hobart?"

She nodded.

"Well, I broke it off this morning."

Settling into the motion of a high-backed wooden rocker, Geneva smiled her understanding. "I'm so sorry, Julie. What happened?"

"I thought it would help him forgive himself, knowing Jenny didn't drown. I thought I could help Renata too. But I couldn't." A great bubble of agony swelled inside my chest. I rose and stalked to the window. "Now everything's so much *worse*. I wish I'd never heard of Jennifer Susan Pearl, or Pearls Along the Lake, or Renata Channing . . ." My voice flattened to a whisper. "Or Micah Hobart."

Soft footsteps padded behind me. With gentle hands, Geneva turned me to face her, and I stared into sympathetic eyes beneath a cloud of soft, golden-brown curls. She shook her head. "My, my, you've taken an awful lot of responsibility onto these slim shoulders. Do you really think God has left it up to you to do what only He can do?"

I drew my eyebrows together in an unspoken question.

Geneva slid her hands down my arms until she clasped both my hands in hers. "It doesn't matter if you're Jenny Pearl, or Julie Stiles, or the Queen of Sheba," she said with a laugh. "Micah's and Renata's pain is their own, and their healing is between them and God. There's nothing you or I or anyone else can do to make it happen." Her lips skewed into a troubled frown. "Much as we wish we could."

A commotion outside the window drew our attention. Neither of us could suppress our laughter as an angry jay dive-bombed a squirrel dangling by its toenails from the highest bird feeder. The squirrel finally dropped to the ground and darted up a tree, while the jay cackled in derision.

Geneva hooked her arm through mine and squeezed. "Do you think that squirrel's going to give up on those tasty sunflower seeds just because a noisy old bird chased him off?"

Even as I shook my head, the squirrel scampered partway down the tree trunk and made a flying leap to the top of the nearest feeder. Birds scattered and sunflower seeds tumbled over the lip and onto the ground. The squirrel made another leap and munched on the fallen seeds while practically grinning in triumph at the birds.

"What did I tell you?" Geneva chuckled as we returned to our chairs. "As the old saying goes, where there's a will, there's a way."

"But you just said it wasn't up to me to help Renata and Micah."

"It isn't." She quirked a brow. "Was that squirrel looking to help anybody but himself? No. He was just being the creature he was created to be and taking advantage of the banquet I set out."

"That sounds so selfish."

"There's nothing selfish about being who you were meant to be." She rocked slowly, deliberately, pushing with the toe of one foot. "The point is you need to accept *who* you are and *where* you are in the life you've been given, and do the same for Micah and Renata. Allow them room to come to healing in their own good time."

"I know you're right." I closed my eyes and whooshed out a sigh. "Okay, I'll try."

Then my eyes popped open, and I nailed Geneva with a desperate gaze. "There's just one problem. I *still* don't know for sure if I'm Jenny."

Two hours later, after a lunch of homemade seafood gumbo and cornbread, I left Geneva's with a shoebox full of old photographs she'd culled from her scrapbooks and albums. "Take your time going through those," she told me as I laid the box on the floor of the VW. She leaned in the open door to give me a hug. "If you have any questions, call or come over. You're always welcome."

I wasn't sure what I expected to glean from a bunch of pictures of people I didn't know. Notice more family resemblances? Get a glimpse into the family that might have been mine if things had turned out differently? At home later, with the bedroom door closed and the photos fanned out across my chenille spread, I studied them, gazing into each face as if the flat, faded images could speak to me.

Unlike my own stash of photos, unorganized and unlabeled, Geneva's collection had been carefully notated, names and dates penned neatly on the backs. I came across shots of the Pearl family at Renata's various birthday parties, at Jenny's dedication ceremony, at Christmases and Thanksgivings and school programs. There were grandparents, aunts, uncles, and cousins of all ages. A few looked a little like me—tall, fair, curly-haired.

And equally as many did not.

At the bottom of the shoebox I found one of those fold-out photographer's displays, the kind containing several different poses from one sitting. The subject was Jennifer Susan Pearl, age eighteen months, according to a penciled caption on the back flap. I sat on the edge of the bed, letting the lamp on my nightstand illuminate the photos as I spread the folder open. A dainty toddler in a pink checked dress sat cross-legged on a fuzzy white rug. She wore a fluffy bow in her golden hair, and her jade-green eyes glimmered under the studio lights.

I ran my finger along the edge of the first portrait, and a smile crept across my lips. Was I looking into my own face from over twenty-six years ago?

Brynna stirred from her nap on the braided rug and gave a whimper. A second later a *tap-tap* sounded on my door, then Grandpa's voice. "Julie Pearl? You up?"

"Come in, Grandpa."

He ambled into the room, thumbs hooked in his belt. His gaze swept across the bed. "This what Miz Nelson sent home with you?"

I pushed the photos into a pile and invited him to sit beside me. "Look here, Grandpa." I stretched out the folder across both our laps. "Can you see anything of me in these pictures?"

He tilted his head up and down, getting the best angle on his bifocals, then rubbed his chin. "Got your eyes and dimples, that's for sure. But I don't know. Somethin' just don't seem right."

Pressing my lips together, I looked closer at the little girl in the portraits, examining each minute feature until my gaze settled on Jenny's fine, straight hair.

Then I saw what Grandpa saw. And I knew.

RENATA

March, 26 years earlier
Hot Springs, Arkansas

"Jennifer Susan Pearl! Hold still, for pity's sake. Rennie, can't you help at all, you lazy girl?"

"I'm trying, Mama, I'm—*ouch!*" Four sharp baby teeth clamped down on Rennie's finger. She yanked her hand back. The toddler clapped her hands and giggled.

Mama eyed Rennie in the dresser mirror as she spoke over a mouthful of bobby pins. "Oh, she didn't hurt you. Now keep her hands down or I'll never get all these pin curls done. You want your baby sister to look pretty for her portrait, don't you?"

Rennie sucked in a sharp breath and wrapped her arms around the squirming child. "Sit still, sweetie. Please won't you, for your big sister?"

Jenny would look just as pretty without the Shirley Temple ringlets Mama insisted upon, but try telling Mama that. A shudder crawled up Rennie's spine as she recalled the semiannual torture her mother used to put her through—her hair pulled taut around tiny permanent rods, ammonia solution stinging her scalp and sliding into her eyes. Then the stiff brush slashing through knots of frizzy curls. Those were actually the good days, compared to Mama's harrumph of displeasure when the process went wrong and Rennie ended up with a random mass of limp waves. She'd thanked her lucky stars when Mama finally gave up on the permanents and settled for chopping off Rennie's hair pixie-style.

"Ow, ow, ow!" Jenny wriggled one arm free of Rennie's grasp and slapped at her mother's hand. A bobby pin skittered across the floor.

Mama staggered back, arms beating the air like the wings of an angry vulture. "I give up, I just give up!" With a choked sob, she mumbled something about needing her "nerve pills" and stumbled from the room.

"Hurt me, hurt me." Jenny tugged at the two messy pin curls Mama had managed to complete.

"Here, honey, let me." Rennie turned the toddler's chair to face the mirror and gently slipped out the pins. Taking the brush, she smoothed the silky, stick-straight strands off Jenny's temples and then fastened them with a lacy white bow at the crown.

Jenny reached up to hug Rennie's neck. "Aw pwetty."

"Yes, all pretty." Rennie smiled over her sister's head at their reflection in the mirror. She fingered the baby-fine locks and prayed her mother would leave them be awhile longer.

JULIE PEARL

Present Day

I knew it was late, but I had to call anyway. An unfamiliar voice answered Renata's private phone number. I hesitated. "Felicia?"

"Ms. Beaufort is no longer employed here. This is Alice Fitzhugh. May I ask who is calling, please?"

Just like I'd thought, Felicia's days at Channing Castle were numbered. "This is Julie Stiles. I need to speak with Renata."

Renata's new watchdog (and no doubt Larry's latest distraction) tried to give me the runaround, but I wasn't having it. "Just tell her who this is. Tell her it's important. Tell her I *know*."

Alice's tone became suspicious. "I beg your pardon?"

"She'll understand, believe me." I drummed my fingers on the cool surface of the kitchen table. "Go on, get her. I'll wait."

Without so much as a thank-you-ma'am, the line went dead, and I could only hope she'd put me on hold. I watched the seconds tick by on the chrome-framed stove clock.

Exactly three minutes and forty-eight seconds later, Renata

picked up. "What do you want, Julie?" Her voice rang cold, impatient, bitter.

I'd promised myself I'd remain calm and controlled, but the first words out of my mouth cracked on a stifled sob. "You knew. All this time, you *knew* I wasn't Jenny. *Why?* Why did you lead me on like you did? Me and everyone else?"

She didn't reply right away, but I could hear her measured breathing. I clenched one fist, my eyes squeezed shut, as Grandpa stood behind me patting my shoulders.

"What difference does it make?" she finally blurted. "You got a new wardrobe out of the deal, didn't you? And a rich, handsome boyfriend, to boot."

"So what was I, just another of your rescued orphans? Another deprived little girl you could play dress-up with? Charm with your elegant mansion and fancy parties?"

"You could have had it all, Jenny, everything I own—"

My fist hammered the wall. "It's *Julie*. Julie Pearl Stiles. I am not your sister, never was, never will be. You need help, Renata. Serious psychiatric help. I hope you get it." I took two strides across the kitchen and slammed the receiver onto the hook. My hand remained on the phone, my whole body trembling.

Grandpa wrapped me in his arms. "Come on now, Julie Pearl, it's over. It's gonna be okay." He led me to the sofa, and I rested my head in the hollow of his shoulder. The fuzzy warmth of his plaid flannel shirt caressed my damp cheek. "I think we should say a prayer for her," he whispered against my hair.

"I don't think I can pray for Renata right now. I'm too angry."

"All the more reason." He wove the fingers of his free hand through mine. "Oh Lord, finder of lost souls, You alone know what's in the heart of Renata Channing. Help her come to grips with her boatload of pain and regrets. And help my Julie Pearl to let go of her anger and to forgive this woman for the hurt she has inflicted, intentionally or otherwise."

With Grandpa's whispered "Amen," a small measure of peace

settled over me. I knew in my heart that what Geneva had told me earlier today was right. It wasn't up to me—it had *never* been up to me—to "save" Renata and Micah from their childhood mistake.

But that didn't stop me from questioning why. Why let me believe I was Jenny Pearl? Why lead me down this rabbit trail of lies, deception, and broken hearts? What role had I been meant to play in the lives of two people I'd otherwise never have met?

Those were my last troubled thoughts as I crawled beneath the blankets and snuggled into my pillow, Sneezy kneading my arm through the covers and Brynna snoring in her doggy basket beside the bed.

So when Grandpa jostled me awake in the darkest part of the night, it took me a full minute to shake off the grogginess and make sense of what he was saying.

"Julie Pearl, you gotta wake up, girl." He flicked on the bedside lamp.

I flinched and covered my eyes. Peering through my fingers, I glimpsed his bent form clad in striped pajamas. "What's going on? What time is it?"

He threw the covers off me, then pulled me up with one hand while tossing my robe around my shoulders with the other. "Miz Nelson is on the phone. Hurry up. She sounds real scared."

"Aunt Geneva?" Fumbling to stuff my arms into the sleeves of the robe, I groped toward the kitchen, where the overhead light glared against the blackness outside the windows. The phone receiver lay on the counter. Still in a daze, I reached for it. "Hello?"

"Oh, Julie—I can't—" Her words came out in choked sobs, and I could barely understand her. "Please help!"

My skin prickled. I came instantly alert. "Aunt Geneva, where are you? What's going on?"

"It's Renata. I'm afraid she's—oh, Julie, we have to stop her!"

I gripped the receiver with both hands. "Please, slow down and tell me what's happening. Is Renata with you now?"

"No." She sniffled hard and long, and then a ragged breath

shuddered out. "I don't know where she is, but she telephoned me a few minutes ago and I'm afraid—" Geneva's voice broke. "God help us, Julie, I'm afraid she's going to do something terrible." Her next words came out in a hoarse whisper, as if even speaking the thought aloud could make it come true. "I think she intends to kill herself."

The stone-cold grip of fear tightened around my chest. I could hear my own shallow breaths rasping in and out. Shooting Grandpa a desperate stare, I tried to focus, tried to think what to do. His comforting pat on my shoulder reassured me but did little to steady my screaming nerves.

"Okay," I said, forcing a calm I didn't feel, "the first thing we have to do is figure out where Renata is. Did you try to reach Larry?"

"Larry is away on business." The harshness in Geneva's tone left no doubt about her feelings toward the man.

"Then how about her personal assistant?" What was her name —Anita, Alexis? For Pete's sake, I'd just spoken to the woman a few hours ago.

Sudden sick remorse nearly doubled me over. *This was my fault!* My stupid, selfish, ill-timed phone call earlier, chewing out Renata for her deception—had I pushed her over the edge?

I collapsed into a chair, one hand covering my eyes, barely aware I'd dropped the phone. Grandpa rescued it, and when I heard Geneva's tinny voice calling my name, I dredged up the fortitude to reach for the receiver and press it to my ear. There'd be time later for self-recrimination—maybe more than I bargained for if we didn't find Renata soon. "I'm here, Aunt Geneva. What were you saying?"

"I said I've already talked to Alice." Alice Fitzhugh, the personal assistant whose name I'd so conveniently forgotten. "She's worried, too. She told me Renata hasn't been herself at all lately and became extremely depressed after she took a phone call sometime yesterday."

Another tsunami of guilt swamped me.

"Then around nine p.m. she sent for her car and left without telling anyone where she was going. Alice said she thought Renata had been drinking. She didn't want to let her leave like that, but Renata wouldn't be stopped." Geneva whimpered softly. "Julie, she could be anywhere! She might already be—"

"We don't know that. We just have to find—" Instantly, I knew exactly where Renata had gone. I surged to my feet. "I'm hanging up now, Aunt Geneva. I'll call you back as soon as I know something."

Slamming the phone on the hook, I spun around, almost colliding with Grandpa.

He grabbed me by the arms. "Slow down, Julie Pearl. It's the middle of the night. What're you plannin' to do?"

"I have to stop Renata. She's at the resort, I just know it." I ripped out of his grasp and raced to the bedroom. In seconds I was out of my pajamas and yanking on yesterday's jeans and sweater. I fumbled under the bed for my brown suede Birkenstocks and jammed bare feet into them while grabbing my shoulder bag and car keys.

Grandpa planted himself in the doorway. "Julie Pearl, it's foolishness to rush out like this. Even if you do find her out there at them cabins, you can't mess with a crazy woman. What if she has a gun? Call the police. Let them handle it."

"She called Aunt Geneva for a reason, a cry for help. If I can get to her in time, I think she'll listen to me—if it's not too late already." I gave him a quick hug that also served to shift him to one side. "I have to do this. Don't worry, it'll be okay."

My headlights ricocheted off wisps of fog as I sped along the winding back road toward the resort. As I steered into a sharp curve, what looked like a raccoon scurried across the pavement into the woods, and I slammed on the brakes. The VW careened onto the shoulder, tires spinning and clutching at gravel, but the near-miss served to jolt some sense back into my frazzled brain. Continuing with more caution, I rounded the final bend before arriving at Pearls Along the Lake.

When I pulled into the circle drive in front of the main house, I glimpsed an amber glow in an upstairs window. Then I recognized Renata's Mercedes parked at a haphazard angle, rear wheels on the driveway and front wheels sinking into Micah's recently sodded lawn. My suspicions confirmed, I whooshed out a grateful breath. If Renata did intend to take her own life, she'd do it right here, where all this craziness began.

Shutting off the engine, I climbed from the car and stood there for a moment leaning on the open door. My insides quivered like a pan of cold gravy as I imagined what I might find inside the house. Maybe Grandpa was right and we should have just called the police. What if it was already too late?

And it was only getting later with every second that passed. Praying for strength, I started for the front door. Then as an afterthought, I doubled back and snatched my cell phone from my purse. I did promise Aunt Geneva I'd call as soon as I had some answers.

Heaven forbid I'd need to call an ambulance. Or worse.

Phone tucked into my jeans pocket and hugging myself against the damp chill, I tiptoed up the porch steps. Easing open the screen door, I thumbed the big brass door latch and felt the bolt slide open. Quietly I slipped inside, my eyes straining against the darkness shrouding the lobby. I passed through a doorway to where a staircase rose to the second story. Pale light crept across the landing. I stood silent, listening for any sound from above.

Then I heard it, a soft, childlike mewling. "I didn't mean anything to happen to her, Mama. I swear it was an accident, Mama. Please-please-please don't hate me!"

My eyelids fluttered closed, relief draining a measure of

tension from my limbs. Renata was alive. I still had time to help her.

But even as I crept up the stairs, heart thudding in my chest, I wondered what I could possibly say to the woman who'd destroyed so many lives—including her own. *Renata, you're a total screw-up, but don't kill yourself, okay? There's always hope.*

Reaching the landing, I edged toward the patch of light in the doorway to my left. One hand braced against the wall, I peered around the doorframe. Renata sat cross-legged with her back to me in the center of the empty room. She looked to be wearing one of those modish, psychedelic-print caftans from the '70s, and her beautiful mahogany mane was gone. Hunks of it lay strewn all around her, a pair of long-bladed scissors nearby. The vicious hack job she'd done on her hair brought a muted cry to my throat.

Keening softly, Renata hunched over, and I saw she was meticulously lining up a row of tiny pills along a seam in the hardwood floor. Amidst the scattered tresses, three empty pill vials rolled on their sides, and I could only wonder how many—and what kind—she might already have taken.

My cell phone suddenly belted out "Call Me Maybe," and I nearly clawed a hole in the plaster. While I fumbled to silence the annoying ring tone, Renata whirled around to stare at me in numb surprise. "Jenny?"

"Hey, Renata," One hand extended in a calming gesture, I sidled into the room. "I'm here now. Everything's gonna be okay."

"Yes, it will be. After tonight." She nodded solemnly and picked up a pill. Pinching it between her thumb and index finger, she lifted it toward the ceiling light and studied it. "I like the yellow ones best," she said before popping it into her mouth.

I lunged forward then caught myself when she recoiled. "Renata," I said, forcing a shaky smile, "can we just talk for a bit? How about I come over there and sit beside you?"

She picked up another pill, and my heart rolled over with a thud.

"Don't, Renata. Please don't." I kicked off my Birkies and dropped to my knees. The cold, bare wood against my toes made me shiver.

"This is my room. Mama hardly ever comes up here, so we're safe." Her gaze swept the bare walls before she cast me a conspiratorial grin. "I sneak into Mama's room sometimes and look at her jewelry and clothes and stuff. This is her dress. Don't tell her I borrowed it."

I could see now that the caftan was old and faded. "It's . . . very pretty."

Renata's lips quivered. "She died right downstairs, you know. Took a whole bunch of pills and just drifted off to sleep." Tears coursed down her blotchy, mascara-streaked face. "They're all gone now. Mama, Daddy . . . Oh, Jenny, I can't go on like this!"

"You can, Renata. You have to." I crept closer, talking softly, coaxing gently, just like I'd done last summer the day I'd rescued Brynna. Renata's eyes held that same wild, worried look, and I had the sick sense it would take a lot more than sweet words and patience to talk her down from this suicidal cliff.

She swallowed another pill, a pink one this time.

I was close enough now to reach one of the prescription bottles. "How about we gather up those little pills and put them away? You don't need them *all*, do you?"

"I do. The doctor told me I do." Three more found their way into her mouth before I could stop her. "Because I'm just like Mama, you know. I'm sick, and so very tired—"

Headlights swept the front of the house. Car doors slammed, then the front door creaked open. Shooting me a look of panic, Renata scrambled onto her knees and began scraping pills into her hand. But they got tangled in the tufts of clipped hair, and she let out a frustrated moan.

"Julie, where are you?" Micah's voice.

Renata's head jerked up, and for a moment she looked fourteen years old again, a teenager with a massive crush. Then, as she clambered to her feet, her face crumpled into a mask of grief. "What have we done, Micah? *What have we done?* Oh, Jenny, my Jenny!"

More voices below, someone ordering Micah to stay downstairs. Red and blue strobes carved across the front windows. Then someone quietly called to me from the hallway. "Miss, are you all right?"

"I'm okay." I stood slowly, hearing the shakiness in my own voice. "But she's taken a lot of pills. I don't know what kind."

"You won't stop me!" With a feral-sounding cry, Renata spun away from me. Arms waving, caftan sleeves billowing, she plunged toward the window, and I knew if I didn't stop her, she'd smash through the glass.

"No!" Scrambling after her, I caught her around the waist and held on tight. "Please, Renata, let me help you. Don't do this!"

She struggled against me, her mournful wail a terrifying sound. "Let me go, Jenny. Just let me go."

"I can't, Renata. I won't!"

In her struggle to break free, her elbow rammed into the window, shattering the glass. Hitting the window screen, the shards bounced off and littered the floor all around us. I yelped when a piece of glass sliced through my bare foot. Renata slipped from my grasp, and I stumbled backward.

Strong arms caught me and eased me to the floor. I looked up to see a uniformed man and woman restraining Renata, then two EMTs entered with a gurney. Her sobs faltered as they strapped her onto the gurney, as if the fight had gone out of her.

A third EMT knelt beside me. "Let me take a look at your foot, ma'am. You're bleeding pretty badly."

I sucked air through my teeth, trying to ignore the pooling blood—and my heaving stomach. "It's not that bad. Just go take care of—"

"Julie. Shut up and let the guy see your foot."

Only at the sound of Micah's stern voice did I realize who'd broken my fall. Acutely aware of his warm chest bracing my back, I sat straighter and scooted around until I could face him. Searching his troubled expression, I was barely aware of the EMT mopping blood off my foot. "Micah, what are you doing here? How did you know?"

"Your grandfather called me. He was worried." His Adam's apple shifted as his gaze slid briefly to my foot. "As well he should. Why didn't you answer your phone?"

"That was you? I was kinda busy at the time."

He fisted his hand and muttered a curse. "What were you thinking, Julie? Renata's insane. She's a danger to everyone around her."

"I was *thinking* about keeping Renata from killing herself. What did you *think* I was thinking—*ow!*" My whole body jerked when the EMT hit a nerve.

"Sorry. This cut's deep."

Micah stood, then addressed the EMT as if I weren't even there. "Are you taking her to the hospital?"

"Yes, sir, soon as they bring up another gurney."

"I can walk, for crying out loud." I flinched again. "And I *don't* need to go to the hospital."

"You do, ma'am. You need stitches. And you sure don't want this getting infected."

The female officer who'd helped subdue Renata returned. Tugging a note pad from her pocket, she looked from me to Micah. "I need to ask some questions about what happened here. Are either of you related to the woman?"

Finally I could reply with absolute conviction. "No. No relation at all."

Then, stupidly, I glanced up at Micah, and the utter devastation in his eyes sent my heart plummeting through the floor. Shoulders stiff, he drew a hand across his mouth and turned away. Before I could explain, much less temper the blow, he bolted for the door.

JULIE PEARL

T he cold, lavender fingers of dawn crept silently across Lake Hamilton. I shivered and snuggled deeper into the scratchy, doggy-smelling army blanket wrapped around my shoulders. Leaning against the fender of the VW, I peered through gray tendrils of mist enshrouding the big house.

The house that for a time I'd believed was my first home.

I felt a comforting arm slip around me.

"You okay, darlin'?"

"Sure, Grandpa. Amazing what a couple doses of prescription pain reliever can do." I pushed a tangled knot of hair off my face.

"Shoulda taken you straight home from the ER, young lady. No sense you comin' here again after all you been through."

It felt like a nightmare. Just hours ago, I'd been in the room upstairs trying to talk Renata out of ending her life. Watching her swallow pills. Struggling with her at the window.

Informing the police officer—and Micah—that I had no familial connection whatsoever with Renata Pearl Channing.

Which meant Jenny was really dead. I couldn't even imagine how Micah must be torturing himself right now.

"Ain't you seen enough, Julie Pearl?" Grandpa's tone, gently chiding, returned me to the present. "Let's get you home and into bed."

With cautious slowness, I allowed Grandpa to lead me to the old white van, parked behind my green bug. The rough gravel along the roadside bit through the bandage and hospital-issue tube sock swathing my injured foot. I settled into the passenger seat as Grandpa shuffled around to the driver's side and started up the rumbling engine.

"We'll get Sandy and Clifton to come get your car later," Grandpa said, making an awkward U-turn. "I made sure it was locked."

"Thanks."

By the time we got to the highway, I'd drifted into a restless sleep, my exhausted brain skittering through confused images of motorboats, campfires, swimming pools, and a big, wet, yellow dog.

Later, Grandpa tucked me into bed, sitting beside me and soothing my cheek with his warm, soap-scented palm. "Leastways one good thing has come out of this," he murmured.

"Mmmm, what's that?" I asked without opening my eyes.

"Least I know once and for all that you're mine. You ain't no kin to that crazy woman and her family. You're my own Julie Pearl, my sweetest, dearest treasure."

I smiled, but as I drifted off to sleep, Grandpa's words danced in my brain: *"You ain't no kin to that crazy woman."* How long before the old, agonizing question about who my real father could be started nibbling at my soul all over again?

More exhausted than I realized, I slept most of the day. Good thing it was Thursday and there wouldn't be much happening downstairs at the Swap & Shop. One less thing to feel guilty about, curled up here in bed and leaving all the work to Grandpa and Clifton.

But plenty to feel guilty about when the hammers, saws, and drills started up. How could we let the Swap & Shop renovations continue when Micah and I weren't together anymore? I was surprised Grandpa hadn't run the workmen off already, stubborn and prideful as he could be. Except I had a feeling Micah's own stubborn pride, combined with an even heavier helping of guilt, would drive him to finish this job no matter what.

Along about suppertime, Grandpa tapped on the bedroom door and peeked inside. "You waking up yet, sweetheart? I got some of Katy's homemade chicken noodle soup on the stove."

I rolled on my side and wiggled my fingers in a weak wave. The aroma of chicken and vegetables simmering in a savory broth wafted into the room. "Hi, Grandpa. Smells wonderful."

We'd just sat down at the table when I glimpsed a shadow outside on the landing. I tucked my robe around my waist. "Looks like we've got company."

He opened the door to Geneva Nelson. Her cap of brownish-gold curls shimmered under the porch light. "I probably should have phoned, but I had to see for myself that Julie's all right."

"Come right in, Miz Nelson." Grandpa stepped aside and held the door. "We're just having some soup—homemade chicken noodle. Can I offer you some?"

I stirred oyster crackers into my bowl. "It's really good. Please join us." I was glad she'd come. Perhaps she could offer more glimpses into the mind of the woman who'd let me believe a lie, who'd nearly killed herself and all but destroyed the man I loved.

"I must say, a bowl of homemade soup would surely hit the spot. I spent most of the day at the hospital, and eating was the furthest thing from my mind." Smiling her thanks, Geneva took the chair Grandpa indicated while he ladled another bowlful.

I dipped my soup spoon and blew across the steaming broth

before taking a bite. Keeping my eyes lowered, I asked, "How's Renata?"

"Physically she'll be fine. But—" Geneva reached across the table and tenderly touched my hand. Moisture pooled in the crinkles beneath her eyes. "I am so sorry for how she's hurt you, Julie. What she's done to Micah. If I'd only stepped in when she was a young girl, somehow made her get the right kind of help before—"

I laid my spoon aside. "Please don't blame yourself, Aunt Geneva. Aren't you the one who told me we can't fix other people's problems?"

"Oh, Julie." Her voice cracked. "That you'd still call me your aunt after all this, it touches me in ways I can't even put into words."

"I'll always think of you that way." I rose and went to her side, pressing my cheek against her springy mass of curls. "You—you and my grandpa—have been my islands of sanity."

Grandpa gave a loud *ahem* as he took his seat. "Best eat up now. Nothin' worse than cold soup."

We finished the meal in relaxed silence, and afterward Grandpa poured decaf for himself and Geneva.

She stirred a dollop of cream into her cup and cast me a sad smile. "Seems strange to think back to when I saw you for the first time behind the Swap & Shop counter. Who'd have thought we'd all end up like this today?"

Grandpa took a noisy slurp of coffee, then sat back in his chair. "Has to be a reason for it. God don't make mistakes."

"Of course." Geneva gazed into her coffee. "But sometimes, like now, it's awfully hard to make sense of it all."

Shifting sideways, I rested one arm on the edge of the table. "Tell me more about Renata's family. Maybe it would help me understand."

"I've told you some about her father—my brother, Everett. He was a decent, hardworking man, but unfortunately in even deeper denial about Lucille's mental problems than the rest of us. Appearances were everything to her, *everything*. Poor Renata, try as she might, never could please that woman. If I'd known then what I do now, how sick my sister-in-law was—" Her mouth twisted into an angry frown, and she hammered a fist against the tabletop. "I wish—oh, how I wish I'd done something sooner. Maybe all this tragedy could have been prevented."

Grandpa covered her knotted fist with his callused, age-spotted hand. "Now, now, Miz Nelson, no use dwelling on might-have-beens. I sure learned that the hard way." His throat worked, and he slanted me a crooked smile. "All those years I had my doubts and suspicions about where Julie Pearl came from. If I'd looked into it back then, or somehow got my poor, sweet Angie to tell me more before she died, there'd been no reason for Julie Pearl to mess with Renata Channing in the first place."

He rose and shuffled to the window, staring into the darkness beyond. "Leastways now we know the truth. And the Good Book says the truth will set you free."

Geneva sniffed and brushed wetness from her cheeks. "I know you're right, Mr. Stiles. The hard part now is finding a way to live with it."

When the Swap & Shop opened Friday morning, I went downstairs intending to work, but with my brain still muddled by extra-strength painkillers, it was clear I wouldn't be much use at the cash register. Grandpa decided we should let Clifton take over our new-and-improved front counter, with me coaching from my barstool. Good old Clifton was turning into a jack-of-all-trades. I kept a watchful eye on him as he made the consignment ledger entries, but before long he seemed to get the hang of it—as long as he had a calculator close by.

I shook my head as he rang up a sale. "And you were so lousy at high school math."

"Hey now, Julie Pearl, not in front of the customers." He winked at the rosy-cheeked, touristy-looking lady across the counter and handed her a plastic bag containing her purchases. "She's teasing, ma'am. I was a star student, I assure you. Check your receipt if you have any doubts."

"I trust you completely, young man." The woman laughed and waggled a finger at me. "You'd better hang onto this one, honey. He's a keeper."

I could only roll my eyes and grin. "Oh, he is at that."

The woman left with a jaunty spring in her step. I elbowed Clifton in the ribs. "Charmed another one, I see."

"You go telling Sandy how I'm flirting with the customers and I'll see to it she asks someone else to be her maid of honor."

I scooted farther onto the rattan barstool seat. "Any closer to setting a wedding date?"

A crimson flush crept up Clifton's neck. "Hoo-eee, this whole idea makes me nervous as a cricket at a toad convention. But Sandy has her heart set on a Christmas wedding, so I s'pose I'll have to get used to the idea."

"Christmas! That's just a few weeks away." I glanced at the fraying gauze covering my foot. "At least I should be all healed up by then so I can fit into my dancing shoes."

Clifton fixed me with an accusing stare. "Man, Julie Pearl, how could you be such an idiot, risking your life to save the likes of Renata Channing."

"Why, Clifton, I didn't know you cared." My mocking tone was a poor attempt to squelch a sudden return of the horror of that night.

"Julie Pearl, you're my best friend in the whole wide world. I love you like a sister." Sniffing loudly, Clifton swiveled sideways. "I wish you *was* my sister. I'd have never let you run off to Little Rock to live with that she-devil. I'd have sat you down and talked some sense into you. I'd have—"

"Stop, Clifton." I stretched one arm around him and laid my head on his shoulder. "I could beat you up in junior high, and I could do it again now if I had a mind to."

"Yeah, well . . . not till your foot heals anyways." He brushed the underside of his nose with the back of his hand. "So what are you hanging out here for? I got this cash register business down cold. Get out of here. Go see that Micah guy. Don't you have stuff to settle with him?"

Clifton's words nailed me. The flea market remodeling issues aside, Micah deserved to know how I'd determined I couldn't possibly be Jenny Pearl.

I kissed Clifton on the cheek. "I should go see Micah. You're right—much as it pains me to admit it."

"'Course I'm right. But, uh . . .'" With one raised brow, Clifton eyed me up and down. "Number one, you might have some trouble operating a clutch just yet. And number two, I ain't no fashion expert, but I'm pretty sure the style police will write you up a ticket if you appear in public wearing that get-up."

"What's wrong with my clothes?" This was my favorite granny dress, a '70s classic with billowing sleeves and maxi skirt.

Then I glanced down and realized what Clifton referred to. I pinched the sides of my skirt and did a klutzy little one-footed dance. "So you don't think the pink fuzzy bunny-rabbit slippers quite go with the red calico print?"

He gave an exaggerated shrug. "Your call, Jules, but if you ask me—"

The brass bells announced the arrival of another customer. Clifton directed the stocky gent to Herman Trapp's used paperbacks booth and then hooked his arm in mine and propelled me toward our brand new elevator. "Go. Change your outfit and put on some decent shoes—if you can find any that'll fit. I'll get Katy to cover the register while I drive you over to Micah's office."

Which now took up two rooms behind the check-in counter at the resort. Did I really want to return there so soon? On the other hand, what choice did I have?

I went up to the apartment to change, but doubted I looked much better in a baggy fisherman's sweater, brown bell-bottom cords, and Grandpa's scuffed moccasins over thick socks. Then, as I wove my hair into a messy braid, all I could think about was Renata chopping off those beautiful dark waves I'd envied for so long.

Clifton drove me toward Hot Springs, but before we turned onto the road to the resort, I stopped him. "Take me on into town. I want to go to St. Vincent's."

"What's wrong, Julie Pearl? Your foot feelin' worse?"

"No, it's fine." I pulled my lower lip between my teeth. "I need to check on Renata."

Clifton snorted. "Now, why on earth would you want to do that?"

I couldn't explain it. I only knew I wouldn't be able to let all these bottled-up feelings go until I faced her again. "Please, Clifton, it's just something I need to do."

"All righty." He shrugged and continued on into town. A few minutes later he pulled up at the main entrance of St. Vincent's Hospital. "I'll park and wait for you, okay?"

"No, don't. I have no idea how long I'll be." I patted my purse. "Got my phone. I'll call Sandy to come get me."

"Julie Pearl—"

"Please, Clifton. Go back to the Swap & Shop. Grandpa needs you more than I do."

He finally relented and drove away, while I limped inside and made my way to the information desk. "I'd like to ask about a patient, please. Renata Channing."

"Sure, I'll look her up." The volunteer checked her computer screen, and then her smile slowly faded. "Are you a relative of Mrs. Channing?"

"I, uh . . . no."

"Then all I can tell you, dear, is that she is no longer a patient here."

"She was released?"

The volunteer pursed her lips. "Mrs. Channing has been transferred to another facility."

Like I couldn't guess what kind. Had Aunt Geneva made those arrangements? It would be reassuring to believe Larry had cut his business trip short so he could take care of his wife, but somehow I suspected that wasn't the case. I thanked the lady and shuffled away.

Plopping into an empty chair in the hospital lobby, I fished my cell phone from my purse and hit the speed dial for Sandy's cell. As I counted the rings, I wondered if Sandy would even be working today. For all I knew, Micah may have changed his building plans all over again, now that his intention to restore the resort for "Jenny" no longer had any relevance.

Sandy answered on the third ring. "How's it going, girlfriend? You up and at 'em yet?"

I watched an elderly man in a hospital-issue robe scoot by with his walker. "I'm up, but hardly *at 'em*. Where are you?"

"At the office. We had some repairs and cleanup to do after . . . you know."

For no good reason, I dropped my voice to a whisper. "Is he there?"

"Yep." Sandy lowered her voice, too. "And as maniacally workaholic as I've ever seen him."

I heard Micah's gruff tone in the background. "Is that Julie? Let me talk to her."

My stomach lurched. I gripped the phone with both hands. "Don't, Sandy. I'm not ready—"

Muffled sounds, Sandy's feeble protests.

Then Micah's voice. "Julie. Where are you? We need to talk."

JULIE PEARL

It wasn't twenty minutes before Micah's maroon pickup pulled up at the entrance to St. Vincent's. Micah stepped from the driver's side and waved to me across the hood. By the time I hobbled outside, he had the passenger door open. I slanted him an uneasy smile as I levered myself into the seat.

Sliding behind the wheel, Micah started to fasten his seatbelt, then noticed I was fumbling with mine. With tenderness he removed my trembling fingers from the buckle and snapped it into place. For a moment our gazes met, and in the depths of his clouded gray eyes I read regret, anguish, love.

He broke away, his Adam's apple working furiously as he steered the pickup toward the highway.

I noticed we were heading west. "Where exactly are we going?"

"No idea. And I don't care, so long as it's as far from the resort as we can get."

Considering the autumn chill in the air, I came up with an idea. "How about the science museum? We're headed that direction, and it shouldn't be too crowded on a school day."

I couldn't have been more wrong. Apparently every elementary school in the county had decided today was perfect for a field trip. A line of bright yellow school buses dwarfed the few passenger vehicles parked in the lot.

Micah slapped the steering wheel. "Any other suggestions?"

"Just park. Let's go in." I brushed away a trickle of wetness from my cheek. "Getting lost in the crowd sounds pretty good right now."

After Micah paid our admission, we wandered into the exhibit hall, dodging hordes of laughing children as they darted from one display to another. Teachers and chaperones meandered through the melee with deer-in-the-headlights stares.

I slipped my hand into Micah's as we paused near the pendulum, watching it trace gentle arcs with trickling sand—so long as the motion wasn't disturbed by impatient kindergartners. I sensed Micah's impatience, too, in the tension in his forearm, the grim set of his bearded jaw.

And why was I so reluctant to be alone with him? How could things get any worse than they already were?

"Come on." I led Micah toward the stairs. We bypassed the rowdy concessions area and exited to the outdoor deck, where relative (if chilly) quiet reigned under soughing pines and leafless oaks. I slid onto a picnic bench, and Micah settled beside me. At least this way I didn't have to face him, but the warmth of his thigh against mine was almost as unnerving.

"Julie, I—"

"Micah, there's—"

"Okay, you first," he said with a hoarse laugh.

I shivered, and he drew me into the shelter of his arm. I took a deep breath. "I know what set Renata off. It's because I told her I knew—" I choked, barely able to get the next words out. "It was all a huge mistake, Micah. I . . . I'm not Jenny after all."

"So I gathered." His gaze slid my way. "You saw the DNA results?"

"No, but something else just as convincing. Some old photos Geneva Nelson gave me."

He kept his arm around my shoulder, but he inhaled long and slow. "I think I always knew. It seemed too good to be true."

I braved a look to search his face. "Are you okay?"

The muscles in his cheeks knotted. He pulled his arm away and fisted both hands on the scarred surface of the table. "That woman—what she did to you, to us—it's unforgivable."

I covered his hands with my own. "Don't you understand, Micah? Forgiveness is the only choice we have."

He shot me a look of utter disbelief. "You're saying you can forgive Renata for the way she strung you along all this time? For playing with our lives? For creating this crazy fantasy that Jenny hadn't died?"

"If I want to stay sane, yes. I have to forgive her. Like I said, it's our only choice."

"You want choices?" He clambered to his feet, then shook his fist at me. "How about hating her? How about demanding she pay for what she's done? How about—"

"Stop, Micah. Stop and listen to yourself." I swung my legs to the other side of the bench, wincing when my injured foot scraped the corner. Rubbing the pain away, I continued, "What have you gained by despising Renata all these years, besides ulcers and a broken heart?"

"I wouldn't have a broken heart if she weren't so vindictive, if I'd never gotten involved with her in the first place. And Jenny, poor little innocent Jenny—" His gaze settled on me, and his face contorted with renewed grief and guilt.

"Micah, don't." I rose and wrapped him in my arms. "I'd give anything if I could bring Jenny back for you. But I can't. And you can't, either. Not by holding on to your hatred for Renata, not by rebuilding the resort."

"But—"

"No, listen to me." I took his face between my hands, the rough feel of his beard so familiar, so dear. "We can either forgive Renata and put the past behind us, or we can let bitterness eat us alive.

Don't waste any more time hating her or yourself, Micah, not when you could be spending that time loving me."

He pulled me close and kissed my forehead. "I do love you, Julie. When you walked out on me, when you said we couldn't be together anymore, something inside me died."

I took a half-step back. "Don't look to me to complete you, Micah, because I can't. I meant what I said before. As long as you're holding so tightly to guilt and hate and anger, there's no room in your heart for love." My voice broke on a sob. "There's no room in your heart for me."

I don't think we said five words to each other on the drive back to the resort. Micah offered to take me all the way to Caddo Pines, but I didn't think it was such a good idea under the circumstances. His nearness only worsened the pain of letting him go. Again.

He parked the pickup next to Sandy's car in the paved parking area beside the house. When he shut off the engine, the silence settled over us like a heavy quilt, yet neither of us made a move to get out.

Finally I reached for the door handle. "I should go. Tell Sandy I'll wait for her in the car."

"Julie . . . help me."

The words were barely a whisper, torn ragged from a parched throat. I jerked my head toward Micah and saw the brokenness in his staring eyes, trained on some object beyond the windshield.

Before I could answer, he continued in the same rasping voice. "When Jenny drowned—such a precious little girl—nothing about my life made sense anymore." He sighed long and loud, his gaze sliding sideways to meet mine. "Not until I met you, Julie. Your spunk, your sass, your determination to rescue that mama dog and her pups." A tiny chuckle vibrated his Adam's apple before he turned sober again. "But your eternal optimism—it scared me. I wasn't ready to let go of the past . . . or maybe I just didn't know how."

I swallowed against the tightening in my throat. "Will you ever be ready?"

"I'm trying. I want to be." He pressed clenched fists into his eye sockets as his chest heaved on a choking sob. "I need you, Julie. Help me!"

I stretched my arms around him and tucked his head beneath my chin, already wet with my own tears. "It's okay, I'm here. Always."

Always.

JULIE PEARL

If I'd had a voice for singing, I'd have been belting out the "Hallelujah Chorus" that day. But healing the heart can be a slow process, and Micah's wounds had festered so long that it would take much more than a single afternoon to set things right.

So we took things one step at a time, starting with convincing Micah to come to church with me the following Sunday and meet my friends. I knew I could trust them to welcome him without judgment, and they didn't let me down. Coincidentally (or not), Pastor Ed just happened to preach on my favorite scripture, the parables of the hidden treasure and the pearl of great price. Then he ended with the verse that says, "For where your treasure is, there your heart will be also."

Micah squeezed my hand, his warm breath tickling my ear. "My treasure's sitting right here beside me," he said, and my heart filled to overflowing.

For Thanksgiving, Micah invited me to his mother's house in Fort Worth. I hesitated leaving Grandpa and the Swap & Shop during one of the busiest shopping weekends of the year, but Grandpa insisted that between him, Clifton, and Katy Harcourt, they'd manage just fine without me. Even so, I made Micah promise we'd be back late Friday.

Micah's mother turned out to be a lovely lady, a widow once again since Mr. MacDonohoe had passed away three years ago. She made me feel right at home, although she wasn't very subtle with her hints about Micah and me tying the knot one of these days. Micah would get extra quiet, and I'd keep my eyes lowered and hope I wasn't blushing too bad.

I made it through the visit *and* a wild and crazy weekend at the Swap & Shop, and things started settling into a comfortable routine. With Clifton taking over several of the more demanding tasks around the flea market, a spring had returned to Grandpa's step. He looked rested, serene, like a king surveying his realm. By nature he always had to be doing something—dusting a shelf, straightening a display—but there was an ease about him I hadn't seen since before our lives got turned upside down last June.

Then Christmas came, and I was blessed to watch another dream come true.

"Okay, folks, it's that time." A computerized fanfare accompanied the DJ's announcement. "All single gals to the dance floor."

Micah nudged me with his elbow and grinned. "I believe that includes you."

I crossed my arms and tried to look hurt. "What? I thought I was already spoken for."

"Oh, you are. You definitely are." His grin became lecherous, and I had to suck in my breath at how handsome this guy looked in a tux.

"Julie Pearl Stiles, get yourself out here right this minute!" This, from the woman in white who reigned over today's festivities. Sandy hoisted her billowing skirt and trotted up the three carpeted steps at the right of the Pedersonville VFW hall stage. Flinging the long folds of her tulle veil over one shoulder, she surveyed the giggling single girls jockeying for position under garlands of silk flowers and red crepe-paper streamers.

"Best not keep the new bride waiting," Grandpa said. "Clifton's looking mighty anxious to get his honeymoon started."

"Grandpa!" I'm sure I blushed an even deeper shade of crimson than my antique velvet bridesmaid's gown.

Grandpa winked. "Facts is facts, ain't they? Now go catch that bouquet."

I minced across the scuffed parquet floor in my pointy-toed, too-tight, dyed-to-match satin pumps. On the stage, Sandy casually waved her gorgeous white calla lily bouquet as she inspected the hall for any single female stragglers. Ushered over by her three gawky preteen granddaughters, a sixty-something widow joined the fray, and I quickly found myself engulfed in a sea of satin, lace, velvet, and lamé.

"Okay, I believe we're ready." Sandy nodded to the DJ, who did an extended reprise of the electronic drum roll. With a quick but studied glance in my direction, Sandy turned her back to the dance floor.

"Wait!" came a high-pitched yell from behind me. "Unfair advantage. Julie's too tall."

I huffed. "Like I can do anything about it."

Sandy cast me an accusing glance over her shoulder. "You know she's right, Julie. It's not fair to everybody behind you."

"Okay, I'll move to the back." *And why am I suddenly so resentful about this?* It wasn't like I really wanted to catch the thing. Neither Micah nor I needed the added pressure.

The "sea" parted, and I reluctantly stepped to the rear. I'd barely turned around and planted my feet when a collective gasp went up from the crowd. I looked up to see a white missile zooming right at my head. I heard a scream—*did that come from me?*—and the next thing I knew, I was crushing white calla lilies to my red velvet bosom.

"Yes!" Sandy.

"Nooooooo!" Every other female on the dance floor.

"Very clever, grasshopper." I touched foreheads with Sandy, the mangled bouquet between us. The lush scent of calla lilies filled my nostrils.

"Hey, didn't I always tell you one day you'd be thankful for your height? You made a perfect target."

Clifton rested a possessive hand at his new bride's waist. "So when are you and Micah going to make it official?"

I waved a hand. "Please, Clifton, it's too soon to even think about."

"Think about what?" At the sound of Micah's voice, I nearly dropped the bouquet. He caught it with one hand, offering me a plate with the other. "After your amazing feat of Amazonian athleticism, I thought you could use another piece of wedding cake."

Clifton rocked on his heels. "We were just asking Julie when you two are planning to tie the knot."

Put the guy in coat and tails, comb his hair, stick a beautiful brunette on his arm, and he thinks he can get away with anything. "Clifton . . ." My voice rose on a plaintive edge.

Micah cleared his throat, eyes downcast. I wanted to melt through the floor.

Sandy came to our rescue. "Oh, Cliffy, honey, look at the time. We need to hit the road soon." She squeezed his bicep and cast him a meaningful glance.

Clifton's eyes widened along with his silly grin. "Well, all righty, then. Let's get out of these fancy duds and blow this pop stand."

While the happy couple disappeared to change into traveling clothes, I resumed my maid-of-honor duties by overseeing the distribution of rose petals and tiny, tulle-wrapped plastic bottles of wedding bubbles. My smile was beginning to feel like lockjaw, but at least the activity gave the nervous tension between me and Micah a chance to cool.

Forty-five minutes later, with Clifton and Sandy on the first leg of their romantic getaway to a beach condo in Pensacola (courtesy of Micah's extensive resort connections), I busied myself in the VFW kitchen helping Mrs. Doakes and Mrs. Monroe pack away the leftover hors d'oeuvres and wedding cake. I glanced through the pass-through to see Micah, tux coat removed, perched on a stepladder ripping streamers from the ceiling and handing them down to Clifton's dad. I sighed, unable to stifle a twinge of envy that my two best friends were now happily married. Could it really happen for me and Micah someday?

"That should do it, Julie Pearl." Sandy's mom burped a Tupperware lid on a bowl of mixed fruit. "Thanks so much for all your help, sweetie. And you tell your grandpa I'll be more than happy to help out when the time comes to plan your wedding." She drew me into a hug. "Why, you're like a second daughter to me, darlin'."

"Thanks, Mrs. M. I love you too."

"Julie, you about ready?" Micah stood across the counter, shrugging into his tux sleeves.

"I thought I'd ride home with Grandpa. We're so close, and you've got the drive back to Hot Springs yet."

"Already spoke to him. He said to tell you he'll see you at home later . . . and no hurry."

No hurry, huh? Was everybody ganging up on us?

I stepped around the counter and let Micah drape my white wool shawl around my shoulders. "About what Clifton said, I just want you to know I—"

Micah silenced me with a finger to my lips. "I hadn't planned it like this—I was going to wait till New Year's Eve. But here we are, all dressed up for a wedding, you looking like a royal princess and me looking like . . ." He chuckled and lifted his shoulders. "Well, like the maitre d' at the Four Seasons. Anyway, what I'm trying to say is . . . Julie, you've changed my life."

A bubble of warmth swelled under my breastbone. "No, Micah, it was your willingness to finally let go of the past."

"Okay, but it was your love that made the difference, pushed me into realizing I *wanted* to change."

"Well, maybe, but . . ." My warm, fuzzy feeling fizzled into a fog of indignation. "Now just a cotton-pickin' minute. *Pushed?* Don't you *ever* go telling people I set out to *change* you. We may have had a few differences of opinion, but you know I've always loved you for yourself. Please! Like *anybody* could ever—"

He gave a frustrated groan. "Will you just let me say this, please?"

My mouth fell open and immediately snapped shut. Leave it to me to start running off at the mouth when my nerves kicked in. Was I ready for what came next?

Another deep breath. He took both my hands in his. "Like I said, I was going to do this on New Year's Eve—you know, the whole 'new year, new beginning' scenario—but seeing how happy Sandy and Clifton are, I realized I don't want to wait a minute longer."

Still holding my hands, he dropped awkwardly to one knee, and my heart flip-flopped. "Julie Pearl Stiles," he began, his voice growing husky with emotion, "will you do me the honor of becoming my wife?"

I swallowed—*hard.* I opened my mouth, but nothing came out except this little tiny squeak that had to suffice for something halfway between *Oh my goodness, is this a dream?* and *Grandpa, get the preacher back in here, pronto!*

Mrs. Monroe's laughter and twangy voice rang out from the kitchen. "Oh, my heavens! We've finally found the man who can leave our Julie Pearl speechless."

Planning a wedding—*me*? How many years had I doubted this day would ever come, much less that I'd meet the man who could claim my heart, soul, and spirit so completely. Micah's love had somehow quieted the lifelong hunger to find the man who'd fathered me. But even with Katy Harcourt and Sandy's mom stepping in to help with the wedding stuff, I couldn't help missing all over again the mother I barely remembered. And I thought I detected the same regret in Grandpa's eyes.

Then one day in April, as I was on my way to meet Micah at the florist shop to pick out our wedding flowers, I pulled up next to the Swap & Shop mailbox to retrieve the day's mail. I flipped through several bills and advertising flyers before a richly textured cream-colored envelope caught my eye. The letter was postmarked Little Rock. The return address, engraved on the back flap, was Renata's.

My hand trembled as I slid a fingernail under the seal. Since the night of Renata's attempted suicide, I'd tried hard to put her out of my mind. I'd learned through Geneva Nelson that Larry Channing had committed his wife to a mental hospital. It broke Geneva's heart to see her only living niece reduced to such a condition, but at least Renata would finally get the help she'd needed for longer than anyone wanted to admit.

Still, a letter from Renata, after all this time? What could it mean? My throat ached with the memories of last summer and fall.

I slipped a stiff, creamy sheet of personal stationery from the envelope, and with it another envelope, sealed and folded in thirds, with my name typed on the front. I tucked it behind the letter while I read the message penned in Renata's graceful script.

Dearest Julie,

I doubt you ever expected to hear from me again—and maybe you never wanted to. As you may have heard, I've spent the past several months at Rosewood Acres Mental Hospital. Part of my therapy has been to face up to the wrongs I've done, and—where possible—to make amends.

But how can I begin to apologize for how I've hurt you? Words will not suffice. Instead, I offer you this gift—the answer you were seeking when you first came to me last summer. True to my word, I have never looked inside, never needed to, never wanted to. My answer, my truth, lies in my heart.

Whatever your truth may be, rest assured of this one thing: My Jenny could not have been more loved, could not have grown up to be more lovely, could not have lived a happier, more fulfilled, more perfect life than what you have known.

Julie Pearl Stiles, you are the woman I would have wanted Jenny to become. You are a treasure beyond worth.

Always,

Renata

Eyes welling, I held the letter to my face, certain I could detect a lingering scent of the spicy Oriental perfume Renata always wore. Despite how angry I'd been with her, how much I regretted everything that had happened between us, I'd forgiven her long ago—for my own sake and for Micah's.

With a steadying breath I tore off the end of the sealed envelope and shook it gently. A folded sheet of white paper slid out.

The DNA results.

ANGIE

December, 24 years earlier
Tulsa, Oklahoma

Angie rocked the listless child and glared at the gruff old man whose knees vied with hers in the cramped space between the rows of chairs. The free-clinic waiting room teemed with patients, many whose racking coughs, festering wounds, or twisted limbs probably should have sent them straight to the ER. Angie could only shield little Julie Pearl's face and pray they didn't leave here with something far worse than what they'd arrived with.

"Stiles? Julie Stiles." The beleaguered nurse behind the front desk scanned the waiting room through smeared bifocals.

"Here." Angie waved the clipboard with the paperwork she'd been filling out. Balancing Julie Pearl on her bony hip, she worked her way over to the desk. The nurse took the clipboard and gave it a perfunctory glance before directing Angie through a side door.

Another nurse, this one noticeably more compassionate, showed Angie into an examining room. "What's the problem with this sweet little thing?" she asked in her lilting Oklahoma drawl.

"She's just so weak. Losing weight, no appetite, pale as a white cotton sheet." Angie stroked Julie's hair—or what remained of it. The few downy-soft strands barely covered the little girl's head anymore. "I've tried to take good care of my baby"—she sniffed, her lower lip trembling—"but I'm scared I'm doing something awfully wrong."

The nurse gave her an appraising, but not unkind, look. "Let's see what's going on with your little one." She shook down a thermometer and tucked it under Julie Pearl's armpit. "I'm sure the doctor will want to run some blood work, maybe a few other tests. You have time to stay awhile?"

Angie bent over her precious little girl and kissed the cool, dry forehead. "We got no place in the world to be but here."

The late-afternoon sun slanted through the streaked front window, casting garish shadows on the few remaining clinic patients. While Julie Pearl dozed in Angie's lap with her thin legs stretching onto the empty chair next to them, Angie struggled to keep her eyes open. Surely the nurse would call for them soon. She wouldn't leave here without answers.

The inner door creaked open. Angie's head snapped up. The tall, sandy-haired doctor who'd examined Julie Pearl that morning frowned in their direction. "Ms. Stiles, bring Julie on back."

This time Angie hugged her baby girl close as she perched on the edge of a pink molded-plastic chair. "What'd you find out, doctor? Is it serious?"

The doctor cocked his hip against the side of the examining table and heaved a sigh. His drawn expression registered frustration, disappointment, accusation. Angie shrank back.

It was true. Whatever was wrong with her baby was all her fault.

"Things could be a whole lot worse, Ms. Stiles, but your

daughter's condition is treatable. Bottom line, she's malnourished. She's suffering from a severe vitamin deficiency." He selected several brochures from a display rack attached to the inside of the door, then passed them to Angie one by one as he explained the information she'd find within.

From a cupboard on the opposite wall he retrieved several sample packs of children's vitamins and slipped them into a small paper bag. "One a day, with breakfast. A *healthy* breakfast, not leftover French fries or white bread and jelly." With a stern look, he added, "By all rights I should report you to Child Protective Services. This borders on child abuse."

"No, please! I'll do everything you said, I promise. I love this baby like—oh, doctor, Julie Pearl's my whole life." Tears streamed down Angie's face. She should have known she wasn't cut out to be a mother. Things had gotten bad enough while Ray was still around. But alone, broke, living in shelters? What chance did she have?

And the headaches sure didn't help. They just kept getting worse. She ought to ask the doctor about them. Maybe he could give her something.

No, if he knew she was sick, he'd have CPS take her baby away for sure. First get Julie Pearl all better, then Angie would worry about herself. She ran a trembling hand over the pale pink scalp. "What about her hair? Will it grow back all pretty again once she's better?"

"Yes, yes, of course." A tiredness tinged the doctor's voice, suggesting he'd seen cases like this too many times to count.

"Okay. I'll be home soon, Daddy."

Outside the 7-Eleven, Angie gazed down at the green-eyed toddler clutching her leg and lightly touched the springy fuzz of golden-brown curls. *Oh my Julie-love, my precious little turtle dove.*

The doctor in Tulsa had been right—a couple months of vitamins and healthy eating, and Julie Pearl's hair had grown right back, only instead of soft and fine and straight like it used to be, it came in all curly and thick, so much like Angie's now that no one —especially not Daddy—would ever guess the baby wasn't her own natural child.

For however many days the Lord granted her, Angie Stiles would bless the day that big, yellow dog brought this precious baby girl into her life.

43

JULIE PEARL

Present Day

I don't know how long I sat there at the end of the driveway, the VW engine rumbling, exhaust fumes drifting through my open window on the cool April breeze. Did I really care what this flimsy sheet of paper could tell me? As Renata had always insisted, she didn't need a piece of paper to tell her what her heart already knew.

So what difference could it make, seeing the results for myself after all this time? I knew with more certainty than ever that it couldn't change who I was, or who I was about to become—Mrs. Micah Hobart. Above all, it wouldn't change my identity as a beloved child of God.

But curiosity got the better of me. With clumsy, trembling fingers, I unfolded the report. My heart clenched as I read the undeniable truth. A truth I realized, deep down, I'd believed all along. That Jennifer Susan Pearl hadn't drowned in Lake Hamilton. That God in His infinite wisdom had made sure that little girl would grow up undiscovered in a flea market and have the best life ever.

Renata, oh, Renata. If only my wounded, tortured sister had been raised by a fine man like Otto Stiles, what a different person she'd surely have become!

When the tears finally subsided—tears of grief, tears of relief—I refolded the page and methodically tore it into confetti-sized pieces. With my left hand dangling out the driver's-side window, I hit the accelerator. I spread my fingers wide and watched the fragments float away in my rear-view mirror . . . float away on the breeze like a hundred weightless pearls.

I hope you enjoyed
ALL SHE SOUGHT

If you did, please spread the word among your reader friends and wherever you share about books on Facebook, Twitter, Instagram, or other social media.

I'd also be most grateful if you'd post a review on Goodreads, your blog, and/or your favorite online bookstore. A review doesn't have to be lengthy or eloquent, just a few brief words sharing your honest impressions. Reviews and personal recommendations are the best ways to help authors get discovered by new readers.

To receive regular updates about my books and special events, be sure to subscribe to my newsletter (signup form on my website).

Visit Myra online:
www.myrajohnson.com

ACKNOWLEDGMENTS

I owe my husband, Jack, a huge debt of thanks for all the years he has encouraged and supported me along this roller-coaster writing journey. Thanks for reading my manuscripts, helping with research, and for taking over so many of the daily household tasks so I could spend more time writing. I appreciate you and our beautiful daughters, Johanna and Julena, so very much for the many ways you have expressed your confidence in my dream.

I remain grateful to Drs. Erv Janssen and Kathleen Klaassen for answering my questions about psychiatric disorders during the early development of this story and for giving me greater insight into my characters. Any discrepancies are strictly my own.

Thanks to my daughter Julena for your assistance with editing and proofreading the original version of this book (published under the title *Pearl of Great Price*), and to author Melissa Jagears for her assistance, encouragement, and cover artistry in giving the story new life in this retitled and updated edition.

Native Texan Myra Johnson is a three-time Maggie Awards finalist, two-time finalist for the prestigious ACFW Carol Awards, winner of Christian Retailing's Best for historical fiction, and winner in the Inspirational category of the National Excellence in Romance Fiction Awards. After a five-year sojourn in Oklahoma, then eight years in the beautiful Carolinas, Myra and her husband are thrilled to be home once again in the Lone Star State enjoying wildflowers, Tex-Mex, and real Texas barbecue!

Married since 1972, Myra and her husband have two beautiful daughters married to wonderful Christian men, plus seven amazing grandchildren and a delightful granddaughter-in-law. The Johnsons share their home with two pampered rescue dogs and a snobby but lovable cat they inherited from their younger daughter when the family was living overseas.

Find Myra online:
www.myrajohnson.com

facebook.com/MyraJohnsonAuthor

twitter.com/MyraJohnson

instagram.com/mjwrites

bookbub.com/authors/myra-johnson

goodreads.com/MyraJohnsonAuthor

pinterest.com/mjwrites

BOOKS BY MYRA JOHNSON

CONTEMPORARY INSPIRATIONAL ROMANCE

Autumn Rains

Romance by the Book

Where the Dogwoods Bloom

Rancher for the Holidays

Worth the Risk

Her Hill Country Cowboy

Hill Country Reunion

The Rancher's Redemption

Their Christmas Prayer

The Rancher's Family Secret

CONTEMPORARY ROMANCE COLLECTION

The Horsemen of Cross Roads Farm

Three full-length novels:

A Horseman's Heart

A Horseman's Gift

A Horseman's Hope

FLOWERS OF EDEN HISTORICAL SERIES

The Sweetest Rain

Castles in the Clouds

A Rose So Fair

---

1. Previously published as *Pearl of Great Price*; see author website for details

www.ingramcontent.com/pod-product-compliance
Lightning Source LLC
Chambersburg PA
CBHW021100110726
47900CB00007B/1961